Disorderly Men

Disorderly Men

Edward Cahill

EMPIRE STATE EDITIONS

An imprint of Fordham University Press   New York   2023

Fordham University Press has no responsibility for the persistence or accuracy of URLs for external or third-party Internet websites referred to in this publication and does not guarantee that any content on such websites is, or will remain, accurate or appropriate.

Fordham University Press also publishes its books in a variety of electronic formats. Some content that appears in print may not be available in electronic books.

Visit us online at www.fordhampress.com/empire-state-editions.

Library of Congress Cataloging-in-Publication Data available online at https://catalog.loc.gov.

Printed in the United States of America

25 24 23   5 4 3 2 1

First edition

for Mark

Disorderly Men

Part I

Rebellious subjects, enemies to peace,
Profaners of this neighbour-stained steel,—
Will they not hear?

—*Romeo and Juliet*

Why do you kids live like there's a war on?

—*West Side Story*

1

On a winter's midnight in Greenwich Village, Roger Moorhouse, gray-flanneled and whiskey-flushed, felt almost comfortable. The room was hot and overcrowded, but no more so than usual for a Thursday. The regular company of older fairies lined the near end of the zinc bar, talking with exaggerated emphasis and appraising the slender hips and nascent whiskers of the bartender, a surly kid from Spain, rumored to be straight. Some of the younger men twisted obscenely by the jukebox to Del Shannon's rough falsetto, while the shyer ones anchored the bar's gloomy corners, hoping to be either noticed or ignored. The other patrons at Caesar's preened and posed like film stars, or snaked back and forth across the room for no apparent reason, or huddled confidentially around the small tables that ran the length of one wall. To Roger, they were mostly ridiculous, despicable pansies. But after so many monthly forays, he'd somehow grown accustomed to the abnormality of it all.

He loosened his necktie and smiled at the young man under his spell, a sinewy college boy, perhaps not quite twenty-one, who'd evolved with remarkable speed from nearly catatonic fear to a conscious knowledge of his own superior attractions. Roger had found him stooping near the front door, fidgeting with a matchbook and trying not to hyperventilate. But once he'd explained through several well-timed hints that winning looks and flowering manhood always bestowed a place of privilege in a queer bar, the boy's breath gradually slowed, his spine straightened, and his mouth cracked a bashful grin.

After sharing a couple of drinks and one or two tangible proofs of virility, they were getting on famously, like the only two men at a bridal shower.

While they chatted, Roger allowed his arm to bump up against the boy's every so often, and once he left it there just long enough to show that it was intentional and perhaps to elicit another grin. But after a quarter of an hour, he began to grow tired of the small talk and silly games and looked up at the gaudy neon Schlitz clock above the bar.

"It's the witching hour," he said.

"Oh, I don't need to be back until—well, anytime," said the boy, whose name was Andy. "Heck, I can stay out all night long if I want to."

Roger smiled at his misunderstanding and reminded himself that he needn't be so impatient. He'd taken a comfortable suite at the Iroquois, where he could expect perfect anonymity. After catching a catnap and savoring a veal chop and a Corby's from room service, he'd come downtown in search of something he'd been anticipating every day since early January, and it had taken him less than an hour to find it.

"I suppose if you still had a curfew, I ought not be whispering in your ear," he said, leaning in close enough to smell Andy's Skin Bracer, sharp and mentholated.

The boy pinched closed his soft brown eyes, as if weighing the propriety of such intimacy between men, then answered with a dopey, open-mouthed chuckle.

"You know, you're really quite adorable," Roger said, but then immediately wondered if he hadn't sounded too fey or, worse, too maternal.

Such superfluous adverbs and dainty adjectives had only recently crept into his speech and stayed, at least when he came to places like Caesar's. Although so contrary to the terse language of men that he'd learned as a boy and always used at home, at work, and everywhere else, he liked the way they stretched out and livened up even the shortest, dullest sentences. It wasn't that he necessarily wanted to sound unmanly, but he rather resented the law that said he must never seem less than thoroughly masculine.

"No one's ever called me that before," Andy said, cheeks ablaze.

"Not even the girls at school?" Roger said, after draining his glass.

"Well, not to my face."

"I bet they adore you all the same."

As Roger put his hand on Andy's shoulder and squeezed, he felt the tingly promise of strange flesh, even through the thick knit of an Irish fisherman's sweater. Andy flinched at first, but just once, and after finishing his own drink, he seemed to relax. Maybe no one had ever squeezed his shoulder before, either.

But instead of enjoying the moment, Roger grew restless again and felt an itch to leave. The Christmas lights still hanging from the ceiling after six weeks were tawdry and depressing. He'd had enough of the smoke and the heat, the smell of stale beer, and the fairies whose voices had grown even louder and shriller than the music. He hated how they could be so aggressively animated one moment and so ostentatiously bored the next. He wanted only a quick exit into a waiting Checker cab and a cozy ride back to the Iroquois, where three hours alone with Andy would infuse him with enough youth and vitality to keep going for another month, even if the whole affair would only seem to have lasted three minutes when he remembered it a week later.

"What do you say we go for a walk?" Roger said, although a Nor'easter was just then blanketing the city.

"In the snow?" Andy asked.

"Or we could go back to my hotel."

The boy let out a nervy guffaw. Then he darted his eyes left and right, scratched his sandy flattop, and fell into a sinking sigh that might have led to any number of answers but eventually resolved into a grave nod.

In his bulky sweater and snug corduroy trousers, Andy looked so fresh and unspoiled. His jagged brow and wayward ears were more attractive for their imperfections. Even the subtlest movements of his body were glorious spectacles. When he clipped his thumbs onto his belt and stretched his back, he let his shoulders hunch forward like angels' wings. And when he slackened again and shifted his weight to one side, he raised his smooth cleft chin, turned his neck ever so slightly, and formed half of his ass into an almost perfect globe.

"Let's get out of here," Roger said breezily, as if it weren't the greatest of mercies in a merciless world that he was about to get his wish.

A minute later, he held up Andy's duffel coat, marveling as the boy pulled back his arms and slipped them into its sleeves and thrilled by the miracle of their mutual consent. But as they put on their hats and turned to leave the bar together, the thrill suddenly came to an end.

A spray of flashlights pierced the front door as a chorus of pea whistles shattered the smoky air. The hum of banter gave way to gasping and shouting and the crash of breaking glass. Instinctively, Roger pulled Andy away from the lights and scanned the room. The Spanish bartender, perhaps the first to understand what was happening, quickly dropped behind the zinc bar and disappeared. As the police burst in, wielding batons and barking curses, some of the patrons began clawing their way toward to the toilet, whose single hopper window, Roger knew, offered no means of escape. Others flew to the back door, where more officers were likely stationed. The old fairies at the zinc bar only swallowed their drinks and hung their heads like martyrs to an ancient faith.

Roger had never seen a police raid before. He'd always assumed he'd be lucky or clever enough to avoid one. But the odds of getting away safely seemed long, and the confidence that had enabled him to walk into Caesar's that night and lay claim to the best-looking boy in the place began to falter. Fragments of his very good life—the fancy new office overlooking lower Broadway, the house in Beechmont Woods, Corinne and the children—all presented themselves to his imagination as fitting sacrifices to the selfish pursuit of pleasure. It was the house he saw most clearly, a center-hall Colonial with white clapboard and black shutters, a scarlet door, a yew hedge, and a stately, slender elm in the front yard. It was a trophy, a fortress, a bulwark against blame.

But when an errant beer bottle thudded at Roger's feet, the images vanished and he thought of the Spanish bartender, young, adroit, and unwilling to be caught.

"Follow me," he said to Andy as he began pushing his way across the room.

A red-faced, bottom-heavy officer swung his baton at a rush of fairies who dodged and shrieked at the outrage of it all. Roger slipped around them, flung himself over the zinc bar, and pulled Andy after him. From the floor, he spotted the empty space between shelves of glasses where a panel had been pulled to one side. He crawled after Andy as they wriggled through the passage into a cold and dusty stairwell.

"What the hell?" cried Andy, looking at Roger.

On his hands and knees, his eyes bulging and his mouth sucking the air, he looked almost like a child. On any playing field, he'd have been a formidable presence. But in the filth of a queer bar under attack by the police, he seemed as feeble and frightened as Roger's eight-year-old Henry after a nightmare.

Roger sprang to his feet and pulled Andy up with him, charging him with a hard look to find his courage. "Just keep moving," he said. "Don't stop."

They raced up half a dozen flights of stairs, their footsteps falling strangely into unison as they reached the roof. When Roger threw open the creaky steel door, snowflakes fell silently around them, and a burst of cold air washed away the close stench of the bar. Several men ahead of them were jumping, one by one, onto the building next door, then disappearing into the darkness. Roger jogged over to the edge and saw that the gap was only about four feet across and the fall would be only a foot or so more. It would be easy enough, even in the snow, even for a thirty-nine-year-old.

As he steadied himself, he felt the relief of near freedom and almost smiled at the idea of such a daring escape, the stuff of movies and dreams—though really nothing compared to landing a five-ton Hellcat on a short floating runway. Of course, this wasn't a tale he could ever tell. Not to Schuyler, his best friend, or to Richard, his older brother, the heart surgeon who thought sympathy was a kind of coronary disease. Certainly not to his father, whose starched rectitude would crack wide open if he ever found out the truth about his second son. That truth, Roger remembered, was still his secret to keep. He hadn't yet made any fatal mistakes. All he had to do was jump and his very good life would be spared. He thought again of the house and the elm tree, of Corinne, Henry, and Lizzie. He felt the warmth of their promise, the promise of a happy future that would still be there for him tomorrow.

He turned to look back at Andy but saw the boy standing frozen, his shoulders slumped, gazing blankly into the night, his future ended even before it had begun. Although he easily could have sailed over the distance and absorbed the fall without a care, he seemed stuck in place, weighed down by something heavy and mournful. Roger could tell by the shell-shocked look on Andy's face that his fiercest pleadings would have been useless.

The roof door creaked open again and the fat, florid officer, panting and wheezing, ordered him back from the edge. Even at a distance, Roger could see a triumphant gleam in the man's eyes. He knew that to hesitate for another second would do nothing to help Andy. He owed it to his family, his friends, and everything that mattered to save himself. He could almost feel in his arms and legs the force of that obligation goading him on. And yet—somehow—Roger froze, too. The feeling in his arms and legs wasn't pushing him forward so much as holding him down, sapping his will, reckoning his whole sorry life in one dismal moment. He felt all the shames of youth and manhood, the trials of daily endurance, all so familiar and exhausting. He saw Schuyler's trusting eyes, Corinne's patient smile, none of it deserved, none of it ever really his. Even the house in Beechmont Woods seemed only a ruined castle in the air. As the officer's heavy footsteps closed in behind him, Roger looked to the edge and the sure path to safety, and then again to poor, helpless Andy. But in the end, it was a feeling more of complicity than of kindness that stayed his urge to jump.

2

A bough of dusty mistletoe hung over the entrance to the toilet, near which Julian Prince hashed out an argument with his latest boyfriend, Gus, who was the most appealing man he'd ever met but now upset for reasons entirely beyond Julian's control. To make matters worse, a stream of patrons passing to and fro were bearing indelicate witness to their private contretemps. One even winked at Julian, as if to make some prospective claim on his interest should the quarrel render him suddenly available. Though Julian wasn't exactly a regular at Caesar's, preferring smarter places like the Cork Club or the Mais Oui, he was something of a known quantity at the West Village bar and in truth, he didn't entirely resent the attention. That night, after three sedentary hours of *Così fan tutte* at the Met, he was glad for a little downtown adventure and thought he looked quite dashing in his black blazer, turtleneck, and peggers. If his bright, intelligent face wasn't perfectly handsome, he thought it highly interesting, and he had a casual slouch some had called aristocratic. Unfortunately, Gus, a serious-minded painter from Wisconsin, seemed unimpressed by these charms, and as their argument persisted, Julian noticed the toilet traffic slowing, like highway drivers mooching past a wreck.

"Come with me," he said, giddy with the fear and freedom of a couple's first real argument. "When this is over and you kiss me, I'd like us to be alone."

"Gosh, J.P.," Gus said in a husky North Central accent that sometimes made Julian's knees wobble. "You're acting like someone who never wants to be kissed again."

Julian took Gus by the hand and led him down a short passage that dead-ended at the ladies' room, which had long been closed for repairs but faced a small alcove, where they discovered a passable privacy amid mops, buckets, and semidarkness.

When the police arrived and panic rang out only seconds later, Julian knew at once what was happening. He'd been at the Trap Door a few summers before when they'd broken in like storm troopers. A lovely old drag queen named Star Bright had been thrown to the floor and died of an aneurysm, and some poor Negro kid was nearly beaten to death, though the police later claimed he'd fallen during the melee. Julian had had the good fortune to slip out through a back room, past a trio of frantic men zipping up their pants as they stumbled toward a fire exit. But this time, he feared, would be different. Peeking beyond the alcove toward the top of the passage, he saw the backs of several people being lined up by the police—a floppy-haired hustler he'd noticed before, a middle-aged suburbanite he hadn't, and a person of considerable girth in silver lamé who was taking none of it in stride.

Julian raised a finger to his lips. Gus seemed to be bearing the bad news with philosophical detachment, though it was possible he had little real idea of what was happening. In fact, Julian wondered if he didn't see the raid as a kind of needlessly officious health inspection. But as the initial cries and groans faded into an intermittent series of gruff commands and hopeless sobs, it became impossible to tell whether the police, having made their point, were getting ready to leave or merely settling in for the tedious bureaucratic work of arresting dozens of people all at once. After a while, all Julian heard was the smooth purr of Gus's breath and the shallow scrape of his own.

"Are you planning on staying here all night?" Gus asked. The fact that he whispered probably meant he was beginning to understand their predicament.

Julian took his hand, a plea for patience and discretion. Then together they inched their backs down the wall and squatted, Gus over a metal bucket, Julian on his haunches. For ten long minutes, nothing happened. While Gus played with a dirty mop head, weaving its frizzled strings into an artful thatch, Julian only listened. He heard a soft moan, a shuffle of steps, a distant murmur of conversation, then more silence.

"You still haven't given me a reason," Gus said in a voice so faint Julian wondered for a moment if it wasn't his own sense of guilt speaking.

Their argument had been about Julian's apartment. Gus needed a place to stay for a week or two while he looked for something more permanent and hoped Julian wouldn't mind putting him up. He'd been living with a Swiss art dealer at his topping Fifth Avenue penthouse in a maid's room that was apparently very small but had excellent natural light. The situation, fraught from the beginning with ambiguous expectations, had grown particularly uncomfortable in recent days. After unwelcome gifts of liquor and cologne were followed by intrusive questions about bedroom habits, Gus decided it was no longer tenable. Julian had probably made too many teasing jokes about the likely expectation of some quid pro quo, and that night when he refused to give Gus shelter—at least until after the weekend—or to explain himself, Gus leapt to the conclusion that Julian either was being extremely selfish or had already made romantic plans with another man. The real reason was something he was still unprepared to share with Gus or anyone else.

"An old friend's in town," he said, relieved that the truth sounded so innocent, even when whispered. "It's an obligation more than a pleasure."

"Uff da!" Gus said. "I couldn't care less who it is. I just need a place to sleep and stow my suitcase."

"What about your studio?"

Gus narrowed his eyes crossly. He shared a modest-sized room in the back of a print shop on West 37th Street with a few other painters, a ceramicist, and an earnest young woman from Texas who sculpted in broken glass and Ready Mix. It was a crowded, often chaotic place that Julian had visited only once before. There was barely enough space for easels and paints, let alone beds, and, according to Gus, the building's owner, a cranky Bavarian widower with time on his hands, often made surprise inspections to discourage overnight stays, which were strictly verboten.

It should have been easy enough to tell Gus about Pen, who came down for the weekend from Boston on the second Friday of every month. She certainly would have liked him, and he'd have liked her, too, since she taught history at Girls' Latin and had a passion for modern design. But it was impossible to explain that she was, at least technically, still Julian's fiancée. In what had begun as a rather spontaneous and perverse experiment in heterosexuality, he dated her casually during graduate school at Harvard, and though they'd never even attempted to make love—a bad experience with a high school boyfriend had apparently left her squeamish about sex—their conversation was always lively and substantial, and he found her sly wit and occasional nihilism an agreeable antidote to the stuffy pretensions of Cambridge. Right before he moved to New York, she unexpectedly proposed marriage and, unwilling to hurt her feelings, he accepted, though they never once concerned themselves with setting a date for the wedding or even buying an engagement ring. It was all so improbable and bizarre, he knew. Except for Pen, he hadn't feigned interest in girls for years. Still, for reasons he didn't understand, she continued her monthly visits, and for reasons he preferred not to dwell on, he allowed this last vestige of conventionality in his life.

"I'm sorry I can't help you," Julian said, when nothing else came to mind.

"Really, J.P.?" Gus said, no longer whispering. "That's the best you've got?"

Julian urged him with anxious eyes to lower his voice.

"You know I wouldn't ask if—"

"Please be quiet!"

Gus suddenly stood up, kicking the mop and knocking over the bucket as he stepped into the hallway. Julian jumped up after him, pulled him back, and hugged him tight. His body smelled of mineral spirits, tar soap, and a sweet, slightly musky scent that reminded Julian of the desert. When he listened again to see if the noise of the mop and bucket had given them away, it was almost as an afterthought. But there was nothing to hear except the swift and sturdy beating of their own hearts.

They'd been nearly inseparable since they'd met, just five weeks before. Julian's one-bedroom faculty apartment on West 113th Street was spacious, comfortable, and private enough that it didn't matter if two men entered or left together on a regular basis. In fact, their lives had become quite harmoniously entangled without either one of them getting in any way jumpy about it. On their first date, they stayed up late smoking marijuana and discussing Saigon and Schoenberg, and the next morning they saw the *Modern Allegories* show at MoMA and read poetry on the floor at the Gotham Book Mart. One weekend they borrowed a car from Julian's friend Hugh, the art historian who'd introduced them, and went to a house party in Rye, where they drank gin fizzes, listened to Brazilian bossa nova music, and felt extremely clever. Julian even taught Gus how to play squash, while several of his students watched from the bleachers. It had been a busy, carefree time, and their romance, no matter how long it might last, was the happiest Julian had ever known.

Most of his colleagues didn't seem to give a fig about his private life. Some even had private lives of their own, though none ever discussed them openly. There were, of course, several senior men so rigid in their morals or repressed in their own queerness that the least whiff of sex gave them the vapors, and a few others who were all too apt to ask Julian if there weren't some sort of Pen in his life. But by and large these people could be avoided or ignored as circumstances required.

Gus didn't seem to understand why anyone would have an opinion about what other people did with their bodies. Physical love, he'd once confessed, was no less fundamental to him than food or air and just as easily enjoyed without self-conscious awareness. At eighteen, after a candid conversation with his draft board landed him a 4-F classification, he'd left behind the suffocating insularity and churchy rancor of his family in Manitowoc—he called them the Frozen Chosen—and came to the city to find truth and beauty or die trying. Although he sometimes received letters from home filled with pious allusions to Satan and Sodom, they did little to discourage the man who believed that self-doubt was worse than plagiarism or banality.

"Can we go now?" Gus asked. "As you know, I've got to find a place to live."

When Julian peeked into the hallway again, all he could see was the corner of the zinc bar, against which stood a handsome, blond-haired, blue-eyed man, perhaps in his midforties, wearing a black woolen topcoat and a bright red plaid scarf, and snuffing out his cigarette in a half-empty highball. In his self-contained Nordic vigor, he might have passed for one of Gus's uncles, if he'd had any who smoked or wore bright scarves. The man appeared to be in charge, but the placid expression on his face and slow and easy movement of his hands somehow made him seem out of place. Julian wondered whether perhaps he regretted the raid as an unfortunate aspect of the otherwise honorable business of police work. He even seemed to look across the room, as if toward a line of handcuffed men, with a kind of sympathy.

"Lieutenant?" someone called out, and the man suddenly turned toward the men's toilet.

Julian ducked back into the alcove, rebuking himself for having been so careless and so naïve. Sympathetic or not, what the man was doing was vile. If Julian and Gus were arrested, their names would be published in the newspaper, Julian would lose his job and his apartment, and criminal convictions might hound them for the rest of their lives. He thought about all the good judgment and careful pains that had brought him from the wasteland of Phoenix to New York City and the halls of academe and taught him to believe he'd found a way to meet his peculiar destiny without too much suffering. Now all of it would be squandered because he'd been caught in a janitor's alcove with a brilliant young painter who'd asked for nothing more than to stay with him for a couple of weeks.

"You must see how ridiculous this is," Gus said, as if reading his mind.

Julian admired his refusal to compromise with the world's petty mores. It wasn't that he himself lacked courage. He certainly wasn't like those self-loathing men with oblivious wives who stole into the city for clandestine sexual relief. He hoped Gus saw him as too wise to worry about other people's morality, too brave to fear their judgments, and too honest ever to dissemble. But he knew that he wasn't, like Gus, entirely free.

"I'm leaving," Gus said suddenly.

"Please don't!" Julian said, raising his arm to stop him a second time.

Gus shot him a determined smile, then pushed his arm away.

"Sorry, J.P.," he said, "I'm just not in the habit of hiding from people."

As he stepped out into the hallway, the man in the topcoat emerged from the men's toilet, lit another cigarette, and began walking back toward the zinc bar. Gus marched off after him, pointing with his left hand, and with his right making a fist he could have had no real intention of using.

"You there!" he shouted. "You've got no right—!"

Before he could finish his declaration, a uniformed officer came out of the toilet, swung a baton at the back of Gus's head, and knocked him to the floor. It all happened in a second or two, but Gus's body collapsed in a slow, outrageous blur.

Julian flung himself from the alcove and raced to his side. He cradled his head in his trembling hands, then leaned in close to interpret his rasping moans and whisper apologies into his ear. When he heard the scuff of shoes, he looked up, still stunned that a man could be struck so casually and that it could happen to someone so blameless. The cop and the man in the topcoat only exchanged curt nods and walked away as if nothing had happened. Julian called out several times for help until it became clear that none would be coming. Then he waited on the floor, stroking Gus's freckled cheek and straddling the miserable edge of catastrophe and relief.

When Gus opened his eyes a moment later, Julian choked back grateful tears, made a pillow of his blazer, and found a clean bar towel to apply to the bloody lesion. As soon as Gus was able to stand, they wrapped their arms around each other and hobbled toward the door, past a half dozen officers with their absurd blue costumes and superior expressions. But for Gus's sake, he only looked straight ahead with a hard, impassive smile.

"You were amazingly brave," he said as they left the bar. "I plan to give you a medal."

"I guess it wasn't much of a protest," Gus said.

"No, very David and Goliath."

"I don't think David was the one who got hit in the head."

"Don't be so literal, baby. You've got to conserve your strength."

They joined a sad pageant of defeated men filing out onto Bethune Street, where snow gathered on the sidewalk and exhaust from the green police vans spiraled into the pitiless dark. Since it was late and quite cold, there was hardly anyone there to witness the abysmal scene. Some of the men threw their coats over their heads anyway or hid their faces in their hats. But Julian kept his eyes locked on Gus, glad beyond measure to be his protector and trying hard to avoid the terrible question of who would be his.

3

Though dancing was strictly against house rules, Danny Duffy had been twisting his heart out near the jukebox with his best friend Gabriel and "wa-wa-wa-wa-wondering why she ran away," when he got blindsided by a cop's swinging fist. As he checked his cheek for blood and smoothed his ginger pompadour, the choice before him seemed clear. He could let himself be taken like a criminal or start swinging back, probably take a few more hits himself, and get dragged out kicking and screaming like a man. Normally, he knew it was dumb to take on the cops, no matter how bad they treated you. But that night it was his guts, full of beer and bitterness, that had their way. So he ducked and struck, hit someone on the nose and took a hard lump to his chin and another above the ear. When he felt someone's rough hands around his neck, he threw a few sticky elbows into the guy's ribs. Then some lard-ass grabbed him by the arm, threw him to the floor, and sat right on top of him. And as he lay there catching his breath, imagining Gabriel somewhere in the bar throwing sloppy punches and getting some rough revenge, he realized he felt disappointed. The whole thing was over way too fast.

After patting Danny down, the cops yanked him out of Caesar's and tossed him into a happy wagon like a sack of spuds. His head hurt in three places, and when he opened his mouth to hurl curses at the cops who'd done the damage, he realized he was too wrecked to keep up the fight. In fact, it was the second one he'd lost that night, though he felt more beaten down than beaten up. He craned his neck to look out the rear window for a glimpse of Gabriel, but when he didn't see him, he just folded his arms, leaned against cold steel, and watched as the other men were thrown inside with him.

The first guy was at least fifty, shoe-faced and ash-skinned, like a dead salesman, crying one moment and cursing the next. Then came a rich kid in a tuxedo that fit him like black-and-white paint. He smirked and tried to look smart, but you could tell he was scared, like he'd just driven his beautiful Ivy League life into a ditch. One poor fellow crept in holding a bloody rag to the back of his head, with another following right behind him, not exactly steering but never letting his hand leave his friend's shoulder. They were lovers, Danny realized, or at least it seemed so by the way the one worried so openly about the other. Behind them came a boy with a big head of light brown hair, probably underage, and definitely for sale. He looked pretty cocky in his rabbit fur vest and bright red pants, like he'd done it all before a thousand times. Then there was a pair of older gents, frail and shabby but highly respectable in their silk and Vitalis. One was black, though you could hardly tell because they both hid behind their hats. Eventually, the cops brought in the last two casualties before locking the door. The first was another kid, tall and sporty but shaking like a salmon, and the second was a man in a gray suit, older and kind of suave, though he looked like he might start giving orders. But except for Shoe-Face, no one made a peep. After all, it was pointless to protest and disgraceful to try to make the best of such a miserable situation.

Danny himself didn't have too much left to lose. Just his job at Sloan's on Columbus and 84th, where he was due the next morning at seven sharp. He'd been there nearly five years and risen through the ranks to assistant manager in charge of produce. As a job, it was as straight as they came and he rarely mentioned it to his friends, who mostly preferred to work in restaurants or beauty salons or department stores, though some like Gabriel preferred having no job at all. Working at a supermarket was a far cry from the gay life, but there was something Danny liked about slipping back and forth between the tidiness of the one and the wildness of the other. Sloan's was never an ass-breaker, and it paid better than anything he'd done before. And he was good at it, so it made him feel like a success. He liked figuring out how to minimize wastage and keep his margins up. He knew nearly everything there was to know about fruits and vegetables, even exotics like kumquats and kohlrabi. He liked the people too, and not just the cute boys who stacked fruit and carried boxes and reported to him directly. The other assistant managers, who all had wives and kids, were decent and never called him Shorty or teased him about his hair or the tunes he hummed while he worked. Even the manager, Mr. Di Stefano, an all-business Sicilian, seemed to respect him just as he was.

Of course, Danny knew that if any of them found out about his arrest, he'd be canned for sure, no questions asked. If that happened, at least there'd be nobody at home wishing Danny had never been born, since they'd all made their feelings known earlier that night and, technically speaking, he no longer even had a home. No one would thank God that Danny's father—Pat Duffy, who was sometimes a saint in death but usually a drunk and a prick and a windbag while he lived—wasn't alive to witness his disgrace because such thanks had already been given.

Over breaded cutlets in their Parkchester two-bedroom, Danny had been accused, judged, and banished in short order. What began as a snide remark from his second-eldest brother, Quinn, soon turned into speculations about Danny's inexperience with women. Their mother, Margaret Duffy, who'd been drowsing over her plate, perked up when she heard the word "virgin" and glared at no one in particular. She hated vulgarity and sex talk, and though one sharp look usually put the kibosh on either, this time its effect was only temporary.

"We all know what kind of guy wears a purple tie," Quinn said.

Danny was surprised by the boldness of the attack, especially at a Thursday-night family dinner, when it was traditional to call a general truce. He'd recently taken to brightening up his work clothes with a skinny plum Wembley, a touch of color to make himself feel a little stylish without attracting too much attention. Though his other best friend Rafael had warned him it might be too Oscar Wilde for the Bronx, in Manhattan nobody seemed to care.

"Blow it out your ear!" Danny said, before looking at Ciaran, his eldest brother, who'd always defended him against Quinn's needling.

But Ciaran only closed his big baggy eyes and shook his already-balding head, while his wife, Mavis, rubbed her pregnant belly and laughed like it was just another joke she didn't understand. Ciaran was no heartthrob—he was as generous as St. Nick, as tough as St. George, and as homely as a baboon—but no one knew what he saw in Mavis except her ready fertility.

Margaret Duffy glared at Quinn. He was the handsomest of them all, with warm hazel eyes and a smile people often mistook for friendliness, though usually not for long. She was annoyed, Danny knew, not just because her first glare hadn't ended the argument but also because what Quinn said was innuendo, though she probably didn't understand what it meant any more than Mavis did. And if their mother hated vulgarity and sex talk, she couldn't tolerate innuendo. But she also couldn't stand to hear a harsh word against Danny. It was a well-known fact that she'd always loved him best. He supposed it was because he was the smallest and looked the least like his father and nothing at all like his brothers, who were nearly six feet tall. When he was little and they lived on St. Ann's Avenue in Mott Haven, she'd sometimes whisper in his ear that he was her favorite and Saint Jude would always look after him and never let him down.

"That's quite enough," she said softly but firmly, before turning back to her plate and muttering, "Lord help us."

When it seemed she'd brought the contest to a draw, Danny took care to not show any pleasure in seeing Quinn silenced or relief that the danger had passed.

"Enough of what, Ma?" Bill suddenly asked, with all the appearance of sincerity, as if he hadn't been paying attention and suddenly wanted in on the conversation. "And what's all this business about ties?"

The middle son, on a week's leave from the army and newly engaged to be married, Bill had perfected the art of innocent troublemaking. But he winced when Michael—a redhead like Danny and only half as mean as Quinn but mean enough still—kicked him under the table. Michael's foot must have ricocheted off its target because Mavis winced too. Danny knew the kick was more for rebelling against their mother's dinner-table rule than for fueling the dispute with Quinn. But since Bill had fueled it, everyone suddenly looked at Danny, even Margaret Duffy.

"For Christ's sake! Can't we eat our dinner in peace?" Danny said, hoping his mother would overlook the profanity since it was used in the name of good manners.

In high school, he'd successfully kept up the illusion that he was young for his age, still more interested in school than girls, a late bloomer who'd eventually come around. The fact that he didn't get good marks and had started shaving when he was a freshman didn't seem to matter. They all saw what they wanted to see, and when no one was looking Danny sang and danced in theatricals, mooned over hunky movie stars, and jerked off several times a day. Since he was brave and could fight and often did, especially after Pat Duffy died of cirrhosis and they moved to the Patterson Houses with Negroes and Puerto Ricans, he was rarely called a sissy to his face. After he graduated high school and there were still no girls, the mask probably began to slip. But except for Quinn, none of his brothers ever said a word. Danny figured they'd decided that his queerness was either Father Frank's problem or God's but not theirs.

"I'm pretty sure there's only one kind of guy wears a purple tie," Quinn said.

"Go choke yourself!" Danny said.

"Just one kind."

They all waited for Quinn to say the horrible word, the way you waited for the answer on *Quiz Kids*, even though you already knew it. Ciaran wrinkled his mouth and merged his fuzzy brows, while Mavis played with her Brussels sprouts. Bill and Michael only watched, like it was a ballgame between two teams they didn't care about.

"I won't listen to this nonsense," Margaret Duffy said. "Lord help us."

"Look then, Ma, if you won't listen. Look at him!"

Quinn pushed his chair back, stood up, and held his hand out at Danny, like he was introducing him. Ed Sullivan with an ax to grind.

"He looks fine," she said.

At first, she didn't turn toward Danny, either because she thought she already knew what he looked like or because she was suddenly afraid to find out. But when she did turn and a smile of relief softened her normally tight, dull mouth, Danny put on a small show of embarrassment for good measure.

29

"Are you kidding?" Quinn shouted. "Look at his hair! Look at how he dresses!"

A creepy chill crawled up the back of Danny's neck. He did wear his pants a bit tight because he liked the way it looked and felt, and he'd definitely let his pompadour mushroom recently. Now he realized that the purple tie had been a reckless choice for Thursday-night family dinner.

"At least he doesn't *wear* dresses," Michael said, producing a snort from Bill.

Ciaran closed his eyes again and said nothing. Two years of fighting communists in Korea had kind of snuffed out his candle, and now he seemed torn between holiness and goodness, though goodness was clearly losing the battle.

"Oh, I'm sure it's the style these days!" Margaret Duffy informed Quinn, raising her voice to the point that it cracked. She wasn't used to being loud or making pronouncements on style. But she didn't like being contradicted by her sons, either.

Danny felt as if a thousand old, well-guarded secrets were about to spill into the room like water from a leaky ceiling. Years of going unnoticed had convinced him he was safe from suspicion. But he'd gotten too comfortable, and his free pass seemed finally to have expired.

"And the music he listens to!" Quinn went on. "Doris Day, Ma! Doris Day!"

When Danny was a kid, taking a keen interest in beautiful blondes was an indisputable sign of manliness, but over the years the rules had changed significantly.

"All the young men like her, I'm sure," Margaret Duffy said, though when the tail end of her sentence fell flat, Danny—who *used* to listen to Doris Day—who used to *love* Doris Day—knew she'd begun to lose hope, and then so did he.

As a last resort, he looked Quinn in the eye to let him know that he'd never forgive him unless he stopped right then and there. But it was too late. Quinn only clicked his tongue and waited to be sure their mother's willful ignorance was obvious to Michael, Bill, and Ciaran.

"No, Ma," he said. "All due respect, they don't."

"Lord help us" was all she said.

What happened next somehow took less time and fewer words than it should have. Quinn didn't call Danny any names. Had he been too specific, it might have forced Margaret Duffy to choose between her favorite son and her least favorite, and while those contests had rarely gone Quinn's way before, his case this time was more solid. Instead, he just declared that it was high time Danny moved out of the apartment. He was old enough to live on his own and stop being a burden to their poor mother, who wanted privacy now that all her children were grown. It didn't seem to matter that Michael, who was ten months older than Danny, still shared the second bedroom with him, though he made good money selling wholesale hardware. Or that Danny had been helping with the rent for nearly five years. Or that privacy was something their mother had never had in her entire life and probably never even thought to miss. But when nobody said anything at all, it was clear a decision had been made. Ciaran sighed helplessly, while Mavis buffed her belly and Margaret Duffy stole fretful glimpses at Danny's tie. Bill looked half-relieved and half-regretful but stayed mum. To his own sad surprise, Danny did too. Any more protest would've only forced Quinn to paint the picture, and he knew he could neither deny the truth, which self-respect wouldn't have allowed, nor admit it, which would've only made things worse for his mother. If she hated innuendo, her peace of mind often depended on insinuation.

So Quinn relished his victory, while Margaret Duffy stared at her cutlet and Danny, almost stupid with disbelief, looked around and said a silent good-bye to the place he'd called home for nearly ten years. The limp, yellowed lace curtains that had been carried from apartment to apartment since before he was born. The old litho portrait of the Blessed Virgin hovering over the mantel, with the gilt frame he used to think was made of real gold and proved his family was rich as well as pious. Even the new leatherette sofa they'd all chipped in to get their mother for Christmas, cheaply made but dearly bought. He worried that he'd miss it all like crazy and it would haunt him in his dreams. But when Margaret Duffy's tears finally came and she retreated to the kitchen, Danny went to his bedroom, packed his duffel bag, straightened his tie, and left the apartment without saying good-bye to anyone.

31

He caught the IRT at Castle Hill Avenue and made his way down to Chelsea, where Rafael had a one-room apartment on the fifth floor of a six-story, cold-water walkup, which was usually freezing in winter but always clean and comfortable. They sat down on the little couch that Raf had turned into a makeshift bed with one cotton blanket for a pillow and two woolen ones for warmth. Danny cursed Quinn's wickedness, Ciaran's cowardice, and Margaret Duffy's betrayal, and Raf listened with the right balance of sympathy and resentment. Later, they drank beer and ate mofongo, then blasted a joint and ogled the latest issue of *Tomorrow's Man,* its glistening models like beings from a happier world. After Raf told Danny he could stay as long as he wanted, they agreed to meet Gabriel downtown and blow off some steam. Raf liked a good time and was easy on the eyes, though when they went out together he usually came home early and alone. Danny knew he needed to get a few strong drinks in him that night or he'd come unglued, and that if he didn't get a little rowdy, too, he'd feel sad and scared and all alone in the world.

◉ ◉ ◉

"Here's what's gonna happen, ladies," the hustler said once the happy wagon started moving. "First, there's what's called initial processing. You get patted down again and whatever you got on you gets vouchered. But if it's nice stuff, just consider it a donation to the PBA. Then you get charged and interviewed for pedigree. That's your name, address, birthday, and such." Here he looked at the Suave Suit: "Don't worry, gorgeous, the truth's gonna set you free! Anyway, then you get fingerprinted and photographed, though believe me, it's not a picture you're gonna wanna send your momma."

Danny admired that the hustler didn't care what anyone thought. But he also wondered how many of these speeches he'd given before. Though the information seemed helpful for a first-timer, the way he shared it was pretty depressing, since getting arrested and thrown in jail could only be funny business if you'd done it so many times that you didn't care about anything anymore.

When the happy wagon stopped in front of the police station on Charles Street a few minutes later, Danny looked out the rear window again and watched snowflakes swirling in the lamplight, which somehow reminded him that Raf had left Caesar's around eleven thirty and been spared. He felt especially grateful for this fact when the door opened and two cops grabbed his wrists and chucked him onto the street—since, for all his good qualities, Raf wasn't what you'd call tough. But he wasn't nearly as meek as the Two Gents, who squeaked like mice when the cops snatched them by their elbows. The hustler hopped out on his own, cool as a sno-cone, but Shoe-Face took a tumble, slipped in the slushy gutter, and started sobbing again, until one of the cops told him to pipe down. The Rich Kid and the Suave Suit came out quietly enough, but the tall boy seemed like he was about to lose his marbles or his dinner. When the injured guy and his lover finally stepped onto the pavement, they were still thick as thieves, though more like condemned ones headed for a noose and a long drop.

But Danny was strangely calm as he stood without his coat on the sidewalk and they were all made to form a line. He looked up and down the empty street and out into the blizzard-dark sky. The big limestone building seemed more like a swanky hotel than a police station. It had a pair of marble columns and right above a second-story window there was a stone eagle perched on a shield between a pioneer and an Indian, as if joining them in a peace treaty everyone thought would last forever. When an old Buick muffled by, the driver looked confused, like he couldn't understand what these harmless-looking men were doing there in the middle of the night. And when he drove away without saying something nasty, Danny felt grateful again.

A hawkeyed officer with a frosty sneer that made him look like a Nazi from *Stalag 17* strutted out of the station and marched them all inside. The lobby was full of beat cops, plainclothes detectives, and about a dozen others, most of whom minded their own business. The only exception was a desk sergeant with a face full of pimples and hair stained midnight black with Grecian Formula, who leered at the prisoners as they filed past, probably just to scare them. When it was Danny's turn, he was relieved of his wallet, his watch, his keys to the loading dock at Sloan's, even his belt and tie, in case he decided to off himself. Then, just as the hustler had said, he was photographed

33

and fingerprinted, though for rebellion's sake he screwed up his face for the camera and smeared his fingers on the fingerprint card and nobody seemed to notice. Eventually, the Nazi Cop led him down a corridor toward the back of the building and up a flight of stairs to a long row of cells. Most were filled with sorry-looking men standing around, sitting on benches, or lying on the floor. Some looked like they'd been at Caesar's that night, though Danny only recognized a few of them and there was still no sign of Gabriel. When they reached the last cell, the Nazi Cop shoved him inside, slammed the door behind him, and marched back down the corridor. His broad jaw jutted out over his chest and he swung his arms high like he was dreaming of Hitler and the glory of the Reich.

The place smelled of rust and sweat. The gunmetal-gray bars, scuffed white cement floor, and graffiti-scratched brick walls made it look like most of the jail cells Danny had seen in movies or on TV. In fact, it was too familiar to be very scary. So he claimed a corner for himself and squatted on the floor, wondering how long he'd be there and whether he'd get out in time to make it to work the next day. Some of the other men were bawling, yelling, or quietly saying good-bye to the lives they thought they'd just lost. The Suave Suit had a real conniption before he started acting like he owned the place. But Danny felt relaxed, even a little hopeful. Though he'd been evicted and arrested all in a single night, he knew he had no reason to panic yet.

He thought of Doris Day in *The Man Who Knew Too Much* and imagined the Nazi Cop coming back to their cell, all smiles and dimples, sashaying through the door with a lighthearted song to cheer them up. As Danny hummed "Que Sera, Sera" to himself and fingered the part of his collar where his purple tie had been, something told him he'd be fine, no matter what. He wasn't even that angry at the cops anymore. It was only the thought of Margaret Duffy's tears or being laughed at by Quinn that bothered him a little, though he knew there was nothing he could do about either. Whatever would be, would be. Despite what anyone thought of him and everything that had happened that night, Danny knew he'd always had a genuine talent for being okay.

4

When the cell door slammed behind Roger, it rang out like a cracked church bell and hard, broken notes quavered down his spine. But as he gripped the bars to steady himself, shock soon gave way to a churning, analytic dread. His visits to places like Caesar's had always depended upon his ability to leave without any trace of his ever having been there. Now an accident of bad timing had brought him face-to-face with the awful solidity of brick and steel. The other men with him—some in tears, one bleeding from his head, most of them fairies or delinquents or both—only made things worse. The line separating Roger from such people would soon disappear completely, and his name would be added to theirs and made part of a ruinous permanent record.

Another cell door crashed. Someone began whimpering softly. The sour smell of unclean bodies confirmed the indignity of it all. Roger felt a hollow heaviness inside him, pulling at his vital organs as if he'd swallowed poison. He thought back to the moment he'd left the hotel that night to go downtown, so spiffy and eager in his favorite chalk-stripe suit—now stained with sweat on the collar and grime on the cuffs. If only he'd avoided Caesar's or stayed in his hotel room, gotten drunk, and taken care of matters himself. If only he'd gone home to his wife and honored his marriage vows. If only he'd been the kind of man who took pleasure in doing that. He jammed his forehead into one of the bars, as if it might help the impossible magic along or split his brain in two and solve the problem once and for all. But after a while it only made him feel more trapped and more foolish, since wishing had never once helped Roger.

It was regrettable that he hadn't tried to comfort Andy when the boy had an attack of nerves on the way to the station, babbling about his tuition at NYU and the town of Pelham, where he lived and everyone knew him. Instead, Roger only straightened his back and stared vacantly at a welded seam of the police van's interior. But as they were brought into the cell, he remembered that Pelham was only minutes by car from New Rochelle, and then the boy's fears suddenly became his own. Word of his arrest would spread quickly through Beechmont Woods, and the small private life he'd so sparingly allowed himself would be made extravagantly public. Richard in Baltimore would telephone to say he'd always known it would come to this. Roger's sister Audrey in Hartford would probably send a telegram, but she'd still call him a degenerate and promise never to speak to him again for the sake of her children. His father, Elliot, twenty miles north in Darien, would only shake his distinguished gray head and kill Roger from a distance with contempt. Of course, Schuyler would deny the accusation at first, challenging anyone who dared to repeat it, but only until tangible proof finally forced him to cut his best friend, sharply and swiftly. Roger's boss, Edgar, might bridle at the impertinent ambiguity of "disorderly conduct," but in the end he'd fire him just as certainly. And poor, trusting, blameless Corinne would be undone. Pitied by the neighborhood, ridiculed as a dupe and a fool. Her mother would hurry down from Litchfield, sparing the children from taunts they couldn't yet understand and removing them from the big white house with the elm tree and the yew hedge, which was no longer a home and never really had been.

As Roger watched the keen-eyed guard disappear back into the stairwell, sweat spilled down his forehead and stung his eyes. He had to open his mouth to get enough oxygen into his lungs. His knees ached, as if they might break under the weight of so much despair. He knew gripping the cell bars made him the very type of the abject prisoner, but he needed to steady himself enough to think. If only there were some plausible way of making his arrest seem like an unlucky mistake. He might insist he'd only gone into the bar to use the toilet, having no idea what kind of place it was. Or say he'd been

36

innocently strolling down Bethune Street when a couple of officers mistakenly seized him and threw him into the police van. But it was all nonsense. There was no explaining away what had happened.

He'd been wrong not to jump when he had the chance. Staying on the roof with Andy had helped no one. He was wrong to have gone into the bar in the first place. His furtive trips were always motivated by a shameful, puerile lust, one he should have long since mastered. He was wrong every time he'd stolen a glance, told a lie, hid a secret, or feigned a feeling. He'd been wrong so many times in his life that he'd come to believe being wrong for him was like being weakhearted or asthmatic—an essential and incurable deformity.

One of the men in the cell began shouting for a guard, as if he thought the one who'd put him there might suddenly admit he'd made a mistake and set him free. Out of the corner of his eye, Roger saw a young preppie in a tuxedo go around begging for a cigarette. He heard the whimpering behind him grow steadily louder. It sounded like Andy, but Roger had already helped him more than he ought to have. They were all in trouble, no one more than himself. He had no responsibility other than to survive the night and face the morning bravely.

"*You* must have a cigarette. I'll go stark raving mad if I don't find one."

It was the preppie, who looked like he'd been at a deb ball that night. He smelled of gin and halitosis, and although his face was handsome enough, there was something in his throaty, clipped voice that Roger detested. It wasn't merely the effeminacy, which he usually did his best to tolerate. What really bothered him was that the boy's voice was so easy and free. It fit him as comfortably as his tuxedo.

"Get away from me!" Roger roared.

"Charming!" the preppie muttered, before swerving to his next mark.

Roger hadn't meant to be so loud or so harsh, and his loss of self-control seemed a needless sacrifice of whatever little dignity remained to him. Fortunately, the other men in the cell didn't seem to notice, which came as a relief—until he realized that they probably had noticed but had also ceased to care about such things as a loss of dignity.

"Gua-a-a-ard!" the first man shouted again.

Roger let go of the bars and turned to the man. His suit was cheap and rumpled and his head much too large for his body.

"Shouting won't help you, sir," Roger said firmly. "And it certainly won't help anyone else. So please stop."

The man seemed ready to call yet again for the guard, but before the words were fully formed, he apparently thought better of it, turned away, and sat down on one of the benches to ruminate more peaceably.

Somewhat revived by this small exercise of leadership, Roger cast about the cell for another opportunity to improve on a bad situation and then eventually walked over to Andy, now no longer whimpering but only staring silently at his shoes. Despite his muscular physique, he was doubled over and as droopy as a rag, the very reverse of the winning boy Roger had met less than three hours before. He felt pity, of course, but no attraction and no particular obligation. He'd neither seduced Andy nor invited him to the bar in the first place. Although he'd certainly intended to commit a felony with him, that intention, however urgent at the time, now seemed ludicrous.

"Try not to worry," Roger said.

It seemed like good advice, but Andy only dropped his chin to his chest, and Roger didn't know what else to say. Since he couldn't predict the future and refused to sugarcoat the truth, he tried to stay focused on the facts.

"I'm sure they'll let us make a phone call," he said.

Andy looked up. "Who the fuck am I gonna call!" he screamed, bursts of spittle spraying from his mouth.

Roger felt ashamed and walked away. Of course, Andy had a point. Unless one had the telephone number of an especially open-minded attorney, there was nobody to call. But it had been unwise to speak to the boy while he was in such a hysterical state.

"We get to make a phone call?" a mellow, lamb-like voice suddenly asked.

It was one of the older fairies, a Negro, huddled with his friend on a bench. Although he was quite the dandy, his threadbare velvet suit smacked as much of poverty as effort, and he had the sere, lackluster face of someone who'd lived a hard life.

"I'm sure they'll let us know soon," Roger said with a charitable smile, ignoring the half-heard gibes of the young man sprawled across one of the benches, whose long hair and provocative clothes made him look very much like a prostitute.

Back in the police van, he'd treated them all to an absurd speech about jailhouse protocols in a manner that was somehow swishy, crude, smug, and jaded all at once—and inaccurate, too, since Roger hadn't yet been charged or fingerprinted but was only photographed and held in a small room by himself before being taken up to the cell.

After the Negro smiled his thanks, Roger noticed him wrap his pinkie finger around that of his friend, who then let the tail of his long, frayed silk scarf fall over their joined hands. There was something rather silly in such a tender show of affection between two old men. But there was something oddly decent about it, too, a sign of solidarity under conditions that might otherwise have made people selfish and mercenary. Roger always liked the way Schuyler squeezed his shoulder or tackled him with a bear hug whenever he was too happy to contain himself. He could never initiate such gestures himself for fear that in the moment his feelings would escape his vigilance. But he'd never had to take the lead. Schuyler, a great lover of women, was always at his ease in the arms of men and rarely passed up an opportunity to be affectionate with his friends.

There was another man in the cell, probably in his early thirties, being similarly free with his attentions to a younger man who'd been injured in the raid. As he caught a glimpse of the first man's face, Roger realized that they'd met before and remembered that he went by the rather pretentious-sounding name of Julian Prince. He didn't hold his friend's hand, but he did whisper in his ear occasionally and kept refolding the bloodied towel he'd been holding to his friend's head to find a clean spot to apply to the wound. The second man, attractive but grave-looking, didn't seem to be in any real danger and at least once hinted that he no longer required such intensive care. But Julian Prince didn't seem willing to take any chances.

Roger hadn't noticed him in the police van, so shocked and distracted as he'd been at the time. But when he pulled a spare handkerchief from his pocket and offered it, Prince looked up, smiled his recognition, and accepted the gift with polite thanks before returning to his ministrations. Although Roger couldn't help but envy the confidence the two men shared, he took pleasure in the idea that he'd at least momentarily joined them in a respectable fellowship of insulted but honorable men.

"Do you think they'll let us go by morning?" Prince asked, after an uneasy silence. His friend nodded at Roger, either to echo the question or in belated appreciation for the handkerchief.

"I don't see why not," Roger said. "They can't have any interest in keeping us here all weekend." He supposed it might not be that simple, but he was glad to sound so self-possessed.

They'd met about a year before at a Midtown hotel, Roger remembered, though he'd forgotten which one. It wasn't especially seedy, nor was it very fancy, but it was known for being a place where men of a certain taste could meet and, if both parties agreed, slip upstairs and go to bed together. They'd been standing near each other at the bar that night, each drinking dry martinis, and the trifling coincidence seemed reason enough to strike up a conversation, which was surprisingly frank and free of the typical façades and prevarications. But somehow it led to nothing. Prince was attractive in a striking sort of way, though older and more urbane than the kind of men Roger preferred. He seemed pleased enough with Roger, but he made no obvious overtures. So when the prospect of more than talk began to fade, so did the conversation itself, and soon the two men made their excuses, shook hands, and parted.

"Okay, Girl Scouts, listen up," the prostitute suddenly said as he sat up from the bench and resumed his lecture. "Sometime before breakfast, you'll be carted downtown to the famous Manhattan House of Pleasure and Detention, also known as the Tombs. Then, unless you got your own lawyer, you'll see a public defender, who won't even look you in the eye, so as to protect his chastity."

This time, Roger wanted to tell the little punk to keep his obscene thoughts to himself. But because he'd already shouted at two fairies that night and feared that shouting at a third might make him an object of suspicion, he only listened and sneered his disapproval.

"Next, you're gonna go in front of the judge, who's likely to offer some hard remark about your wicked ways before making you plead guilty as charged. Then, assuming you don't already got a record, you'll pay your fine, collect your crap, and get released. With any luck, you'll be home before the pot roast is cold."

Here he performed a little bow and looked around to see whom he'd frightened or affronted. "I can answer any questions if you got 'em," he added, as he buffed his fingernails on the collar of his outlandish fur vest.

Before anyone could take him up on his offer, all attention shifted to the keen-eyed guard who was coming back toward the cell, swinging his arms and whistling atonally. He seemed a dullard and a bully, Roger thought, though perhaps the right type of man for the job. After he opened the cell door, he looked at Prince and his friend, then passed his eyes over Roger and the two older men, then Andy, the man in the rumpled suit, the prostitute, and a small, canny-looking redhead who sat in one corner. At last, the guard pointed his finger at Roger, who despite a sudden wave of queasiness felt almost eager to face the enemy. Far better to be the first man shot or set free, Schuyler had once said, than to be kept waiting.

◎ ◎ ◎

In a windowless room, a pair of men in civvies sat at a rubber-topped table without looking up. One of them looked at least sixty years old with a red bulbous nose, a shiny bald pate, and broad ox-like shoulders that loomed over the folder of documents he was reading. Next to him was a smaller, younger man, wiry and alert, possibly of Mediterranean descent. He looked more like a boxer than an amanuensis, but he'd already written a quarter page of notes in a straight, even hand. When it seemed they had no immediate intention of speaking, Roger looked around the room. On the wall behind the two detectives was a large, faded map of lower Manhattan, a dented black filing cabinet, and a noisy radiator. Above them hung a fluorescent lamp whose hard white glare seemed ready to expose all forms of criminality. He wondered if the door directly behind him had been locked.

"Roger Moorhouse. New Rochelle. Born May 1, 1922," the older detective finally said. His expression was cold and humorless as he lay down the driver's license and then fished a business card out of

Roger's billfold on the table in front of him. "Chemical Bank New York Trust Company. 165 Broadway." There was a lift in his voice as he named the bank. "And your position there is?"

The card plainly offered the information, but he seemed to want Roger to tell him anyway, perhaps to savor the irony of such a tragic fall from grace.

"I'm a senior vice president in our commercial loan department," Roger said, wondering how long it would remain true.

"I bet you have quite a number of men working under you," the detective said.

He leaned back in his chair and raised one of his woolly eyebrows as the radiator began to knock. Whether he'd meant merely to imply that a man arrested in a queer bar was a poor role model or something more vulgar was unclear. So Roger only stared back at him and waited for an actual question.

"So *do* you have a number of men working under you?"

The second detective stopped writing and sucked in his lips, apparently to keep from laughing. It was nothing more than a juvenile game of double entendre, and Roger realized he couldn't expect any honor or integrity in the business that followed. Despite their suits and ties, these men were no different from the brutes in blue who'd already treated him so callously.

"Yes, I do," he said, glad at least to have regained a bit of moral high ground.

"How many men, exactly?" the first detective asked.

"Approximately twenty."

"Fine, now tell us about your wife?"

Roger felt a return of the hollow heaviness inside him. Of course, they might have assumed he was a married man, despite the absence of a wedding ring, which he'd left back at the hotel. He knew few bachelors his age and none who were senior vice presidents. But then he noticed the band of pale skin around his left ring finger, and as he looked up, the older detective, who'd obviously noticed it too, smiled for the first time.

"What exactly would you like to know?" Roger asked, bracing himself.

"Is she pretty?" the older detective asked.

"Most people say she is," Roger said.

"But what do *you* say? That's the question, isn't it?" The light from the lamp glinted off the detective's scalp.

"I can't see how that's any of your business," Roger said, insisting to himself that the shadowy space between appreciation and desire was his alone to navigate.

"There's nothing like a pretty girl," the older detective said, turning to his colleague. "Isn't that right?"

"Truer words have never been spoken," the younger one said.

They watched Roger's stifled outrage as another tense, wordless quarter minute passed. It wasn't clear if they were taking an early break in the interview or still trying to unnerve him before the formal interrogation began. But when the younger detective began tapping his pen, the older one suddenly stood up and told Roger to do the same. Then he handed him his billfold, wristwatch, housekeys, necktie, tiepin, and belt, and immediately went to open the door, which hadn't been locked after all.

As they left the room together and walked down the corridor toward the staircase leading back up to the cells, Roger wondered why the interview had ended so abruptly, why they'd given him back his belongings, and why no questions had been asked about the raid or his presence at Caesar's that night or even his proclivity to frequent such places. But instead of climbing back up to the cellblock, they turned at the stairwell and walked down another corridor that seemed to run across the rear of the building and terminate in a large steel door. Roger hoped it might lead to the room where he'd be allowed to make a telephone call, and he began to rehearse the awkward apology he'd have to make to his not-so-open-minded attorney for disturbing him at such an hour with such a disgusting account of the night's events.

When they arrived at the door, the older detective put his hand on Roger's shoulder. "Mr. Moorhouse, you seem like a highly respectable member of the community," he said with a flat smile. "But in the future you ought to take care not to find yourself again in any more situations that might compromise your reputation."

Roger didn't know if it was advice or a threat. But the notion that he still had a reputation to protect seemed as strange as anything the man had said to him that night.

"Do you understand what I'm saying?" the detective asked.

Roger did not understand, nor did he think that he was meant to. He could make no sense of the brief and demeaning interrogation. He didn't even know the names of the men who'd conducted it. He only wanted to make his phone call, get back to the cell, and try to sleep for an hour or two if he could.

But when the detective opened the steel door, all Roger saw was a short staircase leading down to a narrow alley, dark and empty except for a few white-frosted garbage bins. Falling snowflakes nipped at his uncomprehending eyes. His insides instantly grew lighter and fuller, as if whatever poison he'd swallowed had turned out to be harmless after all. And then he realized that everything he thought he'd lost—all the people and possessions he'd been grieving since midnight—might be safe, untouched by the night's violence, still his. But hesitation wasn't a mistake Roger was going to make twice. So he stepped down into the alley, started walking briskly toward Washington Street, his best oxfords slipping on the snow, and he didn't even look back when the detective called out to him one last time.

"Without his reputation, a man ain't worth shit."

5

At first, there was no sound but the silent heft of snow settling around him. Then a truck groaned down Washington Street and then it was quiet again. It was also dark and cold, and without his coat, Julian's turtleneck and blazer had ceased to keep him warm after only a minute or two. He and Gus had agreed that, if separated, they'd wait for each other at the Waverly Restaurant on Sixth Avenue, which was open all night. But there was no telling whether Gus would come out through the same door, perhaps right behind him, or be held for hours and taken downtown to the Tombs, as the hustler had predicted. Julian knew if he stayed where he was, he'd freeze to death and be of use to no one, but if he went to the diner and Gus never showed, the long, lonely night would be unbearable. Either way, the thought of not knowing where he was or what was happening to him pulled icy tears from Julian's eyes. He almost felt as if someone had died, someone young and full of promise, and because he'd been so foolish, he'd failed to save him.

He thought of Gus's wan face and the blood that had matted in his ash-blond hair. It had been horrific, of course. But something about him lying on the floor of the bar was strangely beautiful, too, in the way a painting of Saint Sebastian riddled with arrows was beautiful, though more one by Botticelli or Bronzino than El Greco or Il Sodoma. Kneeling beside him, Julian had felt the bizarre urge to kiss Gus's wound, clean it with his mouth, honor the blood and the man who'd spilt it with the humblest of ablutions, and then spit it all into the face of the goon who'd struck him down.

"I'll be fine, J.P.," Gus had said as they sat on one of the benches in the cell. "It's probably just a bruised parietal and a minor concussion. If you were hoping for blunt force trauma, you're gonna be disappointed."

He often cracked wise with the medical vocabulary he'd picked up in his anatomy studies, which Julian understood as a kind of satire on the prestige of expertise. Yet the words brought back the moment of the baton and the blood, and Julian reached out instinctively before checking himself. He knew that appearing to be a couple could have put them both in jeopardy. But the desire to touch Gus was almost uncontrollable.

Julian's analyst, whom he'd been seeing twice a week for several years, had observed that, while he might take a sexual interest in any attractive man, the only ones he ever expressed any romantic interest in were those he considered superior to himself. He'd had plenty of affairs—with lawyers, doctors, writers, musicians—and with men of all types—short and tall, gorgeous and homely, foreign and domestic. But whenever he'd had any real feelings for someone, it always came with a strong sense of not deserving him, and the desperation it bred invariably killed the rose in the bud. Of course, the unfortunate corollary to such a perverse principle, which Julian's analyst had had the decency not to mention, was that with every other man he'd felt all too superior.

So when they'd begun seeing each other, Julian assumed that Gus would eventually reveal himself to be either impossibly good or unacceptably bad. In a few weeks, he was sure, the verdict would be in. The signs might come in the form of Gus's anxiety-inducing perfections or otherwise in his faulty sense of humor or objectionable hygiene, but come they would. Julian had never expected it to last.

But something was different this time. Gus was without a doubt the better man. He was smarter, kinder, better looking, more ambitious, even more modest. And yet somehow none of these advantages left Julian feeling wanting. They didn't make him uneasy or in need of reassurance, only grateful and proud, as if he'd been given special dispensation to deserve someone like Gus despite his own shortcomings. It was like being an otherwise unremarkable person who'd inherited vast amounts of money.

Since entering the cell, neither had paid much attention to what went on around them. There was certainly a lot of traffic and noise, but Julian and Gus mostly kept their heads down and made a kind of whispering refuge of their own. When a churlish young journeyman in the rough trade said something impertinent to Gus, they ignored him. A few times, Julian thought about his job at Columbia, his mother in Arizona, and his future, which he knew might now turn out very differently than he'd expected. But none of it seemed more urgent than the danger of Gus's wound, the liquored scent of his breath, and the intricate curves of his left ear.

"Would you behave yourself?" Gus said when he caught Julian staring at him. "You're in a jail cell, for gosh sakes! What'll the other prisoners think?"

"Very unclean thoughts, I suppose," Julian said.

"I guess you need a cold shower."

"Only if you'll join me. There'd be safety in numbers."

It was campy stuff, but it had an analgesic quality to it. Like Dilaudid tablets, it didn't quite take away the pain, but it made it a lot more bearable.

Then Julian heard a voice and looked up. One of their cellmates was offering them a clean white handkerchief to replace the bar towel, which had become a foul mosaic of garnet and burnt umber. Julian recognized him as someone he'd met about a year before at a hotel bar. Although he couldn't recall his name, he remembered that Julian hadn't suited him well enough to take things any further than conversation. For his own part, he'd found the man quite physically appealing, despite his somewhat advanced age, but there was something in his manner that seemed a bit weary, as if he struggled to stand up straight and meet the world every day. It made talking with him more fatiguing than pleasing, and when he made a sudden show of mere chumminess, Julian had taken the hint, and that was the end of it.

As he accepted the handkerchief and thanked the man, who called himself Roger Moorhouse, Julian remembered that he worked at the one of the big city banks. But now it was clear that he expected repayment for his kindness in the form of sympathetic talk from a likeminded fellow. Although Julian had no wish to break up his tête-à-tête with Gus to make room for a third, he knew, even without looking around, that for someone like Roger, he was probably the only man in the cell who'd do.

But the conversation never happened. The hustler began an encore performance of his carceral sophistication by enumerating all the further indignities they could expect to endure in the coming hours. It was a colorful account of due process, which, like the one they'd heard in the police van, sounded perfectly justified if you thought the way most people did but perfectly Kafkaesque if you didn't. Julian still didn't understand why he'd been photographed but not, like Gus, also charged and fingerprinted. But he chalked it up to police incompetence and only hoped they wouldn't be separated a second time. When the hustler's lecture was over, Roger shook his head in pique, but Julian and Gus merely exchanged covert smiles, tacitly agreeing that, although it would probably be a long and miserable night, they'd suffer it together.

"Ope. Looks like he's coming our way," Gus said a moment later.

It was the one thing they'd both taken care to notice. The same surly guard who'd brought them inside the station had been conveying people in and out of cells since they'd arrived. He seemed to take pleasure in manhandling his prisoners, often adding a jarring shake or a swift kick when none was necessary. As he entered their cell and scrutinized each man, Julian held his breath. When the guard finally pointed at Roger, who only nodded and left with a surprising show of dignity, he finally exhaled. He knew it was probably wrong to feel such intense relief, but he did anyway.

Over the next few hours, the men around them were escorted out and some were brought back again, but Gus and Julian remained. A pesky kid in a tuxedo was taken after Roger, followed by two older men, who wept openly when they were separated. Next was a small, stoic-looking redhead, who marched off like Cato to face Caesar's army, then a shambling middle-aged fellow, who seemed to expect the rack or the wheel. Eventually, both the older men reappeared with dry but mistrustful eyes. Then the hustler left, singing profanities, and the redhead came back, bruised, staggering, and no longer stoic. But Roger, the middle-aged man, and the kid in the tux still hadn't returned.

Finally, the guard, now a confirmed sadist, pointed at Julian.

"Don't worry," Gus whispered. "We'll both be fine."

Julian was suddenly choked with fear and managed only a broken smile. As he walked down the corridor with a rough hand on his arm, he turned several times to catch a last glimpse of Gus. But when the guard took offense and jerked his shoulder to win back his attention, he dropped his eyes to the floor, listened to the echoes of their footsteps, and struggled to resist the terrifying idea that he might never see Gus again.

They arrived at a small, brightly lit room, and as he sat down in a chair across from a young detective in a cut-rate blue Dacron suit, he wondered if his fear had been an overreaction. His interviewer, who may have been Italian or Puerto Rican, looked up briefly and smiled but then continued to write what seemed to be meticulous notes, even after the guard had left the room. Julian tried to gauge whether the delay was unplanned or an intentional means of disconcerting or assessing him. But sitting in front of this benign-seeming person somehow began to restore his equanimity. After a while, he felt almost as if he were camped out in the dean's office awaiting his annual review.

When the detective stopped writing, he looked up and smiled again. Then he took Julian's wallet from a box on the table, glanced at his driver's license, and wrote down a few more notes.

"Mr. Prince," he finally said, "May I ask you a few questions?"

Julian nodded, surprised by the politeness.

"What's your occupation?"

"I'm a college professor," he said, then wondered if the tone of self-importance that sometimes found its way into that declaration had been audible.

"You're a professor! No kidding? Of what?"

"Literature."

"Wow, I love literature."

"Renaissance literature," Julian added, to return the man's interest with a detail most people found gratifying.

"Isn't that something. So what's your favorite book?"

Julian hesitated. The friendly chat, the strange line of inquiry, was too out of place to be what it seemed. It was the second time that night that he'd stupidly given a policeman the benefit of the doubt. When he took a closer look at the man's notes, he saw that they weren't notes at all but merely the same line of cryptic nonsense—"My mistake was in telling a stranger my private business"—over and over.

"Have I been charged with a crime?" Julian asked, regretting that he'd waited so long to put the question to someone who might have the answer.

"No, no, no," the detective said, as if the idea were unthinkable.

"Then how long do we have to remain here?"

When the detective's eyes bloomed, Julian knew at once that he'd used the wrong pronoun. It was a mistake he rarely made, even in the most casual conversation. But in the muddle of that appalling night, he and Gus had, in fact, become a *we*.

"I just need to ask you one more question. Then you can go."

Julian was so stunned he almost laughed. The prospect of being set free, and without being charged, was an extraordinary piece of good luck—that is, until the relief was blighted by the realization that he'd be leaving without Gus.

"Professor Prince," the detective said. "You're a man of some reputation, wouldn't you say?"

It didn't seem possible that this was a reason to single him out for lenience, considering why he'd been brought there in the first place. He was used to enjoying certain privileges that came with being a professor. Sometimes he was given preference on the squash courts and better tables at restaurants near campus. A few of his colleagues had even been pulled over by the police for driving while intoxicated and escorted home with only a warning and a wink. But he knew that, while respectability could excuse many sins, homosexuality wasn't one of them.

He nodded to summon the promised final question. But then without any explanation, the detective suddenly stood up, handed Julian his belongings, and ushered him out of the room.

"Get warm soon," he said as he left Julian in the snowy alley a moment later.

He stood there coatless and confused for almost twenty minutes, shuddering in the cold, puzzling over his deliverance, and agonizing about Gus. If he went back inside the station to wait, his presence might antagonize anyone who remembered him and lead to his being taken into custody a second time. But when the chill finally began seeping into his bones, he swallowed his fear and jogged through the drifting snow over to the Waverly, arriving sweaty and out of breath a few minutes later.

At nearly four in the morning, the restaurant was quiet but hardly empty. An assortment of beats, hoods, and odd girls took refuge from the storm and filled about half the red-cushioned booths, while a few old pensioners hunched over the counter. Above them, the walls were lined with signed photographs of eminent patrons like Whitey Ford and Kim Novak. There was only one waitress on the floor, an elfish woman of uncertain age who managed the work without any fuss, and when Julian sat down at one of the smaller booths, she brought him a menu and a cup of coffee.

Though he was grateful his own ordeal was over, he couldn't pretend he hadn't been roughly handled, and the overwhelming dread he'd suppressed for much of the night began to rake his nerves. It was something that had terrified him since childhood, the theme of countless nightmares. Of angry courtrooms, filthy prison cells, violent inmates, and unending misery. It was perhaps in part to foil the grim prediction of those bad dreams that he'd worked so hard in school. No one would ever put a valedictorian in jail, he'd assumed. But then it occurred to him that gay people, even clever ones, were always closer to the criminal world than they realized. Who you slept with, how you socialized, even what you said and how you said it might suddenly bring the law into your life just as fast and as hard as if you were a thief or a murderer. You might forget about it most of the time, but the reality never changed. If you were gay, you were illegal.

He ordered banana cream pie, but when the waitress brought it, he couldn't manage more than a few bites. The thought of Gus still in jail left him feeling so wretched he even pushed away his coffee. To stave off despair, Julian told himself repeatedly that Gus might walk through the door any minute, and together they'd take the

51

subway back to his place, where they'd go immediately to sleep in a warm embrace and begin the next day with some tolerable mixture of resentment for all that had happened to them and relief for all that hadn't.

Except that Julian had two classes to prepare for and teach, which would occupy him for most of the day, and Pen would be arriving in the early evening and staying all weekend. He'd have no time for Gus, no means of nursing his wound or simply being together in a way that would make everything better. And no matter how Julian and Pen spent their time, being with her while Gus was stuck at the Y, injured and friendless, would be excruciating. But then he remembered that Gus might not be released as quickly as he himself had been, that he might be taken downtown to be arraigned. Then there'd be no telling what might happen to him, how long he'd remain in custody, or where he'd go after he got out. Pen might already have arrived, and Gus might be too proud to telephone Julian after he'd made it so damned clear that he needed his privacy that weekend. His concussion might have been more serious than they'd realized. He might be despondent about his arrest or the fine he couldn't afford to pay. And if he had paid it, he might be short on cash and decide to sleep in a flophouse, or worse, to go back to the art dealer's apartment.

"Are you all right?"

Julian felt his nostrils flare as tears coursed down his face. Then he looked up at the waitress, eventually understood her question, and smiled.

"I'm fine," he said, as he snatched up a napkin and dried his eyes. "Thank you."

"Okay, sweetheart," she said, smiling back, as if he weren't the first person to weep in her restaurant that night.

The knowledge that Julian might actually be fine took him by surprise. Or if he wasn't precisely fine, he realized that, despite everything, he somehow felt magically buoyed on his sea of troubles. He thought about how brave Gus had been at the bar, how frightened he must have felt as the baton struck his head, and how vulnerable he probably felt now, alone and uncertain in jail. But somehow these awful thoughts brought Julian a strange but undeniable pleasure.

When he pictured the divine filigree of Gus's ear or imagined him in the shadow of the Tombs, his half-naked silhouette reeling against a concrete monolith, the images filled Julian with a terrible tenderness and a magnificent rage.

As he sat back in his booth, he finally understood what it meant. It should have been obvious to him, since he'd been stirred and soothed and sustained by it all night. But it was as uncanny as anything he'd ever felt before and he simply hadn't recognized it.

6

It was almost dusk by the time Danny left the Tombs, and though the snow on the sidewalks had already begun to turn gray, it was a relief to be outside and feel the cold air on his face. Rafael stood on the other side of White Street, dark and lean in the day's last shadows, his head tilted in sympathy and a few black curls peeking out from under his wool cap. He waved a red-mittened hand and held up an old brown pea coat. But Danny was too sore to wave back. The bruise under his left eye was so swollen it made his head feel lopsided and his right flank felt like it might collapse. Even worse was the slaughter in his pants—burning, throbbing, disgraceful—which he did his best to hide as he crossed the street, and the rumbling tremor in his chest, which made his breath feel weak and unsteady. He'd been a prisoner for almost seventeen hours and he only wanted to go home—to Raf's home anyway—and get some sleep.

"Look what you've gone and done now," Raf said, in a decent imitation of Jack Benny, slapping the red-mittened hand to his cheek as he handed Danny the pea coat with the other. Normally, Raf spoke with that nice blend of Latin flair and perfectly correct English that you heard in some Puerto Ricans, but he did jokey voices, too.

Danny nodded his appreciation, then buttoned up the coat and put on the Russian army ushanka hat and old suede gloves that he found stuffed inside the pockets. Back at the police station, he'd used his first phone call to get a message to Sloan's answering service that he had the flu and wouldn't be coming in that morning. But his second call was to Raf, and now it seemed the more important one by far. Just being with him there on White Street made Danny feel safer and sounder.

When Raf noticed his black eye, he reached for Danny's shoulder, which made him flinch and sent a sharp shudder down his side that he couldn't hide. He stooped a bit as he tried to breathe away the pain.

"Me cago en la madre!" Raf muttered with a bitter shake of his head as he looked up at the great Halls of Justice looming in front of them.

They both knew it was what cops did sometimes, especially to gays and PRs and black people. Raf had nearly as many brothers as Danny, so he'd seen it happen before more than once.

"I know, dahling," Danny said, as he straightened himself with a little flip of his hand. "Art Deco ain't my thing either. But I'm fine as French fries so let's go home."

Rafael eyed him doubtfully.

Whenever Danny lied, Ciaran had once told him, he smiled too much and arched his brows without realizing it, and it seemed that Raf was finally onto him, too. So he frowned and lowered his eyes, then took Raf's arm to show he still had his strength and pulled him west toward Broadway. He had to walk carefully, with his thighs apart like a cowboy, but he managed it all right and was glad Raf didn't seem to notice.

"Have you heard from Gabriel?" Danny asked, gingerly straddling a ridge of chunky snow to cross the street.

"Oh, Miss America came by around one with the news," Raf said. "She looked like the cat who ate the damned canary."

"Damn" was the only curse word Raf ever allowed himself in English, so when he used it you knew he was really annoyed.

"And what was his story?"

"That you were dancing right next to him and then suddenly disappeared into thin air. He says he made it to the roof and jumped to the building next door. Probably laughing all the way. Pendeja!"

Raf accepted Gabriel as Danny's friend, but Danny knew he didn't like him much. Gabriel was often ridiculous, usually obnoxious, and always unreliable. If he said he'd be somewhere, he probably wouldn't be. When they went out together, he talked too loud and camped it up, and he never cared what looks he got. And he got plenty of them, especially when people heard his laugh, which was loud and raspy, like a barking seal or a broken accordion. Wherever they went with Gabriel, they'd be late getting there, since he was sidetracked by every shiny object he saw, whether a heartthrob in dress blues or a tchotchke behind the window at Gimbels. He was supposed to be an actor, but he rarely went on auditions and couldn't hold down a day job for more than a day. Despite frequent cash donations from his Orthodox Jewish parents in Riverdale, he was mostly broke, borrowed freely from Danny, and never paid back a cent. The best thing you could say about Gabriel was that he was devoted to his friends. Which meant he was always happy to get into trouble but never easy until he had someone to do it with.

Raf was the opposite. He was totally earthbound and regular as the mail. In fact, he had a good job at the post office on 42nd Street. Which is why Danny loved them both. Sometimes Raf and Gabriel were like the angel and devil floating over Donald Duck's head and fighting for his attention. In the end, Danny usually sided with Raf, who was more reasonable and more persuasive. But Gabriel made life a gas, and when Danny sometimes chose cheap thrills over good judgment, Raf was rarely a scold.

As they crossed West Broadway and arrived at the IRT, Danny stopped at the top of the stairs. It was weird not taking the train home to Parkchester. But having been arrested, jailed, beaten, and convicted somehow made the memory of being evicted less painful. Once word got out about the raid, assuming it did, there'd be no way he could sue for peace with Quinn or reassure his mother that he wasn't what Quinn had almost said he was. As they went down into the station, Danny realized that the first part of his life was probably over and the next one just about to begin.

"How come you're not talking?" Raf asked, as they waited on the platform. "What's wrong? Why don't you want to tell me?"

He liked a good story, and he often asked questions in threes when he was worried.

"About what?" Danny said, as a southbound train roared into the station and the noise forced a welcome pause.

"About everything, loca!" Raf said, once the train had squealed to a stop. "Don't be tiresome. I want to know what happened."

Danny was glad for the excuse of the noisy rush-hour crowd as it pushed out of the train and swarmed past them. Telling the story would've been too much like reliving it. He needed sleep before he could do that. When the northbound train finally came and they slipped inside and grabbed their straps, Raf pleaded one last time for a morsel of information to tide him over, but Danny just looked around the packed car at the mob of strangers and shrugged.

Ten minutes later, they slogged up Eighth Avenue, past streams of brown-skinned, wool-clad people heading home for the day, then turned west at 19th Street, passed through a pair of rusted iron gates into Raf's red-brick tenement building, and climbed up four flights of stairs to his apartment. Once inside, Raf headed straight to the corner of the room he called his cocinita, which was really just a Simmer Crock, a hotplate, a small icebox, and an even smaller basin, while Danny took off his coat and hat and went into the toilet in the opposite corner, then closed the door behind him.

There was only an antique commode and a rusted hand sink—Raf shared a bathroom and telephone with the three other tenants on his floor. But the little room was spic-and-span and perfumed by a fresh bar of Dial soap, and there was an old, chipped dressing mirror on the back of the door. In his reflection, Danny saw how his pompadour sagged and his face looked haggard. The swollen stain to the left of his nose nearly matched his tie. He looked older than he had just a day before, with some of Quinn's meanness in his eyes and Michael's cynicism around his mouth. Unbuttoning his shirt, he saw the bruises on his right side, which had spread like a bouquet of roses against his pale skin. Then he slowly unzipped his pants and tugged on his briefs. His dick was normally a pink, sprightly thing, a little bigger than average. Now it was dappled in dark reds, blues, and browns and swollen in the middle like a sweet potato. He could almost see the mark of the hand that had done the damage, and when he cupped it in his palm, he felt sick and sorry the way you do when you look at a dead baby animal.

◎ ◎ ◎

It was nearly ten at night when he woke up and saw that Raf had laid out a meal of pernil, rice and beans, plantains, and hot tea on a little table by the apartment's only window. He was sitting nearby in his rocking chair, wearing blue pajamas and a fuzzy yellow shawl that looked like it had been his grandmother's. Danny blew a cloud of steam into the cold air and gathered his blankets around his shoulders as he remembered the bad dream he'd been having about being trapped in a dark room filled with cockroaches and big concrete Art Deco walls moving in to crush him to death. He normally paid attention to his dreams, which sometimes showed him the truth about his deepest feelings and maybe even gave a vague prediction of the future. But this one was suddenly wiped away by the rush of actual memories. Of Quinn and Ciaran, the Nazi Cop, the Tombs, and the unfairness of everything. Danny felt so angry he wanted to punch the brick wall behind him. But his chest rumbled, his head throbbed, his dick burned, and a burst of stings in his right side told him he'd probably cracked a few ribs. So he closed his eyes and let the pain chase away the anger, like the memories had the bad dream. Then he carefully pulled himself off the couch, went over to the little table and took a sip of tea.

"Okay, blanquito," Raf said after a while. "Tell me."

The more Danny said, the easier it got. He talked about his tussle with the cops at Caesar's, the ride in the happy wagon, and his first hours in the station. He described some of the other men in his cell, especially the Two Gents, the poor guy with the head wound, and the chatty hustler who was their tour guide, and he explained how they were all taken out one by one and brought back a while later—all except for Shoe-Face, the Rich Kid, the Suave Suit, and the poor guy's lover, who never came back at all. Finally, Danny recounted his interview with a big, red-nosed, old bull of a detective.

"You're in real trouble, Mr. Duffy," he'd said, eyeing some papers in front of him and looking pretty pleased with himself. "Assaulting an officer. Resisting arrest. Lewd and indecent vagrancy. Soliciting men for the purpose of committing a crime against nature. Boy, that's a lot."

Danny struggled to understand the charges. Gabriel's ass-shaking twist could be lewd and Danny's wasn't strictly decent, and men dancing with men was no more legal in New York than it was anywhere. But he knew cops used a special language for hassling gays without having to be specific about what they'd actually done wrong. Even "soliciting" sounded more like work than play, and a "crime against nature" only made him think of burning down forests or using science to change the weather. He also thought he heard a bluff in the casual, cocky way the Old Bull read out the charges. He didn't think the cop he'd smacked had gotten a good look at him. The only one who might have was Officer Lard-ass, but all Danny did was struggle under the weight of his flabby carcass, which probably was "resisting," though no one could've blamed him for it.

"If you're convicted, you'll get six months, maybe a year," the Old Bull said.

It was meant to scare him, Danny knew, to make him fold like a towel. But the Old Bull didn't seem to say it like it was going to happen, and Danny figured there was more to come.

"But if you plead guilty to disorderly conduct, you can either pay a ten-dollar fine and go home or spend a week in jail. The choice is yours."

It was probably what he was telling everybody. The threat of felonies and sex offenses was supposed to make the misdemeanor seem like a late Christmas gift for naughty boys who should have gotten lumps of coal instead. Most of the fines probably made their way into somebody's pocket, Danny thought. With such a good price on their heads, it was no wonder the cops were always rounding up homos like wild horses.

"It's a damned racket," Raf said.

They'd known other guys who'd been arrested before. A waiter at the Fawn on Jane Street had been caught wrestling with some millionaire in the back seat of a limo in Hoboken and did sixty days for sodomy. And Raf knew about a black kid in Florida who got fifteen years for "unnatural sex acts," while the white man he was with only got thirty days. Gabriel himself once got busted trying to make it with an obviously eager plainclothesman in a Central Park toilet, which left him paying a twenty-five-dollar fine *and* spending ten days in Riker's. After he got out, he convinced his parents it had only been a youthful mistake and one he'd never make again. But a week later he went right back to the same toilet and, so far as Danny knew, had been going there ever since.

After Raf sat back in his rocker and adjusted his shawl in a show of patience, Danny told him about making his phone calls and feeling pretty sure at that point that he could handle a night in the Tombs. But when the Nazi Cop came to take him back to his cell, something didn't seem right. The man stood as puffed-up and plank-straight as he'd been earlier that night, but he now looked hopped up, too, like he'd swallowed a handful of Dexedrines. There was a shine of sweat on his face and his hawk eyes gleamed amber in the corridor's bright white light.

As they reached the stairwell that led back up to the cellblock, the Nazi Cop slowed to let Danny go in front of him. But when he turned around to see if he should start climbing, the Nazi Cop punched him hard in the face, connecting just under his left eye, and sent him flying into the staircase. Then everything went dark and he felt weightless, like an astronaut drifting in space. He heard a dull thumping sound that seemed to be coming from inside him, and then a sudden crack of pain in his head and on his side reminded him of where he was and what had happened.

He opened his eyes and tried to push himself to his feet, but his knees buckled and he doubled over again. The Nazi Cop pulled him up by his armpits, wrapped a hand around his throat and pinned him to the wall. Danny figured he was about to get another blow to the head and wondered if he'd be able to take it. But all the Nazi Cop did was lean in close with his face, like he might give him a kiss. His amber eyes looked dead and his breath smelled of whiskey and cigarettes. When his other hand slapped Danny's crotch and squeezed, it seemed like something one of the boys at school might have done, a prank meant to embarrass him. Or maybe the Nazi Cop just wanted to get his jollies and whatever came next would be more gross than painful. But then the hand began to tighten, like the clamshell of a shovel crane biting its quarry. When it finally closed, a river of misery flooded Danny's veins.

He'd known real pain dozens of times, like when Quinn stabbed him in the calf with a pencil or when he split his chin open on St. Ann's Avenue. So he knew how to separate the physical part of it from the panic and fear by counting his breaths until the pain, however bad, became familiar but impersonal, a mere feeling instead of an idea. But what he felt now was worse than anything he'd ever felt before. It was more than words could say or breaths could count. It felt like the end of everything.

He barely remembered what happened next, only that the Nazi Cop dragged him back upstairs and told him to stop making such a bother. As they turned down the cellblock corridor, Danny thought he saw a few of the other men offer sorry looks, but most didn't seem to notice. Once inside the cell, he stumbled back to his corner and with help from the Two Gents, lay down on the floor. He was too confused to speak and too scared to cry. When one of the Gents covered him in a velvet jacket, Danny noticed that it was stained and missing a button. Then he closed his eyes, thought about Raf, safe at home but starting to worry, and prayed to Saint Jude that it wouldn't take too long to die.

When he opened his eyes again about an hour later, he wasn't dead, but something inside him was different. It was as if the pain that still raged in his groin and his side had sharpened his wits. He no longer found the people around him amusing. He didn't think they were panicking without reason. Now nothing looked like it did on TV. The idea of Doris Day singing in a jail cell, careless of whatever would be, was stupid kids' stuff. Everything around Danny seemed dirtier and uglier, less like a collection of facts accidentally scrambled up in the confusion of the night and more like a trap, a plan, a system for keeping people in check. Somehow he knew he could only have been treated like this because he was weak and vulnerable and that the cops were part of a scheme to keep him that way. It was an honest-to-goodness, real-life conspiracy, and in the face of it, Danny's genuine talent for being okay was bullshit.

He didn't mention any of this to Raf. And he said nothing about getting cold-cocked and cock-wrenched by the Nazi Cop, but rather let him believe he'd gotten his bruises during the raid. There was nothing Raf could have done about it and knowing the truth would've only upset him. But more than that, Danny just couldn't think about it anymore. Not about the fist on his cheekbone or the knife-edge of the stairs against his ribs or the monstrous grip of the Nazi Cop's hand. So he only sipped his tea and made Raf wait again until he could pull himself together.

The judge was a wrinkled, mole-like man with flat gray eyes, a run-away hairline and no chin to speak of. Although his black robe made him look solemn and official, nothing about him seemed especially intimidating until he started talking.

"You stand before me accused of disorderly conduct," he said in a droning robot voice. "How do you plead?"

When Danny opened his mouth, nothing came out. He knew he hadn't done anything wrong, and though he'd agreed to plead guilty and understood the consequences of not doing it, he couldn't say the word. It was like when Quinn pinned his head to the floor with his knee and tried to make him say "uncle," which Danny had never done once, no matter how much it hurt or how long Quinn waited.

"Mr. Duffy," Mole Man said, squinting in his direction when Danny's silence went on too long. "You're in my courtroom today because you were found cavorting in a disorderly establishment. You should be grateful that you've been given this opportunity to mend your reckless ways. But that can only begin when you admit that they're in need of mending. So let me ask you once more, how do you plead?"

Everyone waited for his answer. The public defender, a scarecrow in horn-rimmed glasses, seemed embarrassed by his client's lack of cooperation and tapped his skinny white fingers on the table. Mole Man scowled at Danny as if wasn't just a cavorter but a murderer of children and nuns.

"Guilty," he finally said. The word seemed to come from somebody else.

"Very well," Mole Man said. "And your client will pay the fine?"

The public defender promised he would, and the court clerk shuffled some papers. It looked like it was over. But then Mole Man squinted at Danny again, this time with a craggy look of disgust, like someone had just taken a shit in his courtroom.

"Young man, I'll not demean myself by speaking of the deplorable moral condition that brought you to my court today. But I will advise you to consult your priest. Next case!"

Just as the image of Father Frank resolved in Danny's mind—ham-faced, freshly barbered, always so sour and conceited, and probably gay himself—someone grabbed him by the arm and led him out of the courtroom, and within the hour, he'd gotten back his belongings, paid his fine, and left the building. As he caught sight of Raf standing across the street, he knew he only vaguely understood the huge chasm that existed between the absolute authority of the judge's words and their obvious absurdity. But he was pretty sure that he and Raf and Gabriel would now live in that chasm, always despised and sometimes abused, for the rest of their lives whether they liked it or not.

Raf thanked Danny for the story, told him how sorry he was, stroked his cheek with the back of his hand, and went to clean up. Then Danny limped back to the couch and slowly tipped over onto his side. As he listened to the clatter of dishes, he thought about his morning shift at Sloan's. He'd have to fake a few lingering flu symptoms, but his clothes would hide the worst of his injuries. If he didn't move quickly or lift anything too heavy, he hoped no one would suspect anything. He didn't know how he'd explain the black eye or whether it would be taken as a badge of honor or a sign of trouble. He'd never felt "deplorable" in his life, but now that he'd confessed to sexual perversion, it was hard to imagine not feeling that way when he explained the higher price of cauliflower or taught one of the new boys how to stack apples. His separate worlds had collided, and he wasn't sure either would survive the wreck.

As he felt the weight of his body sink into the cushions, he pictured Ciaran and Margaret Duffy and his old bed in Parkchester that he knew he'd never sleep in again. He thought about the shame his dead drunk of a father would've felt if he'd learned his son was both a queer and a convict, which Danny hated caring about but did anyway. He'd been branded a deviant before he'd even had much of a chance to be one, and now even the thought of sex seemed tainted with something foul. But after Raf finished the dishes, sat down on the couch, and draped his arm over Danny's curled-up body, his angry, rushing thoughts eased up enough to make room for a few kinder, calmer ones. And when he knew Raf's arm would stay there for a while, he finally cried his eyes out.

7

Roger feared he'd never get to sleep. After a hot shower had washed away the stink of the jail cell, he pulled the curtains to block out the night's ambient glow and the glare of the sun that would soon rise. Then he got into bed and closed his eyes, willing himself to forget, just for a few hours, what he'd done, what had been done to him, and what it all now meant. But there was simply too much to think about. His unaccountable luck in being freed without an arrest record was a gift he knew he hadn't deserved. A second chance that still looked to the rest of the world like a first. He swore to himself that he'd never succumb to temptation again, that he'd smother all future urges before they became compulsions. Then, because he'd sworn such an oath and failed to honor it so many times before, he searched his mind for some reason to believe that this time might be different. The children were getting older, and they'd need their father more and more. Roger was getting older, too, and he was certainly old enough to sacrifice ephemeral pleasures for lasting stability. Above all, there was Corinne, whom he owed far more loyalty than he'd ever given her. If only he could see how worthy she was of his faithfulness and appreciation—of his desire—and let the truth of her goodness warm his cold heart and remake him as a man of his word.

As a teenager, whenever he masturbated thinking of another boy, he punished himself afterward with hundreds of pushups or dozens of laps around the school track. In college, he sometimes had sex with nameless men at a Scollay Square theater in far-off Boston but then fretted about it for weeks and gave half his monthly allowance to the Salvation Army as penance. After he married Corinne, his infrequent but inevitable trips to bars in Manhattan sometimes resulted in a troubling attack of nerves. But in recent years, as he settled into more regular visits, he struggled against his guilt by working harder at his job and being tenderer with his wife and more patient with his children. If doing these things couldn't fix him fundamentally, he hoped they might at least make him less of a failure.

Once plans for his moral reformation faded in Roger's mind, stingy sleep finally parted with a few restive hours. When the front desk called to wake him at seven o'clock, he rose, dressed, and packed his suitcase, leaving the soiled gray suit behind in a waste bin. Then he ate breakfast at a nearby diner, quickly and without enjoyment, and took a Checker cab downtown to the Chemical Bank building on lower Broadway. He rode the elevator to the sixth floor, greeted Nancy, his secretary, in as calm a manner as possible, and found refuge in the distraction of paperwork for the rest of the morning, while steadfastly refusing to entertain a single thought about the night before.

Just after one o'clock, Edgar poked his hairless, bespectacled head into Roger's office, where he was poring over financial statements in what felt like a highly productive trance. It was consoling that the numbers stayed in their columns so reliably. They rarely lied or postured and almost always added up just as they were expected to. The fact that Roger didn't start at Edgar's interruption was also encouraging, since it suggested he wasn't as rattled as he thought he might be.

"Steady as she goes?" Edgar asked.

He employed nautical metaphors frequently, and it was generally understood that, whenever he did, he expected an immediate and affirmative response.

"Ship shape," Roger said, with a smile that promised calm seas ahead.

Among other aspects of his job, he worked on the continuing expansion of the bank's business in Japan, where the postwar miracle saw hundreds of new enterprises clamoring for credit. Though he'd spent most of his war years flying sorties over the Pacific, he'd never actually set foot in that country and had no plans ever to do so. He hadn't thought much about the Japanese as a people or about how they saw the world now and what they wanted, since that was the job of men in the foreign offices. Roger's was more a series of mathematics problems that required only accuracy and thoroughness but little imagination, which was exactly how he liked it.

"Carry on, then," Edgar said, casting his eyes around the room.

Roger wasn't quite sure how he felt about his new office, with its sleek rosewood desk and credenza, low hopsack sofa, and chrome and leather armchairs. It was all rather austere, but it was considered fashionable by those who understood such things, and it boasted an enviable view of Broadway and the East Side. It looked every bit the reward for hard work well done that it had been, even if the pleasure of that reward now seemed like a distant memory.

As Edgar closed the door behind him, it occurred to Roger that his boss rarely stopped by on a Friday afternoon, and he feared that his distress that morning might have been more visible than he'd realized. Although Edgar's wonted dullness of manner—he wore the same style of navy worsted suit every day without fail—might conceal any intention he wanted kept secret, Roger eventually convinced himself that the visit had been a mere whim and there was nothing to worry about. But as he returned to his orderly columns, he soon grew as suspicious of his confidence as he'd been of Edgar's visit. If Roger wasn't extremely careful, it might lead him to stray again and squander his unaccountable reprieve. He wanted so much to be free from his troubles, but such freedom seemed too distant to believe in. True relief, after all, was for the innocent.

◎ ◎ ◎

Corinne was waiting in the parking lot of the Larchmont train station, smiling mischievously from the window of their new Chrysler—a jazzy New Yorker, midnight black with a wide grill, slanted head-lights, and steep fins—as if his planned and punctual arrival were somehow their own private joke. Her hair was a short brown swirl, and her small, sloping nose accentuated the perfect symmetry of her emerald-green eyes. She was always luminously tan, even in winter. These were things he never failed to notice about her. He certainly did think she was pretty.

"How was Philly?" she asked as he slipped into the passenger's seat and kissed her cheek.

For a second, it sounded like an accusation, but he was too glad to see her to indulge any suspicion. In fact, he'd always liked the way she said "Philly," as if the town, which she hadn't visited in years, were an old friend. It was one of the many ways she claimed the world as her own, even if she rarely strayed far from Westchester County.

"Uneventful," he said.

"Did you get done whatever you needed to get done?"

"Let's just say I'm awfully glad to be home."

They talked of ordinary things—the new snow-plow man, Roger's nephew choosing Milton Academy over Deerfield, something the babysitter had said about Henry—and the triviality of it all pleased him. So did Corinne's competence. She was so self-assured behind the wheel and able to carry on the most involved conversations while maintaining a keen focus on the road. She could also fix a flat tire, play Chopin and Satie on the piano, and plan a large holiday party. She'd only taken up tennis the previous summer and already played better than all the women and most of the men. The finesse with which she did nearly everything made Roger feel lucky rather than envious. There was so much about her to be grateful for.

"Did you see the *Standard-Star* today?" she asked.

The sudden image of a newspaper report of the police raid gave him a sharp stab of fear, but again the feeling lasted only a moment, and he soon realized she was talking about Cuba and the trade embargo. He liked to follow her interest in public affairs. The fact that she was a good deal smarter than him was like having an insurance policy against his own bad judgment.

"I just wonder if disengagement is the best way to make people act differently," she mused.

"How do you mean?" Roger asked, happy to hear her elaborate.

She looked at him curiously. "Are you all right? You seem a bit, well, off."

"No, just tired, I suppose," he said, giving her what he hoped looked like a hearty smile but wondering how he could have betrayed himself so quickly.

"Anyway, it seems a little counterproductive to me, and a bit ruthless, too. Though I don't pretend to understand it all."

She'd studied history at Wellesley and, having impressed her teachers with her excellent memory and eye for detail, even considered getting a master's degree. But only a year after the war, she met Roger at a summer pool party in Oak Bluffs and, by their third date, had made her intentions clear. The following June, they were married from the parlor of her mother's sprawling Victorian up in Litchfield and honeymooned in Niagara Falls.

Corinne liked to tell the story of their meeting to friends. But when she did she always omitted the fact that Roger was only at the pool party because he'd been invited to spend a week on the Vineyard with the family of a former classmate. Mudge Collins was rich and handsome, intimately connected with the Dulles brothers, and ever since their junior year at Brown, madly in love with Roger, who'd returned his affection only in anxious fits and starts. After college, Mudge had been wounded in the liberation of Czechoslovakia and during his convalescence had repeatedly invited Roger to visit him at his family's beach house. Roger, who'd only just returned from the Pacific himself, managed to put his friend off for a year while he organized his life in New York. If Mudge was clever, charming, and generous, he could also be careless with his words and emotions, and Roger scrupled at the idea of putting his reputation back in the hands of someone so capricious. But when Mudge finally admitted that his femur had been shattered by a bullet and he was now so patched up with steel rods and screws that he walked with a cane and a limp, Roger was filled with feelings of tenderness and hurried north on a train.

On the morning after his arrival, as household staff opened umbrellas and set up tables around the pool, Mudge tossed his cane aside, took Roger's arm, and ambled barefoot down the boardwalk to the beach. And when they found sanctuary behind a steep-sloped dune, Mudge sat between Roger's legs and leaned back into his chest as they stared out together into the folding, flaking surf.

"Paris would be awfully cheap," Mudge said, after suggesting they buy two one-way tickets to some foreign land and never return. "And Greece would be even cheaper. On Mykonos, you can get a small pension overlooking the Adriatic, with a gruff manservant, a sleepy dog, and a daily supply of bad wine for practically nothing."

Roger inhaled the smell of Mudge's hair, a delicious brew of cedar, candlewax, and sea salt. His arms were still strong and firm despite a year of sedentariness. It was easy enough to envision them living a private, happy life together, protected by such perfectly humble desires. But he also knew that Mudge's talk of running away, like all the beautiful things Roger felt sitting with him there in the sand, was merely the kind of thing one imagined rather than a real possibility, and less humble than extravagant.

"Wonderful," he said. "Because nothing is precisely what we'd have."

It was true that their money would run out fast enough and that no disbursements would be forthcoming from their outraged parents. *Nothing* was the amount of respect even such a downtrodden people as the Greeks would afford two American men living together as a couple. It certainly described the odds of their affection surviving daily hardships in a distant land without friends, work, or income. They might feasibly live on nothing in such a place for a while, but it would cost them everything.

As the distant chatter of arriving party guests drifted over them, Mudge turned his head, hooked Roger's chin with this finger, and pulled him into a long, slow kiss that seemed to be aimed precisely at making real that which was not—and somehow it worked. Mudge's mouth felt like a magical portal into all the hoarded joy in the world. As Roger shifted his weight to accommodate the injured leg and allow the freedom his own body craved, he wanted only to dissolve with Mudge into the dune or fix the beautiful moment like a butterfly on a board and make it last forever.

But then they heard a short, faint scream above them on the boardwalk. It was obviously a woman's voice, no doubt carried by the wind but still close enough to claim their attention. Roger was instantly brought back from his delirium. He smiled at Mudge, who shook his head, as if to say that the cry of some unknown female could have nothing to do with the rapture that was transpiring between them.

"Let someone else," Mudge said.

Whether it was merely a long-ago inculcated sense of responsibility to come to the aid of any woman in distress or there was something particularly compelling in the voice he'd heard—perhaps a real vulnerability tempered by an unwillingness to exaggerate what was probably not a tragic accident—Roger wasn't sure. But when he looked at Mudge again, it was with the eyes not of a lover but of a gentleman. As he rose from the sand, honor-bound to put aside private pleasure, he smiled gamely and reached to pull Mudge up with him. They were both still awkwardly aroused, and there was even a telltale spot on the front of Mudge's Bermuda shorts. They'd made this abrupt shift between secret and social worlds many times before and it was hardly surprising that they'd have to do it again.

"We'll come down again tomorrow," Roger said, allowing a trace of mere friendship into his voice, not to be cruel so much as to help along the transition. As they straightened out the fronts of their pants and climbed back up the dune and onto the boardwalk, Roger tried to discern whether the grimace on Mudge's face was from the pain in his leg or the pain of disappointment.

Ahead of them on the boardwalk, a young woman in a ruby-red shift and yellow headscarf was sitting boyishly on her rear end and examining her bare right foot. Suddenly, he felt himself compelled by something he didn't quite recognize, a desire not only to help another person but perhaps to help himself, too. So he left Mudge to his own devices and jogged toward her.

"Are you all right?" he called out.

"Nothing a simple bandage and a daiquiri won't fix," she answered bravely, peering out over large, round red sunglasses.

He saw the fragments of a broken champagne glass on the boardwalk and a piece of its stem glinting in the sea grass nearby, and with a twinge of guilt remembered that he and Mudge had celebrated rather carelessly on the very spot late the night before.

"May I?" he asked, as he kneeled and reached for the offended foot.

She leaned back on her hands as he inspected the shard, which was smaller than a dime and seemed to be lodged only a quarter of an inch in her heel. When he brushed away some sand and carefully plucked the glass free, a thin stream of blood flowed from the wound, but not quite enough to give any cause for concern.

"I think you'll probably live," he said, grinning.

"You seem to be very skilled at this," she said, in a tone that was amiably ironic but lacking any of the obvious flirtation that Roger so disliked in women.

He looked behind him to see Mudge hobbling in their direction. "Say, give us your shirt, would you?" he said.

Mudge's face went flat with dejection.

"I'm sure that's not necessary," the young woman said.

"I'll get you a new one, for goodness' sake," Roger said.

He knew the imputation of stinginess was unfair, for Mudge of all people would have given anyone the shirt off his back and thrown his cufflinks into the bargain. He also knew there was something flamboyant about wasting a perfectly good and undoubtedly expensive shirt when a two-cent Band-Aid would have sufficed. But having assumed the role of the magnanimous hero, he now felt obliged to fulfill it.

He waited as Mudge unbuttoned his shirt, slipped it off his lean, summer-cured body and handed it to Roger, who then tore it in half, ripped one of the halves into several strips, and tied the strips, one at a time, around the young woman's heel and across the top of her foot, securing them at the ankle. As he worked, Roger wondered if Mudge was bitterly weighing such a trifling injury against his shattered femur and thinking that whatever sympathies had privileged the one over the other had been grossly misplaced. He pictured his friend standing behind him, silent, shirtless, and deeply unhappy, and he knew that he was the one in the wrong. But the young woman's accident had offered up to his imagination what seemed like a safer and steadier kind of love, and in that moment he decided on her as spontaneously as she seemed to decide on him.

Roger tied the final knot on his makeshift bandage. "How does that feel?"

"It's a perfect fit," said the young woman, who called herself Corinne.

As he offered her his arm, Mudge held back, then limped to the house behind them, and wasn't seen for the rest of the day. He was heartbroken, Roger knew, and never spoke to him again after that weekend, despite several letters begging his forgiveness. But if such a hasty exchange of lovers had been impulsive, it had also seemed prudent. For on that day in Oak Bluffs, Roger began life together with Corinne in a fog of optimism and determination that had more or less sustained them ever since.

◉ ◉ ◉

As they careened down Chatsworth Avenue, they talked about Cuba and Kennedy, Castro and Khrushchev, and the precarious state of the world. But when they eased into the driveway of their house on Rockledge Place, the only world Roger found he cared about was the one with the yew hedge and the elm and the black shutters and the scarlet door. All still there, still standing, still his.

Later that evening, after a welcome-home dinner had been eaten and Henry and Lizzie had been praised, corrected, cuddled, and put to bed, Roger and Corinne lay together in bed and made love. They always did it on the night he returned from a business trip, whether legitimate or not, and it was more or less the same every time. The room was dark but for a thin bar of light under the bathroom door. He drank Drambuie on the rocks and offered her a sip from his glass. Then he climbed on top of her, carefully avoiding her breasts, and kissed her neck for several minutes before beginning. It reassured him that he could still perform as a man and that Corinne had no cause for suspicion on that score, though he knew it was this feeling of success in the marriage bed—of duty virtuously honored—that was his main source of pleasure. Corinne's body was trim and soft and perfectly lovely, but when he held her by the shoulders and moved in and out of her, it wasn't his wife he thought of so much as himself, or rather some alternate version of himself whose powerful feelings had led him to this woman. It was this idea of a virile, normal, desiring man, so unlike Roger but somehow intimately bound to him in the act of love, that made the act itself possible.

But then he sensed something was wrong. Corinne had shifted beneath him several times, pulling her stomach in, and making small moans that suggested more discomfort than pleasure. And now he could see it in her wincing face, though she seemed torn between saying something unpleasant and pretending it was nothing at all.

"What is it, Rin?" he asked.

"It's just that it's hurting a little."

She'd complained about the pain before. At first, he assumed it might be a medical problem, one she should see a doctor about. But he soon realized that, without specifically criticizing him, she'd meant to suggest that his approach—*technique* is what they called it now—left something to be desired.

"What exactly am I doing that you don't like?" he asked, with a tone of masculine rationality he knew would quickly bring things to an end if he persisted in it.

"You're pressing too much," she said. There were few words to describe what they did that seemed fit to speak to one another.

"How?" he asked, wondering if, after the events of Thursday night, he wasn't somehow overcompensating.

"On the top," she said, looking away.

"Oh, okay," he said, as if it were only a minor mechanical difficulty and easily overcome with a small adjustment.

Then he started again, slowly, delicately, careful to avoid pressing on the top, though he wasn't sure he knew quite what that meant. He felt ashamed that the region in question was, even after fourteen years of marriage, still a mystery. It wasn't simply something he'd never taken the time to explore, like a museum or a botanical garden. It was something he was expected to crave, a celebrated fount of life that, whenever Roger dared to think about it, left him feeling like life's enemy—not just a hater of women but a lover of death.

"Is that better?" he asked after a moment, suspecting that, despite his efforts, he'd made no real improvement.

When another wince broke Corinne's smile, he stopped again and rolled over. "I'm not sure I understand what you want," he said.

"It doesn't matter," she said, stroking his unhappy face.

But it certainly did. It wasn't merely that his technique was bad. The fact that he was causing her pain, that he'd done it before, perhaps many times, could only mean that he made love to her without the natural male urges that love-making required. If he was unskillful

73

and clumsy, it was because he was ignorant of the secret knowledge that only came with authentic need.

For half a minute, they lay side-by-side, no longer touching, separately enduring a weighty, expectant, potentially fatal silence. In the back of his mind, Roger heard the cruel insinuations of the detectives. *There's nothing like a pretty girl.*

"Let's try again," Corinne eventually said, with surprising firmness, which jolted him out of his self-pity but then only made him feel worse.

He was afraid if he tried again he'd only fail again. But if he refused her, it would confirm what she was probably already thinking about him, perhaps what she'd known for years. The only way to create the possibility of another, better outcome was to do as she asked and hope for the best. If he could only relax and not expect so much of himself, it might show her that he was merely an awkward lover, in the way that some people struggled to learn a foreign language or play bridge. Rather than a great failure, it would only be a minor foible.

So he again rolled onto Corinne's trim, soft, perfectly lovely body, and kissed her neck. Once he was back inside her, he felt some of the release he'd been hoping for. This time he thought only of his physical insides—blood and bone, straining muscles and pulsating arteries, the heat of friction on his skin—and as he did, he began to feel a rising momentum. He saw that Corinne seemed pleased, and she even pursed her lips slightly as if she were about to say so, but then he closed his eyes because he didn't want her to say or do anything that would distract him. He needed to stay exactly where he was, within himself, a merely corporeal being, and to keep the idea of them, of man and woman, husband and wife, at a safe distance. He knew it was another unnatural cheat. But as his body began to stretch and careen toward the modest summit of its vitality without much effort on his part, he also knew that it worked, and that if he remembered it and practiced it, it might somehow save him from himself.

◉ ◉ ◉

Around nine thirty the next the morning, Roger, Corinne, Henry, and Lizzie ate breakfast at the kitchen table, which was covered in a red, white, and blue striped cloth that Roger had once liked for its patriotic cheerfulness but now seemed somehow false, like a stage prop. Outside the sky was almost charcoal gray and a gusty wind blew sleet and dead leaves against the windows. The roads would be slick with ice, and they'd all have to stay indoors. The only upside to the bad weather was that they'd now be justified in canceling a long-dreaded dinner with Roger's parents in Darien. But the greatest downside was that Corinne would inevitably sense his foul mood and realize that the previous night's troubles hadn't been an anomaly.

"So how will my two men spend this dismal day?" she asked, with a smile that precisely resembled the one she gave Henry whenever he was upset about something.

"I haven't given it any thought," Roger said.

Henry just sighed, somewhat musically, which had lately become his habit whenever he didn't like a question asked of him. Lizzie, not quite six and normally alert to signs of marital unrest, having wolfed down her bacon and eggs, prattled obliviously as she combed the frizzled hair of her naked plastic baby doll.

"There she goes, there she goes, there she goes again," she sang to herself, almost but not quite to the tune of "Row Your Boat." She had her mother's eyes and nose.

Roger hoped he loved his daughter as much as any father could. But the things that mattered most to her—dolls, dresses, and games of make-believe—often left him with a feeling of mild revulsion. And he worried that this feeling was a symptom of the larger problem, a general aversion to the feminine.

"Hairly, hairly, hairly, hairly, hairly all the way."

It was certainly the case with Henry, an especially sensitive child who hadn't spoken a word all morning. When he was a baby, he seemed to Roger a kind of boy-king, perfect in every way and destined to become the comprehensive man he himself could never be. But by the time Henry was three or four and still cried over the least distress, the ideal had begun to require adjustment. By five, he'd developed an intractable stutter that made most communication a challenge and was a frequent source of public shame. And when a few years later Roger insisted he play baseball, Henry was immediately found to be the worst player on the team, striking out every time he was at bat, even though the boys still hit off a tee at that age.

"Hairly, hairly, hairly, hairly, hairly all the way."

Henry's manner wasn't particularly effeminate, and thankfully he showed little interest in Lizzie's dolls. But he was manifestly gentler, weaker, and less capable than other boys his age in the neighborhood, some of whom had recently started calling him a sissy. The appalling force of that word tore through Roger's heart and revealed to him just how divided he was about his son. At times, when there was peace and quiet at home and the prying eyes of the world looked elsewhere, he felt only compassion for poor Henry and his endless trials. But more often, his son's humiliations became his own, and every stammered word and tearful tantrum was a stinging reproach. Henry was a sissy, Roger had to admit, and it was no coincidence. The son had not only failed to escape the father's curse but seemed to express it with redoubled force.

"Well, aren't you two quieter than a barrel of monks!" Corinne said to Roger and Henry, with a look that clearly invited conversation.

Both children now seemed acutely aware of the morning's strangeness. Their mother's sense of humor was normally something Roger appreciated, but when she gave him another of her patronizing smiles, he decided he'd had enough. Of course, his own father would have given his mother the benefit of the doubt. He'd have laughed at her joke and complimented her cooking. He'd have played his part, no matter the cost. Elliot Moorhouse wasn't always kind, but his manners were impeccable.

"There she goes, there she goes—"

Roger suddenly rose from the table and dropped his napkin on his plate. "I'm going for a drive," he said, when nothing else occurred to him.

"In this weather?" Corinne asked.

He heard only derision in her voice.

"As you see."

"Henry, please tell your father he's being very silly this morning."

Henry only sighed.

Roger took the car keys from the old burlwood bowl by the telephone, grabbed his parka off the brass hook in the mudroom, and opened the door to the garage. As he sat down in the driver's seat of the Chrysler and turned the ignition, he tried to imagine the best angels of Corinne's nature listening to his account of Thursday night, understanding all that had happened to him, and accepting the truth of what he was. But his mind balked at such uncommon generosity, conjuring only a dire blankness, like snow on a wonky television, which only made him despise her the more.

8

Early Friday afternoon, Julian sat at the head of a long table in a seminar room in Hamilton Hall, surrounded by old wooden bookcases and fifteen freshmen boys striking a range of poses from eager to indifferent. They were discussing St. Augustine's *Confessions*, which Julian hadn't taught in several years and had intended to reread earlier that week but somehow ran out of time. So he began by leading the class through one of the better-known passages of the text—on the author's youthful theft of the pears in Book II—and asked a series of general questions about Augustine's idea of sin. He was relieved when the conversation that followed seemed sufficiently logical and coherent without being especially difficult or strictly Socratic. He'd certainly faked his way through classes before, but he always told himself that, once he began in earnest, his performance was less the fraudulence of a charlatan than the improvisation of a jazzman. That afternoon, such informality seemed well suited to the task at hand since it allowed him to hold in reserve that part of his brain—whether the hippocampus or the amygdala, he couldn't remember—that could think only of the spiritual trials of the other, far more important young man named Gus.

Julian had waited for hours at the diner the night before, watching occasional passersby and chain-smoking Pall Malls from a pack left on the table next to him by a distracted beatnik. As the night wore on, he pictured Gus in increasingly dire circumstances—fainting in his cell, bullied by fellow prisoners, stabbed with a shiv. He negotiated a series of complex bargains with a God he didn't believe in, offering up anything that might keep Gus safe and Julian deserving of him. After forcing down a club sandwich, he began to doze off, several times knocking his head against the brass rail next to him and then waking up again. Once the snow subsided, the sun rose, and the sidewalks began to fill, the kindly waitress told him her shift was over and it was time to pay, at which point he roused himself, left her treble the tab, and took the subway home.

Two hours later, in front of his office in Philosophy Hall, he ran into T. R. S. Sterne, a portly, affected scholar of Middle English ballads, who occupied the office next to Julian's and was often a wellspring of departmental gossip.

"You look like you're in a hurry," Sterne said, apparently with the intention of slowing Julian down.

"Running behind today," he said, as he opened the door.

He'd only had time enough for a quick shower and change of clothes before taping a message for Gus on the front door of his building and racing over to campus to cobble together some last-minute notes for his classes. With only an hour left before the first one, a lecture on *A Midsummer Night's Dream*, he suspected that some part of it would be lost to Sterne's prattling and the rest to his own muddle-headed confusion.

"You've heard, haven't you, about Harcourt?" Sterne asked.

Julian knew only that Tristan Harcourt was a young lecturer on modern fiction, a leggy, ostentatiously heterosexual refugee from the Deep South, whose gothic eloquence had beguiled more than a few of his colleagues, men and women alike, though Julian found himself completely immune to his charms.

"I'm afraid I don't have time to ask for the details," he said, dropping his book bag on a chair and taking off his coat.

"He's been accused of writing term papers for students!" Sterne cried, his principled outrage quickly dissolving into puerile tittering. "For his own students! And for money! Oh, the little stud has had it!"

Such glee over Harcourt's imminent demise was hard to interpret. Sterne's guise of jaunty bachelorhood had never fooled anyone, particularly not the small number of his colleagues who privately joked that T. R. S. stood for Totally Repressed Sodomite. His attentions to

Julian had usually fluctuated between coquettish and contemptuous, so it was never entirely clear whether he saw him as an object of desire or a younger and more attractive rival. Sterne was surprisingly popular with undergraduates, whom he seemed to view as too pure to corrupt, and at times his genial pleasantries conveyed the sense of a decent man reconciled to a rather contracted moral life. At other times a conversation with Sterne left Julian feeling that he'd just come face to face with his own bleak future.

"I really have to get to work," he said.

"Very well, very well, if you must. But mark my word, his end will come soon, and it promises to be quite a spectacle!"

After practically closing the door in his face, Julian sat down at his desk, opened his *Kittredge Shakespeare*, and thought briefly about his unusual junior colleague who, if the accusations were true, would be soon cut down by his own folly. Then, instead of reading *Midsummer*, he only turned over the heavily annotated pages as he parsed the various means, hopeful and desperate, of finding Gus before Pen arrived that evening.

He knew the play almost by heart and had always taught it more or less the same way. But as he addressed his sixty or so students for over an hour in an auditorium two floors beneath his office, guiding them through the characters, themes, and motifs of the first three acts, the lecture itself began to feel something like a dream—as if the rigid law of Theseus's Athens haunted his own forest of love and even the soberest of fairies flitted between ecstasy and disaster. When Julian arrived at the scene in Act 3 in which Oberon's magic causes Titania to fall in love with Bottom after Puck has given him the head of an ass, it suddenly seemed crueler and more grotesque than he'd remembered. "O monstrous! O strange!" Peter Quince shouts in the text, and as Julian spoke the words aloud, he felt the urge to toss aside his notes and walk out of the building. But the moment soon passed and the lecture eventually ended, and as the students left the hall, all he wanted to do was lie down on the dais and go to sleep.

Shortly after one o'clock, he lumbered across College Walk and lunched on chicken pot pie in the faculty dining room, doing his best to ignore familiar faces who might want conversation, while skimming his paperback of the *Confessions*, again without taking in much at all. He kept turning back to the book's cover, which featured a stained-glass image of a handsome, violet-robed young man in deep spiritual contemplation. With his eyes closed, head tilted forward, and one arm across his chest, he was the picture of asceticism, indifferent as much to the agonies of existence as to its joys. But his angular face and severe blue-black Caesar haircut also made him look like he might be suffering silently, worn out by deprivation, beaten down with sorrow. Julian wondered what state Gus was in at that moment and whether staring at a book cover and hoping for the best counted for anything at all.

It was only when he finally abandoned his half-eaten lunch, ducked past a solemn table of deans, and made his way over to Hamilton Hall that he felt any relief from his doubts. As he passed the statue of the building's namesake guarding the entrance, he saw that the celebrated Founder stood upon his plinth in a pose strikingly similar to that of the paperback saint—eyes deep in concentration, right arm raised as a shield—except that he held his head high and strode forward with indefatigable boldness. At least, Julian thought as he climbed his way upstairs, it seemed a friendly omen.

"Lit Hum" was a survey of the great works of Western literature, a discussion-oriented seminar, and a notoriously challenging part of the university's core curriculum. Julian hoped he might zip through the first half of the *Confessions* in under an hour and end class early that day. When their discussion of the pleasures of teenage "wickedness" grew somewhat unruly, he jumped to the famous entreaty to God in Book VIII—"Give me chastity and continence, but not yet." After a round of snickers, one student remarked that virtue postponed was hardly virtue at all, and another countered that the desire for virtue was probably better than nothing. Having thus established a plausible dichotomy of opinion and noticing that the clock on the wall seemed to be moving more slowly than usual, Julian rushed the students to a passage in Book X, which they hadn't even read yet but he remembered because it had been quoted in a lecture on Proust given a year before by his colleague, Mr. Trilling.

"'And men go abroad to admire the heights of mountains,'" Julian read aloud, "'the mighty billows of the sea, the broad tides of rivers, the compass of the ocean, and the circuits of the stars, and

81

pass themselves by.'" Then he nodded to the scrawny, hard-favored boy directly opposite him, clad in pristine Brooks Brothers, who'd proven himself a reliable if cautious source of intelligence. "Carter, what does he mean?"

Carter wrenched his thin, chalky lips to one side of his mouth, then spoke: "Uh, that maybe the greater wonder of the world is, uh, man himself?"

"Fine, so how's man the greater wonder?" Julian said, hoping the boy's answer might make the point succinctly, while leaving his fellows with some gravitas to ponder as they called it a day.

"Because of his powers of memory," Carter said, pointing to a line in the text. "'I by seeing draw them'—that is, um, the mountains and rivers and stuff—'draw them into myself,' into my—uh, that is, my 'large and boundless chamber.'"

Several of the other boys smirked. But Carter sucked in his teeth and flushed with excitement, as if realizing that his homeliness and puniness were entirely irrelevant to the question, and that he, too, might contain the whole world inside him.

Gus had once said that, as a painter, his job was first to absorb the world and then to put it on canvas. It was why he liked living cheaply and roughly, mixing with all sorts of people, and avoiding the deadening routines of conventional life. But as Julian listened to Carter bravely hold forth on the powers of the mind, he thought about Gus again, wherever he was, and wondered how much of the world would be too much, an excess of cheapness and roughness that left the artist's tools broken and his spirit exhausted.

◎ ◎ ◎

He ended class a respectable ten minutes early and checked his watch to confirm that three hours remained before Pen would arrive. When he stopped back at his office to see if anyone had left a message, Millie, the department's young assistant secretary, looked up through large silver cat-eye glasses and shook her head. Hurrying home, he tried to persuade himself that he'd find Gus standing in front of his building, waiting with tired eyes and an ironic smile, having folded Julian's desperate note into a beautiful origami crane. Turning the corner onto 113th Street, he even chuckled at the relief he was sure he'd feel once he knew that Gus was free and unharmed and all his worry had been wasted. But a moment later, he saw the note fluttering in the breeze, his taciturn old building super hacking away at scabs of sidewalk ice with a mangled snow shovel, and an angry taxi driver arguing with an even angrier truck driver who'd double-parked and apparently had no intention of moving.

It was another blow, another bewilderment. There was no obvious means of finding out where Gus was or getting in touch with him. He had no telephone because he had no place to live. According to the hustler's speech, he'd already have been released from jail, but Julian couldn't bring himself to visit the Tombs or go back to the Sixth Precinct station to find out for sure, since they'd certainly demand to know who was asking and why. Just the thought of the police brought on a fearful cringe. But if Gus wasn't still in custody, it wasn't at all clear where he might be. It seemed impossible that he'd gone back to the loathsome Swiss art dealer. The studio on West 37th had no cot to sleep on or any means of bathing. So with only one likely possibility remaining, Julian pleaded with the truck driver to back up just enough to free the taxi driver, then rode downtown with him to 34th Street, fighting off the creep of fatigue as he stared out the window, and imagining Gus sitting alone in a small, spare room and brooding in a pitiable Augustinian funk.

The Sloane House YMCA was a massive red-brick asylum of four-teen stories and nearly fifteen hundred rooms, one of which cost only five dollars a week to rent and was a good deal cleaner than most of the crumbling hovels Gus had lived in. It even had a highly respectable lobby, full of prim yellow sofas and pewter ash stands, into which Julian wouldn't have been uncomfortable bringing his own mother. But other parts of the building could be noisy, rambunctious, and wildly unsupervised. Various transients and local adventurers passed through its corridors day and night, though some stayed for months and others just a few hours. Julian had once visited an out-of-town friend there and was thrilled by the carnival of sex that took place in both the private rooms and the common areas, and he remembered with particular pleasure a friendly exchange with a Serbian merchant marine in the steam bath. Gus, too, had stayed at the Sloane House several times over the years when he found himself without permanent lodging. Now it seemed too chaotic a place for someone in his circumstances—not a bad one, to be sure, but not the right one for the man Julian was so worried about.

At the front desk, a clerk—thirties, thinning copper hair, obviously musical—sized him up, then brushed his lapels with an apparent aim to please and offered his assistance. But when Julian inquired if a Gus Magnusson had registered that day, he was told in the most apologetic terms that it was against house policy to reveal the names of guests.

"I wish I could help you," the clerk said, with admiring eyes.

"Surely you'd have noticed him," Julian said, after describing Gus's rugged build and freckled good looks. "If he didn't notice you first," he added.

It was a cheap ploy and ought not to have worked, but somehow it did. The clerk pushed his mouth to one side in pensive indecision, looked around to see that no one else was observing him, then winked at Julian before studying several pages of a registration book. After a moment, he smiled sadly and shook his head.

"Once they're in, they can do as they please," he said. "But everyone's got to register."

Julian thanked him and silently cursed the fact that there were only two hours left before Pen would arrive. As he turned to go, he instinctively flagged an attractive man sitting cross-legged on one of the sofas. The meeting of their eyes was swift and charged. Apparently in his early forties and wearing a dark suit, he was casually flipping through the pages of *Look* but obviously posing to advantage. Then, as Julian noticed the man's blond hair and deep blue eyes, he suddenly realized it was the lieutenant from the raid, the one with the black topcoat and red plaid scarf. He turned away and felt his face grow hot. He remembered the sound of Gus's groaning as he lay on the floor of the bar and the callous clip of the man's footsteps as he walked off without a word. Some part of Julian was determined to confront the man and demand answers about Gus; but another, no less substantial part only wanted to get out of the lobby as quickly as possible.

"I'll be here again tomorrow, if you'd like to check back," the clerk said.

Julian looked up in confusion, but when he turned again toward the sofa, he saw that the man had put his magazine down and was offering up a knowing smile. It wasn't the lieutenant at all. His hair was the same color, but he was narrower in the chest and no older than thirty-five. Julian felt ridiculous for making such a paranoid mistake and ashamed for being so ready to flee. He felt even worse about having invited the attentions of someone other than Gus. In such situations, an abrupt change of heart normally demanded some small gesture of apology or regret. Instead Julian only hurried out of the building, careless of the feelings of one man because he'd been so careless with the feelings of another.

◎ ◎ ◎

In most ways, Pen's visits were easy. She didn't like to be met at Grand Central and insisted she was perfectly capable of taking the Shuttle to Times Square and riding the IRT up to Morningside Heights by herself. Although Julian gave up his bedroom for her and removed to the sofa, she always woke up early and never left any trace of having been there, not even a fugitive hairpin or a hint of perfume. But that night he feared his weariness and agita would be difficult to hide and impossible to explain.

"Hey, kiddo," he said, bussing her cheek and taking her overnight case as she came through the door.

There was something strange in Pen's appearance, something unusually defiant in her expression. She was taller and more athletic than most women, with pixie-short auburn hair and a slightly crooked mouth that always seemed either mildly displeased or on the verge of cutting laughter. But now, even in a simple skirt suit, she looked almost radiant with rebellion.

"Hi, Jules," she said, tilting her head to accept the kiss.

During the first visits of their engagement, she'd always stayed at the Millbrae Hotel for Women on Central Park West, which was convenient though expensive and dreary. After putting off the blessed event for more than a year, she declared that saving money was more important than satisfying the outdated mores of far-off parents who'd never know the difference anyway.

"Your train was late?" he asked, grateful for the extra time.

"Yes, and the subway was dirty and crowded!" she said, with feigned shock.

Pen smiled as she handed him her coat and surveyed the living room, as if confirming her pleasure with its contents and their arrangement, especially the bentwood Aalto chaise—purchased by her father, a tyrannical architect in Brookline, as an engagement present—which sat before the room's largest window, amid a tangle of philodendrons in spare ceramic containers Pen had bought herself. Julian liked that she stared for a studious quarter minute at his Bernard Buffet print, *Tête de clown*, which she'd seen before, and whose quirky irreverence Julian thought complemented both the room and his taste. But he was especially pleased that she also seemed to admire a more recent acquisition, the George Nelson eye clock hanging nearby, which looked as if it had just popped right off one of Picasso's Dora Maar paintings. Julian no longer believed Pen ever expected to live with him, let alone marry him, but he was glad she wanted him to live stylishly, even if he did it without her.

After she freshened up in the bedroom, he poured two gin and bitters on ice and they sat together on the sofa for a conversation that usually began a bit stiffly but quickly become a pleasant exchange of interesting news and urgently held views. Pen talked of the Democrats' obsession with Havana, her growing boredom with teaching the French Revolution, and the towering piles of snow on Codman Square that the city refused to remove. Then she mentioned the new Basil Dearden picture playing that weekend at the Forum, which she thought they might go see together, as well as her father's worsening temper and her mother's worsening hip. Finally, she lit a cigarette, blew a perfect vortex of smoke rings, and declared that Project Mercury was the only thing that made her feel patriotic anymore. To ward off any suspicion about his fractured state of mind, Julian talked about the progress he'd been making on his book and the vague rumors about Harcourt. Pen seemed to be in too good a mood to notice anything amiss.

Later that evening, they walked five blocks to La Tribunal, a Spanish restaurant on Amsterdam Avenue, where the crowd was a motley mix of adventurous faculty and noisy Europeans and a guitar player in white ruffles picked out a baroque fandango. Pen admired the dimly lit, dungeon-like walls, strewn with crimson pennants and iron chains, while Julian exchanged nods with a nebbishy Philosophy colleague and his skinny brunette girlfriend. It was the kind of self-consciously au courant place she liked to patronize when she visited and the kind Gus had little patience for. As Julian followed her to their small candlelit table, it was impossible not to think of an actual jail cell, which made the restaurant's penitentiary theme suddenly seem vulgar and ill-conceived.

After they ordered Rioja and paella, Pen continued to carry the conversation, though not at all in the way he expected.

"Are you happy, Jules?" she asked, as if she'd been waiting for the right moment.

"To see you?" he answered. "Of course."

"That's not what I mean."

"Well, then I invite you to clarify."

"Do you think you know how to be happy? It's an important question."

It was an obnoxious one, too, in its tendency to underscore the wisdom of the asker and the benightedness of the answerer. And it was an odd one coming from Pen, who'd always been quick to laugh at such banal abstractions. Was she herself happy in her spinster's life? And how could such a flat concept as happiness make sense of the endless compromises one inevitably made simply to avoid being unhappy?

A waiter appeared with the wine, briefly diverting Pen from her interrogation. After he had loosened the gold wire cage, uncorked and poured the Rioja, and crept away, they offered each other a wordless toast. Recalling that he'd seen a copy of *The Prophet* on his bedside table, Julian realized that she was either reading it herself or intending that he should. Regardless, it seemed a little unfair that she would impose her self-exploration on him like that.

"Do you know what Gibran says about marriage?"

So he was right about the book but also certain he hadn't heard her utter the M-word in over a year. The only possible explanation was that she was preparing the ground for an escape from that barren old illusion of theirs and growing impatient for the means. Quoting popular pabulum just wasn't her style.

"He writes about maintaining 'spaces' in the 'togetherness' of relationships. Pouring generously but drinking from different cups. Trying but not too hard."

It was one way of describing their engagement, but it tended neither toward naming a date for the wedding nor calling it off. And Julian was in no mood to be reminded of the need for romantic self-renunciation. It was impossible to moderate his love for Gus when the feeling was so quickening and the man so imperiled. It was absurd to consider creating spaces in their togetherness when they were neither together nor certain of being so any time soon. And it made him miserable to think of not trying too hard when he was trapped in a restaurant and had no means of trying at all.

"You don't seem to be in fine fettle this evening," Pen said. "What gives?"

"I didn't sleep well last night," he offered, as casually as he could.

When it came to intimate matters, they'd always seemed to have a tacit agreement to tell as much truth as possible but no more than necessary and avoid asking questions that might move the boundary. He supposed that his not sleeping would be attributed to insomnia, the cause of which would simply be too personal for Pen to inquire about.

"Well, I hope you're not down in the dumps," she said.

She reached out and took his hand in hers. It was one of the few things she ever did that publicly proclaimed an intimacy between them, and Julian guessed that to most of the restaurant's patrons they looked like a young couple in love. As if proof were needed, an older woman sitting nearby with a bluish beehive and a cigarette holder dangling from her mouth nodded approvingly at them. Julian nodded back, feeling every bit the fraud, and was just about to pull his hand away from Pen's when the waiter arrived with the paella and gave him an excuse to do it anyway.

Amid so much deceit and so little desire, it seemed that Augustine was wrong—the real sin wasn't lust or wickedness but misguided chastity. In Julian's mind, Gus's brooding image wasn't crying out "not yet" but rather "no more," and he felt ashamed that he couldn't answer the call. But as he looked up at the fake stone walls and the dust gathering on the pennants and chains—a ludicrous memorial of tormented confessions—he promised himself that when he woke up the next morning he'd finally tell Pen the whole truth about himself, Gus, and the horror of the raid. And then having released himself from the person he didn't love passionately, he'd devote all his time and energy to finding the one he did.

9

Max Sloan had also been an orphan of sorts and he'd turned out all right, Danny thought as he climbed out of the 79th Street station and walked toward the big red letters that spelled out the store's name. He was sent away to a foster home when his mother died and his father couldn't care for him, then left school after eighth grade and sold fruits and vegetables from a pushcart on the Grand Concourse. By the time he was twenty-five, he had his own successful wholesale business, and now Sloan's Supermarkets were bustin' out all over Manhattan. Danny had heard the story so often it almost seemed like a parable from the Gospels. Hard work and pluck made good luck.

Though he'd never spoken more than a few words to the man, Danny admired his obsession with getting things right. To compete with the greengrocers, whose produce was often fresher, you had to handle everything carefully and throw away whatever looked bruised or past its prime. If there were Puerto Ricans in the neighborhood, you made sure the store sold guavas, mangos, and papayas, and he knew Negroes ate Swiss chard and mustard greens, not just collard greens. He also knew that white customers didn't want to feel confused by things they didn't recognize, so the more unusual stuff had to be put to the side rather than mixed in with the carrots and the lettuce. But no matter if you were black or white or brown or chartreuse, Max Sloan always said, he wanted to sell you groceries.

When Danny walked into the store on Saturday morning at seven in his pea coat, ushanka, and purple tie, he still felt bound for success in that same open-minded but determined way. Nothing was going to interfere with his future. Not being kicked out of his home or getting arrested. Not the Nazi Cop's attack on his manhood, which still ached in his pants, or Mole Man's insulting words, which still buzzed in his head, or the tremor in his chest, which still made his breath feel shallow and uneven. And certainly not being gay, which was nobody's business but his own.

Unless a newspaper notice about the raid made it everyone's business. But even that didn't seem very likely. Earlier that morning at a kiosk on 14th Street, Danny had flipped through copies of the *Times*, the *Herald-Tribune*, the *Daily News*, and the *Daily Mirror* and found nothing to worry about. He'd seen plenty of raid notices before, which usually gave the name, age, address, and employment of the men arrested—so there'd be no mistaking who it was—as well as the name of the raided establishment. In fact, that was how Danny had learned about his two favorite bars, Glennon's and the Bleecker Street Tavern. But he thought it was unfair that the only time he read about gay people in the paper was in a crime story, and it didn't matter who the victim or the perpetrator was. The homo was always the guilty party.

Once when Danny was little, Quinn danced around the apartment on St. Ann's Avenue, waving a copy of the *Daily Mirror* and shouting about the "ten thousand faggots" somebody claimed were working in the federal government. Ten thousand of anything was a lot to imagine, and all Danny knew about the government was that it was something people complained about a lot, like the weather. But a "faggot" was even more mysterious. It was a sort of monster, but one you laughed at and beat up instead of running from. It was sort of a boy who was sort of a girl, which was how Danny figured he probably wasn't one himself, even though Quinn said so to his face. Years later, no matter how often he heard the word, it still had an angry, cutting sound that made him feel ashamed for something he hadn't even done.

After Danny got one of the stock boys set up on the floor, his first order of the day was to warn the other one about punching in late twice that week. Roddy Faherty was a Wexford-born kid with a face full of acne scars and a ferocious underbite. He was a natural-born comedian, especially when he told Irish jokes, like the one about the dying man whose last request to his wife was to "please put down that damn gun." He seemed to take pleasure in his work and sometimes even winked at Danny when he passed by to show that he did. But he also chatted up customers for longer than necessary and wasn't respectful enough to his superiors. As Mr. Di Stefano had said, he was too comfortable on the job for someone who'd only been at it for a couple of months.

"Are you feeling better, Danny Boy?" Roddy asked as he plopped himself into the only other chair in the assistant manager's office, which was really more of a storage closet with a desk but something Danny was proud of regardless. "Did you tell that old flu what's what and who's who?"

"I'll ask the questions," Danny said. "And you can call me sir or Mr. Duffy, but if you call me anything else, it'll be the last thing you call me."

He knew he sometimes talked and acted tougher at Sloan's than he did in other places and with other people, especially people like Raf and Gabriel, who often appreciated some swish and a little lah-di-dah. But it felt good to be accepted as one of the boys and not be excluded as an oddball or looked down on as something worse. It certainly wasn't any phonier than what most men did to prove themselves to each other.

"Okay, boss," Roddy said, folding his hands in his lap.

He was somehow nice to look at, awkward but cute, like a wolf-hound puppy, and when he reined himself in, you could tell it took some effort.

"You were late again today," Danny said, holding up the boy's timecard.

"Only five minutes!" Roddy said in a burst of righteous feeling, as his hands flung apart then slapped his thighs in protest.

"Tuesday it was fifteen minutes. And that wasn't the first time."

"I know, I know," Roddy whined, calming himself for a penitent moment, then winding up again with a touch of brogue. "But in the bigger scheme of things, Mr. Duffy, your most honorable ex-cellency, what are a few minutes here and there? Haven't we all got better things to do in this short and precious life of ours than to be counting minutes?"

Roddy often resorted to the kind of bunk Irish philosophy that made Danny smile. Pat Duffy's attempts at it had always sounded stiff and rehearsed. But whenever Ciaran or Bill did it or when he heard some old bit by Jimmy O'Dea and Harry O'Donovan, it gave him a warm feeling inside. He liked the way it played with your emotions and even made you enjoy being worked on a little. How it left you knowing secretly you weren't the only one, that the world was full of soft touches and there was nothing wrong with being soft at all. In fact, there was something a little queer about the Irish, Danny knew. Centuries of being poor had taught them to laugh at pain and suffering, especially their own, and their best jokes always seemed to take the hot air out of things that were too fancy or proper. Danny's Uncle Steven did an impression of de Valera boycotting the Queen's coronation that made people's sides split. Which really wasn't so different from the way Cormac O'Connor—the only other gay kid Danny knew in Parkchester— could use an ordinary handkerchief to out-widow any Italian granny who'd ever lost a husband.

"You've had your two strikes, Roddy. If you're late again, you're out," Danny said.

"Even if it's just by accident?" Roddy asked.

"Even if a piano dropped on your head. Company rules," Danny said, handing Roddy his timecard and turning to his stock book to show that the meeting was over.

"Would you cry for me, Danny, if I had a piano dropped on my head?" Roddy asked, his eyes trained on his prey.

The more you resisted boys like Roddy, the harder they tried, even to the point that their needling was hardly any different from flirting. But Danny knew it was all just a game and one Roddy played with the other guys, too.

"I'd cry for the piano," he said. "Now get back to work. You've wasted enough of my short and precious life."

Roddy laughed and stood up, then gawked at Danny's black eye, like he was seeing it for the first time. "What's the other guy look like?" he asked.

"Like you if you don't scram."

"Later, alligator," Roddy said with a wink.

***

The morning came and went. Danny blew his nose and wiped his brow a few times for the other assistant managers to see. His bruised parts still smarted, but he delegated any task that would've been too strenuous and no one else said anything about his shiner. Winter always left his department with less variety and therefore less work to do, so he had the boys clean out the bins and scrub the baseboards every week instead of twice a month. But he also let them take a second break in the afternoon if they were working hard and things were going smoothly. And it was during such a break that Danny found Roddy and the other boy, Nunzio, one of Mr. Di Stefano's many nephews, huddled around a table in the lunchroom. They were often scheming about something, usually related to baseball or comics or girls. But since Roddy was the only one technically on break, Danny whistled Nunzio back to work and watched as the boy tore himself away.

A short while later, when Danny saw Roddy himself back at work, he went into the lunchroom to see if he could discover what all the fuss had been about. That's when he remembered the afternoon papers were just as likely to betray him as the morning ones and that people often left them lying on the tables, as much out of laziness as a willingness to share. His pulse jogged when he spied copies of the *Journal-American* and *World-Telegram* on a corner table in front of two checkout girls drinking coffee and smoking cigarettes. Without asking, the younger and plainer of the two pushed both papers toward him and turned back to her friend. He made a small show of indifference, then took the papers, found a seat in the opposite corner of the room, and began turning the pages. He could tell the older, prettier girl was eyeing him suspiciously, but after a few minutes he found no mention of the raid, so he put the papers down casually and strolled out of the room.

There was still the afternoon *Post*, so he decided he'd better make up some excuse to run to the newsstand across the street. But when he went to get his pea coat from the office, he found Roddy waiting for him there, not smiling or laughing but picking at his cheek with one hand and tucking the other one behind his back.

94

"Did you forget how to use a broom?" Danny asked.

Roddy held up a copy of the *Post*.

"It's in the back," he said. "Next to last page."

Danny's face flashed hot as he searched his brain for some explanation or smoke screen or anything to deflect the truth. He knew that by simply taking the paper he'd practically admitted it, but he couldn't think what else to do.

"I'm sorry, Danny," Roddy said, turning to go.

The fact that he made no jokes or remarks, and even seemed to dislike being the bearer of bad news, only made Danny feel worse.

He went back to his office, closed the door, and on the next to last page of the paper found the article: "Police Raid Pervert Nest." It was a brief notice and the headline took up nearly as much space as the single sentence that followed: "Early Friday morning, New York City Police arrested thirty-three men on charges of disorderly conduct at Caesar's, a tavern on Bethune Street, after having received numerous complaints that homosexuals and other immoral persons were loitering on the premises." Then there was a list of names and right near the top he saw his own: "Daniel J. Duffy, age 23, 120 Starling Avenue, Apt. 8B, Bronx, New York, grocery manager."

Seeing his name there was almost like finding out he had an evil twin running around town ruining his rep. He knew he'd given the cops all the information himself, but reading it on the page, so correct and precise—even the J. for Saint Jude, who seemed to have given up on him—was a real shock. He didn't just feel exposed. He felt dead. More than anything else, the notice looked like an obituary.

A hurricane began to rage inside his head, as if all the anger in his body was trying to come out through the top. The fluorescent lights seemed to be pulsating, the walk-in refrigerator hummed like a turbine, and shouting over the noise were the accusing voices of Quinn, the Old Bull, and Mole Man. *Cavorting in a disorderly establishment.* Danny knew he had to get away from the storm and the stink of his shame. So he shoved the newspaper into his desk drawer and hurried out of his office and onto the floor, then sped over to the checkout counters and back around to the butcher. He went by the freezer case, the dairy case, and the bakery. But the storm and the stink followed him everywhere, and once he realized there was no escaping them because they were inside him, he went back to his own department.

Unless he walked out right then and quit before he could be fired, there was nothing to do but go back to work. As the hurricane began to fade, he offered help to a couple of customers who might not have needed it. He explained the difference between scallions and shallots and apologized that there'd be no rhubarb until April. He pulled a few dingy russets from a bin and picked a cabbage leaf off the floor. Each time he did something, he forgot what had happened for a short while. But when he was done and he remembered it again, his stomach rose, his throat tightened, and his hopelessness returned, like pigeons to breadcrumbs after someone passed by on the sidewalk.

He couldn't help but imagine what was happening elsewhere in the store while he puttered aimlessly around his produce. Nunzio might sit on the news for an honest minute or two before telling one of the boys in groceries, who'd immediately spill the beans to a checkout girl, who might wait until her own break to pass the information along to Miss Crudup, the bookkeeper, who'd waste no time at all in taking it to Mr. Di Stefano. Danny tried to conjure up a more heroic scenario, one where his boss suddenly appeared in his department demanding to know where the notorious pervert was, and then Roddy and Nunzio and all the other employees, even Mr. Blavowski the butcher and the two girls from the lunchroom, came to his aid, stepping forward and declaring one at a time: *I am Danny Duffy! I am Danny Duffy!* But it was just another dumb attempt to distract himself and it barely lasted a few seconds before the pigeons came scuttling back.

Nothing but more gradual forgetting and sudden remembering happened until the end of the day. No one whispered as Danny walked the aisles. There were no looks or sneers and no one came to tell him to report to anyone. After the store closed and Roddy and Nunzio had punched out and gone home, Danny was in the walk-in, wondering if there was anything he'd forgotten to do, anything that might make the smallest difference between having a future at Sloan's and having nothing at all. When Mr. Di Stefano came through the heavy door, there was still every reason to believe he was just saying good night. He had no newspaper with him and no look of annoyance on his face.

But as soon as he sat down on a stack of pallets and let out a foggy sigh, there was no longer any doubt that the old man had heard the news.

"That's quite a bruise," he said. It was always his habit to say something friendly before coming to the point, especially if the point happened to be unfriendly.

"I had a disagreement with someone, sir," Danny said. "But I didn't look for it."

"No, I'm sure you didn't," Mr. Di Stefano said, glancing up at the ceiling, down to his shoes, and then back to Danny. "You've been with us for some time."

"Almost five years, sir."

"You've always done a fine job."

"Thank you, sir. I've always done my best."

Mr. Di Stefano looked up at the ceiling again, blinked twice, let out another sigh, and then finally said what he'd come to say. "You were arrested two nights ago."

"Yes, sir," Danny said, growing colder by the minute.

"You didn't have the flu?"

"No, sir. I was in jail."

Mr. Di Stefano looked as if he expected an explanation or apology. But Danny thought he'd been honest enough and felt no need to say any more.

"It's too bad," Mr. Di Stefano said.

"Yes, sir, it is," Danny said, shivering and rubbing his arms. Now his nose was running, his ribs were stinging, and his groin was having a fit.

"Nevertheless, it does mean I'm going to have to let you go," Mr. Di Stefano said.

"You're firing me?" Danny asked.

He'd fired a few boys himself since being promoted, and whether they were expecting it or not, it was always hard to watch someone learn they weren't as good or as lucky as they'd thought. As their faces went suddenly white or red or sweaty or dry, they seemed to reveal all the sad things they'd ever experienced in life in a single moment. Danny knew his own face was probably doing the same thing, and he wondered how his boss could see all that sadness and then fire him anyway.

"As for me, I say live and let live," the old man said. "But, well, it's been in the papers."

It seemed nuts that being gay was fine so long as nobody wrote about it. Then again, the paper said what Quinn hadn't said at the dinner table and what Margaret Duffy hadn't wanted to hear. And it said it to the whole city all at once.

"Still, I'd like you to stay on for another two weeks," Mr. Di Stefano said, getting up to leave. "That'll give us both some time."

"Time, sir?"

"For you to find another position and for me to find your replacement. It seems best, doesn't it?"

Danny was so numbed by the cold that he couldn't understand how his public disgrace could require both his firing and its postponement. But his boss seemed to want him to say out loud that he accepted these terms.

"Yes, sir," he said.

He was used to taking orders. But it felt like pleading guilty a second time.

◉ ◉ ◉

He'd called Gabriel from a pay phone on Columbus and they agreed to meet at a bar near Verdi Square and then bop it up all night long. But Danny knew Gabriel would take his time getting there. So he pulled his ushanka down around his ears and wandered south along Central Park West, watching the pale light from the streetlamps trim the icy trees and the snow-humped granite walls and trying hard not to feel too desperate. He cursed the sidewalk for being so slippery and some little gray birds for not having flown south for the winter. He wondered why he didn't leave New York himself and go somewhere else in the world, like Peru or Madagascar or Kamchatka. He'd often dreamt about living in the Catskills in a house that he'd built with his friends out of pine planks and spike nails, where they'd grow fruits and vegetables and listen to music and dance and do whatever they wanted, in bed and out. In a weak moment, he even thought about going home to Parkchester and begging his mother's forgiveness, but as soon as he pictured Quinn dancing around the apartment, waving a copy of the *Post*, he promised himself he'd no longer think about the people who'd betrayed him.

"What's your name, son?" asked a silver-haired stiff in a Homburg hat who stopped and stared at Danny as he walked by in the other direction. He had watery eyes and a catfish mouth and Danny almost told him to get bent, but he didn't feel like wasting his breath so he just kept on walking.

Central Park was famous for pickups, especially around the Ramble, where a tree or a bush was all the privacy you got. Danny didn't go for such forbidden pleasures like some guys did, but he'd had his fair share. When he was sixteen, he met an Israeli boy at the skating rink at Rockefeller Center and made out with him in a changing stall across the street at Saks. Once he fooled around with a Negro Ivy Leaguer behind a concession stand at Riis Park beach and ended up sore from all the sand but didn't care. Unlike Gabriel, he didn't think much of public toilets, which were smelly and risky, and he wasn't interested in the older, mostly married men who visited them. He preferred guys his own age, especially from other places and cultures. Sometimes after work, when he was feeling lonely, he'd stroll across to the Soldiers and Sailors Monument and strike up a conversation with whoever happened to be hanging around. If that guy happened to be young and cute, they might swap blowjobs against one of the crumbling marble columns. And even if they only walked together up and down the dark, sheltered stretches of Riverside Drive, it almost felt like love was everywhere for the taking.

Those innocent days seemed over now, and when Danny finally arrived at the Excelsior, he combed his hair, counted the bills in his wallet, and readied himself for the kind of night that would make him forget everything. On one side of the long, narrow room there was a mahogany bar tricked out with liquor bottles of every shape and color. On the other was a wall of sheet music from Italian operas by Giuseppe Verdi, the famous composer, whose statue marked the nearby square. Above it all was an old tin ceiling that sagged and cracked, and somewhere in the back a jukebox played Nat King Cole.

It was smaller and tamer than Caesar's, but on Saturday nights it drew a good-humored gay crowd, and the proprietors never made a fuss about who they served.

"Where *have* you *been?*" Gabriel called out from the bar in his driest Bette Davis. "Come, come. I've been waiting for ages and no one seems to want to buy me a drink!"

Danny laughed and shook his head, then ordered two Rheingolds from a smiling, muscle-bound man in bleach-white shirtsleeves and a crooked black bowtie.

"I won't ask what happened," Gabriel said. "The look on your face says it all."

"And what look might that be, dahling?" Danny asked.

"The look of someone who's developed a taste for jailhouse life and wishes he was still back in the can. Hawh-hawh-hawh!"

Gabriel was a half-foot taller than Danny, naturally athletic, and pretty humpy. The kind of guy who could have been a real ladies' man, if he'd had any interest in ladies. He could swear like a sailor, but he could also squeal like a girl. And then there was his laugh. Danny knew Gabriel wouldn't ask for details about his arrest the way Raf had, and he didn't want to tell him about getting fired either, since Gabriel had been fired too many times himself to see it as a setback. He only wanted to drink away the tremor in his chest and the pains in his groin and side, and when their beers arrived, they blew off the heads, toasted each other, and took great gulps, careless of the mess it made on the bar or the suds that trickled down their chins.

Then Gabriel suddenly slapped his hands on both sides of his face and bugged his eyes. It was Ethel Merman wailing "Together" from the jukebox. And when he heard it, Danny bugged his eyes too because the song seemed like a miracle of good news. They got up from their stools and started singing along arm-in-arm. It was still early and there weren't more than twenty men in the place and a few women, and some of them sang, too. But after a few verses Gabriel was singing the loudest, and before anyone could object, he took his beer in one hand and Danny in the other and they shimmied toward the back of the room. Most of the other patrons got out of the way, though some didn't have time and got bumped by an elbow. Danny's ribs screamed in protest and his groin threatened a rupture, but at that point he just didn't care enough to stop.

"What's the big idea?" someone said as they capered by.

A grumpy-looking man in an orange toupee and a baggy pinstripe suit sneered his offense, while a tiny woman in a ratty mink stole and cheap paste jewelry hid behind him. He looked more like a hole-and-corner queen who forgot to leave his wife at home than an idiot who didn't know what Saturday night at the Excelsior meant.

"It's called letting your wig down, dahling," Danny said. "You should try it!"

He slipped his arm behind Gabriel's back and led him in a wild and woolly cowboy waltz that quickly spun out of control and knocked a pint glass out of Mr. Grumpy's hand.

"Buy yourself another one on me!" Gabriel cried. "Hawh-hawh!"

Mr. Grumpy cocked his head this way and that to get the attention of someone in charge. But Danny and Gabriel kept spinning and singing until they reached the jukebox, then stopped, struck dramatic poses, and belted out what had been their favorite lyrics since seeing *Gypsy* at the Imperial a year before.

No fits, no fights, no feuds and no egos—Amigos!—together!

They hit every note perfectly, like one of those magical Broadway numbers where everyone knew the words and no one had to rehearse. For just a moment, it seemed that a few bars of music and a couple of kick ball changes could redeem Danny's shitty day.

A moment later, Gabriel pulled him into the men's room, where they caught their breath and Danny tried to quiet his throbbing parts.

"You all right?" Gabriel asked, in a rare show of concern.

Danny nodded.

"Well, ring-a-ding-ding, 'cause guess what I have?"

"Beats me. A case of the clap?"

"Oh, no, sister, think again," Gabriel said, as he pulled a small vial from his pocket and held it up between his thumb and index finger, like a miner with a golden nugget. "Hawh-hawh!"

Besides pot, Danny had never tried more than bennies and goofballs. But after Gabriel tapped some of the white powder onto the back of his hand and sniffed it up, Danny imitated his technique, snorted a little pile from his own hand, and soon felt a bitter ooze sliding down his throat and a sense of possibility rising in his head.

"Now how do you feel?" Gabriel asked, tucking the vial into Danny's shirt pocket.

"Like a million buttons!"

"Marvelous! 'Cause I've got something else, too."

This time Gabriel flashed a small white card. It read "Bacchus" in black script and gave an upper Broadway address, which might have been north or south of them but couldn't have been too far from where they were.

"Some old fairy at the Mais Oui gave it to me last night," he said. "She was mum on the whats and wherefores, but she promised we'd have a very gay time."

Danny smiled at the mystery, then tipped the vial on his hand again, took another snort and felt the pain in his sides and groin magically vanish.

"What say you buy us a few more rounds and then we'll go see?" Gabriel said.

Danny licked his lips, gnashed his teeth, and felt like he wanted to light the world on fire and maybe even burn it to the ground.

As they left the men's room and trooped back to the bar, he saw that the whole room had gone quiet. Though "Let Me Entertain You" was playing on the jukebox, the volume had been turned down. No one was singing anymore, and despite Miss Sandra Church's best efforts, no one was smiling either. Mr. Grumpy huffed and puffed and held onto his wife like a life preserver, and the brawny bartender who'd seemed so friendly before was now shaking his head.

"Couple more Rheingolds, if you please," Gabriel chirped.

"You boys gotta go," the bartender said, as his eyes twitched left.

Danny turned and saw a heavyset man with a triple chin and a walrus mustache lumbering toward them.

"Aw, don't be sore," Gabriel said. "We won't cause any more trouble. Scout's honor!"

He was so used to being refused he couldn't see what was happening.

"You tipped the scales," the bartender said. "And they won't tip back. So beat it!"

Danny knew he meant they'd been too campy. They'd said out loud what was supposed to be only hinted at.

"What have we done?" he demanded.

"We don't serve your kind here!" the Walrus snapped, his jowls flapping.

Danny felt a fight coming on again, and though he knew he probably didn't have the strength to win one, he knew he couldn't quit either.

"Oh contrary, Mary! We can see that you do," he said, eyeing the crowd. "These sad tomatoes don't dance as pretty as we do, but they're our kind just the same."

"Hawh-hawh!" Gabriel roared.

"Don't you know who owns this place?" the bartender said with a smirk. "If you don't get lost this second, you're dead meat."

Danny grabbed Gabriel by the shoulder and backed away from the Walrus and Mr. Grumpy until there was a clear path to the front door behind them. Then he turned and addressed the entire bar.

"What a bunch of pussycats you are!" he cried. "You come here to wink at each other and then you shit yourselves if anyone winks back." He looked right at Mr. Grumpy. "You keep your prick in your pocket and mind your Ps and Qs, and for what? To let these crooks sell you overpriced, watered-down drinks? So you can be a respectable eunuch for a few hours once a week? Is this the life your mothers' sons were born for?"

Gabriel looked a little confused by Danny's speech, and Danny himself wasn't entirely sure where his words were coming from. Mr. Grumpy turned white as a bride and his actual bride looked like she might faint. The Walrus sputtered and stammered and the bartender reached for a baseball bat. The rest of the patrons stood back, aggrieved but resigned, as if waiting for the next insult to be hurled.

"Go on, then!" Danny shouted at them. "Gawk and swoon when a faggot dares to act like a man!"

"Come, come, Danny-O," Gabriel said, pulling him toward the door. "Time to beat feet."

What chumps they seemed, these people Danny had offended. Ordinary folks, mostly neat in appearance, not too proud, but totally blind to the devil's bargain they'd made. He'd been too busy enjoying himself to notice that the house rules at the Excelsior were no different than they were at Margaret Duffy's or at Sloan's. That you could only be yourself to a point and then you had to pretend to be somebody else. You might wear a purple tie or sing tra-la-la, but if the tie was too bright or the song was too loud, you tipped the scales and even your own kind felt obliged to remind you that, except in newspaper notices, you didn't really exist.

"Get the hell out of here!" the Walrus screamed.

"Fuck off!" cried the bartender, holding his bat up for all to see.

"Oh, we'll fuck off, dahling!" Danny called out before turning to leave. "Since there's no one here we'd ever trust with the job!"

When they were clear of the door, he and Gabriel locked eyes, breathing clouds of steam in one another's faces, until Gabriel suddenly burst out laughing and Danny, delirious with new knowledge, did too. It felt like they were conspiring against the conspiracy. Then they took off down the street toward Broadway in search of better enemies, arm-in-arm, amigos together, whooping for joy. Though the feeling in Danny's heart was really something closer to fury.

10

On Sunday morning, Roger drove the Chrysler up the Merritt Parkway with the radio on and the window rolled down, letting the
cold air burnish his face and wake his sluggish body after a day of
cloistered brooding and a night of fitful sleep. The cloudless sky
and blazing sun seemed a forgiving respite from the monotony of
winter gloom. The ice that had made the previous day so perilous
had melted, but everything that wasn't asphalt was still blanketed in
white velvet, wind-driven snow. Paul Anka sang about hurting the
ones you love—as if a pouty-lipped teenager knew anything about
it—but somehow it made Roger feel a little less guilty. By the time
he pulled off the highway and sped alongside the frozen Saugatuck,
he'd almost shuffled off his dejection and felt nearly ready to meet
Schuyler without any signs of the trouble he was facing.

When he arrived at their usual spot, a narrow, unpaved lane hidden
between a dilapidated shack and an old fieldstone cairn, he pulled
in behind Schuyler's Country Squire wagon, where a pair of Nordic
skis and bamboo poles leaned against one side and the man himself
curled out of a rear door lacing up his boots.

"You made it!" Schuyler sang out a moment later as he sprung
to his feet. "I thought you might have abandoned me for a day of
poking the pooch."

"Then your blind faith in me is much appreciated," Roger said,
inhaling the resinous pine and minty birch.

Schuyler was tall, barrel-chested, and thick-limbed, but he bounded toward Roger with the agility of a much lighter man. His broad, ready smile was bracketed by deep right-angled dimples, seconded by bright Hollywood-blue eyes, and tinged with a Teutonic rosiness that always betrayed his essential good humor no matter the situation. Although his tidy cap of light brown hair was just beginning to show traces of gray, no man seemed less likely to go bald. Every time Roger saw him, he got a little shock of pleasure, an always unexpected recognition that some part of his best friend's gentle, dependable manliness was his own possession, too.

"How are you, my friend?" Schuyler asked, punching each word with an eager nod, although at first Roger thought he heard him say "How are *you* my friend?"

"Never better," he answered, hoping it might soon be less of a lie.

"It's going to be a fine day," Schuyler said, clapping Roger's shoulder.

When he heard nuthatches and juncos caroling in the trees, Roger took out his binoculars and zoomed in on the familiar drama of flitting and fussing among the snow-laced branches. It was all so peaceful and beautiful and yet so manic and fraught at the same time. How lovely and how terrible to be a bird, he thought. He turned to say as much to Schuyler but found him already clipping into his bindings. So Roger put away the binoculars, hurried to take his own skis and poles out of the Chrysler, and began pulling on his boots, all the while trying to resist the feeling that he'd fallen behind before he'd even begun.

Soon Schuyler was snowplowing over to him with his poles in one hand and a khaki army-issue rucksack in the other.

"Drink up," he said, after he drew a steel thermos from the rucksack, poured a cup of coffee, and handed it to Roger. "Miles to go before we sleep."

Roger wasn't an accomplished skier and had only learned at Schuyler's insistence. In fact, it still amazed him that he could maintain his balance while locked into these queer contraptions of plywood and aluminum. It felt strange to remain upright and move steadily when the snow itself was so slick and treacherous.

"I was thinking we'd go to the reservoir," Schuyler said as he took back the half-empty cup and drank the rest, then returned the thermos to the rucksack and threw it over his shoulders. "It's a dangerous mission, soldier. Are you up for it?"

"I'd ski to Kalamazoo, if my country needed me, Captain Endicott, sir!" Roger answered. The joke was as old and worn as a river rock but a happy reminder that they'd both done their duty and would never have to do it again.

Roger had always admired Schuyler's service in the Tenth Mountain Division, which fought on skis in the Northern Apennines in Italy during the war's last battles in Europe. Although a Fascist bullet had passed cleanly through his hand at Cutigliano on his first day of combat, he otherwise survived unscathed, earned a Bronze Star for heroic action on Riva Ridge, and led the only unit in the division that never lost a man. When he came home to staid Greenfield Hill and settled into the comparatively safe work of running of his father's savings and loan, he began devoting winter weekends to campaigns through the forests of Fairfield County and often recruited Roger to be his comrade-in-arms.

It was nearing eleven o'clock when they took off down the snowy lane, Roger striding and gliding behind Schuyler, whose skis laid the piste that eased his way. After fifty yards or so, they turned into the forest, trading sunshine and small talk for wooded shade and the muffled shush of powder. Then they passed through a ragged stand of cedars and careened down the side of a steep slope into a glen by the river. Although Schuyler seemed to move effortlessly, Roger struggled to get the edge of his skis to bite into the snow. Once he was on flat ground again, he relaxed his knees, remembered to shift the weight of his body from one leg to the other, and eventually picked up speed. A half mile later, as they turned away from the river and climbed a bare knoll, he even began to feel strong and unshakable. It was almost as if time had forgotten the past and all his terrible secrets were hidden away in the smallest niches of his heart.

Being with Schuyler often made him feel this way. They'd met as lab partners in ninth-grade biology class at the Hotchkiss School, when Roger watched with awe as his handsome and fearless new friend ignored the stench of the formaldehyde and the antics of their classmates and sliced right into the frog they'd been asked to dissect, his hand so steady and precise. Roger decided at that moment exactly what kind of boy was truest and best, and after four years together, they'd come to see each other almost as brothers, with Schuyler usually acting as the elder, though he'd been born nearly a year later.

"I'm not going too fast, am I?" he called out without turning around.

"I think I can manage!" Roger answered.

The only problem with skiing behind Schuyler was that it often gave Roger an unobstructed view of his posterior. He'd vowed never to think of his friend in physical terms, and for the most part he'd kept his promise. Even when they showered together at the club, he always made it a point to fill his mind with some abstract idea—an algebraic formula from school or some tricky question of business at work—and avoided the temptation of glimpsing any part of Schuyler's body below the neck. It wasn't so much that he feared being caught sneaking a peek, which probably would have been dismissed as a mere nothing. Rather he worried he'd be unable to look away and might develop a permanent fixation that would be impossible to stop or explain and would ultimately destroy their friendship. But that morning the dazzling spectacle of Schuyler's buttocks wrapped in close-fitting woolen ski pants, and the elegant compression and extension of his muscular thighs, seemed to force themselves on Roger's view. When his powers of resistance failed him, and the seclusion of the forest seemed to invite indulgence, he allowed himself to imagine a few chaste acts of intimacy. A hand caressing the small of Schuyler's back. An arm wrapped around his leg, like a wild grape vine climbing the trunk of a sugar maple. With another man, he might have gone further. But even these tender fancies left him feeling as if he'd violated the one cardinal rule that allowed him to be worthy of such a friendship.

After an hour or so skiing and struggling, of looking and looking away, they herringboned their way up toward a picnic table by the reservoir, where the blue sky split wide open and the noon sun shone hot on their faces. Once they unfastened their skis and brushed the ice-crusted snow off the table and one of its benches, Roger took out his binoculars again and watched a trio of red-tailed hawks angling in the breeze, while Schuyler pulled a piece of canvas from his rucksack, made a place for them to sit, and produced a lunch of four bologna sandwiches, a wax paper envelope of nuts, raisins, and dried apricots, a pair of cranberry muffins, and what was left of the thermos of coffee.

"Marjorie never fails," he said, as he handed Roger his share of the feast.

"She's got a heart of gold," Roger agreed, hoping the cliché wasn't heard as derision, even if it might have been partly intended that way.

Praising his wife's many virtues was one of Schuyler's oldest habits and the only one Roger found irritating. He supposed the praise was fitting enough for a woman who, despite the demands of raising three daughters, found time for half a dozen ladies' clubs and twice as many charities for orphans and refugees. Any annoyance on his part was probably only petty jealousy. But he also knew that, like all normal men, Schuyler's genuine gratitude for his wife was rooted in a feeling he had about women in general, about how they softened the hardness of life, brought sweetness to its sour incongruities, and rewarded manly responsibility with the comforts of home and family. It was when other men spoke of their gratitude to their wives that Roger felt the loneliest.

Schuyler seemed to be counting his blessings as he ate his sandwich and looked out across the sun-streaked ice at the rocky shore and the jagged green horizon beyond.

"How's that young man of yours?" he asked. "Will he play baseball again this year?"

Roger didn't understand how Schuyler could be so obtuse about the boy who turned cartwheels in right field and was existentially afraid of balls of any type or size.

"Apparently not," he said, forcing a smile, and when Schuyler's expression made it clear he didn't understand, he added: "He's turning out to be more of an indoor boy."

"Ah, an intellectual, like his dad," Schuyler said. Then, after a curious tilt of his head, he added: "You don't mind, do you? That he won't be an athlete?"

Roger didn't know whether to be offended by the unnecessary inference or encouraged by its frankness.

"I'm being silly," Schuyler said, before he could answer. "We're both very lucky men."

Although it had long been a commonplace between them, Roger knew that "very lucky," even for Schuyler, was a qualified state of being. If it meant health and wealth, family and friends, and all the benefits of the good life, it also assumed a certain amount of regimentation and boredom. Even at the best of times, even with ski treks in winter and tennis round-robins in summer, it was inevitable that their lives were quieter than those they'd imagined as young men, less exciting than the ones they'd experienced in the war, and far from the romantic exile in Greece that Mudge Collins had talked of so long ago. But Roger knew there was something in Schuyler's nature that made all the trade-offs worthwhile. Some virtue of resignation that was only possible with the authentic love of a woman, given and received, and desire that wasn't merely theoretical.

"Have you ever thought of going back to Italy?" Roger asked, probing for some trace of dissatisfaction in his friend's life, some need unmet, or at least some capacity for small dreams. He envisioned snow-sculpted ridges and a column of white-camouflaged troops schussing across it with stealth and courage.

Schuyler lit a cigarette and exhaled two plumes of smoke through his nostrils. "Why would I want to do that?"

"To ski, of course!" Roger answered, exaggerating his disbelief.

It hadn't occurred to him that Italy might be the last place Schuyler wanted to revisit. He himself had no interest in setting foot anywhere near the Pacific again. But surely Italy was different—it had none of the fetid smells and stinging insects of Saipan or Guam. And perhaps Schuyler ought to go back and see the place again, to view it with new eyes, and to go with a friend who understood what it meant to be brave and to suffer. If they could play snow patrol in the forests of Connecticut, it seemed perfectly reasonable to turn a former war zone into a holiday place.

"We could go together, Sky," he said. "It could be a real lark. What do you say?"

Schuyler looked at him with a flat expression that suggested neither resentment nor regret but might well have hidden either. "I don't think so," he said.

Roger knew he ought to accept such a decisive answer, but it didn't seem fair to dismiss the idea out of hand.

"Why not?" he persisted. "What's to keep us from going?"

Schuyler looked at him as if he'd proposed flying to the moon. "Because Marjorie would feel excluded," he said. "And I think Corinne would, too."

"Would they?" Roger asked, miffed that Schuyler felt he could speak for both their wives so authoritatively. "But we have every right to spend time by ourselves!"

It was an unseemly thing to say out loud, Roger knew. It came perilously close to claiming some kind of equivalence between friendship and marriage. Even worse, he'd said it with a vehemence that betrayed too much need. Schuyler set his jaw and leaned forward, as if he were on the verge of answering Roger's outburst with some indignation of his own. But then he just relaxed again and unwrapped another sandwich.

"Maybe the four of us will go one year," Roger mumbled by way of an apology.

Without answering, Schuyler snuffed out his cigarette, closed his eyes, and bathed his face in the shimmering sunlight. Roger took up his binoculars again, scanning the trees for a pileated woodpecker or a mockingbird or a barred owl. After a while, finding nothing more than a tufted titmouse, he slowly shifted his gaze, refocused, and dared to admire the dome of Schuyler's forehead, the ruddy apple of his cheek, even the purplish creases of his lips. When a raven suddenly cawed above them, he turned back toward the trees, at which point Schuyler gave a gruff sigh of contentment and began putting the remains of their lunch back into the rucksack.

As they clipped into their skis again and headed back, Roger decided to take the lead, which was contrary to their usual practice but would free him from the prospect of troubling sights and might help restore balance to a friendship that he feared often listed too much in one direction. He expected Schuyler to offer a word of advice or make a friendly crack about not knowing the way. But all he heard behind him was the light step and slide of his skis, which seemed a tacit sign of approval.

A quarter of an hour later, as they slid over a ridge toward the river, Roger was regretting his decision. It was too physically taxing to set the pace for a superior athlete and more experienced skier and too mentally taxing to wonder constantly if he wasn't going fast enough or perhaps too fast. He worried that he appeared ridiculous in his pointless bravado, and he hated that he was the kind of man who couldn't even trust his best friend to think well of him. He also couldn't help rehearsing the conversation they'd had about Henry. It was careless of Schuyler to have broached the sensitive topic of baseball, but most of all Roger regretted having called his own son an "indoor boy." It was a repulsive phrase, however accurate. It implied not just a lack of toughness but a real preference for softness that could only mean one thing. He even began to worry it might have been some kind of unconscious confession of his own. Although he could never openly admit he'd been caught up in a police raid at a queer bar, perhaps he'd meant to offer a hint in that direction by betraying the fact that his son, flesh of his flesh, would probably grow up to be a pansy. And perhaps this is what Schuyler had been getting at in the first place when he asked how Roger felt about Henry's effeteness and called him "an intellectual, like his dad."

"Slow down!" Schuyler called out. "No one's chasing us!"

But all Roger heard was the criticism his words implied, and as he sailed over a rise and down the other side, he tucked in tighter, determined to go as fast as he pleased. He knew he was doing everything exactly as he'd seen Schuyler do it. Sitting in a crouch, holding his back straight, dropping his head to lessen the drag. Then it occurred to Roger that every important thing he'd ever done in his life, certainly every act of valor of strength, was little more than a poor imitation of Schuyler. Not only the way he skied but the way he spoke and walked and talked and worked. His best friend, Roger realized, wasn't a role model so much as an obsession.

As the thought detonated in his mind, he lost control of his skis and tumbled head over boots into a steep gully. His cap flew off, he lost a pole, and when he finally landed, he was lying flat on his back, a half-foot deep in powder, with one ski turned in the wrong direction and the other nearly buried.

"Are you hurt?" Schuyler called out.

"Only my pride," Roger said, though he supposed the damage might be extensive.

He tried to turn himself right, but neither his body nor his equipment would cooperate. He began to feel the hollow heaviness inside him again.

"Take off your skis and climb out," Schuyler offered. "It'll be a lot easier."

"I've got it," Roger said, finally wriggling onto his side.

With his one pole, he reached for his cap several feet above him, snagged it with the tip, and put it back on his head, for dignity as much as for warmth. Then he used the pole to dig out the buried ski, stabbing clumsily at the snow, until he gave up and eventually wrested it out with a series of sharp, angry jerks. After he clipped it back onto his boot, he set his skis perpendicular to the slope and pushed their near edges into the snow. But when he tried to stand, the skis slipped out from under him and he fell a second time, sliding another three or four feet into the gully.

"Just unclip them and you'll be up and out in a jiffy."

Roger resented his advice and ignored it. But when he tried to stand up again, the skis slipped and his body fell and slid in precisely the same way. Soon enough, his legs were like noodles, his hands all frozen thumbs.

"Oh, for Pete's sake, Roger! Shall I come down and fetch you?"

"Would you please just shut up and let me do it my way!"

Like a body succumbing to a virus, Roger's mind began to sicken with thoughts of Thursday night. In his friend's voice, he heard only the glib taunts of the bald-headed, bulbous-nosed detective. The resinous pine and minty birch had been replaced by the stench of the bar and of the bodies of men caged like animals. All the nuthatches and juncos had turned mute or flown the forest, leaving behind only the clanging of the cell door, the swishy, smug ravings of the male prostitute, and the hysterical shouting of the man in the rumpled suit. Roger felt the queerness of all those hapless fairies in his own exhausted blood. And he knew it would follow him like a dark shadow for the rest of his life. Whenever he had the temerity to imagine that he'd put his problems behind him, it would rise up again, seize him by the throat, and throw him in a ditch.

A squirrel skimmed past him, air-footed, then swooped up a cedar. The cold began to seep through Roger's ski pants into his bones, even as the heat of the afternoon sun radiated off his cap. He waited for Schuyler to say something more, hoping it might be a saving word and yet dreading another reproach. But when he said nothing at all, and Roger heard only the senseless breeze through the oblivious trees, the silence felt unbearably lonesome. Then he unclipped his skis, took them in one hand and his pole in the other, and slowly crawled back up the steep slope through the heavy, humbling snow.

11

It was nearly ten thirty the next morning when Julian finally opened his eyes. With a female houseguest and a boyfriend unaccounted for, it seemed irresponsible to have slept so long. Since the bedroom door was closed, he supposed Pen was somehow still in bed herself, perhaps sleeping off an excess of Rioja. So after a shower and shave, he tightened the belt of his bathrobe and knocked on the door. While he waited for her reply, he remembered his promise to confess everything to her—about Gus and the raid, about himself—and he was on the verge of putting it off until he'd eaten breakfast when he opened the door, peered inside, and saw the bed neatly made, the overnight case missing, and a handwritten note lying conspicuously on the dresser.

Dearest Jules—
It's awfully rude of me to leave after only just arriving and without even saying good-bye. But you were impossible to wake—in fact, snoring like a grizzly! Suffice it to say that my mother's hip has taken a turn for the worse—or rather she took a turn herself. So I'm off again this morning to do my duty to those who need me more than you do—as you sleep the sleep of the just. Thanks for understanding.
xoxo
Pen

It was a strange letter, not least because the hand was neater than Pen's usual scrawl. Julian wondered how she'd so suddenly come to learn of this unhappy news and whether he ought not call her parents in Brookline to ask for details and offer support, though he didn't relish the idea of enduring her father's cold manner. But then it occurred to Julian that Pen might have used her mother's ever-faulty hip as an excuse to leave because she was upset with him for failing to appreciate all that business about not holding on too tight and drinking from separate cups. Or maybe their understanding had finally become too peculiar and she simply no longer wanted any part of it. Looking around the perfectly tidy bedroom, he saw that her copy of *The Prophet* was no longer on the bedside table. Instead of seeking further clues to the mystery, he thought only of the messier, franker Gus, who'd several times left his dog-eared copy of Gombrich's *Story of Art* in exactly the same place. Then Julian realized that speculations about Pen's motives and a phone call to her parents were needless and officious, that her family, whatever its problems, could take care of itself, and above all, that Pen was not, and really never had been, his responsibility.

Instead he spent the entire day calling everyone he could think of who might know where Gus was and then waiting for the telephone to ring or the intercom to buzz. He first called Syd, an up-and-coming Brooklyn novelist and Gus's sometime drinking buddy, whom they'd had to dinner the week before. Then Dahlia, the girl Friday at a downtown gallery who claimed to be Gus's best friend in the world and was probably in love with him. And Hugh, of course, who offered several plausible explanations for Gus's absence, but like the others had nothing helpful to say. After working up the courage, Julian called seven hospitals, but none had any record of a Gus Magnusson being admitted. As the sun went down, he considered going back downtown to the Waverly, but he worried he might miss Gus if he did. So he kept waiting and made more calls. Sometime before midnight, after eating a late supper of gherkins, chopped liver, and stale crackers, he suddenly remembered lunch dates to postpone and committee meetings he couldn't think of attending until all was well, but moments later he fell asleep on the sofa with the telephone on his chest.

On Sunday afternoon, he taped another note on the door of his building—the first had mysteriously disappeared—and went down to

Gus's studio on West 37th, which was littered with more paint-stained easels and works-in-progress than the room could comfortably hold. He noticed some tattered wicker chairs in one corner, a stack of old *Police Gazettes* in another, and a sharp-eyed tabby cat watching from a windowsill. There were also several longhaired, grass-smoking artists and some rather sophistic talk about Japanese minimalism, but not one iota of useful intelligence concerning Gus's whereabouts.

"He hasn't been here since last week," said the young woman from Texas, without looking up. Her dry brown bangs hung in her face as she broke precise shards of colored glass with a chisel and ball-peen hammer.

"Do you have any idea where he might be?" Julian asked, trying to express a sense of urgency without sounding overwrought.

"No, but it's strange," she said, as she shook away her hair and pointed with her nose. "He's been working so hard lately trying to finish it. Then he just stopped coming."

Julian lifted the sheet that covered Gus's easel. It was a substantial canvas done in thick smears of paint and great earthy planes of color. Although Gus had insisted it was all pure abstraction—or, if he was feeling moody, just oil, pigment, and brushstrokes, nothing more—Julian thought he could see expanses of forest and sod, chalky impasto rain clouds on a gauzy gray sky, and what had to be a kind of dialectical motif of migrating white cranes with golden sunlight shimmering on their wings. Every messy element was somehow perfect, every contradiction uncannily revolved. It was like a picture of Gus himself.

"It's for you, isn't it?" the Texan asked.

"That's what he told me," Julian said.

"Must be nice," she muttered, before turning back to her work.

Julian smiled. It *was* nice. Even in Gus's prolonged and unaccountable absence, he still felt that strange sense of deserving inferiority.

What wasn't nice was seeing the artwork without the artist, and it was frustrating that no one besides the sculptress seemed to express any interest in Gus's whereabouts or concern for his welfare. But then it occurred to Julian that, while they all knew him as a free-spirited artist with no permanent address, they wouldn't have known about his night in jail because it hadn't yet become a matter of public record.

"Ask him to call me if you see him, won't you?" he said, as he threw the sheet back over the canvas.

Ten minutes later, at a kiosk across from Penn Station, he paged through copies of the *Times*, the *Herald-Tribune*, the *World-Telegram*, and the *Mirror*, and it was in the last that he discovered a short, nasty article about the raid, along with the names of nearly three dozen men, fearfully inscribed in black and white, not unlike the victims of the German mine disaster on the front page. Julian felt a wrenching pain in his heart as he read Gus's name. But when he saw that the address he'd given was the Fifth Avenue apartment of the Swiss art dealer, the pain dropped into his stomach.

It was unthinkable that Gus had returned to such a compromising situation, especially given what they'd been through together. Of course, he'd had no other address to give, and Julian had more or less forbidden him from using his own. Because he had to be absolutely certain either way, he hailed a taxi and rode uptown to the flashy Italianate pile on Fifth Avenue and East 85th only to learn from its doorman that Manfred Loosli had left town the day before and wouldn't return until Wednesday.

"Might you recall if he left alone?" Julian asked, pretending to admire the gilt crown molding of the lobby.

At first, the doorman's eyes brightened at the question, but then he shook his head with a self-satisfied smile. "That's not really any of your business, is it?" he said, as if spontaneously remembering his duty of discretion and pleased to have a secret, actual or merely theoretical, to protect.

Julian was stumped. If it was impossible that Gus had taken refuge with such a man as Loosli, it seemed equally impossible that he'd already been released from jail and had failed to contact Julian after getting out. He suddenly felt as if their brief romance had been nothing but a fantastic dream, that Gus's smell, his voice, his beautiful ears had all been merely a projection of Julian's unconscious desires and nothing more. Although he knew it wasn't true, he shuddered at the idea that Gus was now no more to him than a name printed with cheap ink on cheap paper rolled up in his sweaty fist.

Then he said his name aloud, as if he might actually answer. It was ridiculous, he knew, but as Julian walked back across Central Park, he kept saying it over and over in his head as he scanned the fields and hills, like a man with a metal detector or a kid playing Marco Polo, and the sound was strangely soothing—the sound of a game that would inevitably end in finding and being found.

◎ ◎ ◎

The walk to Dr. Ziegler's brownstone office on 101st Street near Riverside Drive was usually a pleasant enough journey, but on Monday it was marred by piles of sooty snow and the slurry of frozen debris, as if the ugly truth of winter had been coughed up on every curb. There was a smoky sharpness in the air that seemed to leave no room in the world for Pen's idea of happiness. As Julian slogged down Broadway, he wondered how he could possibly avoid revealing to his analyst the cause of his angst, and he feared that lying on a couch for an hour was unlikely to relieve it. After he rang the doorbell, he considered making up some excuse about a previous engagement and canceling the appointment on the spot. But when Ziegler greeted him with an amiable smile and a natty Harris tweed jacket that nearly matched Julian's own, he changed his mind.

"Good morning," they each said softly, like two monks passing in a monastery.

Julian had always found most Jewish men to be both intelligent and kind, a pleasing contrast to the dim, crabbed Westerners he'd known as a boy. But Ziegler, who wasn't much older than Julian himself, was unusually attractive. He had dark and gentle eyes that sat placidly behind thick tortoiseshell glasses, an overtly masculine nose, and above it all a full head of curly black hair that cried out to be touched. If the protocols of analysis had left almost everything about his personal life a mystery, Julian had happily filled in the blanks by giving him a charming wife, a multitude of clever and attractive friends, and considerable sexual prowess.

After Ziegler sat down and opened his notebook, Julian eased onto a sleek black leather daybed. Lying horizontal always made him especially conscious of the room, which was otherwise decorated in a lazy Edwardian style, heavy with mahogany and brocade, all probably meant to convey a certain Freudian gravity. It wasn't at all

119

to Julian's taste, and he guessed it wasn't to Ziegler's either but rather the work of some previous occupant or, more likely, the charming wife. But Julian was sure the daybed had been the good doctor's own inspiration, an insistence on modern chic in a life overrun with dowdy tradition. It still gave Julian a passing thrill, despite his bleak mood, to think that the man had probably lain upon it himself.

Yet even the daybed and Ziegler's curls were no longer enough to make the twice-weekly visits feel quite so pertinent as they once had. Many men he knew saw shrinks, some of them trying desperately to change their essential natures. For Julian, who had no doubts about the permanence of his own condition, analysis had been more a soothing retreat from the bustle of the week. He'd liked the ritual of self-reflection, which allowed him to appreciate the complexities of his psyche, and he'd taken particular pleasure in shaping the story of his lonely Phoenix childhood—the early loss of his passive father and endless battles with his domineering mother—into an epic of conflicted manhood, the overcoming of which had, despite its many trials, resulted in impressive prosperity and contentment. But since he'd met Gus, Julian had found himself far more interested in exploring the pleasures of the present than the pains of the past, and the sessions had come to feel not only like a costly extravagance and an undue burden on his busy schedule but even an unwelcome intrusion into his private life.

That he'd never been entirely forthcoming with Ziegler seemed unfortunate but inevitable. Despite the promise of confidentiality, Julian felt reluctant to burden him with what was, strictly speaking, a knowledge of crimes. Although they frequently discussed the men in his life, his most candid disclosures were limited to anxieties, dreams, and juvenile memories. The logic by which he withheld some facts and conveyed others only euphemistically, and then Ziegler either accepted or resisted Julian's withholding and gently translated his euphemisms into something more concrete, was murky at best.

"You don't seem eager to talk today," Ziegler said to the back of Julian's head after the initial silence, which usually lasted only fifteen seconds or so, had stretched nearly to a full minute. "Is there something on your mind?"

It was an old shrink's trick to respond to a patient's reticence by assuming he had too much to say rather than too little. It would have been easy to begin by discussing Pen's visit and its unforeseen brevity, as well as Julian's hope that their unnatural arrangement might be coming to a natural end. But under the circumstances, Pen seemed no more relevant to him than what he'd eaten for breakfast that morning.

"Have you seen your friend Gus lately?"

Ziegler normally didn't ask questions so directly, and when he did, he tended to stick to topics Julian had already brought up himself. So he wondered if this one had been more or less chosen at random or somehow intuited from his anxious appearance that morning.

"Not in a few days," Julian said, covering his worry with a show of lightheartedness. "He's a painter, I think I mentioned. Studied with Hans Hofmann. He does these very impressive abstracts that look a bit muddled and arbitrary at first but then begin to seem quite carefully composed. There's something of the Midwest in them, too, where he's from. Something in their restless fields of brown and green and gray, though I'm not sure he'd like me to put it that way."

"So you like his paintings," Ziegler said, flatly, as if daring Julian to be more honest.

"Well, I like *him*, too," he said, feeling his pulse in his throat. "In fact, I'd even say that I feel, well—a kind of love for him."

Although it took the form of self-revelation, Julian knew he'd meant to invoke something pure and virtuous, like what Phaedrus says about the nobler form of love between men favored by the Athenians and defined by honor and sacrifice. It was a timid, equivocal, ridiculous thing to say, especially because he knew Ziegler wouldn't besmirch such an ideal with intimations of physicality without prompting.

Julian had first read the *Symposium* in the men's room of the old Carnegie Library in Phoenix when he was sixteen. By then he could often sense the queerness of the books he devoured, of friendships becoming intimate, of rebellion getting personal, of candor so raw and unflinching it might admit to anything. He often invented extra-credit projects for himself to justify so much time in the stacks, lingering on the subtle refractions of knowledge and desire amid so much adult opacity.

A disposition to perversions is an original and universal disposition of the human sexual instinct.
The only way to get rid of a temptation is to yield to it.
The scent of these armpits aroma finer than prayer.

As the words cleaved to his brain like night moths on a window, it became possible to imagine a future of fearless love and sweaty satisfaction.

But reading soon proved a sorry substitute for actual armpits. When the *Kinsey Report* appeared, Julian was a freshman at Stanford with a ripening heart and an untamable erection, and for several weekends in a row he took his copy and hid away in the steam works or the eucalyptus grove above campus, weighing the difference between homosexual "response" and "experience" and calculating the likely number of young men in his dormitory who'd felt and done the things he'd felt and done. He thought it logical that all forms of desire lay somewhere on a continuum and even entertained the possibility that he wasn't "exclusively homosexual." But he also knew that being aware of other men like himself wasn't the same as meeting or having sex with them, though that wouldn't happen until his sophomore year.

"What kind of love do you feel for him?" Ziegler asked.

Julian's legs suddenly quaked and he felt the same twinge of pain in his stomach as he had the day before.

Lurking in men's rooms, steam works, and shady groves—it was a pattern. The small, private spaces he'd returned to again and again to live his life honestly but alone. Gus now seemed to offer him the prospect of something shared, open without being shameful, satisfying without being dangerous. But as he struggled to answer Ziegler's question, Julian saw that his own mind was the original small, private space. Even in the cozy confidentiality of an analyst's office, where he might safely spill his secrets to a sympathetic professional, he somehow couldn't do it. Although he wasn't a trapped adolescent anymore, it was as if the trap itself remained a kind of mental structure that pervaded his whole consciousness.

How fitting that he'd finally discovered true love while hiding in a janitor's alcove.

"You seem agitated," Ziegler said. "What are you thinking about?"

Julian wanted to tell him all about Gus and what had happened and how he felt and why it mattered, and had it meant less to him, he might have. But it was simply too much to speak of a relationship that hadn't yet been given air to breathe and might at that moment be dying of asphyxiation. So he quickly cast about for something that Ziegler would find sufficiently symptomatic and Julian could relay without much distress.

"Just a memory," he said. "When I was around nine or ten my mother caught me dancing in the backyard."

"Dancing?"

"Ballet. Though it wasn't much more than a few jetés and pirouettes, and I think she only caught a glimpse of it. She'd taken me to see *Swan Lake* in San Francisco earlier that year and when no one else was around, I sometimes liked to pretend I was one of the dancers."

He remembered the backyard of the squat adobe house in Canal North, the stone slab patio trimmed with a few small, sickly cacti. His grandparents had been at church, his mother had gone shopping, and the wall surrounding the property was high. The place was, for a short while, all his own.

"One of the swans?" Ziegler asked.

"No," Julian said, somewhat annoyed. "Prince Siegfried, of course."

The connection between the character's royal title and Julian's own surname was obvious and familiar. As a child, he'd sometimes imagined himself as a young monarch-in-waiting, surrounded by pomp and circumstance, born to command rather than obey. But now he wondered if Siegfried and Ziegler might be etymologically related and if he'd unconsciously selected the memory for the resemblance. Perhaps this meant that he secretly wished to be Ziegler—smart, good-looking, and above all, straight—or that he simply wanted to be close to such an attractive man, now fitted out in his imagination with muscular legs and a revealing leotard. If that were true, then perhaps Julian really had wanted to be a ballerina—that is, Princess Odette—after all.

"What did your mother say when she saw you?" Ziegler asked.

"Oh, she gave me the third degree. What was I doing? What did I mean by it? She was very upset, though it had been her idea to take me to the ballet in the first place. I think mostly she was just surprised and probably angry for having been made to confront feelings of disgust."

"Do you remember how *you* felt?"

"Embarrassed, of course."

"Why is that?"

"Because I'd been seen. I'd thought I was alone."

Julian knew this wasn't exactly true. In fact, he'd wanted to be seen. He wanted to be graceful and fly through the air and be seen by someone as he did it. He wanted there to be at least one person watching him in his small, private space, and he wanted that person to be his mother, applauding rapturously and telling him he was magnificent. It wasn't embarrassment he'd felt that day, but disappointment.

"She made me apologize," he said.

"Apologize for what?"

"For embarrassing *her*."

"And did you?"

"Embarrass her?"

"Did you apologize?"

Not telling Ziegler about Gus or Gus about Pen, hiding in the alcove at Caesar's, not going back to the police station—it seemed like a pathetic series of cowardly acts in a life so defined by them that the habit could never be broken.

"Of course," Julian said.

◉ ◉ ◉

Ensconced in his office at Columbia with a ham sandwich from the automat, Julian half-blindly skimmed the first three acts of *Much Ado about Nothing*, then turned his dazed inattention to the *Inferno*. He only managed to get as far as Virgil's account of the neutral angels in the third canto when he heard a knock on the door. He assumed it might be Sterne with more gossip to share or Carter or some other eager undergraduate, though his office hours weren't to begin until later in the day. But when he opened the door, the man who appeared was someone he'd never seen before.

"You Prince?" he asked in a weak, nasal voice, the absent verb instantly distinguishing him as a stranger to the groves of academe.

He was a man of middle age and small stature in a grubby brown gabardine suit, like a character from *The Iceman Cometh*. He had the weepy eyes of an old St. Bernard and wore a bushy gray moustache that seemed to belong to someone else. His ashen face suggested a troubled life, though the red veins marbling his nose hinted that he'd brought some of those troubles on himself. In one hand, he carried a canvas satchel and in the other a weathered oilcloth duster. Whatever his business was, he seemed to want to conduct it quickly.

"I'm Professor Prince," Julian said. "How can I help you?"

"I'm gonna tell you how," the man said. He held his mouth as if he had a toothache.

Julian knew at once he ought to get him behind closed doors, and as soon as he did, he peeked back into the hallway to see who might have observed their exchange. There was only Millie, quietly engrossed in *The Brothers Karamazov*, and Harcourt, in an ill-fitting sharkskin suit, pacing in front of Sterne's office and gesticulating with his Dunhill briarwood, as if amid some tortured soliloquy. When Julian caught his eye, a credulous smile suggested he hadn't noticed the visitor at all.

"You surely have the wrong person," Julian said, after he closed the door and turned toward the little gray man, who sighed, put his satchel down, and rubbed his hands in his coat.

"In three days' time, you're gonna give me a thousand bucks," he said, in a way that sounded rehearsed. "Fifty twenty-dollar bills. Half in one plain white envelope, half in another. At exactly ten past twelve on Thursday. I'm gonna knock on the door, take the envelopes and go. And don't tell nobody."

Julian felt stunned by the demand and overwhelmed by the details—the amount, the denominations, the two envelopes, the double negative. "What exactly is this about?"

"Oh, jeesh." The man shook his head. "You gonna make me say it?"

Julian had always been discreet in public and there were no incriminating letters or bitter ex-boyfriends, so far as he knew. "Yes, I'm going to make you say it."

"I got information about you. You pay, it disappears. You don't, it goes straight-away Western Union to the dean of this college and—oh, yeah, to your ma in Phoenix."

Julian wanted to believe that he was being had, that this man was the friend of a friend who'd taken their joke too far or an actor working for the *Candid Camera* show. But the sleazy specificity of the threat seemed to confirm that it was real.

"What kind of information?" he asked, emboldened by a mounting sense of doom. "I certainly can't be expected to pay if I don't know what I'm paying for."

"You and the police last week," the man said with rising confidence. "That enough for you, Professor?"

The weight of that suddenly remembered ordeal felt like lead in his lungs. Now he saw that nothing was as it had seemed. He hadn't been given special treatment. The interview was only a ruse. But then with a rush of hope he recalled that he'd never been arrested or charged with anything, that there was no official record that could implicate him. If it was only one man's word against another's, he had little to fear from the ludicrous threats of a milquetoast.

"There's pictures," the man said, like a gambler showing his winning hand.

Julian remembered the flash of the camera at the Charles Street station and shrank back against his desk. The obscenity of the raid had infiltrated his professional life, threatening not just the sanctity of Shakespeare, Dante, and the young minds in his charge but the whole sphere of his public character and the source of his monthly paycheck. However inconvenient it might be for his "ma in Phoenix" to discover that her son with the perfect grades and manners wasn't so perfect after all, it was nothing to the prospect of losing his job.

"So I can count on you," the man said, like a canvasser for the March of Dimes.

"Get out," Julian hissed, just loud enough to make his point without causing a scene he'd be unable to explain.

The man looked at him as if he were another one of life's many regrets. "See you Thursday, Professor," he said, as he picked up his satchel and left.

Julian was anxious to put a barrier between everything that mattered to him and that which had just threatened to destroy it. But as he reached for the doorknob, he noticed Harcourt leaning against a bookcase, pipe in hand, composed and curious, and next to him, Sterne, his erstwhile antagonist, apparently just as eager to be better informed about the nature of the unusual visitor's errand to their department.

He shut the door, sat down at his desk, and rested his face between his hands as he stared at the wall. When the man came back for his money, he might cause a scandal that would only compound Julian's guilt and gratify the brazen snooping of his colleagues. If he refused to pay, the man would very likely send the threatened telegrams, and Julian knew denying the charges to his mother or his dean would be futile. But he hadn't anything close to a thousand dollars, excepting some utility stocks his father had left him, which were impossible to get at without sounding an alarm. Even if he could borrow the money from some trusted friend, there was no guarantee the first demand would be the last.

As the notion of a successful life spoiled by disgrace began to harden into inevitability, Julian felt as if he were looking into a mirror. On the wall he'd been staring at was a framed photograph of the actor Ingolf Schanche playing Hamlet sometime in the twenties. He'd picked it up at an antique shop in the Village, thinking it might lend ready gravitas to the office of a newly minted assistant professor. But if his scholarly ambitions now seemed absurd, the image of Schanche—his two hands clapping an anxious face, as if mounted on the tripod of his fur-trimmed neck and velvet-sleeved arms—seemed even more so. In fact, his hands were, strictly speaking, not holding his face so much as covering his ears, like the monkey that would hear no evil. And because Hamlet had always seemed to Julian like a bit of a self-pitying wretch, the Norwegian's ghostly, simian fecklessness roused him from his stupor.

◉ ◉ ◉

He canceled his office hours and stopped by his apartment to drop off his book bag and rummage through a closet, then took the subway down to the diamond district on West 47th Street, where after less than a half minute's deliberation he entered the Trans-American Gold Exchange. It was a medium-sized shop marked by several rows of jewelry cases and humming with whispered Yiddish and the high-pitched sound of small, precise machines. There were only a handful of employees, men in baggy black suits who looked nothing like Ziegler, some squinting through special glasses, others dealing with customers. One, an elderly man in a frizzled white beard and drooping yarmulke, approached Julian with a nod and took from him the only other thing his father had left him, an unusual man's ring said to be made of eighteen-karat gold.

"What have we here?" the jeweler asked, with a mildness that suggested he thought it might be anything from a priceless masterpiece to a contemptible trinket.

It was a signet ring of sorts, featuring a grotesque but intricately carved face of Medusa embraced by the arms of a serpent-man and a serpent-woman on either side. It was a gaudy piece, and one Julian never would have worn himself. But it had been purchased in Paris before the Great War by his grandfather, the captain of a merchant steamship, and was signed "G. Fouquet, 1905," so he thought it might be of some value.

The jeweler examined the ring with his loupe, then held it up to the light, looked at it again, weighed it on a scale, and pulled a face. Julian wasn't sure if he was disappointed by the worthlessness of the ring or by the idea that any son would trade his patrimony for filthy lucre.

"How much do you want for it, young man?" he asked, admitting neither knowledge nor interest.

"At least twelve hundred," Julian said. "It's a one-of-a-kind piece, I'm sure. And George Fouquet, well, a leading proponent of Art Nouveau, if I recall correctly."

He felt a little foolish pitching the old man, who probably didn't care to be schooled by an English professor on the value of a gold ring or the history of jewelry design. But Julian didn't want to let humility get in the way of what might turn out to be a fast and easy solution to his problem.

"I can give you four hundred," the jeweler said.

"How about eight hundred?" Julian asked.

"I couldn't sell it for much. There's no demand for such a ring."

"Could you give me seven? It's been in my family for years." Julian didn't know if he was trying to impress the man or soliciting his pity.

"If you ask me, it's melt stuff," the jeweler said, as he handed back the ring. "Four hundred's the best I can do. But you really ought to keep it. After all, it's an heirloom."

Julian smiled faintly and slipped the ring onto his right ring finger, then thanked the jeweler, left the store, and went to buy a packet of cigarettes. Originally, he knew, an *heirloom* was a tool passed from heir to heir and thus a thing of value not to be forfeited in a crisis. Although he'd probably never have any heirs himself upon whom to bequeath the Fouquet Medusa, he felt bad that he'd even considered selling it. He'd always loved his father, who died of ordinary pneumonia when Julian was six. But as he puffed on a Pall Mall and walked to the IRT, it occurred to him that his mother might have sold the utility stocks or hocked the ring but hadn't, and not because the family wasn't sometimes in financial straits. If Claudia Prince, who'd never once been accused of sentimentality, had resisted the temptation to cash out when times were tough, then Julian was not going to be so selfish. And before he reached Seventh Avenue, the same impulse of resolution convinced him that to pay any man who'd threatened him would amount to yet another cringing apology for his life. At the very least, he owed more to the young Midwestern painter with the beautiful ears who'd stood up to tyranny.

12

When Raf pulled open the curtains and a slash of morning light singed Danny's face, he tugged his blanket over his head. It was past seven, he knew without looking at the clock, and if he didn't hurry he'd be late. Although the store was closed on Sundays, it was inventory day, which meant four hours of counting and cleaning, pulling everything out of the walk-in, wiping it all down, and putting it back again. But he was still clinging to his dreams, which were unexpectedly good that night, though he could only grasp at a few phantom fragments—men in leather, the smell of stale beer and sweat, and a messy, powerful, victorious feeling that pervaded everything but attached itself to nothing in particular—all of which seemed like a sign of better things to come.

"I'm going to light a candle that you don't lose your damned job," Raf said.

Danny opened his eyes and saw him, dressed in his best suit and tie, pluck a limp white rose from the crystal bud vase on the little table next to the window.

He knew not inviting Raf to join in the fun the night before had been a mean thing to do, but he also knew that stirring up trouble at the Excelsior with a brown-skinned friend at his side could have made the trouble a lot worse.

"I'm getting up," Danny groaned.

He wasn't stalling because he was tired or unwilling to leave the warmth of his blankets and bear the morning chill. It was because he knew he was no longer the same person he'd been the day before and all his normal expectations about what to think and feel and do no longer seemed to apply. Usually, after a bender, he found relief in the simplicity of his life—of getting things done, keeping his head down. The chaos of night gave way to the order of day and he was so good at following the rules they hardly seemed like rules at all. But now it felt like the rules were choking him and keeping his head down wasn't an option anymore.

"Carajo!" Raf shouted from the toilet for some reason.

Danny rolled off the couch and went to the cocinita, where he grabbed the steaming cup of café con leche Raf had left for him on the counter and sat down at the little table. He looked out past the courtyard at the red-brick grid of rear windows, some lit, some still dark. He felt so different from all the people who were just then making breakfast or heading off to church, who minded their own business, left their enemies in peace, and wanted only what was acceptable to want.

Raf sat down across from Danny to finish his own café.

"So?" he asked.

"So what?" Danny said, though he knew well enough.

"You can be so tiresome."

"I'm barely awake, man."

"*Man?*" Raf said. "Has it come to that, blanquito?"

Danny would've offered up at least some small report, but as usual Raf wanted a story.

"Fine, I'll be here when you get home," he said, before draining his cup, getting up again and pulling on his coat. "But bring back a nice squash, okay? A calabaza, if you still have any, and a kabocha if you don't. I'll make soup and toast the seeds."

"Will do," Danny said, knowing he'd forget it if he didn't write it down.

Then Raf leaned over and studied his face closely.

"What's happening?" he asked. "What are you thinking? What's going on inside that busy red head of yours? Because to me it looks like trouble."

But the trouble Danny had met with the night before was something he couldn't begin to describe in words, and because thinking

131

about it made his skin tingle and seemed to calm the tremor in his chest until his breath grew slow and steady, he knew in his heart that it was good.

The address on Broadway had been a ritzy-looking apartment tower called the Balfour, which was crazy with gargoyles and had a big arched entry and an ivy-covered atrium. Some famous movie actors were known to live there, though Gabriel couldn't remember if they were rising starlets or fading has-beens. But when he and Danny walked into the empty lobby, they found it wasn't nearly as glamorous as they'd hoped. The ceramic floor tiles were cracked and rows of faded botanical prints failed to hide the fact that the flocked wallpaper was parched and peeling.

"What a dump!" Gabriel declared, pretending to file his nails, before flicking his make-believe nail file into the air.

"If I don't get out of here I'll die," Danny cried, glad to play along. "If I don't get out of here I hope I die—and burn!"

"Hawh-hawh-hawh!"

Part of it was the cocaine, of course, which fired your blood and made it hard not to say whatever came into your head. But after getting kicked out of the Excelsior, he and Gabriel had an itch to be someplace grand, and the tired lobby of the Balfour only made them want to scratch it harder.

"I think I'm seeing you for the first time in my life," Gabriel said, as they got into the elevator and he pushed the button for the eleventh floor. "You're cheap and horrible!"

"You think just because you made money you can turn yourself into a lady!" Danny answered. "But you'll never be more than a common frump!"

They roared at themselves until the elevator stopped, and when the door opened they skipped off like a couple of school kids until they reached the end of the corridor, where they found a small card thumbtacked next to the door with "Bacchus" printed on it, just like the one in Gabriel's pocket.

"What exactly is this place?" Danny asked, smoothing his pompadour.

"Come, come," Gabriel said as he pressed the buzzer. "Questions are for sissies."

The man who opened the door was tall and somewhat flabby but had clearly once been a real dreamboat. Cary Grant after a decade of donuts. He gave Danny and Gabriel an oily smile and a speedy once-over, then deprived them of a dollar each and directed them to a kitchen off the foyer. On one side was a stick-thin man in a white dinner jacket, dishing out rum punch and anxiously checking his sleeves for stains. Across from him were three more polished fellows, one in a kind of artist's smock, the second in a striped boating shirt, and the third wearing an opera cape.

"We're here! We're here! Don't panic, ladies!" Gabriel sang out as he claimed two glasses of punch. "We've got everything under control! Hawh-hawh!"

He didn't seem to care that no one was amused. The man in the artist's smock sniffed as if to say he was above it all, while the other two eyed Gabriel like he was a corned beef sandwich. In fact, except for the white Frigidaire and teal-blue cabinets, Bacchus—whatever it was—didn't seem much different from a gay bar.

But as they took their drinks and walked into a brightly lit living room, they found over a dozen men sitting on a pair of long leather sofas in casual conversation or crowding around an upright piano improvising Patsy Cline's "I Fall to Pieces." The drinks weren't watered down and the chance of a police raid seemed as distant as Stalin's gulag. It was weird to see it all happening in what was obviously somebody's home. It wasn't exactly Christmas in Parkchester, but it wasn't completely opposed to it either.

"Fresh guests!" Fat Cary Grant called out behind them, which made Danny feel like summer produce at Sloan's, though not in a bad way.

When half the men in the room turned to look, Gabriel went and sat down on one of the sofas, daring to claim and instantly getting a warm reception. But Danny only stood in the hallway, sipped his punch, and watched. Two men in tweed jackets talked about communism over a red silk divan. Someone he'd seen before at Glennon's stood near the piano in a burgundy evening dress and a brown pageboy, looking like a bona fide woman, even if her baritone gave her away. The best-looking man there was a hunk about Danny's age in plaid shirtsleeves and blue jeans, leaning against a china cabinet like an off-duty Marlboro Man. But the rest were just ordinary guys, most in jackets and ties, some handsome, some not, some swaggering, some reserved. Danny watched as one of the bedroom doors opened and a slick cat came out, grinning like he'd just been given a raise. And no sooner did he emerge than Fat Cary Grant invited another man to go back in through the same door.

Danny noticed someone in a fancy suit trying to seduce the Marlboro Man with meaningful smiles, though without much luck. When he finally gave up and looked around for another victim, Danny realized it was the Rich Kid from the Charles Street station, and the glimmer of recognition must have shone like a spotlight because he suddenly made a beeline in Danny's direction.

"Small world," the Rich Kid said, reaching out his hand. "I'm Barrett."

"It is tonight," Danny said, shaking the hand without giving his own name. Barrett didn't seem especially interested in hearing it.

"Say, have you got a cigarette?" he asked. "I'd kill for one."

"I don't smoke," Danny said.

For a moment, Barrett seemed to study his face and clothes as if he wasn't sure he liked what he saw, though Danny didn't think much of him either. He could tell by the gold ring on his soft white hand that they came from different planets. Guys who wore tuxedos and fancy suits only paid attention to grocery clerks when it pleased them, and it rarely did for long.

"What a night that was, huh?" Barrett said wearily, as he emptied his punch glass. "I've never been so irritated in my life. Thank God they let us go!"

As he swanned off to find livelier company, Danny felt a door blow open inside his brain. He remembered that Barrett and the Suave Suit and a couple of other men never came back that night after they'd been taken from the cell. At the time, he figured they'd been dealt with first because they had their own lawyers but were arrested and arraigned and pled out just the same. Now he wondered if they'd paid off a cop or traded favors with a judge and went home without so much as a warning.

Just then Fat Cary Grant popped out of one of the bedrooms, nodded at Gabriel and waved him over. "Go ahead, boys," he said, before casting an impatient eye on Danny. "Hurry along now. Shyness isn't becoming in a man."

Danny felt committed to hating the Rich Kid and his special privileges and didn't want to be distracted from it so quickly. But something told him that whatever was behind the bedroom door might be worth investigating. So when Gabriel waggled his head at him, he decided to leave his resentment behind and satisfy his curiosity.

"Good golly!" Gabriel whispered, as they stepped inside the room.

It was large and dark except for a few votive candles, and it smelled of gardenias, sweat socks, and spunk. On one double bed lay a trim Madison Avenue type curled up in a sixty-nine with his more muscular black friend. On the other bed was an older, furry, friendly-looking guy in an undershirt and boxer shorts, who nibbled on the bare buttocks of a tattooed blond like they were a couple of Parker House rolls. For just a moment, Danny thought about Father Frank's descriptions of the fiery torments of hell and a strained old voice inside his head told him to leave the room. It was an annoying reflex, the habit of years, impossible either to stop or respect. But then another voice—a newer, clearer one—reminded him that hell was just another lie and he might as well stay and enjoy himself if he wanted to.

When Madison Avenue looked up and nodded at Gabriel, he turned to Danny with eyes asking more for congratulations than permission, then kicked off his shoes, pulled off his clothes, and flung himself into the knotty tangle of flesh. It was a little weird to see Gabriel's fat circumcised dick and watch as he set to work pleasuring his new friends without so much as a how-do-you-do. But somehow it all seemed as natural as a swim at the Y.

"Hey, gorgeous," the older man on the other bed said to Danny.

His voice was deep and kind, and when the blond looked up and seconded the invitation, Danny felt the overwhelming urge to be as wild as Gabriel had been, to be held and kissed and touched, to surrender to someone stronger than he was. But as soon as the swelling excitement in his pants became a burning throb, he remembered what had been done to him and why he couldn't do anything down there until it healed. The cocaine had numbed the pain so much he'd forgotten all about it.

"I wish I could," Danny said, his heart sinking.

When the older man noticed his black eye, he seemed to understand well enough, nodded regretfully, and turned his attention back to his friend's bottom. Then without even looking at Gabriel, Danny left the room. There was nothing at Bacchus for him now and it seemed best to get away as soon as possible. He'd been cheated of a night of pleasure that was his due. It felt like a cruel joke to play on a man when he was down. Saint Jude was AWOL again.

"Having second thoughts?" Fat Cary Grant asked.

Danny ignored him as he crossed the living room and went down the hall toward the front door. But as he passed the kitchen, he nearly bumped into a handsome black guy in a houndstooth suit with a cigarette in his hand and a sly look on his face.

"Slow down, Sunshine!" the man said.

He might have been thirty, with short, wavy dark hair, a neat mustache that perfectly followed the curves of his eyebrows and a tight curly beard that cupped his chin and cheeks without ever meeting his ears. He seemed worldly-wise and way out of Danny's league.

"Sorry," Danny said as he tried to step around him. "I was just leaving."

But the guy stepped with him, like a dancer taking the lead. "Don't be sorry," he said. "Because if you go, that'll make two of us."

Then he quickly pulled Danny into a powder room off the hallway, which was stocked with lots of little soaps and bottles. It seemed too cramped for a private encounter. But the guy put his arm around Danny's shoulder, combed his hair with his hand, and smiled again, like this was the kind of thing he usually did.

"Damn, you're pretty!" he said. "I love redheads."

His breath was sweet with rum punch.

But Danny only sighed, knowing he couldn't take things any further.

"Okay, then, tell me what's wrong," the guy said, with what sounded more like curiosity than disappointment.

Danny looked away. It was too long a story and too personal.

"I'll give you two kisses for the short version."

"It's hard to explain," Danny said, tempted. The man's beard had a fine sheen and his mouth looked as soft as a pillow.

"Roy Lee Davis," he said. "Pleased to meet you."

Danny gave his full name too, and when they shook hands, Roy Lee's grip was so firm and warm he didn't want to let go.

"See, Danny, I'm from Newark. So there's nothing you can tell me I haven't already heard. And I'm a poet. So there's nothing I haven't thought about either."

Danny had never met a poet before, but there was something about Roy Lee that seemed honest. So after he took back his hand, he sat down on the toilet seat and began to talk. He started with his bruised dick and the Nazi Cop, then worked his way backward to the raid at Caesar's and the Thursday-night family dinner in Parkchester, then forward to getting his notice at Sloan's and being booted from the Excelsior, and finally to his flight from the bedroom on the other side of the apartment. He did his best to stick to the facts, but Roy Lee's heartening looks drew out his feelings and before he knew it, he had a ravishing idea of all the wrongs he'd suffered.

"Seems like you just realized where you live," Roy Lee said, putting out his cigarette in the sink. "It happens to white folks sometimes."

Danny wasn't sure what he meant. He felt spent from his confession. But telling Roy Lee helped him see that his problems went beyond having to find another job or being on the outs with his family and weren't even close to being over.

"I don't know what to do," Danny said.

"Mmm, why, you're just like a rosebud aching to blow!" Roy Lee said, as he traced a line down Danny's nose.

Danny wasn't sure what that meant either. It didn't sound like an insult and might have been a kind of poet's mental note. But it felt right. He *was* aching to blow.

Roy Lee checked his watch, then said: "Well, I suppose you've got to decide if you're going to wait for a world that won't ever change on its own or fight back and help it along a bit."

"Fight back?" Danny asked, surprised to hear such hard advice from such a gentle-seeming man.

"You see, it may be true that darkness can't drive out darkness and hate can't drive out hate and all that jazz," Roy Lee said. "But if people can lock you up and beat you up and fuck you up any time they want, then do you really think moral suasion's going to change their minds? Why that's just masochism."

Danny wondered if Roy Lee had fought back against oppression himself, like the people who'd stopped riding the buses in Alabama or sat down at the Woolworth's counter in North Carolina and refused to get up. Or maybe he meant something even bolder. Maybe he was talking about Negroes with guns.

But before Danny could ask him to explain, Roy Lee said, "Will you show me?"

"Show you what?"

"What he did to you."

At first, Danny wasn't sure he should. But because Roy Lee waited patiently, like someone who understood the seriousness of his request, he decided that showing him was really just another part of telling him. So he stood up, unbuckled his belt, unzipped his trousers, and let them fall to his knees. He was about to pull down his briefs when Roy Lee knelt down and took over the job. He slipped his thumbs around the waistband and tugged, slowly and carefully, like he was unwrapping a Chinese pear, until the bruised and swollen mess was right in front of his face.

He looked at it with a kind of humble respect, the way you looked at a corpse at a funeral or at the communion wafer before you took it in your mouth. He touched the shaft a few times, then cradled the whole thing in his palm, and Danny felt wonderfully relieved of its burden, as if it were something he'd been waiting for without knowing it. Then Roy Lee kissed it softly, just barely touching it. In a way, it felt like being kissed on the cheek by Ciaran when he was a little kid, a tender reminder of love and a promise of care, which is why Danny didn't get hard and knew he wouldn't.

"Do you remember what it felt like in jail?" Roy Lee said, looking up. "Locked up in a cage like an animal, accused of nothing that made any sense, and yet deep down in your timid little heart, thinking it's your own fault you're there?"

Danny nodded.

"See, it's their best weapon," Roy Lee said. "Shame."

Danny even felt shame for feeling ashamed. It was a miserable loop.

"But if you understand how it works, you can use it against them."

While Roy Lee talked, he pulled Danny's briefs and trousers back up, slowly and carefully. Then he zipped his fly and buckled his belt. It almost felt like being redressed as a new man.

"How do I do that?" he asked.

"By not being afraid," Roy Lee said. "By turning the shame back on them. By making your enemies face their crimes. That's justice."

"Taking on the cops?" Danny asked, wondering if Roy Lee might be a little touched.

"Toussaint took on Napoleon," Roy Lee said. "Jackie Robinson took on baseball."

Danny squinted. He knew as much about history as he did about sports.

"Resist, little brother, if you've got the nerve. If you believe in your own humanity, you won't ever feel ashamed again." Roy Lee bit his lip and shook his head. "Get real justice once and you'll never settle for anything less."

It sounded righteous and crazy and confusing, but Danny figured it was probably the truth. He was no masochist. When he looked at Roy Lee and smiled, his skin tingled and his breath grew slow and steady, and when Roy Lee smiled back, he felt like both the night and his life had been saved.

Suddenly someone was calling Roy Lee's name from behind the powder room door—a white man's voice, tired and impatient—and the sorry arch of his eyes told Danny that their short, electric meeting had come to an end.

"As you can probably tell," Roy Lee said, "I like to talk about big ideas. But what I just told now you is no bullshit. Okay? Just reality."

Then he leaned over, pressed his lips to Danny's forehead, opened the door and went back to the party. Two kisses, as promised.

◎ ◎ ◎

Danny stood on Columbus Avenue across from Sloan's watching Nunzio throw snowballs at a stray mutt, until Blav came out and told him to quit it and come inside. The sun's glare reflected off the street and the windows and covered everything in a soft white haze but did nothing to make the icy morning feel any warmer. Inventory day had always been a drag made tolerable by the feeling that they were all in it together. But now it would be tedious and lonely work. He pictured Roddy's pitted, pitying face and the clumsy silence of his former friends, all shifting and dodging to avoid the queer. He imagined the coming days, seeing his potential replacements—idiots who didn't know a Bartlett from a Bosc—touring the store, while cashiers and stock boys gossiped about him to pass the time. He looked up at the big red letters and what for almost six years he'd thought was his calling and his future. *It seems like you just realized where you live.* Then he pulled on the flaps of his ushanka, spit into the snow, and headed back downtown.

Part II

Perhaps home is not a place but simply an irrevocable condition.

—*Giovanni's Room*

13

Because taking the train into the city on Monday morning felt like returning to the scene of a crime, Roger did his best to pretend that the crime simply hadn't happened. Corinne helped by being chattier than usual. Zipping through the neighborhood and onto Chatsworth Avenue, she talked about the West German coalmine explosion, the mudslides in Southern California, and how lucky they were never to have been involved in such a disaster. She mentioned how much she was enjoying *Franny and Zooey*, which she'd begun the day before while Roger was skiing, though she thought "prayer without ceasing" didn't seem very practical. She reminded him that the canceled dinner with his parents had been rescheduled as a lunch with his father at Oscar's Delmonico in the city that Friday. And she told him for the third time how pleased she was that he liked the briefcase she'd given him as a Christmas gift, which he held on his lap, stroking the soft black English leather like a cat. She betrayed no memory of his sulking, which had spoiled so much of their weekend. In fact, she seemed committed to the power of positive thinking for the sake of their marriage, as if the new week necessarily meant a fresh start.

As Roger took his seat on the train and began scratching his way through the undemanding Monday *Times* crossword, he felt a vague suggestion of courage lift his spirits. When he finished it ten minutes later, just as the train was passing Woodlawn Cemetery in the Bronx, a genial older man who'd taken the seat next to him at Mount Vernon offered his newspaper, the *Pelham Sun*. Roger thanked the man and smiled at his homeliness—frayed shirt collar, mottled brown hands, a whiff of Barbasol. But when Roger took up the paper, he instantly recognized the face on the front page, smiling earnestly in a high school graduation photo, and blenched at the headline—"Youth Drowns in Bridge Crash." His hands shook as he forced his eyes to read the terrible details: "Andrew Lamb, age 19, resident of Pelham and student at New York University, died on Saturday evening when his automobile careened off the Glen Island Approach and sank in the Long Island Sound. Police report that the victim skidded on icy pavement and no other vehicles were involved."

Roger pictured the poor boy, tears streaming down his frightened face, staring out at the black horizon—ripping through the guard rail and crashing through the ice—water flooding his lungs, his larynx on fire—dying, slowly dying—and finally still as a specimen in the frigid saltwater. He remembered Andy back in the jail cell, his pathetic peeps and snotty hiccups, his frenzied shouting, *Who the fuck am I gonna call!* He thought of Andy's parents, sitting on a chintz-covered sofa in their living room in Pelham, grieving and confused, never to know what had taken their son from them or whether they might have prevented it. Then came Roger's compulsive, retroactive wishing. If only the old man hadn't sat next to him or had taken longer to read his stupid local paper. If only it had been a Thursday instead of a Monday and the *Times* puzzle would have taken Roger longer to complete. He knew he was visibly upset, and he could feel the old man leaning toward him, about to say something sympathetic and obtrusive. So Roger turned away and stared at the Bronx River Parkway, heavy with salt-crusted traffic, streaked with the sun's white glare, and sliced up by telephone poles into a choppy blur.

He remembered Andy standing near the door at Caesar's, twitchy as a rabbit, ignorant of his own charms, of the sharpness of his flattop, the slope of his neck, the easy bulk of his Irish fisherman's sweater. Then Roger knowing at once he could soothe the boy, draw him in and, without doing any harm, enjoy some essential part of him. And then—a drunk punch of guilt, for Andy *had* been harmed, and Roger's lust now seemed not only culpable but causal. The boy probably never would have stayed at the bar for long if he hadn't found him. Perhaps Roger had whispered some self-destructive poison into his ear, possibly the same morbid impulse that had led to his own reckless drive on the iciest day of the year. Andy wouldn't jump four feet onto a rooftop, but he'd had the fortitude to steer his car off a bridge. Perhaps he'd simply been first to find the courage to die.

As the train sped through Harlem and slipped down into the bowels of Manhattan, Roger's own windpipe seemed to swell, his breath grew short and spasmodic, and his head filled with a cold, aching sorrow. Ignoring the old man, he folded up the newspaper and gritted his teeth, trying to force all thoughts of the dead boy from his mind. But nothing he did relieved him of the palpable sensation that he, too, was drowning.

◎ ◎ ◎

Nancy was especially attentive that morning, as if intuiting that Friday's symptoms of distress had been no anomaly. Without announcing it, she seemed to postpone all trivial matters and prioritize only the most important ones. Although Roger might have preferred the distraction of a busier schedule, he doubted he'd have had the energy for it. He felt weak, even sleepy, and was already looking forward to his first chance to escape from consciousness.

The monthly forecast meeting was usually rote business. Although focus was expected, finger sandwiches and coffee were served and, except during sluggish quarters, the mood was collegial and optimistic. For nearly an hour, he managed to listen carefully enough, ask several simple questions, and smile at the appropriate moments. Edgar, blue-suited at the head of the table, nodded neutrally as they discussed the state of the recovery and the new GNP report. Dalton, a podgy, cheerful fellow a few years Roger's senior, waxed spiritedly about the rise in steel orders and plant and equipment expenditures. Then Nick, a graver, leaner, younger man, with whom Roger had something of a friendly rivalry, talked of the recent spike in residential construction.

But when it was his turn to report on international business, Roger felt suddenly stiff and stupid, and when the words came they were like defective fireworks, smoking and fizzling without ever getting off the ground.

"Risk ratings across the EEC, well, they've been, uh, quite steady. But there's every reason to believe that smaller firms—or, uh, those without reliable credit access—what I mean to say is that there's every reason to expect, uh, continuing growth—that is, overall—at least for the next quarter."

He went on for another minute or two, spitting out half-sentences and circling back to the same statistics. He could see by the troubled or amused reactions around him that he was utterly failing. It was as if the carefully prepared notes before him had been translated into a language he didn't speak. His hands were shaking. The whole room went quiet except for a sharp, metallic ringing in his ears. And then all he saw was Andy, tiny bubbles escaping from his lifeless purple lips and fine swirls of blood leaching from his nose into the freezing water at the bottom of the Sound.

"Was there anything else?" Edgar said, as Roger looked up, checked by his boss's imperious scowl. "Very well. Let's tack to retail. Conway?"

He sat back down, but instead of feeling relief that his abysmal performance had come to an end, a wave of heat and blood rushed into his face, pulled at his eyes and squeezed, and he suddenly began to cry.

Of course, to be seen crying at work would be only slightly less scandalous than to be found out as a queer. If it didn't end Roger's career, it might slow it down considerably. So he buried his nose in a handkerchief and blew, hoping it would either hide the tears or explain them as the effect of an allergic reaction, and then shut off the valves of sorrow by dint of sheer will. He kept his head down and scribbled meaningless notes, pretending to follow a mundane report on consumer spending, while listening for any telltale pauses or other signs of concern or derision.

After Edgar called the meeting to a close and Roger finally dared to look up, he was satisfied that he hadn't caused a scandal. Dalton was availing himself of another sandwich, and Nick was already out the door. No doubt they all had better things to do than stare at Roger's face. If he'd performed poorly, he was certainly not the first in the history of Chemical Bank to do so. He'd acquired over a decade of professional goodwill there that he surely might spend on a single, momentary, and perfectly harmless lapse. As he left the room, he smiled contritely at Edgar, an ironic nod to the inevitability of the occasional bad day. But Edgar only grimaced in reply.

Plodding back to his office, Roger thought about losing himself in numbers or staring mindlessly out the window at the constant creep of Broadway or even pulling closed the curtains, easing into his chair, and closing his eyes. So when Nancy suddenly appeared with a doubtful smile, he kept moving, knowing he'd now get none of the things he wanted and feeling that if he stopped to talk he might collapse onto the floor.

"There's a Mr. Harrington to see you," she said, tagging along. "He said he's come about a loan, and when I said you didn't—"

"Just tell him I'm expected on a phone call," Roger said, too weary to hear the details. "Give me fifteen minutes, then send him in."

Nancy nodded and held back as Roger pushed on to his office. But when he saw Julian Prince sitting on the small sofa across from her desk, he felt a jolt of anger. He wanted to scream at Nancy for surprising him this way, but of course she couldn't have known who the man really was. He wanted to scream at Prince for bringing the memory of the raid into his workplace, though judging by his calm demeanor it seemed he wasn't there to make a scene. Every impulse to be furious was thwarted by reason, and when Prince stood up and reached out his hand, Roger knew he had no choice but to take it.

"Just stopping by to chat about that boring old business," Prince said.

"Good to see you," Roger said with a tin smile. "Please come this way."

He shut the door behind them and looked squarely at the unwelcome ambassador from the worst night of his life. "Why are you here?" he demanded.

"I'm hoping we can help each other," Prince said.

Roger knew no one could help him, certainly not an English professor. "You've made a mistake," he said. "Undoubtedly, it was with good intentions. But I'd appreciate it if you would now open the door, shake my hand again, and leave."

147

"Won't you do me the kindness of answering just one question?" Prince asked.

Despite Roger's exhaustion and alarm, the appeal to kindness pinched him. There'd been so little of it in recent days. So he nodded, still unable to imagine what Prince would say but hoping that his own ignorance might somehow protect him from it.

"Did they let you go, too?" Prince asked.

Roger knew at once the question portended nothing good. If it needed to be asked at all, then his ordeal was definitely not over, and poor Andy was only the first casualty.

"After they took me out of the cell," Prince said, "someone interviewed me for no more than a few minutes, then just left me in an alley behind the station. At first, I assumed that—well, that they didn't think arresting me was worth their while."

Prince looked at him like a teacher waiting on a student's feeble comprehension, and Roger realized then that the whole thing had been too easy. He hadn't been let go at all. He'd only been temporarily freed in order to twist in the wind before something else—he hardly knew what—came back to finish him off.

"But this morning a man came to see me," Prince continued. "He wants a thousand dollars within the week. He said if I don't give it to him, he'll send telegrams to my dean and my mother."

He seemed to be telling the truth, Roger thought. Blackmail wasn't unheard of, and it certainly explained the strange interview and unexpected release. Then again, no blackmailer had visited him yet. There was a chance it might not happen at all, and it made no sense whatsoever to get involved before it did.

"They have our photos," Prince said.

Roger suddenly felt sleepy again. He couldn't think. He couldn't make sense of Prince's visit or his news. It was all too much.

"So I thought we might put our heads together," Prince said.

"Please go," Roger said.

"If we could just—"

Roger stopped him with a hard look. Then he opened the door, managed another smile, and shook Prince's hand.

"Thank you for stopping by, Mr. Harrington," he said. "It was good to see you."

As Prince nodded and turned to leave, a twinge of doubt warned Roger that he might have just sent away the only ally he'd ever have in this secret battle for his life. But he wasn't going to repeat the mistake of risking that life to save someone else's. Instead, he shut his door again, pulled the curtains, and sat down at his desk, then leaned back in his chair and closed his eyes.

◎ ◎ ◎

At Hotchkiss—long before Mudge or the trips to the adult theater in Boston—he'd known a hatchet-faced boy named Riley Cross. He was cruel, lazy, and introverted, except when bullying other boys, and the last person in the school Roger might have any feelings for. But late one warm May night, shortly after he'd turned sixteen, Roger stumbled into the lavatory and found Riley leaning over a sink, his pajama bottoms around his knees and a big red blur in his pumping hand, apparently neither waiting for company nor disturbed by its arrival. Roger froze, torn between going back to his room and lingering to discover more. But as he saw Riley watching him in the mirror and smirking, he sensed the growing bulge inside his own pajamas and felt its unstoppable force. Then Riley's smirk softened into a smile. Whatever other unspeakable ideas he was entertaining, one of them, Roger realized, was also resounding in his own mind—*touch*.

A moment later, Riley's greedy mouth was rooting below Roger's belly and currents of impossible pleasure were coursing up and down his legs. It felt as thrilling and necessary as it did nasty and wicked. The monstrous wet heat. The unbearable hardness. When he expended himself after a minute or so, he let out a muffled groan. The final burst felt like an awful combination of peeing and bleeding, and he worried he might have somehow injured himself. But Riley only stood up, wiped his mouth with his sleeve, and went back to the sink to begin again where he'd left off, as if no one were there or ever had been. As Roger pulled up his pajama bottoms, he noticed Riley's skinny legs, pimply neck, and slapdash haircut, as well as the sour grimace he made in the mirror's reflection as he splattered streams of pale jism all over the porcelain in jerky, silent throbs. Then Roger left the bathroom without peeing, crept back to his room and, under cover of Schuyler's rat-a-tat snoring, slipped into bed. But he lay awake for most of the night, first promising God and his parents that he'd never do such a terrible thing again, then crying into his pillow because some part of him already wanted to and because he knew that no matter what he did, he'd be tormented by his desires—always secret and always unsatisfied—for the rest of his life.

Roger thought of Riley Cross as he waited on the crowded platform at Grand Central Terminal for the 5:57 New Haven train, now running ten minutes late. He'd been searching his memory to discover the first cause of all his troubles, or at least to find someone other than himself to blame for them. If he'd poisoned Andy Lamb, then surely someone must have poisoned him.

"Roger Moorhouse," a dry, quivering voice behind him said.

Roger turned to see a short, shabbily dressed man with an unkempt gray mustache tucked under his gin-blossomed nose like an old sponge. More pitiful than threatening, he had the anxious eyes of a novice prisoner. But as he pulled a folded piece of paper from a canvas haversack and handed it to Roger, it became perfectly clear why he was there.

"Just do what it says," the little man said, before waddling off into the crowd.

Roger stared at the poorly typed message, vaguely noting a demand for money, a promise to appear again on Friday, and references to the bank and Corinne. But rather than read it carefully, he simply folded it up again and slipped it into his briefcase as if it were merely a telephone bill or a laundry ticket. For the time being, there was nothing to think about and nothing to do. If his terrible day had gotten even worse, it was clear he was in control of very little of it.

When the train finally emerged from the tunnel and rolled into the station, he imagined stepping in front of it and bringing the whole matter to a quick and certain end. How easy it would be, excepting only the fleeting pain, and then how peaceful, like a warm and comfortable bed. He wondered if Andy had felt something similar—lovely, wretched Andy, who first couldn't jump at all and then felt he had no choice. But as the train approached, Roger only watched and waited, and when it came to a stop, the doors opened and the arriving passengers filed out onto the platform. Eventually, he stepped inside the car, found his seat and, soothed by the familiar droning of the conductor's voice on the P.A., went home to his wife, his children, and his house with the scarlet door, the yew hedge, and the elm.

14

From a pay phone inside a luncheonette on Seventh Avenue, Julian had called the only banks whose names he could remember and gotten lucky on his third try. But as he left Roger Moorhouse's office after their disappointing interview, he realized it hadn't been an auspicious plan to begin with. A man's place of business was where he could feel most vulnerable, as Julian's own experience had shown. And Roger seemed to be taking the raid and his brief incarceration especially hard, even though he hadn't yet been imposed on by a blackmailer or separated from someone he loved. Julian knew it was best not to get involved with such an unsteady character, and as he dropped down into the subway and headed uptown, he regretted all the time he'd wasted and turned his thoughts again to finding Gus, a far steadier man from whom he expected a much warmer reception.

They'd met on the first Saturday after New Year's Eve at the Stable Gallery on East 74th, where Julian had come with Hugh to marvel at the avant-garde before heading down to the Blue Parrot for pleasures of a less disinterested kind. The room was filled with strange canvasses depicting screen-printed newspaper ads, soup cans, and motion picture stills, which Julian thought rather facetious, although everyone else seemed mesmerized by them. Shortly after they arrived, Hugh introduced him to someone he knew from the Art Students League, who'd been gazing at one of the paintings, a legion of Troy Donahues, as if trying to solve a riddle.

"I'd an inkling you two might like to know one another," said Hugh, who loved to play the impresario under any circumstances. "Gus is exquisitely single-minded, and Julian is marvelously dilettantish. So you'll have nothing at all in common and so much to share."

But before Julian could object to either the characterization or the logic, Hugh patted them each on the shoulder and ran off to listen to the peculiar-looking artist holding court in a far corner of the gallery. And when Gus seemed to take Hugh's departure as a sign that the meeting had ended and promptly went back to studying the painting, Julian, eager not to feel too keenly the apparent slight, decided to study Gus.

Although he was immediately taken with the young man's quiet gravity, it was his unusual combination of wholesomeness and elegance that Julian found most compelling. He wore paint-stained chinos, a shabby woolen coat, and what looked like a new, rather expensive blue shirt. He filled out his clothes like a farmer's son raised on hard work, but his fingers, scratching thoughtfully at his unshaven chin, looked dexterous and sensitive. If his bright, lightly freckled face seemed somewhat naïve, his eyes looked knowing and wise. Even the way he stood—his knees a little bent, bouncing lightly on his heels—was a kind of open question. Julian couldn't tell if he'd stay there for a meditative half hour or bolt from the building at any moment.

As it happened, he bolted, and when he did, Julian followed him out the door.

"Was it really so terrible?" he asked, stepping onto the sidewalk.

Gus turned and stopped. "Gosh, is that what you thought?" he asked.

Julian found his Midwestern accent surprisingly endearing.

"I must confess, I didn't look very closely," he said. "I saw something I liked better."

Gus laughed just enough to acknowledge the flattery, then grew thoughtful again. "But the critique of process is really something, isn't it?" he said.

"I gather you're a painter yourself?" Julian asked, wondering if he might also be unemployed and in between apartments.

"Sure," Gus said, as if it would have been absurd for him to be anything else. "What about you?"

Most artists Julian had met loved to talk about themselves, what they were working on, where they were exhibiting, and how they saw the world. Men in general, he'd found, preferred to be the receivers of attention and were often quite stingy about giving it in return. But as they stood talking on the sidewalk, Gus seemed interested only in Julian. In fact, as they talked, he seemed to be examining Julian's face, not appraising it so much as exploring its features, the way a portraitist might before he set to work on his subject.

"Are you going somewhere just now?" Julian asked. He could see Hugh and the Blue Parrot another time.

"I guess I am," Gus said.

As they walked west on 74th Street and then up Fifth and into Central Park, Gus shared a little about himself—his childhood in Wisconsin, a recent interest in theosophy, occasional part-time work for an art mover. Generally, though, he asked questions of Julian. Were his parents still alive? Had music ever made him weep? Had he ever been in love? At first, Julian found himself blushing at Gus's apparent seriousness. But as they strolled side-by-side along a lamp-lit path just south of Turtle Pond toward Belvedere Castle, it became clear he was completely in earnest—that he seemed to take everything Julian shared as if it were not some inert fact but an instance of real experience and worthy of respect—and so Julian decided to meet frankness with frankness.

"No," he said. "I've had plenty of affairs. But I've never been *in* love."

"Sure," Gus said.

Julian wondered whether Gus had meant that he'd comprehended his meaning or shared his relative inexperience. Either way, it seemed they might be well suited to each other—two independent, self-aware men, open to romance, though not in any way overeager. But by the time Julian decided he ought to ask Gus the same question, it seemed too late.

"Systole and diastole," Gus said, as they turned into the Ramble.

"How's that?" Julian asked.

"I guess it's a bad joke," Gus said. "The heart contracts and re-laxes twenty-four hours a day, closing itself off and opening itself

154

up, again and again. It's no wonder we don't always know how to use it properly."

"Ah, but then it's not really a joke, is it," Julian said, smiling.

"Nope," Gus said, smiling back. "Not really."

In the distance, Julian noticed several men leaning against trees or lampposts, either posing strategically or craning to get a better look at someone in the dim light. He felt grateful that the prospect before him that night was so much better than a sloppy tumble in the frigid bushes. He wasn't sure that two men could be together permanently like men and women. But he'd felt almost certain that he and Gus would end the night chastely, see each other again very soon, and perhaps begin a very agreeable affair that might last a month or two or possibly even three.

◎ ◎ ◎

His destination was a small gallery on East 10th, where Dahlia, the young lady who called herself Gus's best friend, apparently spent her afternoons. When Julian had spoken to her on the phone on Saturday, she seemed aloof, as if she thought his concern for Gus meddlesome, a superior claim on their mutual friend that he had no business making. She admitted she hadn't seen him in several days, then pointedly suggested that he might be with another man, since he was free to do as he pleased. At the time, Julian had dismissed the remark as the jealous posturing of a lonely girl. But three days later, he wondered if his quarrel with Gus on Thursday night, despite all that followed, had somehow altered their understanding.

The Tanager Gallery was smaller than the Stable, an artists' co-operative and little more than a narrow storefront above a dive bar, sandwiched between an employment agency and a boardinghouse. When Julian entered the main room, he saw several dozen paintings of various sizes crowding the walls. Most were abstracts—mono-chromatic polygons, swirling tangles of color, manic skirmishes in black and white. Among the three women talking in one corner, two were Julian's age or somewhat older, rather drably dressed, possibly academics. The third was Dahlia, tall, pretty, and chic in a prim sort of way, and when she saw him, she excused herself and came over.

He'd only met her once before, two weeks earlier, when Gus had introduced them at a birthday party for a sculptor in Murray Hill. She'd graduated with a fine arts degree from Vassar, changed her name from something like Eleanor or Gertrude, and, lacking any real talent herself, devoted herself to gallery work and the cultivation, romantic and professional, of artists. She was bright and determined and had already helped Gus get representation with one of the other 10th Street galleries. But she also insisted he was bisexual and hoped they'd one day marry and have children, though according to Gus, this was all strictly fantasy.

"I thought I might see you here," she said. "You seemed so awfully worried on the telephone the other day. I thought you might be having a hysterical fit."

Julian knew betraying any annoyance would only encourage her.

"Have you heard from him since?" he asked.

She seemed to weigh whether his question was cause for real alarm, but also whether giving in to such alarm might require giving up any present advantage.

"No," she said. "But he's perfectly capable of taking care of himself."

"I've called around to all the obvious places."

"Have you tried Loosli's?"

Julian assumed the question, however reasonable under the circumstances, was meant as a kind of taunt.

"He's apparently out of town."

"Didn't Gus tell me he was moving in with you?"

"No, I'm sure he didn't tell you that."

"Well, when did you last see him, for God's sake?"

There were a lot of tricky facts around which Julian was obliged to skirt, but he'd already decided what he'd tell her. "We were supposed to meet at a diner in the Village on Saturday morning," he said, "but he never showed up."

Not showing up wasn't Gus's style, and Julian wondered if the sudden look of worry in Dahlia's eyes might be authentic.

"And you've no other idea whom to call or where to look?"

"You were the last person I thought of."

Her flat smile seemed to take the jibe as fair compensation for those she'd given. "Let me get my coat," she said.

A few minutes later, they took a taxi a mere six blocks to a bar called Dillon's on University Place. Dahlia insisted on paying the thirty-cent fare—she refused to walk in the city, even short distances, claiming it ruined her shoes—and when they arrived, she led the way inside. This was her world, Julian gathered, and it seemed she'd only help him on her terms.

The place was smoky, bohemian, oddly crowded given the early hour, and probably not the kind of place in which a man with a head wound would have sought refuge. But Dahlia insisted it was a fount of artistic intelligence, high-minded and low, and if Gus had been seen at all over the weekend, it likely would have been by one of the painters, poets, and critics who frequented the place. So she told Julian to order her a Manhattan and left him near the bar as she went from table to table, poking her head into private conversations and whispering into the ears of women and men alike. She seemed to know everyone, and everyone seemed to know her. But only once did she linger, talking in a confidential way to a pair of serious-looking young men with beards who huddled in one of the grimy wooden booths. Like most of the people in the bar, they weren't exactly attractive, but they had a certain raw swagger that made them appealing. They were, Julian thought, the very opposite of Roger Moorhouse.

When Dahlia returned, she swallowed half her drink and let Julian light her cigarette, and when he asked if she'd learned any news, she shook her head and blew an impatient puff of smoke. "He could be anywhere," she finally said.

"That was never in question," Julian reminded her, as he lit his own cigarette.

"Someone suggested checking out Judson, but there's nothing going on there," she said with waning enthusiasm. "I suppose you've already been to the Y? You boys are always turning up there. Though I bet he's found himself a cozy guest room somewhere out on Long Island, which is what I'd have done in his shoes."

Julian didn't like Dahlia supposing she knew what it was to be in Gus's shoes. But he could also see she'd already lost interest in the matter, an impression confirmed when she waved at the two bearded men, who seemed to be eagerly awaiting her return.

"I'm afraid I can't offer any more help," she said after finishing her drink.

"But aren't you worried?" he asked.

"Of course, darling, I'm simply beside myself," she said in cold trills of sarcasm.

"Well, then, perhaps you should go be with your friends," Julian said, his disdain slightly more audible than he'd intended.

"You're uncomfortable here, aren't you," she said, narrowing her eyes and pointing her cigarette at him. "You're surrounded by people you don't understand, and it makes you nervous."

Julian laughed and shook his head, confident there wasn't the least truth to the charge. He'd been to such places many times and mixed with all types. He'd seen John Coltrane play at the Five Spot and heard Allen Ginsberg read at Columbia when none of his other colleagues would go. He'd even protested with the folk singers in Washington Square Park. Of course, he'd also twisted at the Peppermint Lounge and gone to drag revues at the 82 Club. He certainly wasn't parochial in his tastes or bigoted in his views the way people like Dahlia could be.

Before she sauntered off, she let loose one final salvo: "I'm guessing Gus simply grew tired of spending time with a bourgeois drip like you. I know I have."

A decade before, Julian might have let such an insult get to him, countering it hours later with speeches of the cleverest esprit d'escalier. But with the experience of age, it was easier to dismiss. He knew he bore no resemblance to the caricature she'd made of him. Only just that day on lower Broadway, he'd seen a true bourgeois up close and knew they were nothing alike. He also knew Gus put no stock in such labels. In fact, it was hard to see how he could have any interest in such a cunning, artificial creature as Dahlia.

After Julian left the bar, he took the subway back uptown and pondered his diminishing options. He could visit the other Ys or go back to Gus's studio or call up Hugh and Syd or the hospitals yet again, but it all seemed hopeless. He reconsidered going back to the Sixth Precinct and demanding to know whether Gus had been charged and, if so, when he'd been released, though he still felt it might be too risky. Eventually, he decided that if he hadn't heard from him by Wednesday, he'd telephone the station and see what an anonymous inquiry might yield.

Yet as he hung on his strap and stared vacantly at the latest Miss Rheingold, he found he missed Gus so much that he began saying his name in his head again and then asking him if he was all right, telling him he loved him, and assuring him that they'd be together again soon. Julian knew it was ridiculous, almost lunatic behavior, but it felt somehow excusable, and he hoped it proved the depth of his feelings. He imagined Gus waiting for him somewhere in the city, smiling bravely, and in Julian's mind, he went from being St. Sebastian, wounded and dying, to Shakespeare's Sebastian, beloved of Antonio, shipwrecked but safe somewhere in Illyria, probably not too far away, only temporarily misplaced.

❂ ❂ ❂

According to Julian's employment contract, which he perused on Tuesday morning in his office, he'd agreed to conduct himself "with due regard to public morals" and to commit no act that might tend to bring him or the University into "public contempt" or "ridicule public morals or decency." There was no telling what these equivocal words meant specifically, but their general import was clear. His employers were concerned about their reputation, and if being rounded up by cops and targeted by blackmailers qualified as contemptuous or indecent acts, then he might well lose his job. If he were fired, finding another like it would be difficult. Certainly, no public university would have taken a known homosexual—Ike and J. Edgar had seen to that. But even private ones were cracking down on what they called the "pervert problem." At Smith, a revered colleague had been arrested a year earlier simply for sharing muscle magazines with his friends, and after betraying those friends to the police and being suspended from teaching, the poor man had had a nervous breakdown. Julian wondered if persecution didn't bring out the worst in everyone involved.

After filing away the contract, he took from his desk the cardboard box that contained his book manuscript and began reading where he'd left off, revising sentence by sentence, sharpening an argument here, removing an infelicity there. He never looked forward to the burden of retyping and had always been lazy about making a second copy with carbon paper, though Millie had urged him more than once to do it. But he found the work of generating so many corrected sheets to be an effective defense against melancholy, both the chronic kind that had sometimes plagued him since his school days, and the more acute kind that had set in that morning.

The book would argue that Shakespeare's *Sonnets* were not merely about real people—whether "W. H." was Southampton, Pembroke, or Willie Hughes, the boy actor, didn't matter—but formal expressions of complex human feelings. The paradoxes of beauty, the vagaries of desire, the profundities of love. When Julian had once tried to explain to Gus what he meant, he turned to Sonnet 29, observing how the "outcast" poet had only to think of his beloved and then his "state, like to the lark at break of day arising from sullen earth, sings hymns at heaven's gate." The lines were sonorous and correct, but they also enacted the emotions they described. The lark, with its melodic morning call, suddenly flew into the air, tracing the very sweep and arc of the speaker's heart-reviving passions as "sweet love rememb'red" magically turned misery into joy and degradation into redemption. While Julian spoke, Gus had nodded with such keen interest that he almost felt his own lark piercing the clouds and soaring into the firmament.

Since he was an undergraduate in Professor Whitaker's class, he'd admired the supple logic of the *Sonnets*, their bold language and astute vision of the heart's machinations, all in three quatrains and a couplet. But it seemed a special dispensation of the otherwise miserly gods that they were addressed largely to a beautiful youth. Although some critics wrung their hands over the question, Whitaker saw it as of a piece with the genius and sublimity of Shakespeare, more a curiosity than an aberration. Certainly, literature was full of loving male pairs—Sebastian and Antonio, David and Jonathan, Damon and Pythias—and if one needn't call excessive attention to their romantic feelings, one needn't despise or ignore them either. Regardless, the *Sonnets* had the imprimatur of the ages, and Julian knew he could safely claim them as his obsession without fear of controversy. If the beautiful youth happened to be the "master-mistress" of the poet's passion, it didn't matter. Hell, it was Shakespeare.

Julian had long accepted such a decorous denial of the obvious because the aesthetic rewards had seemed so great. But as he read page after page of his manuscript that morning, he began to see that he, too, had fallen into the trap of explaining away whatever touched on the carnal. With Schanche's irresolute Hamlet looking on, a number of sentences in particular now seemed unpardonably prudish:

> Such idealized passions were conventional in Elizabethan life and cannot in any way be read as prurient (p. 56).

> The poet's vicarious interest in the young man's sexual reproduction symbolizes his belief in the generative force of nature (p. 63).

> Thus, the love of the youth is figured as a spiritual identification with his beauty rather than a desire to possess it physically (p. 74).

When he'd first written them, such a refusal to take love between men seriously had seemed proper, even rather sophisticated. Now, whatever might have been prurient or possessive in the *Sonnets* seemed central to their meaning, and Julian's callow parsings sounded fatally insipid, the notions of a scholar castrated by narrow professional aspirations—certainly someone made uncomfortable by bohemian morality. Antonio never would have said such things about his love for Sebastian.

He pushed the whole mess of paper away from him like a plate of spoiled food. To take a more honest approach to the material would add months of work, if not years. It also might render the book unpublishable by any university press and jeopardize the golden fleece of tenure. Of course, if Julian's career were about to be scuttled anyway, he had no interest in authoring a book that got one of its most important questions wrong. But then he remembered, with a sudden, lark-soaring pleasure, that there was still at least one good reason to get that question right. So he pulled the manuscript back toward him and then picked and struck at his prose for nearly an hour, replacing whole paragraphs and scribbling minute corrections.

. When a knock on the door broke his concentration, he waited in testy silence, hoping the intruder would give up and go away. But the knocking only became more assertive, and eventually Julian gave up himself and answered it. It was Harcourt, in the same sharkskin

suit he'd worn the day before, and with the bountiful look of someone who'd come to confer a favor rather than ask for one, however
unlikely that seemed.

"Prince, good scholar! Prince of Denmark! Prince of Tyre!" he
sang out in his Yoknapatawpha twang. "We should talk."

"I'm afraid I'm awfully busy."

"Of course you are!" Harcourt said, pushing inside. "But I only
wanted a teensy bit of your time, and as God is my witness, I promise
not to take one second more."

"How much is a teensy bit?" Julian asked without smiling.

Harcourt took the question as an invitation to sit and threw himself into the library chair opposite the desk, slouching like a student,
so that his substantial head bobbed over his lap and his big knees
jutted out into the room. With a thick sweep of mahogany hair and
a ruggedly handsome face, his physical appeal was obvious. But
there was something in his rangy person that made him seem too
volatile, like a man who didn't know his mind and might be led by
circumstances to some sudden act of violence.

"Isn't Miss Millie a peach?" he asked. "An attractive girl, too.
Don't you think so, Prince? Don't you think she's a very physically
attractive girl?"

"How can I help you?" Julian asked.

Harcourt smiled widely, the kind of exaggerated smile young
children often make when someone points a camera at them.

"You've heard the ridiculous charges leveled against me, I suppose,"
he said. Then he pulled his pipe from his pocket and slipped it between
his lips. Julian had never seen him without it, but nor had he seen him
actually smoking it. He usually merely waved it around to accent his
opinions or let it bob in his mouth as a kind of provocation.

What Julian had heard on Friday from Sterne was only casual
gossip, in which he'd taken no real interest. He barely remembered
the details—something about writing term papers for students—and
he didn't want to hear them again now.

"It's all a terrible misunderstanding!" Harcourt cried, brandishing
the pipe. "About which I am quite frankly mortified!"

He went on to explain in melodic detail that the city was so
awfully expensive (for someone just starting out). That he'd taken

on the tutoring of several senior boys (whose parents were quite well off) to earn some extra money. That one of the boys regularly paid him in cash (which was only a matter of convenience, since checks might be lost or mislaid). That this same boy had required an awful lot of help with his history paper on the Marshall Plan (written from a decidedly imperialist perspective). And that he'd earned an A on it (which came as a surprise to both of them) and was so pleased with the help he'd been given that he bragged to his friends that for the low price of twenty-five dollars any one of them might also receive an A in Contemporary Civilization without having to lift a finger.

Harcourt told the story with great verve, emphasizing all its unexpected twists and trenchant ironies as if they referred to someone other than himself. But then he paused, cleared his throat, held his hands up, and spread his fingers wide.

"Now, there have been other suggestions of a base and unseemly nature that I won't dignify by mentioning, except to say that they are categorically false. But I'm quite sure that you, Prince, can appreciate the necessity of having them publicly contradicted."

Julian assumed these suggestions involved what was usually called "interference" with one or more of Harcourt's students. He wondered both why Sterne hadn't mentioned them, given his great interest in both boys and scandal, and why Harcourt was telling him now. Such things did sometimes occur, he knew, though the boys interfered with were often willing enough, and nearly all were, in fact, no longer boys. But he also wondered why Harcourt thought he'd have some particular sympathy for such a predicament. No doubt he'd observed Julian's state of bachelorhood and perhaps even seen him around campus with Gus, which probably also explained the comment about Millie's feminine charms. But it seemed unlikely that he could have surmised anything more than the vaguest suspicions from the previous day's visit by the little mustachioed man.

"If these suggestions are as base and unseemly as you say," Julian said, "then perhaps they ought not be discussed publicly or privately."

"No, Prince," Harcourt said, pointing with his pipe. "I fear I'm to be the victim of a witch hunt—truly a witch hunt!—and need all my friends standing by my side!"

As he spoke, he stared directly into Julian's eyes and spread his legs in a way that prominently displayed a substantial mound of twill just below his waist. Although in any other man the gesture might have seemed unconscious, in Harcourt it looked like a come-on. But neither enticed nor embarrassed, Julian held his gaze, reminded himself that he and Harcourt were not, strictly speaking, friends, and then waited for the request he knew was forthcoming.

"According to the wise and infallible Dean Cavanaugh, there'll be a disciplinary hearing next Wednesday," he said. "The thought of it makes my blood boil! But I would call it the greatest of favors if you would bear witness to my good character."

"You should probably ask someone who knows you better than I do," Julian said.

Harcourt smiled again, slipped his pipe back into his pocket, and looked at Julian with an air that was obviously calculated to unnerve.

"Oh, I believe we know each other well enough, Prince," he said before leaping up from the chair and opening the door to leave. "Quite well indeed."

Julian was astonished that such histrionics and gall had gotten Harcourt so far in life. But he refused to be intimidated and told himself that such a preening, conniving man couldn't possibly make his own situation any worse than it already was.

"By the way," Harcourt said, suddenly turning around and holding out a small pink piece of paper, "Miss Millie said you weren't taking calls today, but I thought this one might be of some urgency and wanting your immediate attention."

He handed Julian a "While You Were Out" message, then walked away with an undisguised aspect of self-satisfaction.

Julian closed the door after him and read the message:

To: Prof. Julian Prince

From: Roger Harrington

Message: Sorry I was out when you dropped by yesterday. Shall we try again tonight? Men's Bar at the Biltmore, 5:30 pm.

In happening upon the message, it now seemed clear that Harcourt believed he'd found some means to extort Julian's support for his case. It was laughable to think so, of course, for its text proved nothing at all. In fact, Harcourt made the clumsy work of the blackmailer seem deft by comparison. But he was young and inexperienced, in a lot of trouble, and apparently clinging to whatever paltry hope presented itself.

Perhaps it was the same desperate impulse that explained Roger Moorhouse's message, Julian thought. He was the very model of the secretive, repressed homosexual. A Kinsey 5 or 6 who told himself he was merely a 2 or 3. It was almost certainly the appearance of the blackmailer that had led to his change of heart. But if Roger was a self-deluding nutcase, as a banker he was probably also well connected and resourceful, and if not particularly bright, at least accustomed to solving problems. Julian could see that the message itself was a kind of apology for the rough welcome he'd given him at his office the day before. Its tone could only be described as affable, and its adoption of Julian's pseudonym seemed a small act of contrition in itself. Undoubtedly, it meant Roger wanted another chance to discuss their mutual dilemma. And since Julian had no other means of extricating himself from it—had, in fact, already given up trying—he decided it couldn't hurt to meet with the man and see what he had to say. Paltry hope, after all, was better than none.

◎ ◎ ◎

The Men's Bar was apparently the safest place Roger could think of to meet another homosexual. Julian had always thought it amusing that masculine exclusivity was such an effective cover for queerness. But hotel bars—like the one in which they'd met a year before, which may have been the Astor in Times Square—were often good places to find a willing partner. They were certainly different from places like Caesar's. Everyone wore a jacket and tie. No quarter was given to swish or camp. You never heard the least high-pitched gasp or shriek. And every exchange happened indirectly. If you met a businessman, you inquired about his business. If you were talking to a serviceman, you asked him where he was stationed. Only gradually did you drop hints about your true motives, and if half the time those hints would be dismissed as innocent chatter, the other half they'd be perfectly understood. Meeting someone at a hotel bar took more time, but it was often a lot more fun. Part of it was the thrill of clandestine activity. But the other part was that it allowed one to imagine, even for a few hours at a time, that the world of men and the world of sex were one and the same.

The Biltmore, on Madison next to Grand Central, was where *everyone* met, often "by the clock" in the gilded Palm Court. The Men's Bar was no less busy, but it was a good deal more intimate. Early that night, as Julian breached the oak-paneled inner sanctum, the din of masculine conversation roared in his ears. He saw a boisterous crowd of slick-haired men swelling in the oval-shaped room—and then, eventually, Roger, sitting alone at a small table. Still in his overcoat, he looked both humbled and irritated, like a fired executive awaiting an entry-level job interview.

"Thanks for coming," he said, without offering to shake hands.

"I didn't mean to shock you yesterday," Julian said.

"You didn't," Roger said. "Well, you did. But it wasn't a good day overall."

When a waiter paused at their table, Roger ordered Cutty Sark on the rocks, not the anticipated dry martini. Julian wondered if whiskey and ice in a squat lowball glass were meant to express an idea of unimpeachable manliness, something the combination of gin, vermouth, and an olive in a slender, fragile stem could never do. He promptly ordered the latter for himself.

"You were right," Roger said, once the waiter had left. "Someone did come. He must have followed me from my office, because he found me on the platform at Grand Central."

Apparently, he wanted to get right down to business.

"What did he look like?" Julian asked.

Roger's description more or less fit the person Julian had seen in his office the day before. "He just handed me a note and then ran off," he added. "He didn't seem happy in his work."

After Roger explained the contents of the note and Julian recounted what the man had done and said to him on Monday, they discussed whether the change in modus operandi held any useful clues and whether it might have been an amateur's first attempt or the work of seasoned veterans. But none of it seemed very enlightening.

"Are you planning to pay the man?" Roger asked.

That was the main question. Either pay and assume the threat would go away or refuse and hope it had all been a bluff.

"No," Julian said. "Though frankly I don't have that kind of money."

Roger looked down at the table, as if he were calculating a new household budget that included the blackmailer's ransom right alongside the monthly mortgage, private school tuition, and his wife's dress allowance.

"Suppose we do pay," he said, after their drinks arrived. "What are the chances that's the end of it?"

"Not good, I think," Julian said. "Why would he stop if there's more money to be had? Then again, it's hard to imagine that odious little man would be very reliable as an extortionist. He seemed more like someone who has trouble remembering to shave."

They lifted their drinks at the same time, and Julian thought Roger meant to toast his witticism. It didn't seem quite apt under the circumstances, but he didn't want to offend or disappoint, so he held his glass out in acknowledgment. But this only seemed to confuse Roger, who promptly put his own glass down and grew serious.

"Why did you come to my office?" he asked. "Did you really think I might know a way out of this mess? Because I haven't the foggiest idea."

This was the man Julian had anticipated—anxious, petulant, self-defeating.

"I thought you might know something," he said. "Or someone."

"Wouldn't telling someone defeat the purpose?"

"What about a lawyer?" Julian said.

He had no real idea what this would mean. But he assumed that, for people like Roger, hiring a lawyer was a common means of getting out of a jam.

"You understand that a lawyer would have to work within the law, don't you? Do you really mean to bring the police into it?"

"I suspect the police are already in it."

"And you mean to call them to account, do you?"

His point was valid enough, though the way he made it was both superior and despairing. It was the tone of a man who thought he was much better than you but still not good enough for the moment, which made you even worse than that.

"I'm afraid I'm out of my element here, Roger," Julian said.

"Well, you were quite wrong to think that I'm in mine."

They sipped their drinks and avoided eye contact, while Julian rapped the Fouquet Medusa nervously against the table. Then he lit a cigarette and offered one to Roger, who at first refused rather crossly but changed his mind for some reason. Julian flicked his lighter and presented the flame to Roger, but again he hesitated, and Julian wondered if, in his warped view of the world, having another man light your cigarette was tantamount to taking it in the ass. Yet just as Julian was about to hand over the lighter, Roger popped the cigarette into his mouth, leaned forward, and allowed him to light it. It seemed that a kind of amity between them was finally about to be achieved when Roger suddenly began choking on the smoke and blushing with embarrassment.

"What about a private detective?" Julian asked, after Roger put out his cigarette. "Frankly, I've only seen them in the pictures, but I suspect they do exist in real life. Perhaps they wouldn't need to work strictly within the law."

Roger frowned and sighed, as if he'd been worrying it might come to this.

"I happen to know one," he said. "Well, an investigator is what he calls himself."

The man was the friend of a cousin, he explained, not exactly in his social circle, but hardly a stranger. He'd gone to law school, picked up side work tracking down cheating spouses and embezzling employees, and finding it a good deal more interesting than his legal studies, eventually opened his own office. Roger had met him at a wedding in Newport in the early fifties, and they'd crossed paths frequently ever since. So engaging him would mean divulging the whole tawdry tale to someone he was likely to see again, perhaps even in the company of his wife, and Roger didn't seem to know if his pride would allow it.

"Do you trust him?" Julian asked.

In agreeing to meet that night at the Biltmore, Roger had already decided to trust someone. He seemed wary by nature, but he'd allowed himself to have faith in a mere acquaintance once, and Julian hoped it boded well for a second venture.

"Do you trust him more than someone you'd find in the Yellow Pages?" he added.

Roger clearly dreaded the prospect of meeting his cousin's friend, but he promised to arrange it as soon as possible. They agreed that he'd call Julian at his office as soon as he had something to report. Meanwhile, Julian would wait patiently and with luck he'd hear back before ten past twelve on Thursday, when the blackmailer was expected to return to campus. He offered to come along with Roger to meet the investigator and share what he knew. But Roger seemed to think it better to go by himself, and Julian thought he understood the reason. It was one thing to admit you were homosexual to someone you knew. But doing it with another homosexual at your side was probably beyond the pale.

As they finalized these details, the sound of applause suddenly rose and clattered across the room, and when Julian looked up, he saw several dozen men clapping their hands at a well-dressed young couple standing near the bar, both man and woman red with confusion. Ladies were not allowed in the Men's Bar, but even innocent mistakes were punished with éclat. Roger shook his head at the spectacle, though it wasn't clear whether his sympathies lay with the intruder or her persecutors.

"How are you holding up?" Julian asked, when the noise died down and there seemed to be no more business to conduct.

It was a fair question and one he wouldn't have minded being asked himself. But Roger either didn't hear him or pretended not to. He only finished his whiskey, set his glass back down on the table, and began to collect his coat and hat.

"I'll be in touch," he said, like a salesman promising to check on an order of vacuum bags.

As they shook hands and Julian watched him leave, he realized the question about "holding up" had been another miscalculation, though a small one. It was unnecessarily reflective, a gesture to vulnerability, which Roger apparently found distasteful. After all, it was a meeting of co-conspirators, not of friends. In fact, they pointedly avoided talking of anything personal. Roger said nothing of his family and asked nothing of Julian's. Of course, the topic they'd steered clear of was also the one that had brought them together—that they were both gay. It was normal not to mention such things casually. But Julian thought it regrettable that two men facing the same calamity couldn't speak frankly about it to one another.

15

Everything that made the West Village like an actual village—the jamming of people, cars, and bikes, the buying and selling of stuff, the freak show—seemed to be in hibernation. The sky was true blue, but it was so cold that morning Danny had to dance in place to keep from freezing. All the windows of the townhouses were still shuttered, and icicles hung unbroken from every awning and fire escape. Except for a few fearless Sunday strollers, the sidewalks were stone quiet. The only noise came when a pair of bundled-up boys went sprinting up Greenwich Street, screeching like baby hawks, until they ran out of steam or interest at Perry Street and dawdled away. But as the fading echoes fled the neighborhood, they only made the silence that followed seem colder and lonelier.

Danny knew it was tempting fate to show his face at the police station again. The cops wouldn't need an excuse to arrest him a second time. Disorderly conduct covered practically anything and always depended on whatever idea of *order* the cops making the arrest happened to have at the time. It was like a municipal version of Pat Duffy's "acting up." Danny's black eye marked him as a mischief-maker, and even on that barren morning some nosy parker might raise an alarm. If it had been warmer, he could have loitered on a stoop with his head down or leaned against a tree with his face buried in a newspaper. But the stoops were frosty with ice and rock salt and the trees were leafless and bad camouflage. So he kept watch at a distance and only passed by the building's entrance every so often, looking up quickly and then moving on.

As the sun cleared the eastern rooftops, people began going in and out of the station. Some were handcuffed and under arrest, like the two blondes in matching fur coats who reminded Danny of Rosemary Clooney and Vera-Ellen in *White Christmas*, except for the way they cursed at each other. Most of the people looked harried or nervous as they went in and then sad or angry as they came out, except for an old priest in a long black cloak, who arrived with a big smile and left a quarter hour later dragging a teenage boy in only dungarees and a cardigan. After Danny bought a donut from a vendor on Hudson Street, he circled back to his outpost on Greenwich, where he almost missed seeing three pot-bellied goombahs get pulled from a happy wagon and marched into the station. He wondered if any of them would be beaten in a stairwell.

He tried not to think about what was happening back in Parkchester, but the thoughts came anyway. After Mass, there would've been bear claws and coffee at Uncle Steven's, who worked for Met Life and lived in a giant three-bedroom. Then cousins and other relatives would've dropped by for a meal and stayed all afternoon. Danny would've been tortured with sports talk by Declan and Colum and quizzed on all the varieties of apples by Eileen, who always praised his talents but, like Mavis, was a naturally boring person herself. Once the food had been eaten and the beer and whiskey drunk and the other visitors had gone home, he might have argued with Michael about whether to watch *Maverick* or *The Bullwinkle Show* on the color TV, and there would've been cursing and threats until Uncle Steven called them both babies and made them watch whatever was left of *Lassie*. But again Danny tried to force these thoughts from his mind as he fixed his eyes back on the marble columns of the station house. His family was ancient history now, just like the pioneer and Indian above the second-story window—and just as phony and unfair.

All afternoon he watched from behind a fire alarm box on Washington Street as more people came and went. He thought about why he'd been arrested for doing what his brothers probably did whenever they went out on the town. Nobody ever raided Keenan's or McEldoo's, and the only punishment Quinn got for dancing and flirting was an occasional slap in the face. But even after being locked up with other men like himself, Danny still hadn't been treated fairly. The Rich Kid, Barrett, had been let off easy, and the same must have been true of the Suave Suit and Shoe-Face, who were probably right then sitting in their living rooms, warm and snug, without any cares at all. And now because Danny's name had been printed in the newspaper, he was standing out in the cold like a desperado instead of taking inventory at Sloan's. None of it was right.

At the Waverly that evening, he took costly comfort in a cheeseburger, fries, and a Coke, and while he ate, he read the *Village Voice* and learned about a "worldwide general strike for peace" and a march against nuclear testing and the "war economy" that had taken place a week before on Fifth Avenue. There were hundreds of people, men and women, beats and suits, teachers and welders and dressmakers, who'd all refused to go to work for one day and hoped to convince others to join their cause and save the world from total destruction. Danny knew the atom bomb could kill anyone at any time, and he liked the idea of so many ordinary folks standing up together for something they believed in. He wondered if his own quieter marching up and down Charles Street was a similar kind of protest and imagined someday reading about himself in the newspaper for being brave and defiant—instead of just being caught.

After the neighborhood emptied out again that evening, the streetlamps flicked on, and the temperature dropped, Danny waited and watched with his collar turned up and his ushanka pulled down. Though he was tired and still achy from head to toe, his head felt as sharp as it had that morning. He noticed the only black-and-white that hadn't moved all day, while others pulled up and drove away and never stayed long. He paid attention to every cop he saw and memorized his size and build and hair color and the way he walked and anything he said. When three of them left the building around ten, lit smokes, and walked east toward Greenwich, Danny was sure one was the pimply desk sergeant with the bad dye job, though he only caught a glimpse of his ugly face.

He'd always had good powers of observation, which mattered when you were short and a moment's woolgathering could get you squashed. But it was Bill who'd taught him the art of patience. Once when Danny was eight, Quinn stole Bill's collection of green stamps and threatened a beating if he tattled. But Bill said nothing about it until a week later when Quinn came home with a new Kodak Pony and Pat Duffy happened to be sober. Then Bill casually mentioned to their father how pricey those cameras were and the whole truth came out in less than a minute, along with compensation for Bill and stripes for Quinn, who was never the wiser about who'd ratted him out.

Bill took Danny aside when it was over. "Silence is golden, shrimp," he said, putting his finger to his lips, which might have been a moral or a threat or both.

Either way, revenge could happen in the blink of an eye.

Only a year later, one hot breezeless day in July, Michael caught Danny playing with his little green plastic army men, which Danny loved but wasn't allowed to touch. As a punishment, Michael sat on top of him, pinning down both of his arms with his knees. Then he pinched Danny's nose closed with one hand, held his head back with the other, hacked up a big loogie, and threatened to drop it right in his mouth. Danny struggled and shouted for help, but Michael was too heavy and no one was home to save him. Margaret Duffy was visiting her dying mother back in Sligo, Ciaran was working the matinee at the Fordham RKO, and Quinn and Bill were at St. Mary's pool. So when the loogie swelled on Michael's lips, drew itself into a shiny glob and began to separate, there was nothing for Danny to do but close his eyes, breathe through a crack in his mouth, and wait.

Half a minute later, Ciaran came home early and poked his head in the bedroom, where Danny still lay on the floor coughing and Michael stood over him grinning madly. No explanation necessary.

"Bare your shoulder," Ciaran said.

"Mind your own business," Michael said sullenly, even as he pulled up the sleeve of his T-shirt.

Ciaran never liked hurting anyone. But he probably lingered in his regret to make Michael squirm a bit and do to one little brother what he'd done to another. Once he'd made his point, he stepped into a boxer's stance, spun his torso around, and drove his knuckles into Michael's arm, giving him a whopper of a charley horse that would hurt for several days and leave a first-class bruise. They stood facing each other in silence for nearly ten seconds. Ciaran to make sure he hadn't done any real damage. Michael to show he could take anything his older brother had to give. Then they parted like prizefighters, and Danny picked himself up off the floor, cleaned his face, and settled for Lincoln Logs. But he understood that cruel actions sometimes brought hard consequences and the strong were meant to protect the weak. He loved Ciaran for what he'd done, but instead of hating Michael, he only pitied him for getting what he deserved.

◎ ◎ ◎

Sometime before eleven that night, as Danny trudged past the Sixth Precinct station for what seemed like the hundredth time, the Nazi Cop suddenly stepped out of the shadows from the other direction and walked right by him. As they passed each other, he felt almost gut-kicked by the memory of the man's sweaty face and crushing grip. He thought for sure the Nazi Cop would recognize him or at least spot the black eye that was his own handiwork. Danny might even have run away if it hadn't been for the hard lump of fear in his stomach. But as the Nazi Cop marched up the stairs, pulled open the door, and disappeared into the building, he just kept walking with his head down, remembering every detail.

He wore a sporty blue mackinaw, a matching wool muffler, and a black fedora. There was something in his manner, too, a sense of ease with a world he expected would treat him well no matter what. Out of uniform, he was the picture of vim and vigor. His chest was nearly as puffed up as it had been on Thursday night and his arms were swinging almost as high. But his big, wide-set brown eyes seemed calm and rested, nothing like amber and more dove-like than hawk-like. He looked like the last guy on the block you'd ever suspect of stealing your mail or running over your cat. At first, Danny doubted what he'd seen. Then he doubted what the Nazi Cop had done to him. He could only think of one explanation for such two-facedness. The guy was a real Wehrmacht man, a shiny killer. Jim Anderson on the outside and Old Man Clanton on the inside.

Danny thought about insides and outsides as he walked up Hudson Street to Eighth Avenue and then back to Raf's place. He regretted that he hadn't gone back that afternoon to leave a note. But he didn't want to involve Raf in what he was doing, not even with the smallest deception or request for help. When he got to the apartment a little after midnight, he found Raf asleep in his bed, the smell of cuchifritos hanging in the air, and Raf's own note propped up against the bud vase on the table.

Where have you been? What have you been doing? Where's my squash?

It made Danny regret the lies he knew he'd write in reply.

That night on the couch he dreamt that someone who looked like Roy Lee—he had the same eyebrows, moustache, and beard—but sounded more like Quinn sat at the piano in the living room at Bacchus playing "Summertime." The place was dark and crowded with leering, thin-lipped men, and Not Roy Lee's playing was lousy and his voice was flat. Danny was so embarrassed he looked away. Then Not Roy Lee suddenly stopped playing and cried: "Who do you think you are?" Danny tried to avoid the quarrel and moved to another part of the room, but Not Roy Lee got up and followed him: "Who the *hell* do you think you are!" Then the woman in the burgundy evening dress came to Danny's rescue and led him by the arm into the bedroom. But as soon as he saw a jumble of naked bodies there, a molar came loose in his mouth. After he pulled it out, another tooth came out and then another, until he was licking every last one out of his pulpy, bloody gums. He wasn't too worried, since he thought he heard a siren fading down Eighth Avenue. But feeling so many sharp, boney bits of himself was weird. No one had smashed them out or pulled them out. They'd come out all on their own because something inside him was sick or broken.

The dream woke him up just after five in the morning, stayed with him while he dressed and crept out of the apartment without waking Raf, and lingered dimly as he leaned against an old bishop's crook on Greenwich Street, sipping a coffee, munching a buttered roll, and watching steam swirl up from a street grate and shuffle off in the wind.

But Danny felt clearheaded and whole again the moment he saw the Nazi Cop come out of the police station and turn east. He looked more rumpled than the night before. His step was slower, his chest seemed a little deflated, and his arms hardly swung at all. Danny trailed half a block behind him as he zigzagged toward Washington Square. It felt like something out of *Naked City* and he could almost hear the tormented chorus of horns and Paul Burke's voice warning him about the danger he was courting. But as they went down into the West 4th Street station and walked toward the BMT, Danny found himself feeling more bored than scared. From behind a steel column, he watched the Nazi Cop sit down on a bench in the middle of the platform, fold his arms, and stare into his lap. When a gang of uniformed private school boys made a ruckus, he only smiled at them and shook his head, more like an easygoing uncle than a thug. Once the train finally came, he stepped aside to let people off, gave up the only free seat to a gray-haired babushka, and joined the strap-hangers without so much as a sneer or a snarl.

At the far end of the car, he held a strap with one hand and smoked a cigarette with the other. Danny had always enjoyed watching people on the subway, especially a choice stud in tight trousers. To avoid being too obvious, he'd sweep his head lazily, like he was only stretching his neck, but then for a quick second he'd home in on the curve of a bicep or the swell of a crotch and fix the image in his mind. That morning, in between glances at the Nazi Cop, he yawned casually and wrinkled his nose like it itched, then looked down at the floor, up over a half dozen hats and bare heads, and then over to a poster of Miss Rheingold, forever expecting men to love her as much as they loved her beer. But by the time the train finally rolled into Queens and the car began to empty out, the man had hardly moved a muscle. He didn't take any of the free seats. After stepping on his cigarette and pulling a *Daily Racing Form* from his mackinaw, he only hung on his strap and read with a smile on his face, like he'd picked a trifecta. It made no sense, Danny thought, sweating in his pea coat. He seemed too happy.

At the Fresh Pond Road station, Danny followed him onto the sidewalk, then fished a rusty old seven iron from a trash can near the entrance, in case things got dicey. But he felt the creep of disappointment as he walked six short blocks to Palmetto Street, which looked no different from the other streets in Ridgewood, which itself didn't seem so different from parts of the Bronx. There were more detached houses and it was a little quieter, but there was a humdrum ordinariness to it that seemed familiar. Low buildings and dull colors, men going to work, women running errands, and kids tramping to school. It smelled the same, too, like roasted chestnuts and gasoline, and it reminded him that he'd never once been beyond the tristate area and probably ought to move somewhere else in the world while he was still young. Maybe Scandinavia or Afghanistan or New Guinea.

When the Nazi Cop got to what appeared to be his house, he stopped and stared at it for a moment, like he wasn't sure he wanted to go inside. It was a plain, boxy, peach-colored, stucco two-story with a tan-and-white striped metal awning above the door. There were two windows on each floor, and Danny might have just glimpsed the shadow of a wife in curlers and kerchief through one of them. He figured if he waited long enough he'd see her come out of the house and go to the market or take their children to school. Maybe she'd be an ugly hag and the kids would be badly behaved or marked with cuts and bruises and other signs of the Nazi Cop's temper. Or she'd be a Donna Reed type, all dolled up and domestic, and their kids would be real cute. One might be a Cub Scout with a lisp and the other a polio victim who walked with a brace. Danny didn't know which would be worse.

Pat Duffy had always wanted to live in a detached house. Space to pass two bodies wide between you and your neighbor was his father's notion of success. "You're never really alone until you don't share a wall," he'd often complained. A detached house was probably Danny's brothers' idea of the good life, too. But standing there, staring at all the ordinary peach stucco plainness, he realized it was an idea that had never included him and never would. Detached or otherwise, houses weren't made for people like Danny—or Gabriel or Raf or Cormac O'Connor or Roy Lee. In some neighborhoods, they weren't made for black people at all. They were made for men and women together, for the raising of children and the comfort of grandparents. He couldn't imagine a house in Ridgewood or Mott Haven or anywhere else that was built for a single man, let alone a pair of bachelors. Only the dream house on a hilltop in the Catskills with all his friends would fit that bill. But a regular house was meant to keep some people in and some out.

He suddenly felt the hurricane of fury churning and roaring in his head again. His hands grew hot and his chest rumbled. He saw himself speeding across the street with the seven iron in his fists, jumping up in the air for momentum, and bringing it straight down on the Nazi Cop's fedora. Cracking open his skull like a honeydew melon, the thwomp of the metal wedge splattering brain pulp all over the sidewalk. Letting the world know there was a high price to pay for arresting and beating an innocent man. *Making your enemies face their crimes.*

But then the Nazi Cop started toward the house, opened the door, and went inside.

Danny felt his heart beating in his neck and, as he gripped the seven iron and tried to calm his breath, he wondered what to do with all the fight left inside him. Once the hurricane finally blew itself out, he imagined Raf telling him to go straight home and forget all about it, and then Gabriel insisting he sneak into the house through an unlocked rear window and stop up the kitchen sink and run the tap. But after a light in one of the upper-story windows came on and then went off again five minutes later, Danny settled on a halfway measure. He crept up to the front door, opened the mailbox, and fished out an unmailed letter, written in a loose, irregular hand that was probably a woman's and bore the Palmetto Street return address of a "Mrs. Harold Blunt." The name sounded too ordinary, and more English than German. But it was something to go on, not just a quirk or a habit but a fact that might lead him to more. Danny didn't need to be rash or reckless, he told himself as he chucked the seven iron into some bushes and headed back to the Fresh Pond Road station. Silence was golden and revenge could happen in the blink of an eye.

◎ ◎ ◎

When he turned the deadbolt on Raf's apartment, he expected to have it to himself. A café con leche with peanut butter toast and some plantains seemed like a good lunch. He thought he might even curl up on the couch and catch forty winks. Although Raf's place wasn't much warmer than the streets of Ridgewood or the Village, it was still the closest thing he had to a home. But when he opened the door, the first thing he saw was Raf himself, hunched over the little table sipping tea, with his granny shawl around his shoulders and looking none too pleased.

"I'm taking a sick day," Raf said, pushing a few stray curls from his forehead. "What about you? Isn't it early for you to be home? Why aren't you at work?"

Danny knew there'd be more questions to come, so he didn't bother answering.

"I went up to Sloan's to get that squash you promised me," Raf continued. "To make the soup I promised you. Puta calabaza! And what did I find there but some smooth-talking Irish boy telling me that they ran out two days ago, just about the time you did, too. You can imagine my surprise."

Raf summoned Danny to the table with a frown and poured him a cup of hot tea. The fact that there was already a second cup and saucer on the table, along with a box of polverones from their favorite panadería, made it clear he'd planned a confrontation. But Danny didn't feel like confessing just yet.

"Gee, I wonder why you went all the way uptown," he said.

"Because you're always bragging about the damned produce at your fancy supermarket, so I thought it might be worth the trip. Dios mío, how wrong I was!"

Danny knew it was all just a prelude to the real argument, and he didn't mind playing along, even if it only postponed the inevitable for another minute.

"Quite a schlepp for a squash, dahling," he said, blowing on his cup.

But Raf waved his hand like he was fanning away the fumes of Danny's bullshit. The prelude was over. "You quit your job, blanquito," he said. As usual, he seemed more worried than angry. Good work was hard to find and a steady paycheck was the key to having a little freedom. Raf never would've walked out on his job.

"They fired me," Danny said.

Raf seemed confused. No one was ever fired for being Puerto Rican. If they didn't want you, they didn't hire you to begin with. So

Danny finally told him about the notice in the *Post* and the meeting in the walk-in with Di Stefano. And then Raf listened and took his part as expected, but the tight smile on his face and the careful way he poured himself more tea made it clear he was still unhappy.

"So I guess you'll be looking for another job," he said, in a businesslike tone he didn't use often. It was fine to sleep on his couch and eat his stews and plantains when Danny was employed, he meant to say. But Danny wasn't Gabriel, and Raf wasn't Gabriel's parents. If he was able-bodied, he had to work.

"Where do you think I've been?" Danny said, lowering his eyes over a frown as he took some cookies.

He was surprised that Raf hadn't called him out about the lie he'd scribbled on the note, about going out with Gabriel after work. It wasn't even a smart lie since Gabriel easily could have dropped by Raf's place and given him up. Although saying he was job hunting gave Danny the excuse he needed to be out day and night pounding the pavement, as he meant to do anyway, it left him feeling like he'd done something unforgiveable. In that moment, he became keenly aware of the room. While it was decorated with a few pretty things here and there—an old, fringed lampshade, a Turkish tapestry on the wall, the bud vase on the table—it was obviously where a man lived without women. And it was one thing to tell a lie in a detached house or a two-bedroom apartment or a police station, where lies were often necessary and sometimes expected. But it was another thing to tell one in a single man's one-room apartment to the single man left in the world Danny knew he could still count on.

16

Corinne drove without her usual focus, staring blankly at the road ahead and only periodically snapping into what seemed like a sudden, irritated awareness of what she was doing, then little by little slipping back into the shelter of her secret thoughts. Roger knew they concerned him, the chaos of the past week, and the questions that now haunted them both, achingly but separately. For two nights in a row, he'd come home in a terrible state that he'd been unable to explain or disguise. On Tuesday, he'd bought a bouquet of daffodils to cheer her with their spring-beckoning optimism, but then he began doubting the gesture as affected and self-serving. Men who brought home flowers were either in love or feeling guilty. So it was no surprise that she seemed to receive them with more suspicion than appreciation. She thanked him curtly, reminded him that Valentine's Day wasn't until the following day, and even made a point of calling the flowers by their botanical name, *Narcissus*.

It was the meeting he'd just had with Julian Prince at the Biltmore that rattled him that night. Although they'd dispatched their business quite efficiently, Roger was awkward and abrupt and entirely failed to make up for his panicked reception of the man at his office the day before. Even at the Men's Bar, he felt the need to project a certain invulnerability, to let the reason for their meeting be merely a technical problem to be solved rather than something that touched in any way on private feelings. There was something in Prince's manner, too, not exactly fey but relaxed and informal, that Roger both liked and disliked. He claimed neither a wife nor a girlfriend and was probably too in love with his own immaculate integrity to stoop to such a deception. Yet he also seemed levelheaded and had a sense of humor and a kind of independent spirit that almost made his being a womanless man seem more attractive than shameful. Roger had never once smoked a cigarette before, but there was something about Prince that made him want to try. As their fingers touched briefly, he felt an oddly stirring thrill, which he knew at once was the release of tension rather than the creation of it. But when his coughing betrayed his inexperience, he feared the whim only made him look foolish.

After the plan to meet the investigator had been resolved upon, Prince asked him a simple question. *How are you holding up?* It was the question of a friend, of course. It announced an unexpected sympathy, an implicit acknowledgement that Roger had suffered. It was the kind of question Schuyler might have asked had he been in Prince's situation—which was impossible to imagine. When Roger heard it, he felt suddenly pulled toward Prince by a hot current of need. He wanted to reach across the table, hold him in his arms and be held in return. But then a barrage of thoughts instantly chilled the feeling. Even Schuyler never would have allowed such a desperate display. Roger wouldn't have allowed it himself. Prince might have allowed it, but that's because Prince was a homosexual.

Roger knew he'd sounded absurdly brusque as he said good-bye. Part of him wanted to stay, to ask Prince how *he* was holding up, to ask a hundred other questions about his life and how he lived it. But when he shook the man's hand, it felt rather limp and moist. His smile suddenly seemed effete, his hair too long, his clothes too arty. And before he knew it, Roger had practically run out of the Men's Bar and into the safety of a Checker cab.

"You're sweating," Corinne said, as they pulled into the parking lot of the train station the next morning.

"I'm fine," he said, dabbing his face with his handkerchief, as if it were nothing.

She slowed the car and came to a stop well short of their usual spot.

"No, you're not," she said. "Stop pretending."

He heard the gravelly timbre that always crept into her voice whenever she was upset. She didn't like to argue, let alone confront or contradict, which is why she'd accused him of "pretending" rather than lying. He could have blamed the pressures of work, the stress of rising expectations and competition from men like Nick, though he didn't think she'd have believed him. He hated lying to her and felt a kind of relief in the fact that he lacked the energy even to try. But Corinne had her limit, too, he knew, and she was telling him she'd reached it.

"I've waited very patiently for you to tell me what's wrong," she said. "But I won't wait anymore."

He knew that to give her what she was asking for would ruin them both. He couldn't even imagine the words he'd use, and when he tried to summon them, he felt as if an enormous sinkhole were opening up in the station parking lot, one that would swallow them whole, Chrysler and all.

"There's nothing wrong," he said without looking at her and in a voice so flat and anguished it wouldn't have convinced Lizzie. "I'm just a bit tired."

"I don't believe you," she said, the words scraping her throat.

He refused to allow any sign of comprehension onto his face and stared out the window as if suddenly noticing a cardinal on a power line. The rain had stopped and narrow columns of sunlight were breaking through the clouds, dividing the world into discrete zones of hope and despair.

"Well, that's a pity," he said. "Shall I get out now, or will you bring me closer?"

"I want you to see a psychiatrist."

The idea had always chilled him. Even when Corinne consulted one for a few months after Henry's difficult birth had left her feeling blue, he'd been unable to ask for any details about her weekly visits. In his own case, he'd always imagined a dark-eyed Jew coercing from him a confession of every nasty thought he'd ever had and every sorry seed he'd ever spilt. He'd once read about aversion conditioning in one of Richard's medical journals—a terrifying combination of pornography and emetics—and supposed it might work for some borderline cases. But he was a dyed-in-the-wool queer if ever there was one, and no doctor of the body or the mind could change that.

"Roger, please don't ignore me," Corinne said, pulling the keys from the ignition.

They'd always been as close to equal partners as any married couple they knew. He thought the main reason she'd chosen him was that he didn't require her to do or be anything she didn't decide of her own free will. Maybe it was the freedom she required in recompense for all normal marital privileges he'd made her forgo. But he also knew that, however insistent she now sounded, she was still only making a request. Her "please" seemed to imply the traditional female acknowledgment that she could only advise and suggest but never command.

"I'm really fine, Rin," he said, turning to face her with a smile he hoped might express all the love and respect he had for her, even though he knew it would probably douse those fine things with kerosene and light them on fire. "Just a bit out of sorts."

When he saw men dashing from cars and the hazy light of the oncoming train in the distance, he grabbed his briefcase and kissed her damp, salty cheek. "I've got to run," he said. "Happy Valentine's Day, darling."

"You're not well," she muttered.

It was possible Roger really was ill after so many years of sneaking and lying. He imagined some pathological accretion of nerves constricting his vital organs, especially his heart. If bad nerves made men queer, it made sense that their queerness could also make them sick.

"Of course I am," he said. "I'm right as rain."

◉ ◉ ◉

They were the same words he'd said to his mother on a long-distance telephone call the afternoon before he shipped out to Pearl Harbor on the *Bunker Hill*. He'd chosen the Aviation Cadets because he supposed navy pilots died more quickly than army combat soldiers, and so long as he had to risk his life for his country, he preferred doing it in a clean and orderly cockpit to sharing a filthy foxhole with a gang of ruffians, farting, crowing, and pretending not to be afraid. And if his plane were shot down over the Pacific or his ship were sunk by a Japanese sub, all his problems would die with him, and the world—even one at war—might be made a little easier.

As he hung up the phone, he wondered if his mother didn't secretly feel the same.

Later that night, in a magenta-carpeted corridor of the Grand Horton Hotel in San Diego, California, he'd found himself standing in a line of nearly two dozen drunk and randy men, some laughing merrily, others moody and restless. Aviators, Roger had quickly discovered, were no different from other servicemen. Many were crass and crude, openly boastful about scoring with women they'd met at dancehalls in Corpus Christi and Norfolk. But whether cocky or shy, nearly all of them believed in the religion of girls—their infinite fascination and saving importance. When the conversation at the base wasn't about fuselages or flying speeds, it was about females.

Ezra Benson was one of the very few exceptions. Although easily the best athlete in the squadron, he was modest and quiet, a devout Mormon from Idaho who wouldn't drink coffee or Coca-Cola, let alone alcohol. He kept to himself, didn't wear a wedding ring, and never mentioned a wife or girlfriend. He never bragged or told stories or even offered opinions about things without being asked. When Roger saw him poring over training manuals late into the night or kneeling in prayer at the chapel on Sundays, he was always still as a statue. But he was more like a real military man than any of them. He got up earliest, worked the hardest, and went the longest, and Roger was always happy when circumstances threw them together. So it was as much a welcome surprise as a perplexing one that Ezra was standing in line next to him that night at the hotel.

They'd all gone there to celebrate their embarkation, and there was an electric feeling in the air. They drank ice-cold beer for a couple of hours—Ezra stuck with lemonade—and when someone announced that the party was moving upstairs, they shifted, sheep-like, and gradually fell into formation along the corridor. At first, Roger had no idea of what was happening, but soon all the blustery girl-talk offered a strong hint, and well before the first pair of airmen sauntered smugly out of one of the rooms, buttoning their shirts and smirking their satisfaction, he understood.

"I frankly didn't expect to see you here," Roger said, after a conversation about the motives of Nagano and Sugiyama began to feel out of place.

"Nor I, you," Ezra said.

It was disconcerting to think that the one man Roger assumed wouldn't be standing in the line on purpose knew exactly what he was doing, and even more so to be pegged as an outsider and without the excuse of religion. But at least it was clear that the man Roger had paid so much attention to for months seemed to have paid some attention in return. Whenever Ezra was around, Roger had always done his best to communicate a likeminded tendency toward circumspection. Even if he were seen roughhousing in the barracks or playing "smear the queer" on the ball field, he tried to show a certain ironic distance from it, as if he'd really rather be doing more serious things. Ezra's keen judgment had probably seen these tortured performances for what they were, but whether he sympathized or scorned them, Roger couldn't tell.

"I suppose I just got swept along with the crowd," he said, hoping it betrayed neither too much enthusiasm for being there nor too much eagerness to leave.

"Yeah, me too," Ezra said, looking doubtfully up and down the line of men waiting in the corridor. "But I don't think I'll stay."

"No?" Roger asked, hoping that Ezra's departure might justify his own.

"It's not really my cup of tea."

It was a daring thing to say, if an equivocal one. Although he'd probably meant that sex with prostitutes offended his morals, it might also have been a subtle invitation. As Roger had learned from Mudge, "tea" had certain queer connotations that signified only to the cognoscenti. Then again, Ezra may have been entirely innocent of such knowledge. In fact, he was the only member of their task group who drank tea, though the herbal kind.

There were plenty of men in the navy who weren't so innocent. At sea, Roger had watched sunbathing sailors romancing each other on the *Bunker Hill*'s flight deck, and drunken ones running around in loud and gaudy packs on shore leave in Honolulu. Although everyone knew it was going on—most of the jokes about life on aircraft carriers involved sodomy—no one seemed to bother too much about it. But from the time Roger arrived at preflight school in Chapel Hill, he'd resolved not to touch another man until the war was over. On his very first day, it was whispered about the barracks that some chuckle-headed ensign from Georgia had been caught fellating a mechanic in one of the hangars and was busted down to a common seaman. It had seemed warning enough.

But there now stood before Roger an excellent reason to break his resolution. He didn't know if it would amount to anything more than an anxious, fumbling, one-time encounter or send Ezra into a moral panic that ruined them both. But it still seemed like the best chance at affection the war might ever offer Roger and one he couldn't squander.

"So what *is* your cup of tea?" he said, hiding his trembling hands in his pockets.

Ezra held his gaze for a moment, then laughed without embarrassment.

"I guess it depends on who's asking," he said.

To Roger, he was the antithesis of boys like Riley Cross and men who frequented pornographic theaters. He was more reliable than Mudge and more like-minded than Schuyler. Although a Mormon, he didn't believe in the religion of girls either. For the first time in Roger's life, the man he wanted was perfectly appealing and apparently willing, and it seemed like a sign that his life wasn't meant to be so lonely after all.

"Why don't we get out of here," he said.

But when Ezra looked at him again, his cold blue eyes gave the wrong answer.

"You should stay," he said, as he turned to go and clapped Roger on the shoulder, the way one teammate would console another after a bitter loss.

Watching Ezra walk down the corridor, Roger felt his heart stiffen against the horror of such an unexpected and unaccountable rejection, insisting to himself that there must have been some misunderstanding. But then he did exactly as he'd been told. He stood in line for over an hour, making occasional small talk with his fellow airmen, each word as if from a long-ago memorized script, inching his way toward one of the doors that promised him all the pleasure a would-be warrior was supposed to crave and deserve. It was like some magenta-carpeted version of the horrible army death he'd hoped to avoid, only worse because it would only maim him but leave no visible scars. He knew he ought to have left soon after Ezra had and gone back to the base or to a motel or just wandered the streets of San Diego. He would have preferred the torture of solitude to the strange and unsavory company he was about to keep. But somehow he was no more able to leave than Ezra had been able to stay.

After all the miserable things Roger would see and do in the two years that followed, it wasn't the raids on Satawan or Palau or even Okinawa that broke him. It wasn't seeing dozens of enemy Zeroes pop, smoke, and fall from the sky, each a nameless victim of his steady aim and callous thumb. It wasn't even the outrageous sight from his Hellcat of thick black smoke spewing from the *Bunker Hill* or learning later that a kamikaze plane had crashed into the flight deck, its bombs blowing up in the ready room and killing every pilot who wasn't in the air as he'd been. Those were moments that Roger had somehow shaped into a memory of the general awfulness of the war and now seemed to have little to do with him personally. Rather, it was standing in that hotel corridor watching Ezra Benson leave that had injured him most grievously and permanently. It was the crippling wound he'd carry with him across the Pacific and home to New York and then up to New Rochelle and back and forth to Manhattan five days a week. After that night at the Grand Horton, he knew he'd never be right as rain again.

⊚ ⊚ ⊚

It helped that Caspar Donovan, who went by Cap, looked more like a lawyer than a private dick. Roger had arranged to meet him Wednesday afternoon at his office in an old limestone building on East 29th Street, which was somewhat primitive but not nearly as louche as he'd expected. When he opened the door, he found an antique Persian rug in the middle of the room, a flourishing ficus on one side, and on the other, an Impressionist painting of a golden hayfield at sunset, which Cap, leaning against a steel tanker desk, seemed to be appraising thoughtfully. The desk was covered with piles of manila folders thick with documents, evidence of actual work. Roger was glad not to feel mocked by framed photos of a contented wife or thriving children.

"Ro-ger Moor-house!" Cap said, turning from the painting, in that sardonic tone with which one greets someone at yet another wedding.

In his midforties, he had a thick brush of dark brown hair and teeth so white they made his ruddy complexion look almost red. He wore a fine blue serge suit and gold cufflinks, which Roger hoped meant business was good. A large, old-fashioned cast iron safe sat reassuringly behind him.

"I appreciate your seeing me on such short notice," he said, shaking Cap's hand and struggling to return such a sunny reception. "I really can't thank you enough."

Cap waved him into one of a pair of Windsor chairs, then took his own seat behind the desk.

"Listen, Roger," he said, the prep school bonhomie turning suddenly matter of fact. "It's one of the downsides of my work that no one who comes to see me is ever happy about it. But I've adapted, so there's no need to be polite on my account."

Roger had assumed that politeness was the only thing that would make their conversation remotely tenable. But he was grateful that Cap didn't mention any of their mutual friends or the last time they'd met in Bar Harbor.

"Let's talk about why you're here," he said.

Roger had thought all afternoon about how he'd present his case, whether to admit he was being blackmailed and let the pertinent details emerge as the interview required, or to tell the whole sordid story from the moment the police came crashing through the front door of Caesar's. But in the end, he'd decided not to decide, and now faced with the task of speaking, he didn't know what to say.

"Ten to one I've heard far worse since lunchtime," Cap said.

Roger felt his heart knocking against his ribs.

"A man has demanded that I give him money," he finally said.

"He's threatened you?"

Again, Roger hesitated. But after a reassuring look from Cap, he nodded.

"With evidence of some kind?"

"Photographs."

"Have you seen them?"

"No."

"But there's reason to believe they exist?"

Roger nodded.

"Okay, good," Cap said, as if they'd already made progress.

Over the next quarter hour, while Cap filled several pages of a legal pad, Roger explained how he'd been accosted by a man at Grand Central, what the man looked like, and how he was dressed. Cap asked some of the same questions in different ways to get at things Roger had forgotten at first, like which train he'd been waiting for and the color of the blackmailer's coat. Several times they went over what the man had said to him, and Cap pressed Roger to be as accurate as possible and to say whether his voice had been gentle or rough, quiet or loud, nervous or confident.

"Kind of rough but quiet. Definitely not confident," he said.

"May I see the note?"

Roger drew it from his briefcase and handed it over. It was strange that he no longer felt the shame of what had happened to him quite so keenly and even experienced a little prickle of excitement to be participating in detective work. The note was evidence, after all.

Cap studied it carefully then put it inside one of the folders on his desk. "Now I'm afraid I have to ask about the night on which the photos were taken," he said.

Roger's shame returned like a suddenly remembered debt. Of course, he'd have to explain everything if Cap were to help him properly. He looked around at the room again—at the ficus, the safe, the painting on the wall—then took a fortifying breath.

"Very well," he said. "Ask away."

"Where were you?"

"A police station."

"Do you recall which station?"

"The Sixth Precinct."

Roger wondered if he were merely confirming a detail or probing for the reason he was there. Cap would have known that the Sixth Precinct was in Greenwich Village.

"Were you arrested?"

"I don't think so. They held me for a while. And they interviewed me briefly. Then they let me go."

"You were never booked? Never fingerprinted?"

When Roger shook his head, Cap looked at him curiously, then cast his eyes toward the ceiling in what looked like a burst of focused thought.

"Would you like to know where I was before the police station?" Roger asked, surprised that he now preferred to get it over with rather than torture himself with anticipation.

Cap stood up and went to the safe behind him, opened the door, which apparently wasn't locked, and pulled out two crystal highball glasses and a bottle of Chivas Regal. Then he came back to the desk, where he poured a finger of whiskey in each of the glasses, handed one of them to Roger and, taking the other for himself, sat down again.

"I'll need to know everything," he said.

Roger took a sip of whiskey, then another deep breath, then another sip. He felt his mouth straining to speak. Then he sniffed and closed his eyes and tried again.

"I was at a bar," he finally said. "Down on Bethune Street."

He felt like he was falling from a great height and there was nothing he could do to save himself and no reason even to try.

"Go on," Cap said, with an encouraging smile.

"It wasn't an ordinary bar—technically, it's not even a legal one."

"I think I understand."

"It was—a queer bar."

"Okay."

"And it wasn't the first time I'd been there."

Roger's hands were shaking so much he had to put down his glass. But once he'd said the words aloud, he was surprised that telling the truth turned out to be easier than lying. He went on to describe the confusion in the bar when the police arrived and his failed attempt to escape, though he left out the fact that he'd been

192

with a handsome nineteen-year-old, now dead of suicide. He recalled the fat, wheezing officer who followed him to the rooftop and then brought him back down, though he didn't explain why he'd been unable to elude such an unfit man and jump to the building next door. He mentioned the police van, the jail cell, and the keen-eyed guard who'd taken him there, but he said nothing about the other men with him. Finally, he told Cap as much as he could remember of the strange interview with the two detectives, then explained how the older one had escorted him to an alley, warned him about his "reputation," and let him go.

Through it all, Cap didn't betray the slightest symptom of unease. When Roger mentioned Caesar's by name, he only asked for the address, as if it were a place of business like any other. And when he recounted the humiliating interview questions about younger men working under him at the bank and his opinion of Corinne's beauty, Cap only listened and took notes as if he were deposing a witness in an ordinary corporate contract dispute.

"They didn't ask you anything about being at the bar? When you arrived? Whom you spoke to? Whether you'd been there before?"

"They didn't seem to care," Roger said.

Then Cap asked for a physical description of his interviewers, and Roger mentioned the broad shoulders, bulbous nose, and bald head of the one, and the wiry, athletic frame, olive skin, and dark hair of the other. Every detail seemed important enough to clarify and double-check.

When they finished, Cap skimmed his notes for a while, page after page, then looked up. "Did you see anyone you knew that night?" he asked.

Roger had so far avoided mentioning Julian Prince, largely out of a sense that their connection might appear unseemly. But it was Prince, after all, who'd persuaded him to seek Cap's help and who'd be eagerly waiting to hear how the meeting had gone.

"There was someone. We were in the same cell at the station, though I didn't see him at the bar. In fact, I told him about you. He's in rather the same predicament."

"Same interview, same alley, same note?"

"Except he was approached first, and I don't think he got a note."

"So you're here on your friend's behalf, as well?"

Cap was probably not used to being retained by two men jointly, but the word "friend" somehow rankled.

"He came to me first. And then, well, I went to him."

Cap drummed his pencil on the legal pad for a moment before speaking again. "What about the others in the cell with you?" he eventually asked.

"I'd never seen them before in my life," Roger said.

He knew he couldn't mention Andy and keep his composure.

"Do you know if any of them were also released?"

"Well, no one else surprised me at my office, if that's what you mean," Roger said, instantly regretting the sarcasm.

"Have you checked the papers?" Cap asked, unfazed.

Roger shook his head. Since seeing Andy's picture in one, he hadn't had the courage to look at another.

"Don't worry. I'll do that. But did you see anyone else that night?" Cap asked. "Anyone else who stands out in your mind?"

Roger had tried so hard to forget the details that he was surprised he'd been able to recall so many of them. But when it seemed he'd said all there was to say, he suddenly remembered someone else.

"There was a man in the main room of the bar," he said, summoning the image in his mind. "He looked a few years older than me, about the same height and build. He wore a black coat, which looked a lot like one I happen to own myself, and a bright red scarf. Some sort of tartan plaid, I think. At first, I wondered why he hadn't been lined up against the wall with the rest of us. But then I saw he had the look of someone in charge."

"And did you see him later that night?"

"Maybe at the station. I don't know. I was rather in shock at the time."

Roger expected Cap to tell him that such vagueness wasn't going to cut it, that if they were to succeed, they needed to be sure of everything. But he only returned to reading his notes, wrote down a few more, then set down his pencil and looked at Roger.

"Do you want my advice?"

"It's only the reason I'm here."

"Ignore the threat. It's as likely to be empty as not. After all, we're dealing with professional liars here. It's what blackmailers do, Roger. All of them, all the time."

Roger slapped the arm of his chair in frustration. After so many mortifying questions and answers, he'd expected something more than passive resignation.

But Cap stayed cool and nodded patiently. "It's usually bad business to give money to an extortionist," he said. "You could expect to pay more than once, possibly for a long time to come. And even that wouldn't protect you."

"You said the threat might be empty."

"It might be. It's always safer to collect from men who are eager to pay than to send actual telegrams."

"And if that's not a chance I'm willing to take?"

"Then you'll need to hire me. My retainer is about the same as what the blackmailer wants, but I'll keep your secrets and only ask for the money once."

Roger couldn't decide whether it was his best move or the only one he had left. But when he saw that Cap hadn't touched his whiskey, even though Roger had swiftly drained his own, he decided to trust him and wrote a check.

Before they shook hands and Cap showed him out, they agreed that Roger and Julian Prince would each give the blackmailer some fraction of the amount demanded—perhaps a few hundred dollars—and promise to pay the rest in a week, which would buy them some time. They'd observe every aspect of his manner and appearance during their second meetings, especially anything that had changed since their first, and ask any questions that might elicit telling answers. Meanwhile, Cap would do some investigating himself and they'd meet again on Friday evening. Each step reassured Roger a little more. There was nothing he liked better than a plan.

"And don't forget to bring your friend," Cap said, his toothy smile suddenly brightening up the room as if he'd turned on a lamp.

It was more truth than Roger had ever shared in a single sitting, but he felt oddly revived by the unburdening and even felt a small flicker of hope. Yet it seemed to burn in two different and almost opposite directions. He hoped, of course, that Cap would come through for him, that the blackmailer would be dealt with by whatever means necessary, and that no one would ever find out about Caesar's or Roger's night in jail. But there was no denying that he also felt a certain eagerness to report everything that had just transpired, to confer on how to proceed, and to share his newfound optimism with the only person in the world he knew who could appreciate it. That is, he hoped Julian Prince was indeed his friend.

17

As he filed into Wollman Auditorium late on Wednesday afternoon, Julian knew he didn't want to be there. The lecture, to be given by a famous James Joyce biographer, concerned the Calypso episode in *Ulysses*. It would surely be marked by careful research and dazzling insights. The audience would smile and nod at every rarefied allusion and at the end there'd be rapturous applause. But when Julian sat down in the stuffy, cavernous room, he felt a headache coming on. Earlier that day in Lit Hum, he'd slogged through the second half of the *Confessions* in a discussion whose only highlight was Carter quoting from memory several lines out of Book XIII and then confessing privately after class that he was converting to Catholicism and celibacy. In Shakespeare, Julian practically force-marched his students through the fifth act of *Midsummer,* but his lecture eventually devolved into a series of vague abstractions and vacant pauses. With still no word from Gus and only tenuous faith in Roger, he had too much on his mind to think about teaching, let alone *Ulysses.* But because the lecturer was a prizewinner and Julian's presence as a junior faculty member was expected, he settled in for a tedious hour.

After an obsequious introduction by the English department chair, the speaker took the stage, made an over-appreciated joke about Leopold Bloom's fondness for organ meat, and then held forth on the pleasures and privations of Trieste in the early years of the century. Julian tried to follow as best he could, but his mind soon began to wander. He thought about Gus's strong preference for walking in the city over taking the subway, even in bad weather, and the time he showed up at the squash courts soaked through. He marveled at how often and without embarrassment Gus asked him about unfamiliar words, especially philosophical ones, like *epistemology* or *nominalism*. Julian remembered the long afternoon they'd spent at home, lolling on the sofa, drinking Earl Grey tea, and enjoying a letter from Manitowoc, which inquired after Gus's health before prophesying the damnation of his soul. They each took turns reading it, giving alternate lines a tragic air in the style of Laughton or Olivier, until Gus seemed to lose interest. When Julian realized it wasn't such a nice a game after all, he put the letter down and kissed him.

It was their first weekend together, the kind Bloom might have envied. On Saturday, they'd gone down to Gus's studio, where amid pot smoke and art chatter Julian read Orwell's essay on Tolstoy and Shakespeare, while Gus daubed and scraped at his canvas—the big, wild, earthy one he'd promised to Julian. Later that night, Julian cooked beef stroganoff, while they drank glasses of Russian vodka, which turned out to be a pairing more congenial in theory than in practice. As they ate, Julian began staring at Gus's soft, pink mouth, the reddish whiskers on his chin, and his smooth white throat, until the idea of dinner suddenly seemed like a pointless encumbrance. When Gus dropped his fork and reached across the table, Julian stood, took him by the hand and pulled him to the sofa, where Gus picked loose the buttons of Julian's shirt, and Julian seized the tails of Gus's and lifted it right over his head. Then they fell into each other's arms, and Gus's weight pressed down on Julian in a heavy, sweat-scented crush. *Your milky stream pale strippings of my life!*

But it was only the next day, in the soberness of a Sunday afternoon, that such a heaven of happiness felt real enough to linger and not slip away like a forgotten dream. Gus sprawled on Julian's Danish shag rug reading the *Times*, while Julian lay in the Aalto chaise, tracing out stories from the front page. Kennedy was confident, Sukarno was agreeable, Glenn was ready. When Julian looked up and saw that Gus had wiped his inky fingers on his cheek, he almost said something but then decided against it. Artists were often smudged up and the silence mattered more. So he went back to the killings in Algeria with a blithe spirit.

"Do you want some tea?" he asked, a few minutes later.

"Nope," Gus said, sweetly.

When Julian noticed a skinny, mottled pigeon shimmy across the window ledge and leap to the fire escape without using its wings, the impressive little feat seemed to mark the moment and call for its appreciation. After all, there was a very fine man lying on his very fine rug on a very fine winter's day. Above them, Buffet's *Tête de clown* seemed to envy so much contentment, and the eye clock, not far away, bore witness to all of it. The air itself seemed to be filled with prosperity.

"What's *uxorious* mean?" Gus asked without looking up.

"What are you reading?"

"Review of a new play. Looks awful."

Gus could rarely afford a ticket to a show or a concert, but Julian thought it wonderfully disinterested that he stayed abreast of the latest cultural news.

"Excessively fond of one's wife," he said.

"Sure," Gus said.

Maybe they'd see *The Aspern Papers* or *A Passage to India*, which Julian had heard good things about, or better yet something Off Broadway, something clever and original. He'd ask Hugh about it and surprise Gus with tickets for next weekend.

"I'm going to make some tea," Julian said, feeling much too generous to lie around reading the newspaper.

So he made the Earl Grey and poured a second cup for Gus, who took it graciously and joined him on the sofa. Which was when he pulled the letter from his back pocket and they took turns reading in grave English stage accents, laughing at so much blinkered bigotry and how far they'd each traveled from their provincial pasts. The eye clock read 2:22 when they stopped reading and Julian kissed Gus softly on the lips.

A roar of laughter jolted his thoughts back to the auditorium. The speaker was saying something about Joyce's letters to Nora Barnacle being more "thoroughly real" than their famously amorous marriage, and Julian knew at once he had to leave. His casual daydreaming was the luxury of old lovers, not new ones. So he snatched up his coat and stepped on the feet of several unhappy people to reach the aisle, where he caught Sterne and Harcourt observing him closely a few seats away. He ignored their supercilious looks as he raced out of the auditorium. It was only when he passed through the campus gates that he realized his headache had disappeared.

◎ ◎ ◎

The doorman at Loosli's building eagerly informed Julian that he'd been expected, and as he shook out his umbrella and took the elevator up to the penthouse, he prepared himself to meet a very light and venal man. If Loosli had left town on Saturday, as the doorman had claimed, it was possible—though still unthinkable—that Gus had come back to his apartment after he'd been released from jail and Loosli had hurried him out of the city to take advantage of his present vulnerability. If so, and Loosli had now returned, then it was likely that he'd brought Gus with him, that he'd moved back into the maid's room on a permanent basis, and that he might even answer the door himself.

But it was Loosli, battle-ready in rouge, eyeliner, and double-breasted silk, who greeted Julian.

"Professor Prince," he said in a breathy Germanic accent. "I am so happy that we finally meet. August has told me so much about you."

He was stout and rather short, vaguely ten years on either side of sixty, with a perfectly round, shiny face that seemed made to utter platitudes. His living room looked like the set of an old Hollywood romantic comedy—many shades of pink, vast in its dimensions, and organized chiefly around the serving of liquor. The Italian and Flemish masterworks that hung on the walls and were ostensibly the focus of Loosli's business seemed entirely beside the point.

"You must be thirsty," he said. "You prefer a dry martini, I believe."

"I won't be staying," Julian said.

"But you must allow me the pleasure."

Julian felt a strong desire to get to the point as quickly as possible and wanted nothing to do with such a sad old queen's idea of pleasure. "I've only come to ask about Gus," he said. "Have you seen him recently?"

"No," Loosli said, frowning. "I have not seen him since last week. But I must confess that I cannot put him out of my mind. Perhaps we are the same in that regard."

Julian wasn't sure if the suggestion of their similarity was a kind of bitchiness or a sign of authentic sympathy. The man was as fey as a bouquet of violets, but he also seemed to possess a kind of fairy-like big-heartedness that reminded one of Liberace or Auntie Mame. It might well have been a guise calculated to seduce young and penniless artists, but it also might have been the simple truth.

"I'm sure he'll turn up sooner or later," Julian said, anxious that he had come to yet another dead end.

"If you give me your telephone number, I will call you the moment I see him."

He said it with such apparent sincerity that Julian wondered how he could possibly have expected such a thing.

"Ah, but let me find a pen and some paper," Loosli said, before shuffling off to an adjoining room.

He attended with such precision to every detail of the stereotype, Julian thought. The suit, the makeup, the excessive cologne, the limp handshake. The suit reminded one of his wealth, the makeup of his vanity, the cologne of his lust, and the handshake of his inability ever to satisfy it. And yet he wore them all as proudly as any general ever wore his medals.

"I believe I know what you are thinking," he said, after returning with a gold fountain pen and a black patent-leather notebook. "I was once young, too, let me assure you, and just as dubious of rich old men. But I really do expect him to return."

As Julian wrote down his telephone number, he decided not to apologize.

"Of course, if you really believed it to be impossible, you would not have come," Loosli added. "But as you see, my apartment is large and comfortable, and as you know, August is a talented artist who has not yet arrived at his success."

It all sounded either very liberal or very calculating—either like nineteenth-century patronage or a twentieth-century exploitation. Again, Julian wasn't sure. But as he shook Loosli's supple, forgiving hand and watched the elevator close on his round, smiling face, a strong sense of being glad to get away led him to a particularly annoying realization. Men like Loosli didn't make life harder for men like Julian, as some of his friends had complained; they made it easier. To the unknowing world, they made being gay a simple matter of appearances. And because they did, they offered indemnity to those more covert types who kept their pleasures and secrets to themselves. Julian knew one day he'd be old, too, just as unmarried, and perhaps just as susceptible to scorn. If he didn't have Gus or someone like him, he might also be angling for the attentions of men half his age—and without the money and a fancy apartment to distract from his wrinkles.

As he went back out onto Fifth Avenue, pitched his umbrella, and waited for a taxi, he wondered how many years it had taken for Loosli's philanthropy to devolve into self-indulgence. But then he wondered how many years it might take him if he were in the sad old queen's shoes.

❋ ❋ ❋

There were still more circles of Dante's hell to revisit and a quiz on *Much Ado* to devise. So Julian headed back to campus to collect his Penguin *Inferno* and his *Kittredge*, as well as the cardboard box that contained his book manuscript, in case the weekend somehow left him with enough focus and energy to revise. But as the taxi sped across the park, he began imagining a catalog of potential catastrophes. Maybe Gus had died of a brain hemorrhage, or been murdered by a junkie in the Tombs, or run off to Long Island to be with some wealthy industrialist, or gone back to Wisconsin to be born again. Julian didn't know which he feared most.

He considered yet again whether he shouldn't simply go to the police. On Monday, he'd promised himself that if he hadn't heard from Gus by Wednesday, he'd make an anonymous call to the Charles Street station. But now it was Wednesday, and he knew he'd put it off for at least one more day. Gazing out the window at the spiky treetops and darkening sky, he couldn't help but believe that Gus might be waiting for him when he arrived at Philosophy Hall or that he'd be there in front of his apartment building, loitering on the sidewalk with his suitcase and a good story, asking Julian to be his valentine. He'd been anticipating Gus's sudden appearance ever since Friday morning as he waited at the Waverly. Since Monday, he'd been silently talking to him everywhere he went, telling him where he'd looked for him, asking him where he should look next, never quite hoping for answers but somehow comforted by the feeling of closeness it brought him. He even thought he'd seen him on College Walk, on the IRT, and again at the automat on Broadway, only to discover that it was someone with a similar head of ash-blond hair or loping gait but not the man himself.

So when Julian passed Rodin's rain-soaked *Thinker*, climbed the stairs of Philosophy Hall, and found someone waiting in front of his office door, for just a moment his heart thought it might finally be Gus, even though his mind knew it wasn't.

"I hope I'm not being a bother," Roger said.

It took a moment for Julian to recover, so he spent it fumbling for his keys. They'd agreed on a phone call to his office, not a visit. In fact, they'd been quite specific about it. Roger wouldn't leave a message but would wait until Julian answered himself.

"It's fine," Julian said, knowing that Millie and the other staff had already left for the day and Harcourt and Sterne would be at the reception for the visiting speaker. But he wondered why Roger would wait in a nearly empty building without any real prospect of finding him there. The only plausible explanation was that he'd felt some need to give the news of his meeting in person, and Julian hoped this meant the news was good.

"Have we hired ourselves an investigator?" he asked, after offering Roger a seat in the library chair.

Then Roger smiled, leaned forward, and told Julian all about the interview with Caspar Donovan. He was deliberate and precise, as if presenting a quarterly report to the board of directors at his bank.

"You trust him then?" Julian asked.

"I told him everything," Roger said, "and he didn't bat an eye."

He seemed to want credit for his candor. So Julian nodded solemnly, and this seemed to satisfy him.

"He asked whether we saw anyone we knew at the bar or in the police station," Roger said. "Anyone else who'd been released without being arrested. I didn't tell him about, well, the fellow you were with. But he'll want to know."

Julian hoped Roger wouldn't press the issue. It wasn't that he was averse to discussing his relationship with Gus. In fact, he wished he could simply refer to him as his boyfriend. Since he was just one homosexual talking privately to another, there was no reason he shouldn't be forthright. Except that Gus was still missing, Julian didn't know if he still *was* his boyfriend, and it would have been too hard to explain it all.

"By the way, is he all right? Your friend?" Roger asked.

"It was just a mild concussion," Julian said, hoping Gus's own diagnosis had been correct.

"He was arrested? You didn't mention that anyone had asked him for money."

"No, he was arrested."

"I suppose he paid a fine or something?"

He probably had, but Julian didn't know. He didn't know if Gus had been taken to the Tombs, what he'd been charged with, when he'd been released, or where he was now. He didn't know anything.

"There was a list of names in Sunday's *Mirror*," Julian said. "I have a copy."

"Oh, there was something else," Roger said quickly, as if the newspaper were the last thing he wanted to see. "Cap was quite interested in the fair-haired detective in civvies, the head man. Do you remember him?"

"All too well," Julian said.

How elegant he'd first seemed in his black woolen topcoat and red plaid scarf. The way he so casually snuffed out his cigarette in the half-empty glass on the bar. Though the glass was only half-empty because he'd forced whoever had paid for it to run for his life. And Julian could never forgive the way he'd watched Gus take a blow to the head and fall to the floor and then walked away as if someone had merely swatted a fly.

When Roger had reported all there was to report and then rehearsed the plan they'd hatched, he wrote Cap's address on the back of one of his business cards and placed it on the desk. But then he didn't rise to leave as expected. Instead, he looked around Julian's office, noticing books and framed diplomas, a few modern prints, the photograph of Schanche.

"Do you like your job?" Roger asked.

It might have been only a friendly attempt at chat to make up for his hasty exit at the Men's Bar. But Julian sensed there was more to it. "I'm hoping to keep it," he said.

"As a place to work, a college must be quite different from a bank," Roger said. "More broad-minded, I'd imagine. Collars not so tight."

Now it was clear. Roger wanted to know if Julian was forced to maintain a façade as an eligible bachelor or if somehow there was no need for any façade at all.

"You'd be surprised," he said. "Keepers of the tradition can be very traditional."

Roger looked down at the floor. He seemed to regret broaching the topic.

"What about the fee?" Julian asked. "How much will this man cost us?"

"Don't worry about that," Roger said easily, as if soothed by the solidity of financial matters. "Anyway, you told me you don't have any money."

"That's true, but I'd like to pay you back my share."

"Very well, but to be honest, I'm glad not to be doing this alone."

It was the first time he'd admitted anything the least bit personal. Julian appreciated his effort to make this meeting, however unplanned, more pleasant than the first two had been, and he found he disliked Roger somewhat less than before.

"Several of my colleagues in the English department are also members of our club," he said. "But everyone's very discreet."

"I didn't mean to pry," Roger said, blushing. "It's really none of my business."

It wasn't strictly speaking Roger's business, but Julian understood why he wanted to know. How men like them got along in the world was crucial information to have, but such trade secrets could be hard to come by without a little help.

As Julian wrote on a scrap of paper and pushed it toward Roger, he realized it was the second time that evening he'd given his telephone number to another homosexual. He hoped the kindness might inspire the Fates to bring about Gus's safe return. But even if it didn't, feeling sorry for Roger left Julian feeling a little less sorry for himself.

"Most evenings it's easier to reach me at home," he said.

18

It took three days of watching and waiting, but the moment Danny saw it, he knew it was what he'd been looking for. If he hadn't been so absorbed in all the bits and pieces of Harold Blunt's daily life, he might have missed it. But after so many hours of fixating on a single idea, he sometimes felt like a swami in a trance, thinking of nothing and everything at the same time. And when it finally happened, it was as obvious as a sudden change in the weather or a stink in the breeze.

Except for the fact that the Nazi Cop worked all night and slept all morning, anyone could have taken him for a normal guy. When he kissed Mrs. Blunt's cheek as she left for the beauty salon or her part-time job at a gift shop on Myrtle Avenue, he seemed proud of her slender, petite figure and the spun-gold bouffant that nearly doubled her size. Since they didn't have kids—not even one with polio or a lisp—he spent most of his free time puttering from room to room or going to the corner store for cigarettes. One afternoon, he went to a barbershop to talk to a guy who was probably his bookie and then to the VFW to sit for an hour playing pinochle with an old man who might have been his father. He drank every night before work at the Admiral's Tavern, which a dozen or so barflies made their home-away-from-home and where they called him Harry.

But as soon as he got to the Charles Street station, Harry Blunt showed his true colors, and like Clark Kent, the metamorphosis needed only a change of clothes. It was part of his job to come outside and help when the happy wagon showed up with more prisoners than the driver and his partner could handle, as he'd done on the night of the raid. On Monday, Danny watched as they brought in three Negro workingmen still in their coveralls, and Harry Blunt was there to punish their cool composure with rough handling. An hour later, there was a sorry crew of vagrants who didn't seem to pose a threat to anyone, but Harry Blunt treated them like bomb-throwing anarchists anyway. Then, on Tuesday, Danny watched from Washington Street as he helped drag out five greasers in dungarees, peaked caps, and leather jackets. In the Bronx, there were Bachelors and Rockets and Dragons, but these were downtown boys, tough and mean, a lot uglier than Sharks and Jets and not nearly so clean or well fed.

One of them, probably the leader, looked up at the full moon hanging ripe and heavy over the Village and began howling like a wolf.

"Oh, for the love of Christ!" the first cop cried, shaking his head in disgust.

"That's enough," the second cop said, apparently less surprised.

But it was Harry Blunt who gave the howler a poke in the chest with his baton, which must have been pretty sharp, because he stopped howling right away. Then a scrappy kid about Danny's size let loose a wail so loud and awful it made Lon Cheney's Wolf Man sound like Petey from the Little Rascals. Soon the others, including the leader, were joining in the choir. For Harry Blunt, it must have sounded like the call of duty because without any warning he socked the little greaser in the face, sending him straight to the ground. Danny nearly choked when he saw it. It was almost like getting punched a second time, and he began to feel the same seven-iron, hurricane rage he'd felt the day before in front of the detached house on Palmetto Street. But he quickly stepped on his feelings, forced himself to concentrate, and crept toward the station to get a better look at the fracas.

One of the greasers, a hulking oaf, suddenly bulldozed Harry Blunt and knocked him over, and while the two other cops tried to grab him, the scrappy kid made a break for it, running west toward Washington Street. For a second, the three cops seemed torn between bringing him back and putting down the skirmish, though after they brandished their batons and made the other greasers lie belly-down on the sidewalk, Harry Blunt and the first cop took off after the runaway. The kid was fast, even in handcuffs, and he blew right past Danny with a wicked gleam in his eye. The first cop was fast too, and as he ran by, Danny hummed "The Man That Got Away," just loud enough to be heard. But Harry Blunt hadn't gotten nearly so far. In fact, he soon slowed to a jog, then to a walk. It was an odd one, kind of careful and tender, like every step was a bare foot on broken glass. Danny was about to turn into the doorway of a mechanic's garage to avoid being spotted when Harry Blunt stopped and turned around.

Watching him go back to the station was like looking at a "What's Wrong with This Picture" cartoon and knowing something was off and then suddenly seeing it. The way he stooped over a little and stuck his ass out and held his hands like claws. He obviously had bad knees, just like Uncle Steven, who walked the same way whenever he overdid it and said he'd still be the best hurler in the Bronx if he hadn't had to give up running. Insides and outsides, Danny thought again. Despite Harry Blunt's chesty, arm-swinging stride and punch-happy fists, he was a secret invalid. With his dark eyes and hateful sneer, he could be terrifying on the surface, but his bones were rotting with arthritis.

❂ ❂ ❂

Fuck Max Sloan.

The bootstrap story of working his way to the top from nothing might have been basically true, but it left out a few things. Sloan was smart and had grit, Danny thought, but only an asshole would fire you just for being yourself. And he wasn't all that open-minded either. Sure, he sold papayas to Puerto Ricans and Swiss chard to Negroes, but he wouldn't hire any of them to work in his stores.

Ducking out of the rain, Danny pushed past the big red letters and through the front door and stalked in the direction of Di Stefano's office. Two checkout girls stopped ringing up customers and sucked their teeth at him, while Blav, weighing a pile of ground round, gave him the evil eye. But Danny just shook his head at them, remembering what Roy Lee had said about turning shame back on whoever wanted him to feel it and hoping that it actually worked.

"Hey-ho, Danny Boy!" Roddy cried from a few aisles away.

He was pushing a dolly full of lettuce boxes and seemed genuinely happy to see him, even if no one else was. Danny wanted to wave back, but he was fuming and proud and needed to stay that way, so he only winked at Roddy and then marched on through the double doors and past Miss Crudup's desk, until a half minute later he was standing in front of Di Stefano himself.

"I'm surprised to see you here," the old man said.

"It's payday," Danny said. "I'm here to collect a week and a half's wages."

Mr. Di Stefano glowered at him. It was a show of emotion Danny had never seen from him before. Probably few of his employees had ever failed to call him "sir."

"We agreed you'd stay on for two weeks," he said. "You left me in the lurch."

"But you didn't give me a choice," Danny said. "I'm not a masochist."

"Well, whatever you are, you were expected Sunday morning and chose not to come."

"You fired me for no good reason," Danny said. "That was your choice."

The excuse that it had been in the papers was a crock. It only meant that Mr. Sloan and Mr. Meyer would probably find out and maybe some customers would too. It might have been bad for business, but then again it might not have been. Danny's customers liked him and probably wouldn't have made much of a bother. Just like with their hairdressers and florists, they'd eventually decide it was easier not to think too much about how he spent his free time. Good fruit was good fruit, even if one was selling it to you.

"It was a business decision," the old man said with a shrug.

"Now we both know that's not true," Danny said, thinking they were some of the most grown-up words he'd ever spoken.

He left the store five minutes later with a hot wad of cash in his pocket and cold pity for those who'd treated him so unfairly. But telling off his boss had also left him feeling even more separate from other people and their lives than he had before, like he was moving invisibly around them or existing in some other dimension. It was a feeling that had been coming on ever since his night at Bacchus and quietly snuck up on him as he haunted Harry Blunt's life day and night, but it had just become undeniable. Now that he was free of his job, his family, and his past, he felt kind of like a ghost.

◎ ◎ ◎

The men's room in the Times Square subway station smelled of mildew, bleach, and damp plaster, along with all the usual toilet smells. The lamps were dimmed with soot and flyspecks. God-knows-what was smeared on the white tile walls and a half-inch of piss-water lagooned in one corner. As you entered, there was a row of urinals to the right, old and cracked like dinosaur fossils. On the left was a big graffiti-scratched mirror, three leaky basins, and five rundown stalls. And in the fifth stall, Danny sat on the toilet seat, listening for footsteps, and grinding his teeth on the last of the cocaine.

There'd been a casual plan, made in their escape from the Excelsior, to go out with Gabriel to the Rumpus on West 4th that night. But Danny hadn't seen him since then and no one at his parents' house in Riverdale was answering the phone. Danny could have spent the evening with Raf, but he wanted to avoid the third degree and having to tell another lie. He also could have called Cormac O'Connor from the neighborhood or Jerry Franklin, who lived in the East Village and played the bass in a jazz band. But Danny didn't feel like music or parties or pussyfooting for hours to decide on Mr. Right-for-the-night. Physically, he still wasn't ready for that sort of thing anyway. And what he really wanted was a lot filthier and more one-sided.

Gabriel loved tearooms, though none of their other friends did. Raf once said he'd rather have sex with an old woman on a pallet than a young man in a toilet. Danny had always thought them pretty awful places to do such a nice thing. According to Gabriel, some of the men who went there were soldiers and sailors who wanted a cheap thrill without risking their reps. But most were old-timers, in their fifties or worse, usually married, the kind who'd never go to a gay bar or a party like Bacchus. There was no talking or exchanging of names, no kissing or gentleness. The sex was fast and physical and dangerous, too, since anyone could walk in at any time. The cute cat wagging his pecker at you might be a plainclothes cop. There could even be one peeking through the ventilation grill behind the urinal and another waiting outside to take you into custody. And a conviction meant as much as a month in Riker's. Again, this according to Gabriel.

"Oh, go cross yourself, Tia Maria," he'd once said to Raf, who'd sniffed at his slutty habits. "It's the only reason I feel good about paying taxes."

"When have you ever paid taxes?" Raf said.

That night, Danny found that he, too, was drawn to the danger. But being there also felt like a protest against all the people in the world who hated filth and pleasure, done in the name of those who didn't mind the one and couldn't get enough of the other. When he first got there, just after six o'clock, the place was packed with commuters, even though it was Valentine's Day. Every urinal was taken and sex filled the air like a spilt secret. Men were fiddling with themselves or glancing up and down at their neighbors. Some even helped each other out with a tug or a tickle. And there was nobody to stop them or say they were wrong. If some stuffed suit came in to relieve himself and didn't like what he saw, he'd have to close his eyes or find somewhere else to go. For a while, the men's room had been commandeered by queers. No holds barred. No prudes allowed.

But there was something else turning Danny on that was harder to understand. When he was very young, just old enough to use a urinal by himself without one of his older brothers standing by, he liked to look at the grown-up men on either side of him—their penises so wrinkled and dark, so big and marvelous. It wasn't until Ciaran caught him one time, yanked him away by his shirt collar and told him not to be such a dirty bird that he realized it was supposedly sinful. Since men rarely noticed what little kids did, he'd kept it up for a few more years without consequences. But now, as he sat in the stall listening to the sounds of people coming and going, the door slightly ajar, waiting for someone to peep inside, he didn't only want to be bad, he wanted to *feel* bad, too. Not sweet or friendly or nice, but rough and foul. It didn't matter if he was ugly or good-looking, fat or fit, old or young. Danny knew he'd invite the first man who showed interest. He just wanted to be a dirty bird and suck a stranger's dick.

One of the other toilets flushed. A door creaked. Then the sound of footsteps and the shadow of someone inspecting the stalls, standing in front of each one for few seconds before moving on. It was a hard game of chance. The next guy who looked in might be a cop or a thief or a psychopath. He might have a social disease or a bad temper. But that night, Danny just didn't care.

Someone eventually appeared in the crack of the door. He had a Roman nose, a broad jaw, and the surly expression of a beat cop. He might have been Harry Blunt's homelier Italian cousin. But he would've had to be a damned good actor to fake the stiffy in his slacks and the ready-made look of regret in his eyes. When Danny nodded, he came into the stall and locked the door behind him. Then he just stood there staring, his hands scratching at his sides like he didn't know what to do next. So Danny unbuckled his belt, unzipped his fly, pulled down his briefs, and watched their contents spring out like a diving board. It was veiny and crooked and jutted from a scraggly patch of thick black hair. Looking straight at it reminded him of Roy Lee kissing his bruises, and he wondered if there was anything righteous in what he was doing, but then he decided it didn't matter. When he pulled the man's cock toward him, he caught a sharp whiff of funk, and when he took it in his mouth, a smack of saltiness nearly made him gag. But as he relaxed his throat and let the man pump away, he soon began to feel just what he knew he needed to feel—dirty and invincible at the same time.

19

When Roger came into the kitchen on Thursday evening and Henry and Lizzie looked up fretfully, he knew something was amiss. Corinne turned away from the oven, wiped her forehead with her apron, and made a short, muffled groan. Schuyler and Marjorie were coming for dinner in celebration of Schuyler's thirty-ninth birthday, and she'd been attempting boeuf bourguignon for the first time. It took a good part of the afternoon to make the stock, fry the lardons, and sear the beef, she admitted with an unfamiliar whine of regret in her voice. But two hours after putting the dish inside a hot oven, she peeked in to check its progress and found the oven barely tepid and the meat still purple and raw in the middle. There'd been some kind of electrical short. She'd tried to fix it herself but to no avail. It was too late to call a repairman or use the stovetop, and just as Roger appeared, she realized she'd have to serve something else.

It was the kind of problem he didn't mind having. There was no significant loss, it wasn't in any way his fault, and there was nothing for him to do about it. Corinne would rally, of course, discover something suitable in the icebox and turn it into a tasty meal and an amusing story. But it gave him a certain pleasure to bear the annoyance with calm. Too often, he overreacted to trifles—like mislaid keys or fuzzy television reception—and offered a poor example for Henry and Lizzie. So the malfunctioning Magic Chef seemed like an excellent opportunity to make up for past mistakes and show himself the mild and patient man he longed to be.

"I'm sorry, Rin," he said, as she pulled the wine-soaked meat from the oven and surveyed her wasted efforts. "I really should've replaced that old machine years ago."

But when she narrowed her eyes at him, it was clear she thought his sense of culpability grossly misplaced. After all, there were far more important things in their lives that needed fixing.

They hadn't spoken once about their argument at the station on Wednesday morning. On the journey home, she offered only indifferent thanks when he gave her a box of expensive Belgian chocolates. And they were both nearly mute throughout the evening, as she finished Salinger and moved on to Peterson's *Art of Living*, while he limped through another Graham Greene. The next morning, as she drove him to the station again, she seemed as relieved as he was that she'd be too busy cooking to pick him up that night and he'd have to take a cab.

Sensing new trouble, Lizzie looked at Henry to learn what else had gone awry.

"Are we stuh-stuh-still huh-having cuh-cuh-cuh-company?" he asked, thrashing his way across a field of treacherous consonants.

"I'm gonna be hungry soon," Lizzie added.

There was, in fact, every cause to be sanguine, Roger thought. It had been a week since the terrible night, and the small dinner party seemed like a bookend, if not an actual end, to his troubles. Schuyler and Marjorie were old friends, Corinne was a talented hostess who never dwelled on her disappointments, and their gathering together was a good sign that life had almost returned to normal.

When the doorbell rang a half hour later and Henry raced to answer it, Roger felt a kind of giddy expectation that he recognized as pride. He wanted Schuyler to bear witness to the abundant riches of his family life. Corinne was as fine a woman as Marjorie and a good deal more attractive. Henry was brighter than anyone in his class. Their home reflected all they were and believed. Schuyler had seen it hundreds of times, of course, but Roger wanted him to understand that nothing had changed. So he was especially pleased to watch Henry open the front door, reach for his friend's hand, and shake it the way he'd been taught. They'd practiced it many times, and if

Henry usually only went through the motions, Roger saw that he could do it correctly when he wanted to.

"Hank, my good man," Schuyler said. "How's tricks?"

Henry beamed and nodded without speaking. Schuyler was the only person who ever addressed him that way, and Roger liked that he did as much as Henry seemed to, hoping it presaged a solid avuncular bond for the future.

"Well, aren't you the little gentleman!" Marjorie cried, not quite letting go of her husband's arm as he reached out to pat Henry's shoulder.

When Henry only sighed, Roger worried that instead of accepting the compliment, he felt ridiculed. For trying too hard, for trying to be something he wasn't, for being little. These were worries Roger remembered well enough from his own childhood, and he hated that he'd passed them on to his son like a congenital disease. When Schuyler tousled Henry's hair, he recovered a partial smile. But Roger was still irked by Marjorie's needless condescension. She wore an ankle-length mink coat and just enough gold in her ears and on her fingers to remind her friends that Schuyler ran a very successful bank. She had life on easy terms and ought not be teasing sensitive little boys.

"Roger, you old son of a gun!" Schuyler cried.

He came forward with his hands aloft and enfolded Roger in another great bear hug, as if they hadn't just seen each other less than a week before.

"Happy birthday, Sky," Roger said, returning the embrace with equal force, refusing to resist as he'd always done in the past.

It was a rare and delicious pleasure to press up against a large, fit, cashmere-clad man, to feel the warmth of his body, to smell the subtle musk of his skin and the sharp sweetness of his tobacco-scented breath. When Schuyler gave him one last squeeze and made a hearty growl, Roger squeezed and growled right back.

"My goodness!" Marjorie cried. "One might think you were a pair of loving cavemen!"

It was a new version of an old joke Marjorie trotted out whenever Schuyler's greetings of other people were more enthusiastic than she liked, which was often. But this time there was a mirthless chill in her voice that put Roger on his guard. Certainly "loving cavemen" was a calculated choice of words. It conjured not only a brute male sensuality, but an absurd impossibility—something that had never existed in the history of the world and, Roger was meant to understand, never would.

"Nonsense," Schuyler said, giving him a bonus triplet of claps on the back before letting him go. "We're brothers-in-arms, bosom companions, and the oldest of great good friends!"

"Well, that's a lot of things for two people to be," Marjorie offered, rather feebly.

"It's certainly not too many for us, dear," Schuyler said.

It was an unusually public contradiction. But Marjorie only smiled to acknowledge her defeat without agreeing with her husband in any way. Then she handed Henry her coat and offered her cheek to Roger, which he didn't quite kiss.

"So kind of you to have us," she said.

"The pleasure is all ours," he said.

"And where's your better half?"

"Still in the kitchen, I'm afraid. We've had a minor mishap. But I'll let her give you the details."

Marjorie eyed him doubtfully, as if whatever it was had been his fault, then went in search of female companionship. But Schuyler, now giving Henry his own coat and a friendly wink, seemed too ready for pleasure to be aware of any tension. And despite the failure of the oven, Marjorie's probably unintended jibe at Henry, and her rather pitiable objection to sharing her husband's affections, Roger still thought there was every reason to believe that a very merry party was in the offing.

◉ ◉ ◉

Corinne poured sidecars as Mitch Miller swung from the Curtis Mathes and the four friends gathered around a tray of cheesy canapés. Roger knew that excessive drinking was considered a telltale sign of queerness, so he'd always limited himself to two glasses, even when he was in the navy, where counting your drinks was also considered a telltale sign of queerness. But around Corinne, he liked how a little alcohol softened his reluctance and made even her most feminine traits seem like tender mercies, and in company a little buzz allowed him to play his part without any more self-scrutiny than was absolutely necessary. It seemed that Corinne, too, had decided that a bit of liquor might be a reliable safeguard against upset. Usually, she only took polite and infrequent sips from her drink or managed to forget about it altogether. But that night, she kept pace with her guests and even slighted the canapés for her cheerful cup.

"You're amazingly calm," Marjorie said. "I'm sure if my oven had failed in the eleventh hour, I'd have hit the panic button and sent out my regrets on tear-bedewed stationery!"

"Hah!" Schuyler cried. "We both know you'd never have told a soul about it."

It was irritating that Marjorie's self-deprecation was always a cue to Schuyler to pay her a compliment, especially any involving an implicit criticism of Corinne. But instead of explaining or defending, Roger laid the groundwork for a more effective kind of vindication.

"She'll have that old oven back up and running in no time," he said.

"You'd really try to fix it yourself?" Marjorie asked. "I know you're a handy girl, but you could get a shock."

"Oh, I like to do things myself," Corinne said, "but I know when to quit."

"You know, I can never get over the fact that you don't have help," Schuyler said, just as Roger knew he would.

Marjorie employed a staff of three—a cook, a maid, and a full-time gardener and handyman—to keep up appearances at the old manse. Whereas Roger and Corinne only had a widow from the neighborhood who stayed with the children for a couple of hours on weekday evenings while Corinne ran errands and fetched Roger at the station.

"Without ours, we'd be sunk!" Schuyler said.

"Well, that's not quite true, now, is it?" his wife protested. "And they do require quite a lot of supervision, I can tell you." She lowered her voice as she spoke and cast a knowing glance at Corinne that Roger understood from experience was meant to imply that Negro employees, however honest and good-natured, weren't always so reliable.

"I only meant that you wouldn't have time for the thousand other marvelous things you do if you had to cook and clean all day long," Schuyler said.

"And you really don't mind?" Marjorie asked Corinne, peering into her eyes as if to coax the truth out of her.

"I suppose I'm just too particular to give up control," she said, with an ease that suggested her sidecar, now almost gone, had taken effect.

Roger was the particular one, they both knew, though he went along with the fiction. Before Henry was born, they'd had a Portuguese housekeeper who cracked the porcelain, scuffed the wainscoting, and left crumbs on the countertops. As did the next seven or eight women they'd hired in her place. Eventually, Corinne hinted that handing out wages and criticism wasn't to her liking. But it was Roger who finally decided they'd had enough of help and would thereafter do the work themselves, which necessarily meant that Corinne would do it. If the decision wasn't entirely fair to her, it had nevertheless brought a semblance of cleanliness and peace to their household and in Roger's mind made Corinne superior to ladies who lolled about while others did their bidding.

"Self-reliance is all well and good," Marjorie said, "but you must want a vacation from it sometimes."

Roger watched Corinne's eyes suddenly sparkle with brandied curiosity, as if a vacation were something she'd never considered before but now deeply yearned for. It was true that, despite the usual summer circuit of weddings, they hadn't had a real one since they'd gone to Miami Beach with his sister Audrey's family two years before, a trip marred by rainy weather and endless indecision.

"Women are always overworked and underappreciated," Marjorie said to Roger, relishing her petty triumph.

"That reminds me," Schuyler said before Roger could answer the charge. "What do you say to the four of us going to Italy this summer?"

Roger almost dropped his canapé in astonishment. Or perhaps the proposal was a kind of apology for the way Schuyler had so hastily dismissed the idea only days before, even if he insisted on including their wives.

"Italy?" Marjorie gasped. "Isn't that a bit far out?"

It wasn't clear if she meant that it was unconventional or at a great distance, but Roger suspected it was a bit of both. Marjorie seemed to be comfortable with neither language nor geography beyond that of southern Connecticut.

"It was Roger's notion," Schuyler said.

"What made you think of Italy?" Corinne asked Roger pointedly, as if she thought the answer might finally offer a clue to all his mysterious behavior.

But as the more recent and more zealous convert to the idea, Schuyler seemed too eager not to answer on his behalf: "When we were skiing on Sunday, the beautiful hills of Fairfield County apparently suggested the sublime peaks of Italy."

Everyone laughed, even Corinne.

"I know absolutely nothing about the place," Marjorie said. "But I do know that it rarely snows in the summer."

"Actually, I was thinking of Lake Como," Schuyler said.

"Oh, I saw just some beautiful photos in *Holiday*," Corinne said. "The stone villas ringing the lake!"

"It's like heaven on earth," Schuyler assured her, before taking Marjorie's hand. "And the water is as blue and lovely as your eyes, dear."

"But how would we get there?" she asked, tossing aside the compliment with the ease of someone sure to get another. "Would we go on an airplane?"

As Schuyler patiently completed the picture, Corinne warmed to the idea and Marjorie offered as many objections as she could think of before becoming a complete enthusiast and praising the brilliance of her husband's scheme. Roger joined in as they all spoke at length about their expectations and preferences whenever they traveled—what "we like" and what "we always insist on" and what "we're careful to avoid"—and soon the desires and aversions of each melded into a happy consensus. When Roger suggested they buy some bottles of Chianti and begin cultivating a taste for it in advance of their trip, Marjorie called it a fine idea, and to seal their agreement they even shared a mutual smile. It felt so heartening to plan the future in this way, to be dissolved into the company of friends and its spirit of adventure. The misery of the past week seemed almost as far off as last year's head cold.

Roger looked at Corinne, hoping for some sign of forgiveness, but she'd turned toward the staircase, from which Henry was poking his head and nodding feverishly. She normally invited the children to come down to say goodnight to their guests, so Roger thought their brief appearance would only heap one blessing upon another. But as they tumbled into the room, he saw that something more was in the works, and he regretted that it would put a temporary halt to their festive conspiring. Lizzie wore a bright canary-yellow tutu and matching leotard, and Henry, old, faded yellow pajamas that no longer quite fit him. It could hardly have been a coincidence, and the way Henry looked expectantly at his sister and tried to focus her attention made it clear there'd be a performance of some kind. So Roger poured out the last of the sidecars, both as a bribe for their guests' forbearance and as an analgesic against the din to come. Thankfully, Henry didn't stutter when he sang.

They all watched as the children positioned themselves, faltered for a few moments, and then began. Roger noticed the way Henry tried to hit every note clearly, even as his younger sister slurred her way through them and struggled with the tempo. "You Are My Sunshine" was a country music song that had been popular during the war, and Bing Crosby's version of it wasn't at all bad. But as the children sang on, Roger became aware of the mature, even desperate nature of the lyrics. The song wasn't at all appropriate for children. In fact, it was unsettling to watch his offspring crooning about unrequited love and fear of abandonment, of shattered dreams and lonely nights. He recoiled at the idea of Lizzie one day crying over some heart-breaking cad. But nor could he help imagining Henry, too, all grown up but still in the same skimpy yellow pajamas, bewailing the same man. It was a repulsive image, yet it wouldn't leave him as he watched his son acting out his childish notion of grown-up feelings—clutching his breast, shaking his head sadly, wiping away pretend tears. Roger wondered if Schuyler was thinking that this was what indoor boys did to amuse themselves.

As soon as Lizzie caught her father's sour eye, she stopped singing. Henry urged her with a nudge as he carried on solo, but it was no use. Although the song seemed to be almost over, Lizzie began to cry and Henry grew red in the face. Once he finished his last tentative plea not to take his sunshine away, Corinne applauded vigorously.

"Splendid!" Marjorie cried.

"Hear, hear!" Schuyler agreed.

As Lizzie ran into her mother's arms, Henry looked skeptically toward his father, perhaps to see if he might offer some similar comfort. But in that brief moment, the idea of embracing his son—his poor, unhappy, girlish chip-off-the-old-block—was more than Roger could bear. In truth, he hesitated only for a second and was sure he'd have come around had there been another to spare. But by then it was too late. Henry was already fleeing the room. Corinne tried to stop him by making space in her maternal refuge, but he marched straight past her in grim, tearless torment, only pausing at the top of the stairs to level his angriest blow.

"Luh-luh-luh-luh-liar!" he screamed, leaving no one in doubt of whom he'd accused, even if the grievance itself remained somewhat obscure.

"Henry!" Roger said. "Henry, come back here!"

In a rapid-fire sequence of emotions, Roger felt embarrassed by the spectacle of his son's outburst, angered by his insubordination, glad to be rid of the parental burden, and—it felt like a saving grace—impressed that the boy had had the courage to disobey the man who'd so wronged him and the discernment to judge him so aptly. It was something he'd never been able to do to his own father, and somehow it allowed him to love Henry all over again, despite everything else.

As he swallowed what was left of his second sidecar, he reminded himself that children's feelings were naturally volatile. Henry's suffering wouldn't last long, and whether or not anyone else had observed the moral failure that was its cause, the moment seemed to pass quickly. Corinne stroked Lizzie's head and cheered her with the thought of spending a week or two in the summer with her grandmother in Litchfield. Then Marjorie began to speak of her own children's periodic fits of pique, and Schuyler praised her extraordinary patience and nurturing instincts. But it wasn't long before the topic of Lake Como reclaimed their attention entirely, and Roger pushed away his guilt, sat back in his chair, and enjoyed the company like sunshine on a winter-worn face.

◎ ◎ ◎

Dinner was only minute steaks with mushroom gravy, boiled potatoes, and an assortment of frozen vegetables. But everyone agreed that it was superb and Corinne was a culinary genius to have concocted it all at the last minute. Instead of the pricey Burgundy she'd bought to go with the boeuf, which she wrapped up and gave to Schuyler as a gift, they drank Lancers and called it just as good. They talked of Italy and Valentine's Day, "A Tour of the White House with Mrs. John F. Kennedy" and the steady creep of middle age. Corinne told a rather funny story about hoop-rolling at Wellesley, and Marjorie told a rather risqué one about a Mountain Day escapade at Smith. Then Schuyler grinned at Roger as if they had far more scandalous tales to tell, and Roger grinned back as if they were tales of the same genre.

"We'll stay mum and allow the ladies to imagine us lifelong saints," Schuyler said with a wink.

Marjorie's placid smile seemed to suggest that all his past errors had been amiably forgiven if not quite forgotten, but Corinne gave Schuyler an oddly sharp look, perhaps something between surprise and annoyance. Roger had mentioned a few wild parties during the war, though no experiences with other women. Excepting the prostitute in San Diego, Corinne had been the only one. He'd always allowed her to believe it was his shyness and somewhat rigid morality that had kept him so chaste. At least, he'd assumed it was what she believed.

"I'm far too old now to regret whatever unsavory past brought me to such a savory present," Schuyler said, as he poured himself more wine.

Again, Corinne looked vaguely uncomfortable, and Roger felt he ought to change the subject for both their sakes.

"We forgot to toast the birthday boy," he said, as he suddenly stood and raised his glass. "To Captain Endicott. My best friend since the ninth grade."

"To Captain Endicott!" Corinne and Marjorie echoed.

Roger was not a great giver of toasts and usually kept them short and orthodox. But the few sentimental words he'd uttered somehow seemed to call for more, though he had little idea of what he was going to say. So he took a gulp of wine, cleared his throat, and spoke: "As we gather tonight on this anniversary of your birth, we who've had the privilege to know you must count ourselves very lucky indeed."

It was a stiff and rather formal beginning, but Roger felt the force of that luck, in combination with the sidecars and the wine, enter his lungs like helium filling a balloon.

"You've always stood by me with great wisdom and affection. In fact, you've been more like a brother to me than my actual brother. And the God's honest truth is—"

His skin began to bristle and he felt dizzy, as if he might lose his balance. Corinne looked worried and Marjorie looked suspicious. Roger knew he ought to stop, that any more gushing might render him unfit for company. But he hoped he could somehow master his feelings, realize them as natural and manly, like gold in his pocket rather than fire in his hands. If he could only get the words out, he felt sure they'd be true.

"—that I couldn't be happier to have you with us tonight in our home —"

His face suddenly flushed, and his head seemed to swell with grief, bitter and hot. Then, for the second time that week, he began to cry.

"Roger?" Corinne said.

"Oh, dear," Marjorie said, looking away.

"Forgive me," Roger said, wiping away tears with his napkin.

"You mawkish old cuss," said Schuyler. "You keep it all bottled up like you do, and it's just going to come pouring out sometimes."

"I don't know what's come over me," Roger said, sitting down.

But he did know. It wasn't the alcohol or even his unrequited love for his best friend that had undone him. It was the excruciating recognition that, no matter how hard he tried, he'd never be as free and affectionate as Schuyler was. He'd never feel merely brotherly feelings for other men. He'd never love Corinne the way Schuyler loved Marjorie. He'd never really be happy. These were failings he'd meant to reject by proclamation, but instead his foolish toast had only validated them. And then like Henry and Lizzie, he'd gone to pieces.

Marjorie shot him a doubtful look: "If you don't mind my saying, Roger, you do seem a bit out of sorts. I noticed it the moment we arrived."

Roger smiled hard, willing the blood from his face. "I'm just a bit tired, really," he said, hating how often he'd lately resorted to that valetudinarian excuse.

Marjorie clucked and shook her head.

"I'm perfectly fine," he said, before turning to Corinne for help.

"What would you like me to say?" she said, coolly.

"Please reassure our guests!"

"Of what, Roger?" Her anger was so apparent it didn't even bother with sarcasm. "I'm afraid I'm completely in the dark about what ails you." Then she turned her head and stared out though the bay window at the yew hedge.

"I don't mean to beat a dead horse," Marjorie said. "But Schuyler said you didn't look at all well last Sunday. I really hope you're not ill."

"Schuyler?" Roger cried. "What on earth could she mean?"

"Nothing at all," he said, glaring at his plate, probably because he was unwilling to glare at his wife. "Perhaps we should talk about something else."

Roger felt he was being ganged up on in his own home. Corinne might have had her reasons, but Marjorie was the one behind it all. For years, she'd made her cutting remarks, which he'd always pretended not to notice. Now, with his maudlin toast, he'd practically invited her to point the finger and call him out for what he was.

"Well, if you have concerns about me," he said, "I'd like to know what they are."

"For heaven's sake, Roger, let it go," Corinne said.

Marjorie pursed her lips, hesitated for a moment, and then shrugged: "He said you looked frantic and grief-stricken."

"Darling, please," Schuyler said.

"Very well. I'll say no more."

"Frantic and grief-stricken?" Roger cried, looking at Schuyler. "Dear me, was I also sallow and tubercular?"

"It was only a mistaken impression. I never should have said anything."

"And yet you did."

"And I deeply regret it."

During a long, strained silence, Corinne refilled her water glass, Schuyler finished his potato, and Marjorie picked at her lima beans, while Roger lowered his head and waited for the crisis to pass, just as he'd done at the Monday forecast meeting. To press the matter further would have been disastrous. Unless he were to admit to some actual physical ailment, he'd have to live with their suspicions.

"You'd tell us, wouldn't you?" Marjorie asked, with a light in her eye. "If something were really wrong?"

The words flew from his mouth before he could stop them: *"Why can't you leave me alone!"*

He hated Marjorie in the same way he hated all aggressive women who provoked and belittled him. Impatient with the limits of their sex, they lashed out at any man who didn't appear limitless. For years, he'd been so blinded by Schuyler's incessant praise of his wife's supposed virtues that he'd failed to see how, despite her smiling façade and devotion to orphans and refugees, she was an ungenerous, perpetually scheming bitch.

Still, she'd won, and Roger had lost. By insisting so vehemently that he was well, he'd shown so definitively that he wasn't. And his real ailment would probably no longer be a mystery to anyone. Although he couldn't blame the alcohol, he knew they'd conclude it had served to uncover the truth he'd been hiding from them for years. The feeble schoolyard retort had practically announced he was in love with her husband. He might as well have told her to *leave us alone!*

◉ ◉ ◉

After Schuyler and Marjorie made awkward excuses and went home, Corinne declined to hear Roger's explanations and insisted on cleaning up herself, while he went upstairs to his study. They'd always done the dishes together after a dinner party. As she washed and he dried, they assessed the evening, recalled its highs and lows, and appreciated one another's good taste and good sense. But that night Corinne said she wanted to be alone, and he wondered if it was a portent of things to come.

As he eased into the chair behind his desk, he eyed the silver-framed photos in front of him. There was Henry, practically swimming in his baseball uniform, Lizzie as a Halloween witch, and the whole extended family under a spreading sycamore in Litchfield. Missing was the photo of Roger himself in San Diego during the war, the splendor of his uniform and flight gear not quite obscuring the hardened sorrow in his eyes. Although Corinne had dug it out of a box and framed it for their tenth anniversary, he'd always found it too upsetting to look at—like the picture of a friend who'd died young—and that Christmas he'd quietly packed it away again.

He reached for the bottle of Cutty Sark on the bureau behind him and poured a glass. As he took a drink and felt it warm his insides, he imagined Corinne coming into the room and asking him for a divorce. He considered how likely it might be for Cap to change his mind about taking the case or inadvertently leak the facts of it to one of their mutual friends. He imagined the blackmailer growing impatient for his money or sending his telegrams out of mere perverseness. He worried that Schuyler would never want to see him again and Henry would hate him for the rest of his life.

Then he picked up the telephone and dialed the number on the scrap of paper Julian Prince had given him. He knew it was too soon to use it and he had no proper reason to call. He would seem unhinged. Frantic and grief-stricken, indeed. But the prospect of a sympathetic ear on the other end of the line kept him from hanging up. He needed to tell somebody and there was only one person he knew who'd understand.

"Hello?" The mellow, manly sound of Julian's voice came as a relief.

"It's Roger Moorhouse," he said, almost whispering. "I'm sorry to call so late. I hope you don't mind."

"Of course not. Is there news?"

"No, no news. I just—"

"Are you all right?"

Julian betrayed no hint of bother. It was, in fact, the second time he'd asked about Roger's welfare. The first time Roger had pretended not to hear it, but this time he knew his shaky voice had made the answer obvious.

"Has something happened, Roger?"

He batted away the images as they flew at him—the flashlights in the doorway at Caesar's, Andy crawling in the stairwell, the look on his face when he refused to jump.

"There was a boy," Roger said. "At the bar. I was about to take him to a hotel."

He saw Andy in the corner of the jail cell, wretched and hopeless. Then the tiny bubbles, the purple lips, the freezing salt water.

"What's this about?" Julian said. "Why are you telling me this?"

"He drove his car off a bridge last Saturday," Roger said. "He was only nineteen. He was beautiful—and terrified. And now he's dead."

Although it brought no relief from the sadness, sharing the news made Andy's death more a thing of the known world and less Roger's private misery.

"I'm awfully sorry, Roger," Julian said. "That's just rotten."

Roger wondered if the death of one man might justify recounting the ruination of another. But to tell Julian all about his horrible evening, his tainted friendship, his faltering marriage, and his incompetent fatherhood—to tell all his troubles seemed pointless. It implied at least some shred of faith in a better, happier time to come, and in this he had no faith at all. So there was nothing else to say, no confessions of guilt to make nor accidents of fate to lament. It would have to be enough that they were in agreement. The fact that a boy was dead for no good reason was just rotten.

"Roger?" Julian asked. "Do you want to meet somewhere?"

"No, I'm sorry to have troubled you," Roger said. "Good night."

Then he hung up the phone, poured himself another whiskey, and stared out the window at the elm tree in the front yard, its limbs darkly dripping with rain, its canopy reaching like a black river delta into the moonless sky.

20

Julian's late arrival at Ziegler's office that morning had distracted him so much that he was unable to begin the session. So after a long stretch of false starts and stubborn silences, they finally resorted to free associations, an exercise he'd never cared for. It was like being punished for having nothing to say by being forced to talk nonstop. Given the pressure he felt to utter every thought that came into his head, it seemed more like a mild form of mental torture than a therapeutic technique. But he also worried it might somehow betray the awful truth he was still unwilling to share with Ziegler.

"I was late for class once in elementary school. Just once, mind you. I'd been daydreaming on the playground or reading in the cafeteria, I don't remember. But then the second bell rang. So I was sent home that day with a note from my teacher, and my mother got so upset that—well, I've almost never been late for anything since. Actually, she loathes public transportation, even more than I do. Gus calls it a sign of our extreme sense of entitlement, which is probably the only reason I took the bus in the first place."

Ziegler took lots of notes when they did free associations, making a transcription he'd refer to later when they discussed in detail what Julian had said. But the steady scratch of his pen was another reminder of the supposed significance of every word. He'd assured Julian that even the most random-seeming things could be important. He should try not to think about the exercise itself. But it was impossible not to edit his words before they came out of his mouth, and in the end, he usually found himself performing a stream of consciousness instead of actually experiencing one.

"But almost immediately after I paid my fare and the door closed, an enormous truck pulled right in front of us, and we were boxed in on both sides by cars and taxis. Nothing was moving for blocks. And after a few minutes, the driver wouldn't let anyone off. So then there was nothing do to but stand and wait."

Julian asked himself why he'd emphasized the size of the truck, whether it might have some connotation of sex or death. Then he noted that cars and taxis weren't mutually exclusive and that the word *taxis* almost rhymed with *paraphraxis*. He suspected it all had something to do with his mother.

Such a tedious train of associations was unlikely to betray his feelings about the raid or the blackmailer or the continuing search for Gus, now absent without explanation for six days. But they couldn't have held much interest for Ziegler either. In fact, Julian's ramblings that day probably revealed little more than an unoriginal need for self-control and a poverty of invention. He needed to try harder.

"You know, Milton has that beautiful ending to Sonnet 19," he said. "It goes: 'Who best bear God's mild yoke, they serve him best. His state is kingly. Thousands at his bidding speed and post o'er land and sea without rest.' And then that great last line: 'They also serve who only stand and wait.'"

He paused to honor the sound and sense of these famous words, to let them swirl and buzz in the air for Ziegler's appreciation and his own.

"Of course, Milton's blindness didn't stop him from writing *Paradise Lost*, so his own yoke couldn't have been too harsh. But then there's that marvelous contradiction between serving and having thousands at one's bidding—"

Julian thought he heard Ziegler clear his throat. He'd been warned that academics doing free associations often began to lecture as a matter of habit, which defeated the purpose of the exercise. So they'd agreed that, were he ever to speak about literature, he'd try to confine himself to the personal thoughts or feelings it provoked.

"Anyway, I remember once in college, on a fine spring day, Professor Whitaker held class outside on a sunny patch of the Oval, at the

229

request, I think, of one very fetching letterman. And then at some point, that same letterman quipped that the line from the sonnet had given him a most poetic rejoinder the next time his football coach accused him of being lazy at practice. Everyone laughed."

Jokes and the unconscious, Julian thought, racing to find the repressed object. Or perhaps jocks and the unconscious, though the letterman in question had meant no more to him than any number of good-looking, wisecracking boys in a school chock full of them. It was more likely that standing and waiting had reminded him of how impatient he'd become spending two hours a week on Ziegler's daybed—that is, *lying and waiting* for some kind of enlightenment—especially when the far more likely source of happiness in Julian's life was still missing.

But just as he resolved to quit analysis once and for all, a strange feeling of tenderness washed over him. He suddenly realized that he'd remembered the class on the sunny lawn at Stanford not because of Sonnet 19 but because of another poem they'd discussed that same day. It was "Lycidas," an elegy written, when Milton was younger and still had eyes to see, for his friend, Edward King, who'd drowned in a shipwreck. Julian knew that poem by heart, too, but the line that suddenly cried out inside him was Neptune's plea for the lost youth.

What hard mishap hath doom'd this gentle swain?

As its sorrowful pentameter echoed across the week's pursuit of an answer, Julian's legs quaked and his chest began to ache as if the systole and diastole of his heart were at war. He opened his eyes and saw the brass ceiling fan, the mahogany bureau, and the brocade curtains, and felt relieved to return to a world in which Gus wasn't yet doomed but only somewhere else.

Then he turned around to see Ziegler's handsome face marred by signs of irritation and pity. He looked like a sober man watching his alcoholic friend take yet another swig.

"Is everything all right?" Julian asked.

"Why don't you tell me?" Ziegler said calmly.

It was clear he hadn't been buying any of it. Apparently, the difference between repression and suppression was easy enough for the trained eye to spot. So Julian sat up and pulled a Pall Mall from the box in his shirt pocket.

"It's been a difficult week," he said, before lighting the cigarette.

"I can see you've been distressed."

Julian's neurotic symptoms had obviously grown more noticeable. In fact, he'd been fiddling with the Fouquet Medusa so much during the session that his ring finger had become sore and inflamed. It seemed he needed analysis now more than ever.

"And I haven't been completely honest with you," he admitted.

"Then why don't you begin right now?"

Julian suddenly wondered why he'd thought it so necessary to hide his problems from Ziegler in the first place. It certainly wasn't to protect Gus or their relationship, he realized. But the truth came to him as quickly as the question had: he was ashamed of what had happened. It seemed impossible to believe that good people were locked up for no reason or threatened with exposure and mysteriously bereft of their loved ones. Such things happened only to marked men. In fact, in happening to him they seemed to have revealed an ugly mark on the otherwise enviable life he thought he'd made for himself, something that no stylish apartment or prestigious job could ever hide.

So in what remained of their session, he told Ziegler all about the raid at Caesar's and the night in jail, the days of waiting by the telephone and the visit from the blackmailer, the hiring of the investigator and the endless, fruitless search for Gus. He spoke as efficiently as he could, weighing which details to include and which to leave out. Every few minutes, he checked the clock. It felt like packing a suitcase in a hurry.

He did his best to acknowledge the full extent of his love for Gus rather than hiding any part of it in the little alcove of his heart, and he confessed without embarrassment that he'd been silently talking to him for days. But he also admitted that his duplicity hadn't spared him as he thought it would. Though most had been lies of omission and had seemed necessary in the moment, in Ziegler's case, as in Pen's, they'd cost him what might have been real consolation during a miserable time. In Gus's, they might have cost Gus himself.

Ziegler didn't offer any advice on how to confront a blackmailer or locate a missing person, but he seemed genuinely sympathetic, pronounced the actions of the police "outrageous" and "terrible," and offered to be available by telephone in the coming days should the need arise.

In the end, he only asked one simple question: "Why haven't you gone back to the police?"

As Julian fumbled for all his excuses—of risking arrest or compromising Donovan's plan—a surge of shame told him the answer was simple, too.

◎ ◎ ◎

It wasn't that Gus didn't like parties, but he had no tolerance for snobs, hypocrites, or fools, and the majority of men who filled Adrian Closter's chic Park Avenue apartment seemed to be at least two out of the three. Julian had been asked at the last minute by his graduate school friend, Mel, a brilliant charmer who'd left the humanities to work in the mayor's office and now made a career keeping big secrets and powerful company. It went without saying that the invitation had come only after all of Mel's swankier friends had declined. But Closter, a rich-as-Croesus Washington lawyer, was known as much for his lavish lifestyle as his high-profile clients, and Julian thought it might be fun to see how the other half lived.

It was a Friday in late January and the winter doldrums hadn't yet depressed the spirits of the plutocrats, bon vivants, and their male escorts who talked and joked and drank as if the world had been made exclusively for them. The apartment was modern and chic and filled with expensive art. Some of the older men were, Julian had to admit, quite attractive, but the younger ones were uniformly beautiful. As Gus observed, they all looked weirdly similar—about five-foot-ten and blond with pearly white teeth and California tans—like they'd been procured from a mail-order catalog or were brothers in a large family of gorgeous gold diggers. One among them stood out because he was darker and slightly older and mingled more easily with the host, though Mel explained that he was not an escort at all but a well-known New York Giants football player. An hour later, as Julian was admiring the apartment's terrazzo floor, he looked up to see *the* Anthony Perkins, who milled around the party for a quarter of an hour, shaking hands and slapping backs, before making his exit with one of the choicest young blonds in tow.

The world seemed full of secret homosexuals. There was J. Edgar and Clyde Tolson, Cardinal Spellman and Roy Cohen, Truman and Tennessee, Tab and Rock, Marlon and Monty, Sal and Dirk, Van and Farley. Nobody knew. Everybody knew. The rules that bound them were ironclad and soft as silk at the same time.

But just as Julian arrived at this paradoxical conclusion, Gus announced that he'd had enough. "I think the room's running low on oxygen, J.P.," he said.

In the time they'd been there, they'd had a hasty conversation with Mel, who soon ran off to fry bigger fish, then a somewhat longer one with a would-be fashion model from Indiana named Rex, until he discovered they were neither rich nor famous. When one salivating lecher learned that Gus was an artist and suggested they go to his studio to see his canvasses, Julian promptly intervened, and the man moved on with little more than a shrug. There might have been one or two guests who were, like them, not on the giving or receiving end of some transaction, but if so, they were impossible to pick out.

"Uff da! You've had your fun," Gus said. "I'm starving."

"You saw the two Klees and the Kandinsky?" Julian asked.

"Yep, and I was exactly as impressed as I ought to have been."

That Julian took even the smallest interest in wealth or status was, for Gus, a minor character flaw. "Cheap, cheap, cheap," he'd say whenever the subject came up. Julian would reply that, as a poor scholar, he was obliged to confine himself to pleasures he could afford. Then Gus would insist that the greatest and most lasting pleasures were free to any who made the effort to seek them out. And finally they'd end in a stalemate in which Gus was a complete ascetic and Julian a total hedonist.

They had, in fact, left the party at just the right time. If they'd stayed a minute longer, Julian knew, it would have become a bore. It had also placed his new romance in a highly advantageous light. There hadn't been a single man in the room he liked better than Gus. Most of them had more money—a lot more—and a few of the younger ones were perhaps conventionally better looking. But leaving with Gus was like choosing Portia's lead casket and claiming the fairest prize of all. Julian sometimes wished his boyfriend weren't quite so poor, and that the inevitable success Loosli was predicting might hurry up and arrive. Still, if the richest, best-looking men in the city couldn't tempt Julian, then he'd done very well for himself indeed.

The thought lingered with him as they walked west toward Madison in search of a dinner suitable to their modest rank in life, when Gus spontaneously grabbed Julian's hand and placed it inside his own coat pocket. He seemed to do it as naturally as if it had been his wallet or his housekeys, something important he didn't want to lose. Julian loved the pressure of Gus's hand wrapped around his own, his knuckles knocking against the warm sturdy flesh of Gus's abdomen. He probably hadn't given it any thought at all. Most likely, he'd simply noticed that, without his gloves, Julian's hands would be chilled in the night air. But taking one of them in public was something Julian never imagined he'd do. One might hold a woman's hand in the middle of Sheep's Meadow on a summer Sunday, but holding a man's hand, even on dark and desolate East 66th Street, wasn't safe. And yet Gus *had* done it and he wasn't letting go. If anything, he tightened his grip and pulled Julian in closer as they walked.

But after a breathless half minute of excruciating delight, Julian pulled his hand away and put it in his own coat pocket. He did it casually, as if merely shifting for his own comfort, which was almost true, and as if unaware of what he was doing, which wasn't. Then he allowed his shoulder to brush up against Gus's several times as they approached Madison and headed north, to show that he wasn't afraid of physical contact. But he knew it was a fainthearted gesture that could neither compensate for the one he'd forgone nor restore the perfect amity that had inspired it.

"Chop suey, baby?" he asked. The words sounded like a lie.

"Sure," Gus said.

They never spoke of that night again and Gus never reached for his hand a second time. But Julian desperately hoped his failure of nerve hadn't been noticed, or if noticed then not minded too much, and if too much, then not in a way he'd come to regret.

At ten past twelve that cold gray afternoon, having again replaced the note for Gus on the door of his building and then stopped by the bank to empty his savings account, Julian stood near the *Thinker*, scanning the area between St. Paul's Chapel and Kent Hall and hoping to intercept the little mustachioed man before he could offer up another spectacle for Julian's nosy colleagues. Scattered packs of students trudged to lunch, while a lone huddle of visitors stared appreciatively at old masonry. The sun picked its way through a jigsaw puzzle of darker clouds and dappled the quad with uncertain light. Julian's teeth chattered and his eyes watered as he rubbed his hands in the steam of his own breath like a rookie cop on his first stakeout.

When the man finally appeared seven minutes after he'd promised to, he was wearing the same oilcloth duster. But as he approached Philosophy Hall, he squinted past Julian without any sign of recognition.

"If I knew your name," Julian said, stepping into his path, "I might welcome you back to campus properly."

Then the man shook his head, turned on his heel, and walked right back the way he'd come, down the steps onto College Walk. His retreat seemed more an instinctive reaction than a rational one, and he tottered as he went, his satchel bobbing on one side, like someone unused to moving quickly. So Julian ran after him, trying hard to look more like a professor late for class than like someone chasing his blackmailer.

"Hold on there!" he called out as discreetly as possible.

The man stopped, looked nervously toward the gate on Amsterdam, then back toward Julian. "Your office, damn it!" he barked. "You was supposed to be in your office!"

"I thought you'd changed your mind," Julian said quietly, as he approached. "Mister, eh, what's your name?"

"Mister, my foot! Now, you—"

"Lower your voice. I'm sure you don't want to make a scene any more than I do."

A moment later, Julian led the man along 116th Street, past the new law school building to Morningside Drive, where they crossed to the terrace and granite memorial overlooking the park.

"You sound like you might be from Queens," Julian said. "Am I right?"

"Never mind that. Where's the money?"

"Yes," Julian said, making a small show of regret. "About the money."

"You didn't do that right neither?" the man said, clenching his eyes in exasperation.

"Have the others been more scrupulous?"

"What?"

"The other men. Have they been better at following directions?"

"That's none of your business!"

"I suppose the police are used to being obeyed to the letter."

"Police?"

"Do they give you a fair cut of the profits? Or do they take the lion's share for themselves?"

"No more questions! Just the money!"

Julian knew he was getting nowhere, so he pulled an envelope from his pocket.

"I can only give you two hundred dollars today," he said, handing it over. "I'll need more time to get the rest."

He wondered if he ought to have sounded more distressed—like someone who hadn't already engaged a private investigator and wasn't now attempting to be one himself. But the man seemed too upset to notice either way. He began pacing frantically in front of the statue of Carl Schurz—the famous Prussian immigrant and friend of human rights who'd succeeded at everything he'd ever done—apparently unmindful of the invidious comparison it implied.

"Maybe I can explain it to your boss," Julian said. "How can I get in touch with him?"

"Stop talking!" the man cried, his face now twisted in a knot of helpless rage.

"I'll tell you what," Julian said. "Let's meet again right here in exactly one week's time. I'll bring you the rest of the money. In two envelopes, just as you asked."

"You better!" the man snapped, before turning and scuttling his way south.

Julian felt oddly calm as he leaned against the stone wall and watched him go. He certainly hadn't learned much. The man was poor, anxious, and short-tempered, though this had all been obvious from the beginning. If there were others involved, he'd offered no sign of it. If he was colluding with the police, he'd betrayed nothing to illuminate the connection. Still, Julian felt a certain satisfaction in what he'd accomplished. He hadn't faltered or lost his nerve. He'd bought himself more time, even if at a relatively high price. When he made his report to Donovan at the next day's meeting, perhaps his account would corroborate Roger's in a way that led to some useful conclusion or other. At least he'd done something other than stand and wait.

As he lit a cigarette, enjoyed the first soothing drag, and readied himself for his next, far more difficult confrontation downtown, he realized that the whole business hadn't been so alien to him as he'd thought it would be. Thinking on his feet, distorting the truth, obscuring his intentions—they were, in fact, something like second nature to him. After all, in a way, he'd been working undercover for most of his life.

21

They stayed in on Thursday night and listened to *Judy at Carnegie Hall*. Raf made arroz con pollo and they drank beer and twice sang every word of "When You're Smiling." Danny didn't mind that Raf had the better voice. He loved the bouncy, winning feeling the song always gave him. Tickets to the concert had been impossible to get, but it was fun to imagine Judy, only the year before so tubby and sick and taking too many pills, suddenly herself again, ravishing in her frowsy black bob and sparkly sequins. Lady Phoenix from the garbage heap.

The night before, Danny had been wallowing in his own mess. In the back of his mouth, he could still almost taste the sauerkraut tang of the construction worker who came into the toilet stall after the Italian, and the milky sweetness of the bashful beanpole who showed up fifteen minutes later. He didn't know if sucking off three strangers in a row made him a revolutionary or just a slut, but he was determined not to regret it. When he eventually crept into Raf's apartment later that night, he expected to see another note of complaint on the little table. But instead he found a light-skinned boy lying in Raf's bed, burrowed into his armpit, and the room messy with beer bottles, Chinese food boxes, and a few splayed issues of *Tomorrow's Man*. Again, Danny wasn't sure what to make of it—whether to be happy for Raf or annoyed for reasons he didn't want to think about. So he quietly lowered himself onto the couch, covered his head in his blankets, and decided not to think at all. By the time he woke up the next morning, the boy was gone, the room had been cleaned up, and Raf had made fried eggs and café con leche without offering any explanations. But Danny was still in a defiant mood, and when Raf asked, just once and pretty civilly, what he'd been up to himself the night before, he'd only grumbled in reply that he wasn't in the market for a new mother since his old one had tossed him out.

So as soon as the day's vital business was done, he made a serious effort at self-reform. He brought home a whole chicken, bags of spinach greens and yuca root, and a handy-six of Pabst Blue Ribbon. Then he stuck a fresh white rose in the bud vase on the little table and straightened up his side of the room. He was just beginning to finger Raf's LP collection when he came home from the post office. And when he saw the groceries and the flower and the neatness of the room, he smiled and said it just had to be Judy. After that, they were nestled together like a pair of pigeons in the comfy little dovecote of their single-man's apartment, and Danny felt like he might be making a comeback, too.

What a day this has been
What a rare mood I'm in
Why, it's almost like being in love

Things weren't exactly normal, though, and Raf probably knew it, too. Though the bruises on Danny's side had begun to heal and the ones on his dick were fading into a lattice of light brown splotches, he could still feel the sting in his ribs if he moved the wrong way or too fast. He sat at the table and put his legs up on a chair like a man of leisure, but he was weirdly aware of everything around him—the smell of the chicken in the pot, the rolling beat of the music, the red flannel shirt Raf had changed into, which was snug around the arms and shoulders and made him look like a handsome lumberjack. But it all felt a bit hazy, too, like a mirage or something he was watching on TV instead of actually doing. He wasn't sure if he was having a perfect night with the best man he'd ever known or just a plain old chicken dinner in Chelsea.

"Are you just going to sit there?" Raf asked without turning around. "Aren't you going to help me? Or are all jinchos as spoiled as you?"

"Gosh, I never thought about it," Danny said with his best country-club smile.

"'Comfort is yours in America!'" Raf sang out.

"'Cut the frabbajabba!'"

If Judy was their favorite star, *West Side Story* was their favorite show. They'd only been able to see it once on Broadway before it closed, but they'd already seen the movie a half dozen times since it opened. Danny loved that the Sharks and Jets had the run of the Upper West Side. That the cops were all dopes, everyone was a great dancer, and there was nothing you couldn't sing about, even being oppressed or going bonkers. He was glad Raf didn't mind how phony all the Puerto Rican characters seemed. They both thought the whole finger-snapping, stage-magic version of Manhattan was an over-the-rainbow *somewhere* like nothing else. And since all the male dancers were as gay as daisies, the story of men and women in love felt like a kind of stand-in for another, better story that couldn't yet be told. It was like being winked at by a sailor on a passing train, but it was better than not being winked at at all.

"You cheap beast!"

"You Puerto Rican tomato! Cha cha cha, señorita!"

"Hijo de puta!"

Danny knew Raf loved small protests but not actual conflict. His family had been evicted from their tenement in San Juan Hill a few years before and were now scattered over three boroughs. Apparently, they thought he was still waiting for the right girl to come along, but since his brothers all had wives and kids, the subject of marriage came up like weeds in a vacant lot. Raf said he always laughed off any question or remark like a dumb joke not worth his attention. Danny figured he was swapping frankness for privacy and thought it a good bargain, even if Danny didn't think so himself anymore.

"Come taste this," Raf said, holding up a spoon.

Danny got up from the table, leaned in toward Raf, and opened his mouth. The yuca, fried in bacon, was nutty and sweet.

"Qué rico, chico!" he said. "I could eat this every day."

He noticed that Raf's face was weirdly shiny and his smile seemed intense and kind of helpless at the same time. Danny felt he ought to say something more about the food, to thank Raf for the delicious meals he'd made him lately and make clear how much he appreciated him in general. But the words felt too clumsy and foolish to speak and the moment got awkward. Raf looked like he was getting ready to say something himself, but Danny suddenly feared it might not be something he wanted to hear.

"I'm gonna call Gabriel," he said, as he turned and ran out into the hall. "He might not come. But then again he might!"

Danny knew that Gabriel's being there would change the mood of their party and that asking him might make Raf feel he wasn't good enough company. He wondered if it wasn't some feeling of jealousy about the boy in Raf's bed that had made him do it.

All the music of life seems to be
Like a bell that is ringing for me
And from the way that I feel
When that bell starts to peal

Then he reminded himself that Raf and Gabriel were his only family now and eating and singing were things to be shared. It would be their own Thursday-night dinner. Besides, it had been days since Danny had heard from Gabriel. After three separate tries, no one had answered the phone at his parents' house. And as Danny stood in the hall calling a fourth time, it just rang and rang, as if for no one at all, and the lonely, grating noise drowned out Judy's song of love.

◎ ◎ ◎

Earlier that afternoon, he'd been loping east along Charles Street, studying the shops and the townhouses, the parked cars and the people, when he suddenly felt caught. At first, he didn't recognize the slim, stooped figure walking in his direction a few yards away, and just before he did, he thought maybe Ciaran or Raf had sent someone to put a stop to whatever foolishness he was planning. The guy, who looked like a young Monty Clift, wore a tweed jacket and walked with his fists tight at his sides. But when their eyes met and he stopped, he didn't seem angry or nervous or guilty. In fact, he looked relieved, like he'd been hoping for an excuse to change his mind about whatever foolishness *he* was up to.

241

"Oh, hello there," the man said, cocking his head with the same trusting half-witted smile that some of Danny's high school teachers used to give him.

It was one of the swells who hadn't come back to the jail cell, the one with the injured lover. Danny wondered if, like Barrett, he'd been set free and never arrested at all. Maybe he knew people in high places or had found a way to pay off a precinct captain or a judge. Or maybe it was like how captured military officers automatically got better treatment than enlisted men. It didn't even pretend to be fair.

"How strange to meet again like this," the guy said. "Though you could say we never did meet the first time. It wasn't the place for introductions, was it? But I felt terrible when I saw what they did to you. Though you look like you're doing a lot better now, so I hope it's true."

He talked like someone who loved the sound of his own voice. Bookish without necessarily being too smart. Totally different from the kind of men Danny generally knew. It was nice that he said he felt "terrible" about Danny getting beaten up, even if it seemed more like politeness than real concern.

"Oh, I'm Julian Prince, by the way," he said.

Danny shook his hand and introduced himself but left off his surname to show how unimpressed he was.

"So what brings you back to this God-awful place, Danny?"

"I could ask you the same question," he said.

He certainly wasn't going to share his plans with Prince Charming, who looked like he had plans of his own he wasn't sharing.

"You were arrested, weren't you, Danny?" he asked. "With the others?"

"Weren't you arrested, too, Julian?" Danny asked, pretending to be confused. As if they all hadn't been penned up like pigs.

"Oddly enough, no," he said, a little flustered. "They just asked me a few questions and sent me home."

"What a lucky break!" Danny said, now not bothering to hide the sarcasm.

"But my boyfriend, Gus, wasn't so lucky. Do you remember him?"

Danny nodded. He remembered the guy holding a handkerchief to his head, his friendly, freckled face, and the way Prince Charming doted on him so openly. It had made Danny consider for the first time what it meant to be another man's *lover*—a word he liked a lot better than the more childish-sounding *boyfriend*.

"Do you recall the last time you saw him?" Prince Charming asked.

Now he sounded worried, which probably explained why he was back down on Charles Street. He was there to find out what the cops had done with Gus.

"We shouldn't be standing here," Danny said, annoyed that now he couldn't dislike the man quite as much as he'd wanted to.

They walked to West Street and under the Miller Highway to the piers. Along the way, Danny explained that, though he hadn't noticed Gus being taken out of the cell or brought back, he was still breathing when they were all put back into the happy wagon together later that morning.

"So he was with you at the Tombs?" Prince Charming asked, pronouncing the name with too much emphasis, like someone who'd never actually been there.

"Yeah, I guess he paid his fine like everyone else," Danny said. "I was out by the end of the next day, so he must have been, too."

"And how much was the fine?"

"Ten bucks."

Prince Charming twisted his mouth and narrowed his eyes. The information seemed to make him both scared and sad without clearing up any of the mystery.

The wind picked up as they walked past Pier 45 and the shuttered warehouses and concrete slabs that jutted out into the frozen Hudson. Danny remembered how busy the piers sometimes got in the summer, with boys in their bathing suits or underpants or nothing at all, stretched out on the ground or jumping in and out of the river, laughing, screaming, and calling each other names. He loved to do back flips off the piles, over and over until his heart was rattling in his ribs, then he'd throw himself onto his towel and listen to the sound of his breath while his body grew warm and calm again.

"Was there anyone else who didn't come back to the cell that night?" Prince Charming asked, before stopping and cupping his hands to light a cigarette.

The question didn't make any sense. If he wanted to know where his lover was, he should have been asking about the men who were arrested and convicted and had their names printed in the paper and their jobs taken away and their lives ruined. But that wasn't his angle.

"Anything you can think of might help," he added.

Danny remembered them all perfectly. The Suave Suit was the first to go and Barrett sashayed out next like he was headed back to his fancy-dress party. Poor old Shoe-Face cried like a toddler when it was his turn. But none of them ever came back.

"One of them seemed to be a friend of yours," Danny said.

"I know about him," Prince Charming said, a little impatiently. "But were there others?"

"I don't remember," Danny said with a shrug.

He felt bad that the guy couldn't find his lover, but he probably still had a job. He probably had a nice apartment or a detached house and a family who'd never think of kicking him out. He probably had more than enough for one person and didn't need Danny's help to try to keep it.

"What about the man in the black coat with the red scarf?" Prince Charming asked. "The one in charge? Do you remember him?"

It didn't matter if Danny had seen him or not. He didn't like being used for something he didn't understand. Whatever it was, Prince Charming's plan seemed better worked out than his own, and he was asking too many questions.

"No, but do you remember the guard?" Danny asked, partly because he was tired of keeping it all to himself and partly because he was tired of hearing Prince Charming blather on. "The one who was making everyone miserable? He lives in Ridgewood on Palmetto Street and his name is Harold Blunt. And don't be taken in by his good looks. He drinks three Old Grand-Dads at the Admiral's Tavern every night before his shift and then he takes his frustrations out on anyone he pleases—"

Danny stopped himself. He knew he was screwing up. For days, he'd been so careful to keep his plan a secret, and now he'd put it all at risk out of stupid self-pity.

"He was the one who beat you up?" Prince Charming asked.

It felt good to hear it said out loud, even on the cold, windy pier, with only a few salty seagulls as witnesses. When Danny nodded,

Prince Charming stepped on his cigarette and shook his head and seemed to curse under his breath, like he was finally figuring out that the world was a pretty bad business.

"I'm awfully sorry, Danny," he said, as if he might have meant it.

They heard the purr of a single-prop airplane flying above them, and as they both looked up, they watched it soar over Manhattan.

"There were two other guys who didn't come back," Danny finally said, once the plane was just a tiny speck in the sky. "The kid in the tuxedo and the sad sack who was shouting for the guard. I ran into the kid the other day. He said his name was Barrett. He seemed to think he was the living end, but I thought he was a real jackass."

"Do you know where I might find him?" Julian asked.

"It won't be too hard," Danny said. "He seems to go wherever he thinks there'll be a party. But I doubt you'll ever see the other guy again."

Shoe-Face didn't seem like the kind of man who normally went to bars. Danny figured he was from the suburbs and had made a rash decision to go to Caesar's that night but wouldn't be making another like it for a long time.

"I hope you find your lover," he said.

Julian seemed confused for a moment, but then he smiled. "Thanks, Danny."

They shook hands again, like soldiers leaving on different missions.

"Are you *in love* with him?" Danny asked.

It was a personal question, but somehow it didn't seem wrong to ask. What was private in their lives had been made pretty public, so the boundary wasn't so clear anymore.

"Sure," Julian answered, like it was obvious.

As he walked away, Danny thought about how selfish he'd been during the past few days and how he didn't want to take Raf for granted anymore or push him too far. He thought about heading home and picking up some groceries and beer for dinner and letting him know he'd come to his senses. Then he wondered why he and Raf had never been lovers and realized he couldn't think of a single good reason.

"By the way, it's probably not worth it," Julian called out from a distance, his voice almost blowing away with the wind.

"What's not?" Danny called back, knowing he didn't want to hear the answer.

"Revenge. It almost always ends in tragedy."

◉ ◉ ◉

He wandered back under the highway, wishing he'd worn his ushanka, and trying not to think about Julian's warning. He knew whatever he decided to do might have no effect at all or make everything worse. Harry Blunt could beat him up again or even kill him. Danny could get caught and sent back to jail for much longer than a day. Raf could find out what he was up to and never speak to him again. It might turn out that Roy Lee's idea of justice was wrong or that Harry Blunt was no different from most assholes and making one cop accountable for his actions was no better than stepping on one cockroach. Maybe it was true that darkness and hate couldn't drive out darkness and hate, and waiting for the world to grow up on its own was the only option, even if in the meantime they could still lock you up and beat you up and fuck you up anytime they wanted.

But Danny knew if he stopped now Harry would only do the same thing to some other schmuck and then to another and then they'd all feel like ghosts for the rest of their lives. He was glad he'd told Julian what he knew about Gus and Barrett and Shoe-Face and he wished he'd had more to tell. He wondered how he could get that kind of help too—not just information but muscle and guts—and whether there'd be anyone willing to give it and where to find them and how to ask. And as he walked south along West Street, he tried to imagine what would've happened if everyone at Caesar's that night had fought back like he had. If they'd all refused to be arrested and had beaten up the cops instead and then stormed the West Village, gathering recruits along the way like a revolutionary army. If it had gone on for days and people everywhere began to see that they were right and then they declared a worldwide general strike against unfair laws and police harassment.

It might not have been a coincidence that the idea came to him right in front of the Keller Hotel on the corner of West and Barrow. It was a seedy sailors' boardinghouse where almost nobody went on purpose, but it had a gay bar that catered to motorcyclists and brawny he-man types. When Danny opened the door, the twangy guitar from "Let's Go Trippin'" tumbled out into the gloom. The place smelled of stale beer, cigarettes, and neat's-foot oil, and it was decorated with a bunch of club pennants, a big American flag, and an even bigger skull and crossbones. There were about a dozen men, wearing mostly leather—silver-studded jackets, peaked caps, and shiny buckled boots—either sidled up to the elbow-worn bar on one side of the room or standing around a pool table on the other, all looking like they were on a fifteen-minute break from doing whatever you did when you wore those clothes.

No one paid Danny much attention when he stepped inside, went to the bar, and ordered a beer, even though his pea coat and purple tie probably violated the dress code. At Caesar's, every newcomer, dishy or not, caused a wave of turning heads and a chorus of catty whispers. But at the Keller Bar everyone seemed to know his own business and mind it, and even the occasional burst of laughter was of the deep-throated, cynical variety. Though a few of the guys looked more like court stenographers in Halloween costumes, others seemed to be legitimate bruisers, like Brando in *The Wild One*, though not as handsome. But all of them looked ready to show the world and themselves that they were real men, never mind their bedroom habits.

The big moon-faced kid who sat on a stool by the door was no exception. Nearly twice as tall as Danny with legs like trees, he wore a black leather vest over a black T-shirt and tight black leather pants. Quinn would've roared with laughter, but Danny admired the kid's confidence and the way he bobbed his head to the music but never took his eyes off the door. Probably a square in high school, he seemed to have found his calling early.

"Quiet afternoon," Danny said, approaching him with his beer.

"Uh huh," the kid said without looking at him.

Danny noticed that there were two windows facing the street, each secured with iron bars and covered in dirty canvas. Besides the entrance, the only other door was next to the bar and marked "private."

"I bet it's busier on weekends," he said. "What about Sundays?"

The kid turned and raised an eyebrow at Danny. "Who wants to know?"

"Someone who'd definitely be better dressed for the occasion."

The kid nodded, then turned his gaze back on the door.

"Sunday's club night," he said. "Riders come from all over the city."

"The place really gets packed, huh?"

"Rest of the neighborhood's going to bed, we're just getting started."

Danny's skin tingled and his breath was slow and steady. Though he didn't want to spread his trouble around needlessly, he thought it might be okay to share it with men who'd take it on willingly. He hadn't started this fight, and even if it ended in tragedy, at least his enemy would face his crimes.

"One more thing," Danny said, after he swallowed the last of his beer and buttoned up his coat. "You never see any cops around here, do you?"

The bouncer's chubby face went tight. One of the nearby bruisers seemed to prick up his ears. It was a risky question, Danny knew, since it cast doubt on the asker. But the jittery response it got was just the one he'd been hoping for.

"Nah," the young leather-man said with a grin, as he started bobbing his head again and burning a hole in the door with his eyes. "Wouldn't have the balls."

22

From five stories up, lower Broadway looked gray and forbidding, though the day was unexpectedly warm. Rows of pigeons lined windowsills across the street like a feathery fungus, and a new glass-and-steel tower going up on Fulton seemed garish and flimsy. From beyond his closed door, Roger could hear the crisp, even snapping of Nancy's Selectric and the amiable chime of the elevators. He resented such blithe and steady routine amid his disaster, and when the urge to scream suddenly rose in his throat, he jammed the sharp tip of his letter opener into the palm of his left hand. The pain raced hot and ragged up his arm.

He'd been sitting at his desk, taking notes on the annual report of a British tool and die company, but the distraction of numbers and columns failed to quell the thoughts that had harangued him all morning. About his sniveling speech the night before, Schuyler's good-humored forbearance, Marjorie's undisguised contempt. The fierce, stifled clamor of Corinne's dishwashing, and the phone call to Julian Prince—his encounters with that man nearly always ended in some kind of sudden and hysterical retreat. Roger felt surrounded by his failures with no means of escaping them. Even the afternoon's itinerary mocked him with the likelihood of more suffering to come. Lunch with his father, another meeting with his blackmailer—*his blackmailer!*—and then one with the expert he hoped would put everything right but probably wouldn't succeed in the end. When Roger's throat tightened and his hands began to shake, he grabbed the letter opener and stepped to the window, as if it might offer a way out.

As he drove the point in deeper, the idea came to him like good news. Monday's thought of stepping in front of the train had been impulsive and fleeting. But now dying seemed the only choice he had left. He had to do it before Corinne or Schuyler or anyone else learned the truth about him. He could never abide their disappointment or disgust. He had to be gone before they found out.

Andy's hadn't been his first suicide. Roger's cousin Tim, a shy, effeminate tennis player, had hanged himself after his freshman year at Dartmouth for reasons nobody claimed to understand. There'd also been a pilot on the *Bunker Hill* who cracked up after a rough sortie and jumped into the North China Sea one night without leaving a note. They, too, had only needed the pain to stop. And yet suddenly Roger wasn't sure if the pity he felt for these men was something he was ready to trade for no feeling at all. In fact, actual death began to seem like a precarious path. It might hurt a lot more than a bit of steel in his hand or cause more suffering to the people he loved than it spared them. He might regret the decision before it had taken effect but after it was too late to change his mind. And then there was the question of means. Killing oneself, he suspected, was harder than it looked.

The desire to die came and went like traffic at an intersection, charging forward toward some inevitable destination and then giving way to feelings tending in another direction. Roger told himself that this proved they were merely feelings and neither substantial nor permanent. It was only his mind seducing him with tricks. But then, just as he convinced himself of their falseness, the feelings returned.

"You asked me to remind you when it was time."

He turned away from Nancy's voice and pulled the letter opener from his hand. The blade had only penetrated about half an inch into his flesh, but blood was flowing freely, so he took a handkerchief from his pocket and balled it up in his fist.

"You'll need to be there in fifteen," she said, poking her head through the doorway. "But it's a nice day for a walk, which should take fewer than ten."

"You're a gem, Nancy."

"Is everything all right?"

Her near whisper said she knew it wasn't. Although he appreciated her loyalty and discretion, he hated that there was now another woman worrying about him and that there would be still more lies to tell.

After she closed the door, he wiped off the letter opener and laid it back down on his desk. He looked around the office at all his new furniture, which now seemed like a present that had been intended for someone else. Then he put on his coat and hat and went back to the window, as if another look might finally explain the problem of life and death. But the whole scene below was strangely quiet and still, almost like a photograph, as if time had stopped briefly to acknowledge his suffering. Until a delivery truck on Broadway boomed its horn and the pigeons on the windowsills struck out in great helices of flight above the city, where the noon sun burnished the dull sky with a thin veneer of gold.

◎ ◎ ◎

When the elevator door closed on Roger, Nick, and Dalton in an unwelcome synchronicity of lunch appointments, it was unclear who would speak first. Dalton, already eating from a bag of peanuts, seemed the least likely, while Nick, in a three-piece suit with French cuffs and silver studs, raised his chin in a gesture that seemed preparatory to remarks of some kind but might also have been intended to suggest that he thought any conversation entirely unnecessary. As the only senior vice president among them, Roger felt a certain responsibility to say something, but he hoped on that day of all days his colleagues might understand him to be in a pensive mood and just stare quietly at the illuminating floor numbers like most people did.

"You seemed rattled on Monday, Roger," Nick eventually said as the number four lit up.

It wasn't clear if he'd seen Roger cry. But he'd no doubt enjoyed watching the botched report and had apparently been waiting all week for the chance to remind him of it. Nick had sought Roger's promotion himself and even dropped several hints that he felt more deserving of the honor.

251

"How good of you to notice," Roger said as the number three blinked on.

When they reached the second floor, Nick was lowering his head, like a leopard ready to pounce. Dalton seemed surprised by the open display of tension but unwilling to get involved. The number one light flashed, and the elevator door opened.

"Oh, everybody noticed, Roger," Nick said as he pushed into the lobby.

Roger followed them out of the building, where the mild air on his face reminded him that seasons come and go. Everywhere water was leaking under piles of snow, dripping over curbs, flowing down gutters, and rushing into grates. Even if spring didn't come right away, it would come eventually. He thought it best to ignore Nick's implied threat. It was probably little more than posturing and not worth his attention. If his reputation really were about to be destroyed and soon everything else in his life wouldn't be worth shit, then the jibes of a jealous colleague hardly mattered at all.

"Can I assume you'll be coming back?" Roger suddenly heard Edgar ask in a sharp and disdainful tone.

Walking toward the building, he wore a new gray trilby, a matching raincoat over his blue suit, and a look of extreme irritation.

"Of course," Roger answered neutrally. "Just going to lunch."

"On Wednesday you left early. Nancy didn't know where you were."

He'd gone to meet Cap Donovan. But it wasn't unusual for him to take late afternoon meetings out of the office and then go straight home. So he was surprised Edgar was mentioning it at all.

"I had a private matter to attend to," Roger said.

His boss took so little interest in people's personal lives that he assumed the mere allusion to his would be enough to end the conversation.

"Business hours are nine to five," Edgar said. "No exceptions!"

He was obviously more disappointed by Roger's report than he'd been letting on, and his absence on Wednesday had been ill timed. But neither peccadillo could possibly account for such a dressing-down.

252

"You're sailing very close to the wind, Moorhouse," Edgar said. "I won't ask the reason because I don't want to know. But you'd better even your keel and soon."

As he stormed off, Roger stood wondering if perhaps Nick, now so clearly more an enemy than a rival, had whispered something in his ear, or if Roger himself had betrayed something without knowing it. Perhaps his guilt was no more hidden than the bloody handkerchief in his left hand.

It was ironic that his business was lending. Whether it was a building loan to a motorcycle company in Hamamatsu or a line of credit to a chocolatier in Bruges, his job was to know who was trustworthy and who wasn't. But now he didn't know if he could rely on Edgar to forgive his few small lapses. Or Nick not to take advantage of them. Or Nancy to keep the reality of his distress to herself. Or Cap to solve the problem that was its source. There was even no telling if Schuyler and Corinne were preparing to cast him out as a liar and a leper. Everyone who could help him or hurt him was a risk he couldn't analyze. When he imagined them all staring at him in bitter judgment, their faces became mere blanks. No features, no expressions, just terrifying ovals of skin.

◎ ◎ ◎

What in Fairfield County they called "lunch with father" was meant to suggest a moderately happy occasion wherein men who'd battled on unequal terms for over two decades suddenly, upon the twenty-first birthday of the younger, forgot their prior animosities, exchanged hatchets for fish forks, and agreed to a truce in which all future interactions would be said, even in advance of the event, to have gone swimmingly.

All morning, Roger had worried that his father would see signs of trouble in his eyes or somehow smell the foulness of Charles Street on him and then admit that he'd already heard the whole shameful story from some well-intended friend. But as Elliot Moorhouse sat heavily in his chair at Oscar's Delmonico, cleared his throat several times, and complained to a nearby waiter about the warmth of the room, Roger realized that his worries had probably been unfounded. Their conversations were invariably the same, so there was little risk this one would veer into realms unknown. Lunch would be over in an hour, and he'd survive it intact. Assessed, judged, and humbled but largely unscathed and ready to face his next mortification. So Roger pulled his crisp white napkin across his lap like a seat belt and aimed his cutlery at the criticisms he knew he'd be consuming along with his lobster Newburg.

"How are Corinne and the children?" his father asked, wiping his broad brow. No wastrel of speech, his social inquiries were usually collective and invariably came with an expectation that their answers would be both similarly brief and unambiguously positive.

"They're all fine," Roger said. "And how's Mom?"

"Never better," he said, before noticing that the table wobbled a bit and waving over a waiter to set it straight.

They went on like this for a few minutes, cursorily but definitively confirming that Richard and his surgical practice were "thriving," that Audrey and her family were "quite content" in Hartford, and that there was not a second cousin or great-aunt in the entire family tree who had anything to complain of. This declaration of universal happiness would, Roger knew, be followed by a discussion of his various shortcomings, personal, parental, and professional, all disguised as unimpeachable fatherly interest.

"How is Henry's stutter?" his father asked, squinting at the menu before pulling out his bifocals.

"The doctor says he'll grow out of it any day."

"Richard's boys are both playing football next year."

"Henry prefers baseball, as you know."

"Does he?"

His father ordered a Tom Collins, Roger, a dry martini, and while they waited for their drinks to arrive, a kind of ritual silence, neither comfortable nor awkward, drifted between them. The old man looked a bit thicker in the face and shoulders than he'd been during the holidays, and he seemed to be perspiring more than usual. But his stalwart expression was drearily familiar, like a Palladian façade or a grandfather clock.

"And all is well at the bank, I suppose," he said, as he cast his eyes across the fusty dining room, probably to show how little interested he was in the answer.

"I'm expecting another good year," Roger said, slipping the blood-ied handkerchief into his coat pocket. He'd already announced his promotion once and dared not mention it a second time.

"Well, you seem to be on track."

It was his father's highest compliment, though it came with two tacit assumptions. First, that you might fall off the track at any time. There were always new milestones to reach and higher obligations to satisfy, and the least inattention to either could lead straight to mediocrity and disgrace. And second, that staying on track reduced a man's life to his achievements. It wasn't even supposed to be fun.

"Thank you, sir," Roger said with an irony he knew would go unheard.

Just as his father began to summon a waiter again—he feared the Tom Collins he'd ordered might be too sweet—he flushed and began to cough. A morsel of bread soon dislodged itself from his throat and sailed onto the tablecloth next to the pepper shaker, but he continued to snort and wheeze, straining at the buttons of his vest. When Roger offered him his own napkin, he brushed it away like a plate of garlic, then drank an entire glass of water.

"Richard's buying a summer house on St. George's Island," he managed to say in between uncouth gulps, apparently determined to share the news before death rendered it impossible.

When his glass was empty, he sank into his chair and stared at the little spray of crocuses in the center of the table as if unable to move or speak. Roger saw a waiter approaching with their drinks and a busboy hurrying over with a water pitcher. But in the seconds before their attentions brought his father back to life, he looked like someone Roger had never seen before. He was no paragon of virtue, and his manners were far from impeccable. He'd somehow become a nervous, fussy septuagenarian, undone by a crumb. Roger wondered how long he'd been this way and why he hadn't noticed it before.

He'd never loved his father and had never felt loved by him. But he'd always respected and feared him, as much out of duty as instinct.

And now that his fear and respect seemed to have vanished with the cold weather, he felt faintly sorry for the old man and wondered whether pity might not be a kind of love.

"What happened to your hand?" Elliot asked.

The wound in Roger's palm, now caked in dried blood like a stigma was plainly visible as he lifted his martini to his mouth.

"I stabbed myself with a letter opener," he said, looking his father in the eye.

"Not a very clever thing to do."

"No," Roger admitted.

◎ ◎ ◎

The doors of the empty 5:57 New Haven train still hadn't opened, and the platform was crammed with weekenders whose presence often turned the otherwise staid commute into something of a circus. A conductress rebuked a group of schoolgirls for singing too loudly, while a cheerless Mennonite family with several trunks in tow plowed through the crowd. To Roger's left, a man spread wide his *Times*, claiming space beyond his due, and to his right, a young bohemian couple kissed each other so passionately that he could hear the smacking of their lips. Yet somehow he didn't mind all the close bustle of humanity. He felt almost steady in his dizziness, somehow alert in his numbness, and surprisingly patient with himself, though only because he'd lowered his expectations to mere survival. All that was required of him now was to wait for the man with the drooping gray mustache.

But at exactly a quarter before the hour, Roger saw a very different person.

"Don't say anything. Just hand it over."

The man reading the *Times* was now gone and in his place was someone Roger recognized as the desk sergeant from the Charles Street station with the unnaturally black hair, though now he was dressed in a bulky greatcoat and cheap, unpolished brogues. The expression on his pockmarked face was cool and arrogant, nothing like that of his jumpy colleague. Taking money from people seemed to be second nature to him, and Roger felt the old familiar tremor of the bully's threat.

He knew his carefully rehearsed speech would have to be improvised. But before he could even begin, the sergeant grabbed him by the lapels, reached into his breast pocket, and pulled out the cash-stuffed envelope. He seemed to know at once that it contained too little.

"Where's the rest?" he asked, as he searched Roger's other pockets then began rifling his briefcase.

"I can g-g-get it," Roger stammered. "But I need more time."

He recoiled as much at the scene they were making as at the foul smell of unwashed clothes and Aqua Velva, and his right fist readied itself instinctively. But the bohemian couple was now staring in dumb fascination. The students had stopped singing and cocked their heads in Roger's direction, and the conductress seemed to be moving toward him, like a mother drawn to children's trouble. To fight back in front of so many witnesses would almost certainly mean getting arrested. It might satisfy his honor, but it would land him right back in jail and ruin him more efficiently than any telegram could. Standing up for himself would be tantamount to giving up altogether. Somehow the paradox came as a relief.

When the sergeant found nothing else that pleased him, he dropped the briefcase at Roger's feet and yanked him by the necktie until they were face to face.

"Monday!" he hissed. "Same time. Right here. Two grand. Or you're finished!"

A second later, he disappeared into the crowd, just as the train doors opened and the people around Roger began pushing their way in.

He quickly snatched up his briefcase and stepped aside, but after dusting it off and checking for marks, he felt a strong urge to flee the scene of his humiliation. His miserable day was far from over, and he couldn't abide any more impertinent looks. So he hurried back into the main hall, dodging crisscrossing streams of travelers, exhausted and clumsy with fear, and finally stopped near the clock to catch his breath.

Looking up for perhaps the thousandth time at the vaulted ceiling and its celestial mural—showing Cancer in the West and Aquarius in the East—he felt once again reassured by the famous error. Since as far back as he could remember, he'd suspected that everything he did was essentially backward, despite occasional appearances to the contrary. It was this backwardness that had made his father dislike him so much. It's what made him prefer men to women, compromised his marriage, and led him to Caesar's and the nightmare that followed. It's what clouded his mind as he'd looked out over Broadway that morning, and unless some long-forgotten luck crossed his path soon, it's what would rob him of his family, his job, and everything he cared about. But whenever he traced the dazzling Zodiac from October to March, he allowed himself to imagine that, in the creation of his soul, he too had been inadvertently transposed, that his backwardness was only a kind of minor technical defect, and that a simple shifting of perspective—not some great revolution of the universe—was all that was needed to make him right as rain.

23

Julian hid his hands under the table, nervously strumming the pages of his paperback *Inferno* with his thumb. It wasn't the same windowless room he'd been interviewed in a week earlier, though with a similar black steel cabinet guarding one corner and buzzing fluorescent lamp overhead, it might as well have been. The sleepy-eyed, day-shift detective in front of him—his bland face crowned sparingly with wisps of silver hair—seemed as deceptively genial as his younger, swarthier nocturnal counterpart. He looked more like a high school principal than a cop. But the file folder he held in his hands wasn't the neutral buff manila Julian had seen before. This one was a very culpable red.

What hard mishap hath doom'd this gentle swain?

"So how can I help you?" the detective asked, after clearing his throat.

"Gus Magnusson was brought here last Friday morning around one A.M.," he said. "I'd like to know what happened to him."

The detective smiled, looked inside the folder, then put it back down on the table. "Do you know the charge?" he asked, though it seemed he already did.

As Julian thought about how to answer the question, he let the pages of his book slip, one by one, over his thumb, all those unregenerate souls fanned into oblivion. Then he eyed the folder and the chubby hand with the gold wedding band that hid the writing on the label. Underneath was certainly Gus's name, and in the folder, not only a charge, but a conviction, a release date, perhaps some other clue. It was all right there in front of him now and might have been languishing in a file drawer for days, awaiting only Julian's resolve.

The Ninth Circle was mainly for traitors, but it included cowards, too.

"What are you doing under there?" the detective asked.

Julian put the book on the table, its orange cover curling upward.

"Oh, yeah, 'abandon all hope,'" the detective said with a chuckle as he reached across the table.

"It's my right to know!" Julian said, slapping the table with one hand and taking back the book with the other.

The detective only shrugged, then he opened the folder and cleared his throat again, as if finally ready to tell him the truth.

"Charged with disorderly conduct," he said, as he scanned its contents. "Pleaded not guilty. Bail posted late yesterday. Should have been released this morning."

"Released?" Julian asked. "From where?"

"Riker's."

The sound of the place name pierced Julian's ears. "What do you mean?" he cried. "Why would he be *there*?"

"Seems he tried to take a swing at a cop," the detective said.

Julian's heart cracked and his legs quaked as he imagined Gus in a filthy cell, now neither St. Sebastian nor Shakespeare's Sebastian but an anonymous prisoner of the state. And he knew that he himself was to blame. He might have posted Gus's bail sooner. He might have found him a proper attorney. He might at least have given him comfort and hope. But he'd put it off again and again, convinced it had been too risky or unnecessary. His guilt felt like a rat lodged in his throat.

He jumped out of his chair, his hands grasping at the air, the room suddenly a cage. Why had Gus never called him? Why hadn't he pleaded guilty? But then Julian stopped himself. He knew his panic was only another selfish indulgence and of no use to Gus whatsoever. What he needed now was information.

"Who posted his bail?" he asked, grabbing the chair for support.

"That I can't tell you," the detective said calmly as he closed the red folder.

"Can you tell me where he was released?"

"The bus lets them off at Jackson Avenue and Queens Plaza South."

Julian scribbled the address on the inside cover of his *Inferno*. "And would they have given him any money?" he asked.

"Eighty-five cents," the detective said. "Enough for three subway tokens and a cup of coffee. Or two tokens and a pack of smokes."

"Is there anything else you can tell me that might help me find him?"

The detective's complacent smile made it clear he'd given so much unhappy news in his career that he'd forgotten how hard it was to receive it. He seemed to have no idea why Julian was so upset. Or why he thought a man arrested for being in a disorderly establishment and trying to assault a cop shouldn't expect to be punished for his crimes.

"Who's this fellow to you exactly?" he asked, rising from his chair.

"He's my lover," Julian said, before he walked out of the room.

◉ ◉ ◉

If he'd had any money left, he'd have hired Caspar Donovan to help him find Gus. Instead, he smoked and listened absently as Roger explained to them both that the man he'd encountered earlier that evening at Grand Central wasn't the same one who'd handed him the threatening letter a few days before but the desk sergeant from the Charles Street station. Roger described the encounter in detail, noting the man's hair, face, clothing, and speech, his anger at being short-changed, and his last-minute doubling of the ransom amount. When the sergeant had gotten a bit physical, he was apparently ready to give it right back to him and surely would have if they hadn't already attracted so much attention on the crowded platform. It was a bit sad to hear Roger puffing up like that, especially considering his wretched phone call the previous night. But for Julian, it all felt beside the point. Although Donovan seemed professional enough, the reason for their meeting no longer mattered as much as it once had.

After his visit to the Sixth Precinct the day before, he'd telephoned Hugh, Syd, and Dahlia a second time, along with a half dozen other people whose connection to Gus was only tangential. He'd called back every hospital and paid another visit to the Sloane House, the McBurney Y, and Gus's studio, where Julian's painting still leaned on the easel, unfinished and neglected. The next day, after teaching his classes and canceling his office hours, he stopped by the Art Students League and the West Side Y, but he found no trace of Gus or anyone who could report having seen him. An invitation to a cottage on Long Island now seemed out of the question, and Julian refused to believe he'd have jumped bail. But unless he'd packed up and gone home to Manitowoc as an accused sex offender, there was simply no other person to call or place to look.

Stopping to teach during so much desperate searching had been almost unbearable. But it wasn't the *Inferno* that had impeached him so forcefully as *Much Ado*. Dante only loved his Beatrice from a distance, after all, whereas Benedick had already squandered one chance with Shakespeare's Beatrice out of vanity and pride and nearly blew it a second time for the same reason. Yet in the end it was the feckless, faltering Claudio, whose confusion nearly cost Hero her life, that had stabbed at Julian's heart and brought his lecture to a frazzled end.

What men daily do, not knowing what they do!

Donovan cleared his throat to claim Julian's attention.

"So when operations like this are unstable at the bottom," he said, "we want to know if higher-ups are taking a cut. If so, it makes them more vulnerable. If not, it can make them harder to stop."

The piles of paper on the desk where he sat suggested he was a busy and competent man. The Impressionist painting on the wall, the elegant Windsor chairs, and the expensive-looking carpet all implied that he'd been successful in the past. So when it was his turn, Julian stirred himself, snuffed out his cigarette, and described his own meetings with the little mustachioed man. He also told them of his chance encounter with the redhead, Danny, and what he'd learned about the two other men released from the Sixth Precinct station without being charged—the brat in the tuxedo named Barrett and the man Danny had only called Shoe-Face. But as Julian spoke, he wondered how any of it—the color of the desk sergeant's coat or

262

the possibility that some callow undergraduate and hapless blunderer were being threatened by the same people in the same way—could matter.

Thinking about Danny, out on the freezing piers, plotting his revenge, made Julian even more depressed. He was just a kid in dungarees, untutored and unconnected. He wasn't like the boys at Stanford or Brophy, who'd had all the avenues of success laid out before them like a choice of ice cream flavors. Though he did remind Julian a little of his student, Carter, puny but passionate and full of surprises. How different Danny's life might have been had he been born to different parents. How much easier Julian's own life had been so far, all things considered. And how strange that one could be both oppressed and privileged at the same time, a kind of pampered pariah. He wondered why it had never occurred to him before.

When he finished talking, Donovan scribbled down a few more notes, then began tapping his pencil like a drumstick.

"So assuming you both still want to proceed," he said after a moment, "then our only real option is to defang them."

Julian assumed it was some jargon of the trade, but he was surprised by how much the idea appealed to him. It seemed to promise some judicious amount of violence but only to prevent much worse. It was what you might do to a rabid dog or a poisonous snake. When he looked over at Roger, he was already nodding his approval.

Donovan went on to propose that he prepare a detailed dossier that included their names and addresses, accounts of their being taken to the police station but never arrested, descriptions of the two blackmailers and their visits, and a photograph of Roger's threatening note. It would also include the names of all the men who were arrested that night and those who, like them, were only picked up and released. Then Donovan would send one copy of the dossier to the assistant chief of police for the Borough of Manhattan, demanding that the blackmailers, whoever they were, cease their threats and promising that, if they didn't, further copies would be sent to the Manhattan district attorney, the state attorney general, and the FBI.

When Julian looked at Roger a second time, his face had fallen, his mouth hung open, and he seemed about to collapse into his chair.

"So we'd put the whole affair down on paper and send it out into the world?" Julian asked. "Isn't that the kind of exposure you're supposed to be helping us avoid?"

"It would practically be making a public confession!" Roger cried.

But Donovan only folded his fingers into a patient teepee. "I understand your concerns," he said. "But to put it simply, risking exposure may be the only way to prevent it. They're counting on your fear. It's their only real advantage. If you refuse to be afraid, they've got nothing."

Julian was surprised by the oddly straightforward logic.

"Don't make the common mistake of assuming you're the only ones vulnerable here," Donovan continued. "Who's more vulnerable than a criminal?"

Roger glanced at Julian, either to warn him against a premature decision or to borrow whatever courage he lacked.

"Would either of you like a drink?" Donovan asked.

"No," they each said firmly.

Then Donovan reached into one of the piles on the desk and pulled out a copy of the *Post*, folded to an article about the raid at Caesar's, with a circle drawn around the names of those arrested.

"Who besides you from that night isn't on this list?" he asked. "What's this Barrett fellow's first name or his last? Who's the other man the kid mentioned? The more names we have, the better our chances."

Julian liked the way Donovan spoke as if they were all in it together and appreciated having the matter reduced to such a straightforward task.

"Why the assistant chief?" he asked, feeling that one more reservation answered might be enough to convince him.

"He'd have to think he had enough to lose," Roger offered. "And the power to make it stop."

Donovan went back to the same pile on the desk and this time fished out a folded copy of the *Herald-Tribune*. Then he passed it to Roger, who held it up to reveal a photograph of a fair-haired, well-favored man identified as Ivan Fischer, shaking hands with the police commissioner while being promoted to assistant chief on

Valentine's Day. In dress blues and youthful in middle age, his chin was angled defiantly upward.

Julian swallowed hard. It was the lieutenant with the black topcoat and red scarf who'd been haunting his mind all week.

"What if the sergeant doesn't want it to stop?" Roger asked.

"Then one of two things will happen," Donovan said, flashing a toothy smile. "Either you'll both be looking for new jobs, or one or two crooked cops will be."

Roger still seemed to be weighing the odds of self-incrimination. But Julian had heard enough. If saving his own skin also meant hindering the man who was chiefly to blame for Gus's suffering, he was willing to try.

It was nearly nine o'clock when they all shook hands and agreed that Julian and Roger would search the most likely bars, all weekend if necessary, to find the two men they were looking for. Then they'd let Donovan know first thing Monday morning what they'd found and whether they still wanted him to send the dossier. Roger clearly bristled at the thought of returning to those scenes that had intruded so violently on his handsome suburban life. But as Julian found himself staring at the painting on the wall—a late summer sun setting on a field of new-cut hay—he felt almost indifferent to the nature of the work before them and knew he'd use the opportunity to continue his own search. Gus was out there in the city somewhere, and he wouldn't stop looking until he found him.

Until then, until love had all his rites, time would go on crutches.

24

If a huge house on a lot the size of a baseball field meant you were rich, and the address Danny had gotten out of the telephone book was correct, then the Golofskis were loaded. Gabriel's father Hersh ran a business in the garment district that made cheap, wrinkle-free ladies' dresses, the kind Gabriel said he'd never be caught dead wearing. For years, they'd lived out in Throgs Neck until a big contract with Bamberger's and a sudden aversion to old country schmutz required moving west to Riverdale into a three-story Tudor mansion on Grosvenor Avenue. "My parents didn't eat grass clippings and wood shavings so my children could live in hotseplots," Gabriel's mother Aviva supposedly once said. It was the biggest detached house on the nicest, most tree-lined street Danny had ever seen up close. It looked nothing like the houses in Mott Haven or Ridgewood—it was hard to believe he was still in New York City. But it also didn't seem like a place Gabriel would ever call home, and even as Danny rapped the door knocker one last time, he knew he wasn't there.

Because it had been almost a week since their night at the Excelsior and Bacchus, Danny wondered if Gabriel had been arrested again or gone on a bender. Maybe he was bopping it up in Atlantic City with likeminded friends or laying low in the Poconos with someone else's sugar daddy. Danny missed his loyalty and his big mouth, which now seemed like less of a shtick and more a kind of faith, like religion or patriotism. After so many lonely hours watching and following Harry Blunt, it would've been nice to hear Gabriel's campy jokes or just appreciate his way of seeing the world. Danny wouldn't have told him what he was planning to do—just as he hadn't told Raf—but he felt that Gabriel would've understood.

He'd counted on the Golofskis being at home for Shabbos well before sunset, which the *Daily News* said would take place that evening at 5:32, after which they wouldn't answer the door at all. But it was nearly half past five. The door was locked, the curtains had all been drawn, and there was no car parked in the wide cobblestone driveway. Though winter had taken the day off and Danny might have killed a few more minutes snooping in the backyard or taking a stroll around the block, he was tired of feeling like a professional loiterer and didn't want to run the risk of being arrested as a house burglar either. So he took one final look at the big leafless oak tree in front of the house and the massive lawn still flaked with patches of snow, then went back down the stone path toward the sidewalk.

But before he got far, he heard a click of the lock and a creak of the door. When he turned around, a girl of thirteen or fourteen was staring at him from just behind it. She was dressed like a schoolteacher but had a dark, pretty face and shiny coal-black eyes. It had to be Gabriel's younger sister, Hannah.

"What do you want?" she whispered, as if people in the house were sleeping.

"I'm here to see Gabriel," Danny said, like a neighbor from down the street who'd only just dropped by for a chat.

"He's not here. And you shouldn't be either."

"Why not?" Danny asked, thinking rudeness must run in the family.

"My parents will be home soon," she said, biting her middle finger.

Danny looked at his watch, then showed it to her. It was 5:35.

"I shouldn't have answered the door at all," she said, then shut it in his face.

When he put his ear to the door a few seconds later, he didn't hear any footsteps in retreat. So he figured she was still there, waiting for him to go away.

"I'm worried about your brother," he called out. "I haven't seen him in a week."

But he heard nothing in reply.

"I think something's happened."

Still nothing.

"Gabriel's my friend!" Danny shouted.

"What do I care?" Hannah said from behind the door.

It was a mean thing to say, but Danny wondered if she'd really meant it or just hadn't been able to think of anything else. She was just a kid, after all.

"Just tell me where he is!"

"I don't know!"

"I don't believe you, Hannah Golofski!"

It wasn't long before she opened the door again, this time letting it swing wide, as if her name had been some kind of magic password. She was tall for her age, thin as a knife and wearing at a least three sweaters. She didn't invite him inside but didn't seem to think he was a threat anymore either.

"I meant I don't know the name of the place," she said.

"What place?"

"I'm not supposed to tell."

"Well, you can tell me."

She looked down at her feet, chewing her lip and sighing, then up again at Danny.

"The hospital," she finally said.

"Why? Is he sick?"

Her eyes drooped with regret. She looked like she wanted Danny to understand her without having to say anymore.

"He's being treated for—his problem."

"What problem?" Danny asked.

Gabriel had tons of them, but few were treatable, except with cash or antibiotics.

"If you're his friend, I'm sure I don't have to tell you."

"Tell me what?"

"That he's—"

"That he's *what*?"

"A feygele."

She turned away, as if the word itself might be contagious, then burst into tears.

Between weepy sniffles, she eventually confessed that her father and eldest brother had found some dirty pictures in Gabriel's bedroom on Saturday night and carried him off early Monday morning—kidnapped him, practically—to some place a few hours outside the city, threatening to disinherit him or worse if he didn't cooperate. Her parents went to see him again on Wednesday, but Hannah hadn't been allowed to come.

"I just want him to get better," she cried.

"What are they doing to him?"

"They give him medicine to calm his nerves," she said, her voice low and wobbly. "And shocks."

"Shocks?" Danny cried.

"Of electricity. But they said it's just little ones!"

Danny knew what it meant, but all he pictured was Colin Clive flipping the switch on Boris Karloff and Tesla coils exploding with sparks. Then he imagined Gabriel doped up on Lithium and watching Lawrence Welk on a day-room television.

"Where did they take him?" he asked. "Which hospital?"

"I don't know," she said, whimpering. "They didn't tell me."

"Where is he!" he shouted.

But then she slammed the door on him a second time.

He kept shouting and rapped the knocker over and over but got no answer. He wanted to break down the door and tear apart the whole house, timber from stucco, smashing every post and beam until there was nothing left of it. He hated the Golofskis for being so cruel. And God for piling so much misery on top of him all at once. And Saint Jude for sleeping on the job yet again. But this hurricane of fury was somehow different from the others, stronger yet more short-lived. When his arm grew tired, he stopped knocking and listened, then, still hearing nothing, gave up, turned around and went back down the stone path, past the oak tree, and out onto the street.

As he retraced the mile to the IRT, he wished he'd known his friend was in trouble and wondered why he hadn't come sooner. But by the time he got to the station, he knew it wouldn't have made a difference, since houses like the Golofskis' were the worst kind of trap for people like Gabriel and him. The whole picture-perfect, trumped-up neighborhood of beautiful mansions was a trap. Single men could never live there. Either they'd be carted off to hospitals or they'd just get sick and die from sorrow.

⊙ ⊙ ⊙

As he stood in the cocinita, where a chicken carcass was simmering into soup, Danny told Raf the whole sad story and added Hersh and Aviva Golofski to his growing list of mortal enemies. Some people—most straight people, it seemed—just couldn't be trusted. Then he wrapped his arms around his friend, buried his face in his chest and bawled like a baby. It was the second time in a week, but he felt no shame about it. Those days were done. And Raf seemed to understand. It was a crime to steal a man like that, after all. It was kidnapping and probably attempted murder. But there was nothing they could do. Gabriel could have been in any loony bin within a two-hundred-mile radius. And even if they found out which one, they couldn't have gotten him out and probably wouldn't even have been allowed to visit. They weren't family. They were just friends, and as far as the law was concerned, friendship wasn't worth a damn.

When Danny felt he'd cried enough, he patted Raf on the shoulder and kissed his cheek, which smelled of Dial soap. But as he stepped back to wipe his eyes, he sensed something odd and looked down. The khaki trousers Raf always wore to the post office were loose and pleated, and his stiffy made a circus tent in the front you couldn't miss.

Raf turned away, red as rhubarb. "I don't know what to say."

"Oh my God, don't say anything!"

Danny knew hard-ons happened for lots of reasons and sometimes for none at all. From middle school to high school, his own dick had been up and down at all hours, like a railroad crossing gate. And even if Raf had gotten a little horny during their hug, Danny thought, he probably hadn't meant to do it. Unless he *had* meant it. He wondered if that would be bad news or good. But he also worried it might mean another big change in his life—and in the solidest and steadiest part of it.

When the doorbell suddenly rang, Raf seemed as relieved as Danny was. He went to look through the peephole. "Quién es?" he asked.

"It's Ciaran Duffy, Danny's brother," the voice behind the door said. "May I please speak with him?"

Danny didn't want his brother barging in on him when he'd been crying and while Raf was still stiff. He didn't want him to be there at all. Though it had been Quinn's idea to give him the boot, Ciaran had gone along with it. But it was more than mere spite that Danny felt. He'd once believed that the two separate parts of his life could coexist, like the dayshift and the nightshift, each getting the job done but never meeting for a moment. Now there was only his old life and his new one and he knew it had to stay that way.

When Danny waved his hands in protest, Raf only made a great pained face and shrugged, then adjusted his trousers and opened the door. He didn't believe in family breaches, even under the worst of circumstances, and he was probably charmed by Ciaran's manners, which usually won people over, despite his homely looks.

"What's new, Danny?" Ciaran said, merrily. He wore dusty work clothes and carried his tool bag in one hand and a stuffed paper sack in the other.

After Raf invited him in, he slowly cast his big baggy eyes around the apartment, like he was taking in the mysteries of the homosexual's lair. If he noticed the remains of Danny's shiner, he didn't say anything. But when his attention seemed to rest on the old, fringed lampshade, Danny decided he'd had enough of his brother's inspection.

"Why are you here?" he asked.

"Just to see how you've been keeping," Ciaran said. "It's been a week, you know. I don't think a week's ever gone by I didn't see you."

It was true, except for when he was in Korea. Even after he'd gotten married and moved into his own place in Tremont, Ciaran stopped by all the time. He'd been more like a father than Pat Duffy had ever been.

"Mavis sends her love," he said.

Danny couldn't have cared less about Mavis's love, but he did want to hear how Margaret Duffy was bearing the loss of him, whether she spoke his name often or couldn't stand to hear it said out loud. He wondered if she regretted what she'd allowed to happen under her own roof. If she missed her favorite son and was asking for the Lord's help to bring him home. He hoped she at least missed the thirty bucks a month in rent he'd been paying for years. But he couldn't bring himself to mention her at all, which would've seemed like a kind of backwardness. Ghosts didn't ask about their mothers.

"I brought you something," Ciaran said, setting his tool bag down. "You left it in the hall closet."

He reached into the paper sack and pulled out Danny's old St. Helena's letterman's sweater, size small, which he'd won for suffering through a single season of cross-country running and proving nothing to nobody in the process. It had a few moth holes in it and the navy felt letter "H" was peeling off. But he'd never worn it once and had left it in Parkchester on purpose, along with the other things that didn't suit him anymore or never had.

"No thanks," he said.

He knew it must have taken Ciaran some effort to get Raf's address. But bringing the sweater made it clear how little he understood Danny.

"Aren't you gonna introduce me?" Ciaran asked, looking at Raf, who'd already gone back to the chicken soup, pretending to mind his own business.

But when Danny said nothing, Raf turned around and smiled.

"I'm Rafael Ramos," he said. "Glad to meet you."

Ciaran reached over and gave him a hearty handshake, probably to show that he wasn't afraid to touch a homo.

"Just tell me why you're here," Danny said, as Raf went back to pretending.

"You quit your job, they said at Sloan's," Ciaran said.

"I was fired."

"Will you get another one?"

"What do you think?"

"Ask me to sit down and I'll tell you," Ciaran said.

Danny hesitated. If he asked his brother to sit, he knew he'd have to hear all the latest from home. Of Bill's wedding plans and Michael's annual bonus or Declan's latest feat of stupidity and Eileen's latest romantic crisis—none of which mattered anymore.

"Oh, just come home, won't you?" Ciaran whined, his bushy eyebrows merging like two caterpillars in love. "I'll buy the beer and you can beat me at Risk!"

272

Raf clucked from the cocinita.

"It's not my home anymore," Danny reminded his brother. "I was made to leave.

"So be made to come back," Ciaran said, "and all will be forgotten."

Danny looked into Ciaran's hopeful eyes.

"What'll be forgotten? What it means for a man to wear a purple tie?"

Watching Ciaran trying to imagine a solution to a problem he couldn't even name was like watching a child trying to fit a square peg into a round hole. He'd already have heard about the raid and the arrest and the article in the *Post*. He must have known it was why Danny had been fired from Sloan's. Everyone in Parkchester probably knew at this point. But Ciaran didn't have the guts to spell it out. Not only couldn't he un-ring the bell, he couldn't even admit it had been rung at all.

"Well, then just come for Thursday-night dinner," he said. "Ma would love to see you."

Raf clucked again.

"I won't," Danny snapped, crumpling the image of Margaret Duffy in his mind like a wad of paper. Then to show that he wasn't just being stubborn, he added: "I can't."

Ciaran didn't ask him why not and Danny knew he wouldn't. He wanted all to be well without anything having to change. He wanted forgiveness without remorse, peace without honesty, and love without pain. And so when there was nothing left to say, he stuffed the letterman's sweater back into the paper sack, picked up his tool bag, and gave a flat smile to Raf and a hangdog frown to Danny.

"You've become an angry man," he said before walking out the door.

But Danny only thought that it was about time.

Part III

I've heard it in the chillest land -
And on the strangest Sea -

—Emily Dickinson

25

Roger stood in a dark recess of the bar, not far from the front door, hemmed in by so many bleak silhouettes but still able to see whoever entered or left the place. He tried to ignore all the flamboyant gestures, the shrill chatter, the morbid laughter, but his biggest concern was that the police might burst in at any moment and the nightmare would begin all over again. He found it impossible to believe that returning to Caesar's wasn't an act of willful self-destruction, but he'd somehow allowed Cap and Julian to convince him that he had to go back to erase the fact of his having ever been there at all.

After their meeting on Friday, he'd called Corinne again from a phone booth on Third Avenue to tell her that, rather than coming home late, he'd decided to stay at a hotel. The important Japanese loans he'd been working on would require his undivided attention all weekend, and he wanted to save her the trouble of shuttling him back and forth to the train at odd hours. He wasn't surprised that she offered no protest. She said nothing about missing Lizzie's tap recital on Saturday or the plans they'd made to see *Lolita* with some of their neighbors that night in White Plains. She didn't wish him luck with his work or ask him to check in during the day.

"Okay, Roger," she said, her gravelly voice rising to accuse him.

But her obvious distrust left him feeling a certain freedom to act without worrying about covering his tracks or justifying his behavior. So with a sense of purpose rather than a conviction of right or an expectation of success, he picked up the spare suit and shirt he always kept at his office, took a room at the Pierre on East 61st, and eventually went over to the West Side, where he muddled his way through the Wayfarer, the Mouse Trap, Faisan d'Or, the Astor Hotel, and the Old Grange near Herald Square. A few hours later, having had no success at all, he went back uptown, took a sleeping pill, and dozed until nearly eleven the next morning. Then he bought a toothbrush at the Pierre's gift shop and BVDs at Bloomingdales and whiled away Saturday afternoon with a long, gin-sopped lunch in the Rotunda Room and an even longer swim and steam at the Athletic Club, whose geriatric clientele on weekends offered few temptations. Finally, after an over-rich dinner from room service, he went down to the Village and visited Lenny's Hideaway, Café de Lys, the Rumpus, Glennon's, the King's Arms, the New Colony, and the Bleecker Street Tavern, all teeming with weekend revelers. But the only person he recognized was the male prostitute from the jail cell, making himself obnoxious on the sidewalk in front of the Hat Box on Seventh Avenue, his outrageous life apparently not having altered a bit.

"This is America, ladies!" he brayed at a group of scandalized tourists, who fled into the street to avoid him. "If you don't like what you see, you don't have to buy!"

For an hour, Roger nursed a coffee at a diner on MacDougal and then read *Popular Mechanics* at a newsstand on West 4th before he finally worked up the courage to walk over to Bethune Street. Cap had told them that, unless it had been closed down, Caesar's was probably the most likely place to look. People were creatures of habit and often perverse in their need to revisit scenes of suffering, he'd said. Like dogs to their vomit, Roger had thought.

Everywhere he looked, there was evidence of what had happened nine days before, though nobody seemed to care. There was a "raided premises" sign posted in the window, but it seemed to function more as an advertisement than a warning. The neon Schlitz beer clock was broken, the Christmas lights were gone, and the aloof Spanish bartender had been replaced by a friendlier Virginian. But the older patrons were again lined up at the zinc bar, chatting and tippling, while the Shirelles warbled on about "days like this." Roger wondered how people could so casually risk their lives and livelihoods or whether perhaps they felt they had little to risk to begin with. Heads turned, mouths sang out with surprise and chagrin, and trains of friends and strangers moved like conga lines through the crowd. Although the odds were against finding either man, Roger assumed the kid would be more likely to show up and easier to spot. He remembered shouting at him in the cell, and though he couldn't remember what he'd said, he hoped it hadn't been too harsh. The other shouter that night would probably never go to a bar again—in that, he had more sense than Roger. But if he did, he'd probably be hiding in the dark too, just like poor Andy had done.

As the thought came to him, Roger realized he was standing in the same spot where he'd first discovered the comely outlines of the young man's flattop. It was the one thing from that horrible night he could recall with any pleasure. The way their first shared smile seemed to soothe Andy's nerves, how he'd flinched when Roger squeezed his shoulder but then gradually grew calmer. Remembering that lovely, life-giving connection made Roger feel a little better, too. After a while, he relaxed his own tight jaw and taut belly and even began to feel a certain grudging affinity with the men around him. Thinking about Andy didn't transport him back to the time before the raid when he was vaguely comfortable around such people and in such a place. But it did help him see that the thing he'd always dreaded had in fact already come to pass. Whether he liked it or not, he was no stranger in a strange land but just another queer in a queer bar, and there was no use in pretending otherwise.

"Have you got a cigarette?"

Roger was about to tell whoever had asked the question to get lost. But when he turned around, he saw a familiar face, grinning smugly, obviously drunk. It was the preppie, Barrett.

"I'm afraid I still don't smoke," Roger said, relieved that the night might soon come to an end.

"Well, good for you," Barrett said. "They say it causes sarcasm."

Roger surprised himself by laughing at the joke.

"So how can I help you?" Barrett asked. "You've been standing here for a quarter of an hour looking for somebody. Not somebody to sleep with, I gather. So I figured you must be looking for me—since I'm sure I'm not your type."

"You've been watching me?" Roger asked.

"I've been celebrating," Barrett said, between sips of a whiskey sour. "You just happened to be in my line of sight."

Even in the dark, Roger could see that he wasn't at all bad looking. Although he wore a too-tight and excessively bright striped shirt, he had a classic Ivy League haircut and a winning smile. He swirled the ice cubes in his glass in exactly the same manner as virtually every male member of the Bonnie Briar Country Club.

"What are you celebrating?"

"My imminent departure from our great metropolis."

"Why are you leaving?"

"Because the winters are so hard! Though I suspect you know the real reason. Isn't that what you've come to see me about?"

Roger was impressed by how quick he was to draw the inference and how calmly he seemed to accept his fate. Perhaps it was the whiskey, but Roger sensed it was something more like mettle. They were two men of the same class and background, each facing exposure and ruin for the same reason, and even may have had friends and acquaintances in common. It wasn't exactly a revelation, but Roger marveled at the notion that, if you considered every school and office in the country, there were probably thousands of men just like them, maybe many thousands, and not just creeps like Riley Cross, but decent fellows like Mudge Collins and Ezra Benson and Julian Prince. All of them out there hiding in plain sight, confronting doubts and suspicions, salvaging a little honor from the wreck of their wants and needs.

"If you must know," Barrett said, "I haven't got enough to pay the little weasel."

"So where will you go?" Roger asked.

"San Francisco," Barrett said with a wink before emptying his glass. "I hear it's a friendly town."

Roger wondered what it would be like to start over in a new place. He thought of streetcars and sailors, palm trees and sunshine. But while it was easy to see Barrett frolicking in North Beach, Roger couldn't see himself there. He saw only a solitary man in a hotel room, someone who'd packed up all his burdens and carried them across the country with him. Wherever his future lay, he knew it wouldn't be somewhere else.

"Roger Sutcliffe Moorhouse," he said, extending his hand.

"James Barrett Buchanan," the kid answered.

They made three quick, vigorous shakes and released at the same moment, just the way Roger had taught Henry to do it.

But now that he had the information he needed, there was no reason to stay. Although he scrupled about leaving so abruptly—running out of bars was a habit he was determined to break—lingering would have been pointless.

"Is there some place you have to be?" Barrett asked, apparently noticing Roger's impatience. "I really meant for you to buy me a drink."

"I'm afraid I have to go," Roger said, pulling a twenty from his billfold and slipping it into Barrett's shirt pocket. "But I'm very glad to have met you."

"And did you get from me whatever it was you needed?" Barrett asked.

Roger shot him a look of admiring disapproval and then squeezed his shoulder.

"If I were you, I'd put off San Francisco for a few weeks," he said. "See how things turn out. You might be surprised."

◉ ◉ ◉

At first glance, Julian's apartment seemed a bit too whimsical—a picture of a clown, a clock in the shape of an eye, an odd sort of chaise made of bent wood. But the living room was nicely open and airy. If there was a somewhat precious attention to detail, nothing about it was overtly feminine. It looked more like Roger's office than anyone's home, but after a while he found he liked it a good deal. When Julian asked him earlier that night where they should meet, he'd spontaneously suggested Morningside Heights, though it was quite out of the way. And as Julian poured a pair of neat scotches, Roger marveled at the idea that he lived there alone in rooms decorated entirely to his own taste. A moment later, the simple fact that they were two men sitting on a sofa together without female company sent goose bumps juddering up his neck and down his arms.

Yet the pleasure ceased the moment he remembered why they were there. He understood how the dossier was meant to work and why it was necessary. But to admit everything publicly—on paper and to government officials—seemed like yet another form of suicide, only slower and more painful. It went against decades of training in patrician reserve and stealthy anonymity and contradicted the very idea of self-preservation. The advice he'd rashly offered to Barrett Buchanan had been premised on the notion that Cap's plan would succeed. But now it seemed a ludicrous risk to take, one that might turn an awful but local problem into an unthinkably federal case.

"I suppose we have to trust the expert," Julian said, sounding even more fatalistic than the day before. That night, he'd been to the Excelsior and the Cork Club, then to the Allendale, the 415, and the Mais Oui—all without any seeing sign of the other man they were looking for.

"What if they call our bluff?" Roger asked. "It's not hard to imagine being visited by government agents."

Julian nodded as if he agreed but then only leaned back and sipped his scotch.

They sat in awkward silence for a while, until the idea of two men on a sofa together began to feel stifling. Then Roger stood up and crossed the room toward the chaise, an outlandish contraption of blond wood curves and tan leather webbing, like some kind of giant spring trap.

"Would you like to try it?" Julian said, gesturing to the chaise.

"Uh, no thanks," Roger said turning away in confusion. "I was just—"

"Go ahead," Julian said, rising slowly from the sofa. "It's Finnish."

Roger looked at him to be sure the invitation was in earnest, then he slowly eased himself into the chair. It cradled him with an odd weightlessness, and from his low vantage point the room looked different than it had, somehow less eccentric and more refined.

"You mentioned Gus is a painter," Roger said. "What does he paint?"

"Oh, he does these big and messy but rather moving abstractions," Julian said, with a solemnity that was modulated by obvious pleasure. "Very easy to stare at for half an hour."

"And he lives here with you?"

Julian seemed annoyed by the question at first but then smiled sadly. "He's been staying here most weekends," he said.

Roger tried to imagine how it all worked—eating, sleeping, friends. But it was hard to picture Julian cooking bacon and eggs and Gus coming into the kitchen in his bathrobe to give him a peck on the cheek. All he saw was two naked bodies in a bed.

"It's all quite ordinary," Julian offered. "Just like men and women, really."

Despite his sedentary profession, the trim suit he wore clothed what must have been a lean and active body. Roger realized that Julian was neither too old nor too urbane for him, that the impulse he'd felt at the Men's Bar to reach out and hold him had been born as much of attraction as of desperation. He imagined touching Julian's legs, his stomach, his cock. He wondered if Julian might ever feel the same about him. If, in the event that he and Gus didn't work out, he might welcome Roger's affections instead. If, after Cap's dossier plan failed and their lives were ruined, they might face the future together, come what may.

"Did you ever think of leaving your wife?" Julian asked.

The question felt like a poke in the eye, and Roger immediately regretted his fantasies. He felt ashamed to be lying horizontally in the chaise. But he was too paralyzed by gravity to get up and too pinned down by the question to evade it.

"I could never do that," he finally said.

He didn't know how he could explain divorcing a woman as fine as Corinne or remaining single when other women might avail. He didn't know where he'd live or work or how he'd spend his time. He tried to picture a happy life in a stylish bachelor's apartment, designed to his own taste, where he might come and go as he pleased. But all he saw was the same forlorn hotel room.

When Roger noticed the pitying look on Julian's face, he grabbed the arms of the chaise, threw one leg over the side and struggled to push himself up. The bandaged wound in his left palm protested with an electric shot of pain up his arm. He felt graceless and indecent, like a crab, and the more he fought the weight of his body, the shakier he grew. Finally, Julian offered his hand and Roger reached up, took it, and pulled himself to his feet, flushed and unsteady.

"Are you all right?" Julian asked.

"No, not really," Roger admitted, for the first time in his life.

He was probably more envious of Julian than in love with him. Envious of his freedom, his nerve, his ability to be himself no matter what anyone thought. But it felt good to be near him, in the same way that it felt good to be near Schuyler, as if some of these virtues might somehow rub off on him.

"The world's changing," Julian said, as they separated. "Slowly, anyway. And there's more than one way to live."

"Maybe," Roger said, tucking in his shirt and straightening his tie. "But I fear if I ever struck out on my own, I'd just end up a lonely old fairy who pays younger men for love."

It was the plain truth. Life was full of compromises. Respectability came at a price. And Roger preferred the pain he knew to whatever waited for him in the grim-seeming future of that untaken road.

He looked at Julian again, hoping to hear that he couldn't be blamed for feeling the way he did, that it was natural, or at least forgivable. But Julian only screwed his face into a rictus of horror. Then he crossed to the other side of the room, looked up at the eye clock, and snatched a set of keys from the coffee table.

"I'm sorry," he said breathlessly. "I have to go."

"What is it?" Roger asked, worried his frankness had offended.

But Julian's eyes flamed with self-accusing bitterness. "Gus spent a week at Riker's Island," he said.

Roger hid his revulsion behind genuine, open-mouthed shock. Then he offered his sympathies while he collected his coat and hat. He tried to remember what Gus had looked like in the jail cell, but the image blended into that of Barrett, ironic and unrepentant, and then of Andy, blue-lipped and lifeless, and then it became just another blank oval, just another ruined young man.

"And where are you going right now?" Roger asked.

Julian pulled his coat off a hook in the hallway and swung open the front door. "To bring him home," he said.

Watching him race to catch a taxi on Amsterdam, Roger felt a vicarious hope for his success, tempered only by the realization that he'd probably never have such powerful feelings for someone else. But the comparison on the score of personal strength made him feel even worse. With both his reputation and the man he loved in danger, Julian had borne twice as much as Roger had and done it all so gracefully. Whereas Roger had merely survived from crisis to crisis, and now all he could do was pull his scarf snug against the cold damp air and hail a Checker cab to carry him back down to the Pierre, where sleep was the only comfort he had left.

But then he saw Schuyler stepping out of his Country Squire a few yards away, dressed in an overcoat, flat cap, and muffler, and glaring at him with livid eyes. It should have been one of those coincidences that made city life seem charmed. But Roger knew it was the opposite, a deadly intermixture of contraries, and he feared the combustion would tear right through his heart.

"Roger!" Schuyler called out bitterly, like a man shouting at his dog.

"Sky," Roger said, hoping the mere exchange of names might somehow summon an old trust.

It couldn't have been a matter of chance that Schuyler had discovered him leaving an apartment in Morningside Heights at midnight. He must have been following him. In fact, he looked as if he'd been at it all night, which a half-eaten sandwich and deformed paperback on the dashboard of his Ford seemed to confirm.

"What are you doing here?" Schuyler asked. "And please just tell me the truth!"

Roger's first impulse was indeed to lie. He knew he might easily concoct some tale about the Japanese loans, a colleague's carelessness, and the necessity of coming uptown to fetch a missing document. But Schuyler, so gruff and stern in the dim glow of a streetlamp, seemed unlikely to believe anything he said.

"Have you been following me?" Roger asked.

"Yes, I have," Schuyler said, his voice curdled with self-righteousness. "Your wife asked me to find out what you were up to."

Roger was both hurt and surprised that she'd betrayed him to his friend, even if he'd driven her to it. Her aloofness on the telephone the night before hadn't been passive resignation but tactical evasion. She wasn't surrendering to her husband's judgment but biding her time until she might more effectively impugn it. Of course, it was typical of Schuyler to assume an unpleasant responsibility with such stoicism. He'd always loved sacrificing for the greater good.

"She seemed quite worried, so I agreed to do it," he said.

"How chivalrous of you!" Roger said. "And what have you learned?"

"That you've gone to at least half a dozen very unseemly places tonight in search of God knows what."

"Unseemly?"

"That's the polite term, Roger. Don't force me to be impolite."

"I was looking for someone, if you must know."

"And the man I just saw you leave this building with, is he the one?"

"No. He's just a friend."

Roger wasn't sure he'd be able to tell Schuyler the whole truth. But he felt an unexpected comfort in relating even a few facts. He had indeed been looking for someone that night, and Julian was indeed his friend.

Schuyler lit a cigarette and leaned against his station wagon, kicking the heel of his shoe against the simulated wood side panel, as if he'd only just discovered its nefarious duplicity. How silly, Roger thought, to drive all the way into Manhattan alone in such a large car.

Then he wondered if he'd mistaken Schuyler's hurt feelings for anger, and if the truth in all its pitiful detail might not inspire in him some compassion. If decades of friendship were worth anything, he hoped they might be called on in a crisis to bear the weight of ordinary human frailty, however unseemly.

"Can I explain?" he asked, imagining what it would feel like to have a lifetime of lies fly from his shoulders like birds off a statue.

"Have you had relations with that man?" Schuyler shouted, snowflakes dancing madly above his head.

"Will you please just listen for a moment?" Roger asked, resenting Schuyler's question as much as his own naïveté.

"No!" Schuyler roared, throwing his cigarette into the gutter. "No, I won't!"

He looked at Roger as if he'd just caught him giving aid to the enemy. His eyes were wet and bloodshot. But it was his tremulous mouth, slick with sweat, that made it clear he felt Roger had betrayed not only their friendship but manhood itself.

"For crying out loud, Sky!" Roger said, beginning to realize that telling his story might never have been as painful as not being able to tell it at all. "Hear me out!"

"Damn it, Roger! We've always trusted each other—I mean, how can you expect me—?"

Schuyler groaned liked a large animal taking its last breath. Then he craned his neck and shook his head defiantly, as if to confirm that there was no place in his mind for such dark and terrible knowledge.

"Schuyler, please—"

"I want you to stop this insanity right now. Go home to your wife and beg her forgiveness. That's all!"

He got back into his car, ground it into gear, and lurched its ungainly bulk out into the street, then disappeared around the corner onto Amsterdam.

A light switched on in the window of an otherwise darkened building on the other side of 113th Street, and Roger stared impassively at the apartment, waiting for some figure to appear, while trying to persuade himself that Schuyler might eventually regret his outburst and come around. Then he felt a sharp burning sensation on his cheeks and around his eyes and realized that they'd probably never speak again. There'd be no more skiing in Weston or tennis at the club or birthday celebrations in New Rochelle and Greenfield Hill. No trip to Lake Como, no blue water, no heaven on earth. What had begun so fortuitously in a biology lab in Lakeville, Connecticut, had ended so inevitably on a deserted street in uptown Manhattan. Their ancient, cherished, physically demonstrative, famously indestructible friendship was finally over.

But when no figure appeared in the window and the apartment went dark again, Roger suddenly discovered that he wasn't as sad as he thought he ought to be and, in fact, couldn't shake the feeling that he'd somehow been set free.

26

When Julian heard the buzzer, he inched out of bed, yawned himself into his robe, and staggered to the living room, where white morning light scorched the edges of the curtains and the eye clock read 8:17. Not exactly early, but certainly too early for visitors. The night before, after his meeting with Roger and Donovan, he'd stayed out late and brought home little more than the dismal perfume of cigarettes and sweat on his clothes. He went to the East Side and searched the Blue Parrot, the Big Dollar, the Grapevine, and the Stop Gap, all without finding either of the men they were looking for or a single person who'd seen or heard from Gus. Although the weather was practically balmy for February, trudging from bar to bar had left Julian so demoralized that the next morning, as he pushed the intercom button, he didn't even have the energy to hope for good news.

It was Pen, who'd left so mysteriously the previous week and whom he hadn't expected to see again until the second Friday in March. Through the crackling speaker, she offered every manner of apology for her untimely intrusion, and when Julian opened the door a minute later, he saw that same unwonted gleam of rebellion in her eye, which now seemed to betray some hidden, though not necessarily unhappy, motive.

"Oh, Jules, I know it's cruel and unusual of me to drop by so early and so unannounced," she said. "But I'm sure you'll forgive me when you know the reason. Or at least I hope you will."

"Is everything all right?" he asked.

"I have something important to tell you."

She handed him her coat but held on to her purse and a small shopping bag. Then he left her to admire the living room while he boiled water for Nescafé, hoping only that whatever she had to say would make their lives easier rather than harder.

A few minutes later, they arranged themselves on the sofa with their cups.

"Now what's this all about?" Julian asked.

"Did you see they put off the mission again?" she said.

"What mission?"

"Atlas 6! In Cape Canaveral. Poor Colonel Glenn."

"And so you're here to commiserate?"

"No, I'm only stalling."

"Stalling about what?" Julian asked, with a tone of impatience meant to hint that he wasn't entirely free of care that morning.

"It's so strange to say it," Pen said, with an oddly kittenish smile. "I fear it might sound shocking and improbable, at first, and yet then be so obvious and inevitable once you think about it."

"Cryptic doesn't become you, kiddo."

"Well, if you really have no idea what I'm going to say, then I've gotten myself into an awful mess."

"Just tell me why you left so suddenly last weekend."

He'd never quite believed the medical emergency. And then there was all the strange talk of happiness and the quoting from Gibran. She'd been a very different Pen than Julian was used to, though he hadn't had time to give it much thought since.

"Well, it wasn't because of my mother's hip," she said. "I'm sorry I wrote that. It was a lazy lie—and I'm so tired of lying. But it's all happened so fast."

He sensed a great change looming. Most likely, she'd found another man, one who'd be able to give her romance and children. But then he remembered his own resolution to tell her everything about himself and Gus and the mess they were in. It seemed like another obligation in his life that he'd put off for too long. And he was on the verge of interrupting her confession to offer one of his own, when she reached into the shopping bag on the floor.

"I bought you something," she said.

"What's the occasion?"

"I'm getting to that."

He received the small rectangular package with uneasy curiosity and picked through the fancy wrapping paper to discover a box from Paul Stuart, inside of which lay a pair of expensive-looking lambskin driving gloves.

"They're beautiful. But why?"

"To keep your hands warm, of course."

"But why now?"

She sighed, shrugged, and looked him square in the eye: "Because one has no idea how to tell one's fiancé that she's fallen in love with someone else."

"Oh," he said, dropping the gloves in his lap.

His first thought was that he'd be seeing her much less often. No man would be glad to share his wife with her ex, even if he were the furthest thing from a rival. His second thought was that his mother would be both annoyed and relieved, since the news of his engagement to a "Radcliffe girl," once the talk of Canal North, had over the years turned quite stale and left her friends asking impertinent questions. But Julian's third thought—he wondered why it hadn't been his first—was that he was finally free of an awkward entanglement and one that had indirectly put Gus in so much danger.

"I'm sorry, Jules," she said, reaching for his hand. "I would have told you sooner, but—my father. Of course, you understand that he's not going to take it well."

"I'm very happy for you," he said, though he didn't understand at all. "And I'm sure it's for the best."

He imagined Pen had found herself a pilot or an astronaut, someone athletic and rugged, bright and ambitious, someone who was her equal. It was hard to see how such a man might not meet even Ron Bollinger's exacting standards. Of course, any man who wasn't a homosexual had to be viewed as an improvement.

"Oh, it really is for the best," Pen said. "For both of us."

It was the closest they'd ever come to admitting their engagement had been a sham.

"So tell me all about the lucky fellow," Julian said.

"Her name is Myra," she said.

Julian cleared his throat to hide his astonishment. Then he snatched up the gloves again and rubbed them between his fingers.

"She's a nurse. She lives in Gramercy Park and has a big Newfoundland dog called Lord Byron. I know you'll love them both."

It certainly was shocking and improbable and yet obvious and inevitable, too. He'd wondered once or twice before if Pen had any tendencies in the Sapphic way, but he'd always dismissed the idea without serious consideration. He'd known few such women personally and supposed they were mostly as mannish or peculiar as the odd girls he'd sometimes seen in bars or the dour spinsters everyone knew but no one ever talked about. Pen had always seemed much too fine a woman to be one of them. But how idiotic it was of him to traffic in crude stereotypes and to ignore all the signs. She was neither a hausfrau nor a glamourpuss. She liked men but had never expressed the slightest physical interest in them. She was liberal, open-minded, and ironic. In fact, although she was smarter than Julian, he liked to think she was a kind of female version of him, which he'd always assumed was why they were such great friends.

"I know it's all so sudden, but she's just taken a position at Lawrence Memorial. We're going to live together."

He tried to return her beaming smile as he thought about two women sharing a life. What had always seemed to him rather outré suddenly seemed perfectly sensible. After all, Boston was probably full of Boston marriages.

"That's wonderful!" he said, relieved to feel his pleasure overcome his surprise.

"You're not angry?"

"How could I be?"

Now he did understand. Pen's father was not a man to brook such a disappointment, and she'd obviously felt she needed to be ready to confront him before she could risk her secret, even with Julian.

There were so many questions to ask—about what Myra was like, where and how they'd met, if Pen had always preferred women, and why she'd ever asked Julian to marry her in the first place—though that last question no longer seemed so pressing.

What men daily do, not knowing what they do!

But there was so much to tell Pen, too, and although he didn't want to spoil her moment of joy, he knew the time for withholding had long passed. It would, of course, be a kind of comic absurdity, the inverse of Benedick and Beatrice in *Much Ado*—not professed enemies admitting they're in love with each other but pretended lovers admitting they're each in love with someone else. Still, he knew that the greater farce would be the one in which he played the understanding and sensitive normal man so tolerant of the plight of clandestine lesbians.

"Aren't you going to try them on?" she asked, looking at the gloves.

Taking what he hoped was his final opportunity to delay the inevitable, he did, and they fit perfectly, like a tough but beautiful second skin.

"You know that I don't own a car," he said.

"But you might one day."

He stood up and circled the room, making fists with his hidebound hands. There was no reason it should be difficult to say. She was an old and trusted friend, and she herself had just shared nearly the same revelation.

"Since we're being so honest, there's something I'd like to tell you, though it feels a bit anticlimactic at this point."

Pen leaned forward with her hands on her knees, grinning and eager, like a blooming bride who assumed all the world's news would flatter her own.

"I've been seeing someone else too," he said.

"Tell me all about him," she said with a sly smile.

The jolt lasted only an instant, as did the chagrin that he'd been foolish enough to think he ever could have deceived her. Then came the warm embrace of Pen's kindly questions and the long, detailed answers that carried him from the Stable Gallery to Caesar's, from Phoenix and Palo Alto to Cambridge, from the Sixth Precinct station to Roger Moorhouse's office and then to Caspar Donovan's. Julian described his deep love for Gus and the agony of knowing what had happened to him but not where he'd gone. Pen listened with concentration and compassion and was every bit the friend he'd lacked in recent days. When he finally got the whole story out, it seemed nothing like the comedy he'd feared it would be, and depending on how things turned out, possibly not quite a tragedy either.

"You really knew?" he asked.

"I knew about you before I knew about me," she said.

"And yet you asked me to marry you!"

"And yet you said yes!"

"I guess we've always deserved each other," Julian said.

They hugged for a long time in the absolving silence, then Pen got up to go. She and Myra would be packing all day and leaving the next morning. Julian asked her if she'd like to have the Aalto chaise, since it had been given by her father with every expectation of receiving a son-in-law in return. But she insisted there'd be no room for it in Myra's car, especially with such a large dog in the back seat, and anyway it had always been his, even if she hadn't made that clear.

Julian's mother would have said they'd used each other abominably. But as he kissed Pen on one cheek, caressed the other with his gloved hand, and sent her on her way, he felt only joy on her behalf, relief that the decade-long charade had finally come to an end, and gratitude that they'd had the sense to lean on one another as good friends should. They really had deserved each other.

◉ ◉ ◉

On a cold, rainy Thursday night in mid-January, he'd traced the golden waves of hair on Gus's paint-stained forearms, studied the field of copper freckles on his upper back, and kissed his inner thighs, pale and smooth like the patina on old marble. He licked the stubbled slope of Gus's neck and tasted the salt of his toes. His skin smelled of mineral spirits and tar soap, his hair of musky sebum, and his armpits—*aroma finer than prayer!* As the radiator hissed, they lay crosswise for a time, Julian's cheek on Gus's firm belly, watching his plump and stately cock pulse in regular fluxes. It seemed criminal that something so lovely should spend most of its life hidden away in the dark, so rarely springing into another man's view, a squandering of beauty and verve.

Then without warning, Gus rocked up from the bed, seized Julian by the arm, flipped him onto his stomach, and fell on top of him.

"I want you," he whispered, with typical simplicity.

"You can have me," Julian whispered back, with atypical surrender.

What happened next wasn't the usual fumbling negotiation of body parts. Gus was neither too fast nor too rough but knew exactly what to do, just how hard or soft, how fiercely or tenderly. With most of his previous partners, Julian had always been ready to vocalize every happy, nervous, silly, or nasty thought in his head. But in Gus's steady silence he felt something worthy of deeper respect. And so with hot whiskers on his shoulder, Julian held his tongue, closed his eyes, and relaxed into the pressure, thrilled by the pleasure of Gus, the far better man, inside him. Every stab and sway seemed to bind them closer together, wrapped in each other's skin and sweat, smells and softness merging, and for a gasping, delirious, impossible fifteen minutes, it almost felt as if they'd become the same person.

When it was over and they were separate again, and Gus's shining body purred next to his own, Julian mused to himself that the mechanics of the act, which could often be sloppy and even a bit revolting, had been so curiously easy and clean. It was just how sex was meant to be. Hardly an expense of spirit in a waste of shame. In fact, in their damp and tangled sheets, what had been so mad in pursuit was so serene in possession. Instead of worrying about whether he'd yielded too much too soon or whether Gus might now lose interest in him or Julian might find himself unworthy of so much perfection—instead of dwelling on these fears or covering himself in the protection of nonchalance, he only listened to the sound of their quieting breaths and felt the waning heat of their bodies and was happy. Their heaven was still heaven, their bliss in proof a proven bliss.

Although he hadn't understood it then, that night Julian's bedroom ceased to be one of the furtive, solitary spaces that had always contained the most vital moments of his emotional life. It became instead something far more real and dangerous and satisfying, and if it seemed he'd lost some part of himself in the process, it was only in the way a rich man donates his fortune to charity or a fat man on a reducing diet loses weight.

The next morning, after Gus had gone off to a job moving paintings for a Midtown gallery, Julian paid a brief visit to the university's law library, where amid the low hum of serious thought and the pleasant mustiness of the stacks, he learned that, according to New York Penal Law Section 690.5, "A person who carnally knows any male or female person by the anus or by or with the mouth" is guilty of "sodomy," which is a "crime against nature." Even if it involved two consenting adults, it was a misdemeanor, punishable by imprisonment for up to three months, a fine of $500, or both. He winced at the odious language and cruel numbers and wondered briefly if he'd sought them out of unconscious fear or conscious defiance. But by the time he'd left the building a few minutes later, he'd forgotten about them entirely, and all he could think about for the rest of the day was seeing Gus and doing it all over again.

❂ ❂ ❂

Finding Loosli's doorman nodding off late on Saturday night, Julian slipped quietly into the elevator and a minute later began banging on the penthouse door. The clamor seemed justified by every outrage, every fear and grief he'd endured in the past week. He felt almost as if he were raiding the apartment in retaliation, attacking a citadel of sin to rescue the innocent and punish the guilty, though with a far greater right and purer intention than the cops had raided Caesar's. For even in his disgraced and outcast state, he needed only to think of Gus and the lark of his passion soared. And as the door opened, he readied himself to make his demands and shake Loosli by his velvet lapels until he got an answer.

But the person who appeared was Dahlia. In a black silk sheath with diamonds shimmering in her ears, she looked like she'd just come from some tony art world affair.

"I thought it might be you," she said coolly, as if she were used to greeting belligerents at all hours, though nothing could hide her triumphant glow.

"I've come to see Gus," Julian said.

"What makes you think he's here?"

He knew she only meant to be obstinate, so he reached over her shoulder and pushed the door open. In the near distance stood

295

Loosli, wearing a remarkably plain cardigan and a somber expression on his face.

"Professor Prince," he said. "The last twenty-four hours have been quite harrowing, as you can imagine. We are only now settling into a routine. But I had every intention of calling you tomorrow morning."

Dahlia looked away from them both, lit a cigarette, and then pretended to inspect an old Flemish still life.

"Where is he?" Julian said. "I need to see him."

"He has been through so much, the poor boy," Loosli said. "But let me assure you, he is getting the best possible care. My physician has already visited him twice."

"What's happened?" Julian asked. "Is he sick?"

Dahlia suddenly turned from the painting. "You've got some nerve!" she cried. "You knew where he was all along! And you did nothing!"

"August is sleeping at present," Loosli said to Julian, in a calming, parental tone. "But please do join us for a nightcap."

Julian looked around the room. On his last visit, it had appeared so rosy and faux-majestic. The furniture seemed to be made of cotton candy, the paintings all obvious forgeries. But this time it looked somehow more sedate and less obviously shady.

"Have you ever tasted Armagnac, Professor?" Loosli asked, holding a bottle aloft.

Before Julian could sneer at the offer, Gus appeared at the end of a hallway at the far side of the room between a grand piano and a large potted fern. He seemed to be in a half-waking stupor. Although his eyes were red and puffy, the rest of him looked ghostly white against borrowed green silk pajamas, and there were bruises on his chin and under his eye. But he was still the most beautiful man Julian had ever seen. He felt as if he'd been holding his breath underwater for days and finally come up for air.

"Gus!" he cried, as he went to embrace him.

He caressed the familiar curves of muscle and bone and thought he could still smell faint traces of mineral spirits and tar soap on his skin. But the expected release didn't happen. Gus stood stiff as a board, his arms at his sides and his face turned away, and Julian could almost feel his love draining out of him like blood from severed veins.

"Nobody wants you here," Dahlia said, her eyes now stained with tears and mascara.

"Nonsense," Loosli said, with a wave of his hand. "You are always welcome, Professor. However, it might be best if you were to come back tomorrow."

But Julian wouldn't be told to leave—not by a girl who loved a man she could never have and not by a sad old queen.

"Talk to me, baby," he pleaded. "For five minutes. Then I'll go, if you want."

Gus pinched his eyes closed, then sighed and nodded.

The maid's room was as small and plain as he'd described it, but with a decent-sized window and a clear view to the north that probably did offer reasonably good light. There was a twin bed, an old, japanned dresser, and a tattered leather club chair. Except for a few sketches and magazine pictures tacked to the walls, the only other object in the room was Gus's suitcase, spilling over with socks and undershirts in a corner.

He eased himself onto the bed and pointed Julian to the chair.

"You don't look well," Julian said with a beseeching smile.

"I've been incarcerated, J.P.," Gus said, his voice weak and hoarse, barely more than a whisper. "What's your excuse?"

"I know I can't imagine what you've been through."

"You couldn't even come close."

"Will you tell me all about it?"

"About my days in the bullpen trying not to get killed or my nights listening to men scream in their sleep? Which would you prefer?"

"I just want to help."

"Well, I guess you missed your chance."

It was precisely what Julian had feared. That their fragile new bond would break under the weight of so much misery. And that Julian's timid attempts to make things right would be all for naught because when he finally found Gus, it would be too late.

Gus coughed, drank from a glass of water on the dresser, and fell back against the headboard. Then he narrowed his eyes and asked: "What's that on your finger?"

As Julian looked down at his hand, the Fouquet Medusa scowled back.

"It was my father's," he said, glad that Gus still cared enough to notice, but realizing that the story of the blackmailer would have to wait.

"But why are you wearing it? Why now?"

He seemed annoyed that the change had happened in his absence, and Julian hoped that this, too, was a good sign. Although he'd worn the ring every day since his visit to 47th Street, he'd never once thought to ask himself why. Then an old Greek word sprang from the recesses of his brain. *Apotropaic.*

"I guess it's meant to ward off evil," he said.

"And has it worked?"

Julian still hoped it might. There in the small, quiet room, face-to-face and finally safe from the evil of the past week, their reunion ought to have been easy. If only they could move beyond their lingering doubts, he thought, the rest would happen on its own.

"Why didn't you call me?" he asked, impatient to learn the answer but careful not to sound too condescending.

Gus sat up, a rush of color in his cheeks.

"Why didn't *you* go to the police to find out what happened?" he cried, his voice raspy and ragged. "Or get me a better attorney than my lousy public defender? Or visit me? You know, even the rapists and murderers got visitors!"

Julian hadn't anticipated any of these things. Of course, the situation had grown dire enough to hire a private investigator. But until just the day before, it hadn't occurred to him that it might also involve defense attorneys, bail money, and prisons. If he was guilty of cowardice, he was guilty of a failure of imagination, too.

"I didn't know where you were," he said, sounding like a lost child.

Gus coughed again, took another drink of water, and shifted his legs under the coverlet. The small, ungenerously furnished room suddenly seemed so unsuitable. Loosli certainly might have provided better for him. But more than anyone, Julian ought to have known what he was worth.

"I tried to call you," Gus said, after a while. "From the police station, I called the operator to get the number of the Waverly. But when I called there, they hung up on me. And then I only had one call left, so I called Dahlia, but she wasn't home."

That their initial missed connection was a result of mere bad luck and not Gus's change of heart came as a relief. And Julian hoped there'd be more to come when Gus learned just how hard he'd tried to find him.

"I waited all night," he said. "Then I called everyone you know. I went to your studio, three YMCAs, a dozen bars. I came here twice. I never stopped looking for you."

But Gus didn't seem impressed. He blew his nose, pulled the coverlet up to his stomach, and muttered, "I'm sorry to have taken up so much of your time."

"But why didn't you just plead guilty?" Julian asked. It was the other question he'd been unable to answer since his second visit to Charles Street. It's what Danny had done and what any sensible person would have done.

"Oh, gosh, J.P., it never occurred to me," Gus said.

The sarcasm joggled Julian's sense of contrition and he felt the moral ground beneath them shift unexpectedly.

"So you spent a week in jail as a matter of honor?" he asked.

"I hadn't done anything wrong."

"You had me frightened out of my mind to prove a point?"

"Ope, that's right. You never let your principles get in the way of your comforts."

Once again Gus meant to define their essential incompatibility. He was the Puritan, Julian was the Cavalier, and any congress between them was now impossible.

"And you didn't think to try calling me again from Riker's?" Julian asked.

"I did think of it, actually. But then I thought better."

"But why? I waited for you! For hours every day!"

Gus lay back on his pillow and pulled the coverlet up to his neck. "You wouldn't let me stay with you when I had nowhere else to go," he said. "I mean, come on, J.P., you wouldn't even hold my hand at night on an empty street."

The ground suddenly shifted back. Julian had indeed refused him, and no amount of effort or intensity of feeling could ever undo that.

"And so you came here?" he said, feebly. "To him?"

"He posted my bail," Gus said. "Anyway, I'm far too sick to be appealing."

How perverse that fear and love were such near neighbors, that only an hour after telling Gus he wasn't welcome in his home, Julian realized that he was in love with him. From being shut so firmly, his heart had cracked wide open—from systole to diastole in a flash.

"I love you," he said, smiling, as if at an old joke.

He was about to say more, to amplify the simple phrase with superlatives, to ornament it with a line of poetry, even to repeat it over and over until they both felt the full measure of its meaning. He thought about admitting that he'd been talking to him like a madman all week, because only someone madly in love would act that way. But he knew nothing he could say would conjure the echo he wanted so badly to hear. Gus only stared back from under sinking lids, blank and aloof, as if he'd decided that Julian's sentimental, all-too-belated declaration was mere melodrama. Cheap, cheap, cheap.

"You know, J.P.," Gus suddenly said, "I'm not the man you think I am. I'm not nearly as virtuous. And I'm not as strong."

"You are to me, baby," Julian said.

"Uff da! That's my point. I know who I was in love with. But I think you've been a little mistaken."

As Julian searched for something to say, he finally saw in Gus's defeated eyes why he'd come back to Loosli's. It seemed to be so much more than a knock on the head and a week in jail. It was a depth of suffering he hadn't thought Gus capable of. It had been easier to believe him a saintly Augustine or Sebastian who'd somehow risen above it all. It was another failure of imagination.

"I need to rest," Gus said, before closing his eyes and turning his head away.

Julian wanted desperately to climb into bed with him and kiss his beautiful ears and somehow make his past-tense love present-tense again. To leave him alone again seemed like another act of negligence he might regret forever. But he knew his five minutes, grudgingly given, were over.

"Can I come again tomorrow?" he asked, fearing he no longer had a right to the question.

But the back of Gus's head didn't move. There was no sound but the soft wheeze of his breath. Julian watched the rising and falling of the coverlet and wondered if he was more angry than tired, more hurt than ill, and which might have been preferable.

"Good-bye for now, my darling," he finally said.

After he closed the door to the maid's room, he tried not to show any of the despair he felt—or the anger or the shame or the relief that the search for Gus was finally over. Dahlia, her eyes still smeared black, peeked out from above a *Vogue* magazine, while Loosli pursed his lips sympathetically, then stood to see him out. There was no point in rebuking the old man for his treachery. Julian wasn't sure he'd ever see him again, but he was determined not to expend his fury on anyone but himself.

"You were right," he said. "He came back."

Loosli performed a little sportsmanlike bow. "Time will tell with our young friend," he said. "And as we both know, Herr Professor Prince, you probably have a good deal more of it than I do."

When Julian arrived at 113th Street, it was just past one in the morning, and he steeled himself for yet another solitary homecoming and the many that would probably follow. The note he'd left for Gus was still taped to the door of his building, fluttering in the breeze like a white flag of surrender. So he took it down, crumpled it into a ball, and tossed it into the waste bin by the stairs.

27

It began to snow again on Sunday night—another Nor'easter, the cashier at Bigelow's had said—and Danny was back on the corner of Charles and Greenwich, just barely keeping warm in his ushanka and the black leather motorcycle jacket he'd bought the previous day. He'd played the whole thing out in his head a dozen times, each action and possible reaction, and calculated fair odds of success. He'd even jogged over to West Street twice—one long block to the east, three short ones to the north—to make sure that club night at the Keller Bar was crowded enough and the distance wasn't too close or too far. But no matter how well prepared he thought he was, it still felt kind of like jumping off a high dive he'd been afraid of his whole life.

Saturday had been cold, too, but as sunny as July in a way that seemed like a practical joke in February. Danny and Raf spent the morning browsing the secondhand shops down on Essex Street. At Diamonds, their favorite, you could find cameras and candelabras, teapots and tiaras, watches and wigs. They liked old things, especially things once loved, then unloved, then magically rediscovered behind a glass cabinet to shine again. Diamonds often attracted other neat and alert young men like themselves. Seekers and collectors who cast sidelong glances at each other while they peered, handled, and appraised. Men who mixed one kind of passion with another like two different versions of the same thing. Danny had brought Raf there to distract himself from the terrible news about Gabriel and to avoid the elephant in Raf's pants from the night before. He hoped that looking at cool stuff and pretty boys together would help remind them that they were best friends and nothing more.

"You know he's probably too crazy for a mental hospital," Raf said, inspecting a bronze statuette of a naked Roman youth. "He'll be out before you can say boo."

Danny stroked the forehead of an old fox fur stole, its glass eyes bulging as if in a permanent state of dying. He wondered if, underneath Gabriel's greedy appetite for life, he didn't have some kind of death wish after all.

"Tell me you're not going to go look for him," Raf said, eyeing Danny closely. "And please don't do anything else I'm going to regret."

"Don't worry, dahling," Danny said as he frowned and lowered his eyes.

"You can be so tiresome," Raf said, apparently not buying it.

As they approached a rack of coats, Danny immediately saw what he'd been looking for, the other reason he'd come to Diamonds. Hanging tough and sleek between a new US Army parka and a used trench coat was the motorcycle jacket, a Schott Perfecto, size small, with snaps and zippers and a silver belt buckle that seemed to mean business. When he tried it on and it fit him perfectly, he knew he'd be spending almost all the money he had left.

The next morning, Raf dragged him to Mass. Danny didn't know exactly why he agreed to go since he hadn't been in over a year. Maybe he wanted some kind of divine permission for what he was about to do and thought St. Francis Xavier's baroque granite jumble on 16th Street was a good enough oracle for his purposes. Listening to the old Latin chatter and staring at the priest's broad, silk-covered backside made him think of Father Frank, who'd never approved of anything Danny liked or did and was never really his friend, despite what everyone said. If he'd consulted his priest about getting arrested at Caesar's, as Mole Man suggested, he wouldn't have gotten anything better than a liquored tongue-lashing and a hundred Hail Marys. But as Danny followed along in the missal, he took one line for a timely sign that his struggle was a righteous one after all.

Judge me, O God, and distinguish my cause from the unholy nation, deliver me from the unjust and deceitful man

If that wasn't enough, while Raf knelt at the altar rail for communion, Danny happened to look at the transept and saw the shrine of Saint Jude, with the medallion of healing on his chest, the flame of the Holy Spirit spitting out of his head, and in one hand, the club the Syrians used to beat him to death. Danny guessed it was meant to remind you that he'd had lots of troubles of his own and understood suffering as well as anyone. But he looked less like a holy man than someone ready to take up arms in his own lost cause.

Danny never prayed that morning. Not for guidance, not for Gabriel—another good man attacked for his beliefs—not even for poor Miss Taylor, lying in a hospital somewhere in Rome instead of shooting *Cleopatra*. As Raf bowed his head next to him and Danny noticed the soft wisps of hair feathering the top of his neck, he realized that he didn't believe in prayer anymore. He didn't believe in heaven and hell either and definitely not the one holy catholic and apostolic church. But since he also wasn't sure if he believed in God at all, it seemed it might not be a terrible sin to believe in himself.

◉ ◉ ◉

His teeth were chattering in the cold and his hands were twitching in his pockets. He wondered how long he had before the small flicker of heat left inside him died away and then he did, too. But he knew Harry Blunt could appear at any moment and once he did, there'd be no time to waffle. The walk from the West 4th Street station was a maze of awkward angles, and while Harry usually turned left onto Charles from Hudson, that night he might decide to come up Greenwich instead. So Danny watched in both directions, looking for any movement or shadow, the bob of a fedora or the flash of lamplight on a mackinaw, though sometimes he really hoped he'd see nothing at all. His angel and devil were circling again. Raf was telling him to turn the other cheek and go home, offering up chicken soup and maybe another sexy hug. But then there was Gabriel, shaking his head and tapping his foot, saying "Come, come, get it over with, tomorrow we could all be dead!" Danny hoped for tingling skin and slow, steady breath, but all he did was shiver and shake. If he was ever going to move anywhere else in the world, he thought, it should be a warm place, like Egypt or Siam.

He saw someone padding through the snow on Charles Street. For all the racket of his hammering heart, he could just hear the muffle of footsteps. He headed west to the station and ducked behind one of the marble columns just in time to catch Harry Blunt passing under the streetlamp at Greenwich Street, his chest out, arms swinging, as easy as a man could be in a blizzard. Then Danny ran toward Washington Street and waited near the fire alarm box. There was no storm in his head this time, but he felt the sloth of fear in his legs.

As Harry approached the station, Danny sang out: "Officer Krupke, you're really a slob!"

The words came out a little squeaky and broken, but they seemed to get Harry's attention because he stopped for a second and squinted into the dark, then kept moving west on Charles Street to the end of the block.

From West 10th, Danny could just make him out. He still looked ready enough to donate a few slugs to any loudmouth punk in need of them, but also kind of wary, like he might get less generous the farther he got from the station. There were still four blocks to go, and Danny didn't want to scare him off too soon.

"Don't be such a pansy, Harry!" he cried, just loud enough to be heard.

At first, he walked slowly, but as Danny began to move a little faster down Washington, Harry did too. By the time they reached Christopher Street, they were both nearly race-walking. The Keller Bar was less than fifty yards away. But when Danny looked back a few moments later, he thought he could see some uneasiness in Harry's step. Either his knees were already giving out or some voice of warning in his head was finally speaking up. When he got to Barrow Street, he stopped at the corner and stuck his big jaw into the air, like he was using it to judge the direction of the wind, and for a moment it seemed like he might go back to the station.

But then he looked west and it was clear he saw Danny. For a half-second, they looked right at each other and the blaze in Harry's eyes seemed to light up his face.

"Does Mrs. Blunt know about you, Harry?" Danny yelled. "Does she know what you like to do to men when no one's looking?"

Again, it worked, and when Harry started moving again, Danny counted five seconds, then turned on his heel and raced over to the Keller Bar, past a row of snow-dusted motorcycles. He pulled off his ushanka, raked a hand through his pompadour, and went casually through the door.

The place was darker and louder than it had been on Thursday afternoon and jammed shoulder-to-shoulder with leather-men of all kinds. They drank and laughed and tapped their boots to the stammering horns of Louis Prima's "Night Train."

"You weren't kidding," Danny said to the young bouncer straddling his stool by the door, who nodded with grudging approval at Danny's leather jacket.

He had no doubt that Harry would soon come through the door, but he worried that someone besides him might get hurt, that the end of his own troubles might be the beginning of someone else's. He'd feel sorry for Mrs. Harold Blunt and imagined her gold bouffant collapsing at the shock of it all. These things mattered to Danny and couldn't be ignored or forgotten. But at that moment, they didn't matter enough to stop him. Just because he wasn't a masochist didn't mean he was a saint.

The bouncer took a second look at Danny and squinched his eyes, like he sensed something was wrong without knowing what it was. But before he could say anything, Harry threw open the door, barged right past them, and wiped his eyes over the crowd. Most of the leather-men turned their heads, as though they recognized an enemy in their camp. One bruiser got off his bar stool and stood tall and fierce, like the Black Knight. Then everybody in the room stopped talking and stared. Despite his workaday clothes, Harry didn't look like someone who'd accidentally wandered in from the street. He wasn't an amber-eyed monster, but he didn't seem like a kindly neighbor either. Under his frosted fedora, he looked exactly like someone who'd steal your mail and run over your cat. And the way he leaned forward with his arms ready and his jaw jutting probably gave him away as one of New York's Finest.

Danny figured there was still a chance that the he-men of the Keller Bar might turn out to be no braver than the wimps at the Excelsior. But as soon as he saw the bouncer reach for a hockey stick and the bruiser step forward with two of his buddies, he knew he'd found the army he'd been looking for.

"This man's a cop!" he shouted. "A cop who likes to torture queers!"

The room rumbled its irritation. The bruiser shouted something and then the bouncer did, too. Hardly a second passed between Harry seeing Danny and coming for him. But at the same moment, Danny crouched, pulled his left shoulder back and drove his right fist straight into Harry's groin, all knuckles and torque. Though it wasn't the soft target he'd hoped it would be, it seemed like the fastest, hardest punch he'd ever landed, and it gave him a feeling of wildness that made him want to do it again and again. But as Harry moaned and fell forward onto his knees, Danny rolled to the side and slipped between the bouncer and the bruiser, who moved in to claim their share of the action.

From the bar, he rubbed his sore hand and tried to catch his breath as he watched Harry disappear into a tangle of leather. Except for a few old veterans who looked on from a distance, every man in the place tried to join in, and some seemed to be paying back debts of their own and with interest. It was all a lot louder than Danny had expected. There was shouting, cursing, and the dull thud of boot-heels on flesh and bone. It was messier, too. A few of the leather-men were lousy fighters. One turned his ankle after he swung at Harry and missed, then twirled to the floor. Another got in the way of a loose fist that broke his nose and left him keening as blood filled his hands. Danny wasn't sure if the night was turning into a tragedy, but people were definitely getting hurt.

He wondered if he'd understood Roy Lee's idea of justice at all. Maybe when it came down to it, he'd just wanted to get even.

Though a part of him felt he ought to stay and take responsibility for what he'd started, a wiser part knew he ought to get out of the Keller Bar as fast as he could. So he skirted the room and pushed past the fringes of the fight. Then, as he reached the front door, he watched Harry Blunt fall between two leather-men and crash to the floor next to the pool table like a beef carcass. One of his eyes was already swelling shut and a gash below the other one was bleeding into his ear. He was still breathing, but otherwise he wasn't moving.

"Don't ever come back here," the bouncer said to Danny, a smear of blood on his hockey stick and tears running down his cheeks.

Danny nodded at him gravely, then ran out into the night.

The roar of the brawl stayed with him for a few blocks, and as it faded, the reality of what he'd done began to settle in. He'd hoped it might feel like a reversal of the raid at Caesar's—an assault on the invader, a rising up of the despised, maybe the beginning of a revolution. But now those ideas seemed sketchy and vague, and except for a couple of bleeders and limpers heading home for the night, no one was taking his cause into the streets. Danny didn't feel any guilt, but he didn't feel any peace either. Instead of ending something, he realized that he'd probably only given it a jump-start. If Harry survived his beating, he'd never report it, since he couldn't explain why he was in civvies at the Keller Bar without raising questions. But he might come looking for Danny and there was no telling when or whether the vendetta would end. Either way, it was just a matter of time before the next police raid happened. And each time it did, Danny knew he'd be fighting back. He no longer felt like a ghost, exactly, but he did feel as though he might have just declared war on the whole world.

He stopped at a dark corner on West Street, where the streetlamp was broken and a few cars were up on blocks, and pissed big looping yellow arcs in the snow. He was glad his dick would soon be healthy again. As he held it in his hand, it swelled a little and filled his fist with a pleasing heat, which didn't hurt as much as he thought it would. He was thinking of Raf, who'd swelled for him, too. Whose dark, lean body smelled of Dial soap and whose single man's pad was a pretty nice place for two. Who'd taken such good care of him all week and who'd probably forgive the lies he'd told but would never understand or approve of what Danny had just done. And as he headed back up to 19th Street, he wondered how, when the fight came again, he could ever have love and justice at the same time.

28

When the hourly scramble at the Larchmont station parking lot came to its inevitable conclusion late Monday evening, Roger found himself the last man waiting. For nearly ten minutes, he'd watched as cars pulled in and parked, couples waved and kissed, and men either wearily clambered into passenger seats or hastily changed places with women and drove off again. Then the last car pulled away and he was alone, standing under the rain shelter's dim orange light, kissing the bloodied knuckles of his right hand, and with his left, feeling the wind beat against his ruined briefcase like a sail in a squall. Salt air rolled in off the Sound and mingled with acrid wood smoke and the flinty dust that always seemed to hover over the tracks of the New Haven line in winter. The last rays of the sun faded into the fretwork of trees and power lines to the West, as inky blue-black clouds spread across the sky from the East. But there were no chickadees or grosbeaks to improve the silence, nor even the whistles of far-off trains. Just the dull hum of the Thruway, the occasional crescendo of traffic on Chatsworth Avenue, and knocking around inside Roger's head, the disquieting thought that perhaps Corinne had decided not to come at all.

On Sunday, during breakfast, she'd said nothing of his unexpected arrival earlier that morning and talked only of the meal itself, making sure Henry ate at least one bowl of Kix and Lizzie didn't have more than two. Then she left the dishes in the sink and spent the morning loafing on the sofa with *The Art of Living*. It seemed unlikely Schuyler had had a chance to communicate his news to her—he'd probably be forced to wait until Monday to telephone her privately. But Roger couldn't be sure. And when he tried to speak to her—he'd done the dishes himself and wanted to let her know—she only shook her head and refused to offer the least sign that her feelings were temporary.

So he went upstairs to his study and began drawing up a list of house projects for when spring finally arrived. There was a cracked windowpane to replace, clogged gutters to clear, and an unruly phlox bed to weed. He rarely managed to get done half the chores he set out for himself, but he knew this year's list was more a talisman against catastrophe than a real plan. As he added a termite inspection and a new oven, he reminded himself that houses had to be maintained regardless of their owners.

He'd left the study door open, in case Corinne changed her mind about talking or felt the need to berate him for his evasions or even to tell him she'd finally decided to take the children and leave. But his only visitor that morning was Lizzie, on an embassy from Henry, to ask if their father would help them put together a jigsaw puzzle.

"It's a big one," she said solemnly. "Henry says we can't do it alone."

"Is that what Henry says?" Roger asked, his heart softly breaking.

"Too many pieces."

So the three of them spent an hour together leaning over the kitchen table and staring at an emerging scene of horses, hunting dogs, and white-haired Englishmen in red riding coats printed on two hundred and fifty bits of cardboard. Henry gathered up all the edge pieces and began snapping them into place, while Lizzie quickened several red coats and a horse's head. Roger made a small show of testing one piece against another, but mostly he enjoyed watching his children as they searched, struck, and lit up with delight, proudly creating order out of chaos. It had been too long since they'd done anything like this as a threesome—and so successfully. Even Henry's stutter almost vanished as he prattled on about fox hunting, the men's handsome outfits, and how cruel it was to chase a poor animal until it died of exhaustion and fright.

"Why would anyone want to kill such a sweet little creature?"

"I don't know," Roger said. "But it suggests a strong character that you'd ask."

Henry smiled and then Lizzie smiled, too. Roger didn't know if their happy afternoon together was a hint of better things to come or the last he'd ever know.

He hoped he'd proven to be a better father than his own had been. He remembered so many things about his children with vivid clarity. Henry's backward tumble down the stairs when he was two. The obsession with salamanders at age five. The time he made sugar cake by himself at seven, perched on the kitchen stool, as focused as a Jonas Salk curing polio. Lizzie, on the other hand, was more a girl of intuitions than of actions. She could search out most lost objects and hurt feelings and predict weather of any kind. Once she'd warned them all that Henry had chicken pox, which ultimately turned out to be true. Roger doubted his father could have remembered such specific things about his own children.

When he called Cap Donovan from his office the next morning, he was thinking of Henry, his indoor boy, and how the stigma of a scandal might warp his development. Whether he might turn out like Barrett, bold and reckless, or Andy, fierce but fragile, or more like Roger himself, a self-armored bastion of solitude. And whether the scandal might also hurt Lizzie, perhaps in some way that could never be healed. Roger hoped that Cap's plan, if it did nothing else, might at least help make things easier on his children.

They discussed his brief meeting with James Barrett Buchanan and the continuing mystery of the second man, though Cap said he probably wouldn't matter in the end. The dossier would be compelling enough with three names and delivered by courier within the hour. It wasn't an easy thing to get information to a man of Ivan Fischer's rank in a fashion that was both timely and discreet. But Cap had certain friendly connections within the police department, and he expected that, given its importance, it would likely receive immediate attention.

"When will we know?" Roger asked. "I mean, if we've been successful."

"We probably won't ever know for sure," Cap said. "But if you don't hear anything after a few weeks, that'll be reassuring."

"And then it'll be over?"

It seemed like impossibly good luck to have everything go just as planned, unless Roger had had so much bad luck lately that he'd somehow earned a bit of good.

"If all goes well," Cap said, "you'll never hear from them again."

Then he brushed off Roger's profuse thanks with a short speech about doing his job and delicately implied that, should they run into each other again out on Long Island or up in Newport, he had nothing to fear in the way of awkwardness. Roger thought such a meeting was unlikely to happen and knew he'd probably try to avoid it.

"Do be careful, Roger," Cap added, before hanging up.

It was obvious what he meant—be more discreet, don't get caught again. Roger knew the price of his indulgence as well as anyone and certainly didn't require the hint. But then he realized that Cap was saying something else, as well. That he fully expected Roger to continue being the man he was. He wasn't going to change no matter how much he wished he could or how violently the world rebuked him. Even if he'd have to find safer ways to satisfy his needs in the future, there was no denying who or what he was.

He left work at five o'clock that day and took a Checker cab to Grand Central, pondering what that future might look like. Schuyler had by then almost certainly called Corinne. Within a day or two, she would leave him and the story would begin circulating among their friends. Edgar would eventually hear the news, too. Then Roger would be fired, and Nick would get his promotion. Unless—he grasped at the shining prospect—unless Schuyler *hadn't* called Corinne. Gentleman that he was, he'd have hated saying such things to another man's wife. When he'd told Roger on Saturday night to go home and beg her forgiveness, he might have meant that he had no intention of telling her anything. When he'd said, "That's all!" perhaps he'd meant only that they were never to discuss the matter again. Maybe, in the end, it would be like Schuyler's eldest sister, hidden away in a hospital somewhere up in New Hampshire and never mentioned by name. Or like the boy Richard had accidentally killed with his car on the night of his eighteenth birthday, now entirely forgotten. Smaller sins could destroy a man, but people often got away with the greatest ones precisely because they were too awful to acknowledge.

As Roger climbed down the stairs toward the platform and the waiting 5:57 train, he wondered how many of the men and women around him were as guilty as he was or worse. Most of them probably had their secret failures, some even less forgivable than his, and in the normal course of things no one would be the wiser. The sounds of a scuffle behind him—of murmurs, angry shouting, a whimper—only seemed to confirm this. When Roger reached the platform, he stopped and looked back in the direction of the noise, though more to avoid whatever nuisance might be coming his way than to involve himself in the business of strangers. On the staircase, an old Oriental woman was clutching her handbag in obvious distress, while next to her, a young Negro man in a ski parka stood chest to chest with the apparent perpetrator of the offense, whose face Roger couldn't see. After the old woman made her escape, the young man, no longer having female virtue to defend, and perhaps thinking it unwise to persist in such a public contest with a white man, stepped aside.

Then Roger saw the black-haired, acne-scarred desk sergeant.

At first, he felt only annoyance. The dossier had been sent, after all. The hounds were to have been called off. Even though it had all just happened that morning, it was still bad business management. But then he felt a sudden swell of outrage and reacted mechanically, as if he had an enemy plane in his sights. He steadied himself, channeled his focus, and then bolted toward the stairs, past the young man, right at the sergeant, who recognized him with just enough time to point his finger.

"You—!"

Roger swung his briefcase at the sergeant's head, clipping his chin with its hard corner. The sergeant wobbled but managed to stay upright. When he countered with a wide, careening fist, Roger held up the briefcase to block the blow. Then he dropped it and grabbed the sergeant by his jacket collar. He shook him once, then pulled back his right hand and swung—one quick, clean cut to his nose, one loud crack—so smooth and exact that Roger felt no pain at all, like a perfectly driven golf ball. The sergeant stooped and groaned as he held his bleeding face. A few women screamed. Several people at the top of the stairs stopped and stared, while those at the bottom hurried off to safety. They all seemed afraid of Roger and he was almost glad they were. He felt strong and untouchable and in control of everything. It was like flying his Hellcat at thirty thousand feet, soothed by the steady bass of the engine, the neighborly warmth of the sun, and the ungodly lightness of the machine in his charge.

When the sergeant stood up again and spread his eyes wide, it looked like he might try to fight back. But then he only bent over again and sighed.

"That was a mistake," he muttered, before fleeing into the crowd.

Roger knew he'd made a spectacle of himself again. But he didn't care that he looked like a maniac. Or that his right hand was now throbbing and his briefcase ruined. He only thought of the blood-ied, bested sergeant—and the fat, red-faced officer on the roof of Caesar's—and the old bald detective who'd asked about his pretty wife. All the men who'd humiliated him and, directly or not, killed a handsome young man's spirit. All of them finally defanged.

He jogged back upstairs into the main hall, ignored the ceiling mural, and searched out a phone booth, then began to dial the number that he'd already learnt by heart. He knew he'd probably never see Julian Prince again, that if they'd indeed been friends, it was only a temporary arrangement born of necessity. But Roger felt they still hadn't said a proper farewell. He wanted him to know not only that the blackmailer hadn't heeded their warning but also that he'd given him quite a licking. That he'd been brutal and reckless in a way that made him feel like a man again. He thought Julian might understand what that meant.

Then Roger looked at his wristwatch, hung up the receiver, and called Corinne instead.

When he told her that he'd missed the 5:57 again and would now be taking the 6:29, she said without any apparent concern that she'd pick him up accordingly. She sounded oddly unburdened of the wretchedness of recent days. He even thought he heard in her words some traces of the confident young woman he'd met long ago at the summer pool party in Oak Bluffs. Her voice, placid and faintly distracted, made him glad he hadn't called Julian, whose life, after all, was so different from his own. Roger's place, he knew, was with Corinne, if she'd have him, and their brief conversation told him it might somehow still be possible.

But staring at stolid, mute Chatsworth Avenue an hour and a half later, he began to think she'd changed her mind. Perhaps she was still at home, stewing in grief and resentment after hearing Schuyler's damning report. Or maybe the desk sergeant had called her directly and she'd already begun the drive to Litchfield. It seemed too much to hope for that she was simply running behind schedule. But as the wind picked up, he thought he heard somewhere in the near distance the resolute chirping of a goldfinch, though it was too far into the evening to have expected it. It made him think of an old poem from school, whose author he couldn't remember, something about hope being like a bird—maybe a meadowlark or a bobolink—perched on a branch, calling into a gale. He'd always preferred birds to poems. But the hope that he might survive his homecoming that night did seem as frail as feathers and yet somehow still alive and singing a tune so soft it could only be heard by someone who'd otherwise given up hope altogether.

◉ ◉ ◉

Corinne didn't explain her lateness or ask how his day had been or why he'd missed another train. But the corners of her mouth seemed to stretch and lift a couple of times as she talked of the weather forecast and the electric bill. She held the steering wheel with a light touch, but her focus through the rain and windshield wipers seemed sharp and constant. Before pulling out onto the road, she'd glanced at the bloodied hand in Roger's lap and the damaged briefcase at his feet but said nothing. He didn't know if she'd given up asking questions or assumed that explanations would come eventually and there was no need to rush them. He noticed her emerald-green eyes and small, sloping nose, wondering again if appreciation and desire weren't so different after all, but suspecting she was too wise ever to confuse the two.

As she slowed to turn left onto Huguenot Drive, he felt the car skid a bit on the icy asphalt. But Corinne seemed perfectly calm and, in fact, wasn't going very fast. He knew how much she enjoyed driving, even at night. The sweet, chemical smell of the Chrysler's newness reminded him of how much fun they'd had buying it from the dealer in White Plains. How she'd taken it on a test drive and asked so many questions about the fireball V8 engine and the power steering and brakes. How they'd laughed at the salesman's corny pitch: "All the full-sized excitement, all the full-sized value."

The sky darkened as they cruised through the heart of Beechmont Woods, over rolling hills that had probably once been filled with Indian villages and wild animals and then gradually became Dutch and English farms and then smaller and smaller parcels of real estate on which enterprising men eventually built Colonials, Capes, Tudors, French Revivals, and split-level ranches, some of them rather modest, others rather grand, all now lacquered in freezing rain. Roger wondered how long the rain would last and whether it might be the beginning of a real ice storm, the kind that pulled down trees and snapped power lines. The metronomic brush of the wiper blades lulled him into a calm, almost meditative state, and he pictured the elm in front of his own house, its slender trunk encased in ice but deep beneath its bark still abiding with summer heat. When Corinne seemed committed to her silence, Roger turned on the radio and eased back into his seat, as LaVern Baker's tearful strain made the world's troubles sound far away.

"Schuyler called this morning," Corinne said suddenly, turning the volume down without taking her eyes off the road.

The car, the talk, the rain, the radio—he'd done it all so many times for so many winters that he'd somehow allowed himself to forget what was surely coming.

"Is that right?" he said, bracing himself.

"I asked him if he knew what you'd been up to all weekend," she said, her tone edging toward anger. "He told me you'd been at your office. And when I asked why, he kindly explained to me that women don't understand how hard men sometimes have to work. He was in quite a foul mood."

Schuyler hadn't told her. It was obvious she knew there was more to the story, and Roger wondered why she didn't press him. He thought about feigning surprise or indifference or even changing the subject. Or he might have acknowledged a regrettable infidelity or, even more obliquely, admitted that he'd always had a "private problem"—which is what he'd told his family doctor when he was fifteen, just before losing the nerve to say exactly what the problem was. If secrecy was a bitter pill that killed you slowly, honesty seemed like a river that carried you swiftly over a cliff. But the impulse to deceive was only a reflex, an old habit, like the car trip itself. How strange for a lifelong liar to have no lies left to tell.

"Did you see the *Standard-Star* today?" Corinne said, after a while.

As she talked about the Negro boycott in Georgia, Roger silently rehearsed his confession so that he'd be ready when the time came. He pictured her listening to every word, weighing grievance against sympathy, revulsion against the stability of the family, then pulling over to the side of the road and weeping inconsolably.

"How sad it is," she said, "carving up the country by skin color."

"It's been that way for a long time," Roger said.

He knew men lied to women for lots of reasons. To shield them from harm, to flatter, to keep the peace. Most thought it as much a responsibility as a right. But now he saw that his own particular brand of male chauvinism was far worse than Schuyler's. Roger had lied not to protect Corinne but to keep her at a distance, to explain away his failures, to make them feel more like her own.

"I wonder if it's fear that makes people prejudiced," she said. "Or is it more a defect of the soul? I mean, people like this Governor Vandiver. Is it something he chose or was he just born that way?"

"I don't pretend to know," Roger said.

"And if you really were a bigot, would you admit it? Or would you spend your whole life pretending you weren't to avoid offending?"

It was obvious Corinne knew. She was far too clever to have been deceived by him for fourteen years. She'd known during all his pathetic attempts at lovemaking. All the days he'd spent with Schuyler, adoring and emulating his perfections. When he'd wept at the birthday dinner, toasting the man he could never have and never be, she'd known.

"Have you noticed Marjorie always lowers her voice whenever she says something about her 'help'?"

If Corinne had known from the beginning, then she'd probably also known about Mudge, who'd run off to Jordan in the early fifties to become a cotton farmer or a Marxist or a lover of Bedouin boys, depending on whose gossip you believed. Roger knew he'd broken his friend's heart, had traded freedom and love for security and approval. He'd never made any attempt at contact, never once asked their mutual friends about him. He'd told himself it was to protect the life he'd chosen. But perhaps it was also to protect the one he hadn't—the small white pension in Mykonos, overlooking the Adriatic, two men living together, poor and despised but in love.

"Loretta, Trudy, and Melvin. Those are their names. When he's not pruning trees and clearing rain gutters, Melvin's a deacon in his church and reads Isaac Asimov. I bet you didn't know that."

Perhaps she'd known she was taking a risk in marrying Roger. Perhaps she'd told herself that his condition was no different than having a war wound or a birth defect. Or she'd thought she was offering him a clear choice between happiness and misery, even if she didn't know he'd take so long to make up his mind and that the choice wouldn't be so clear after all.

"Anyway," she said, with sudden calm, "I'd much rather live among strangers than fear them at my fence."

Of all the lives to wreck, he'd picked an exceptionally lovely one. But his reason had been simple enough. He'd wanted a lovely life, too.

"I'm sure you're right," he said, "but you've always been good with strangers."

He suspected she might be willing to give up their comfortable, compromised marriage for a chance at something better, but he couldn't be certain. Although he'd lived with her for years, he didn't know her well enough to predict. He also didn't know if he was honor bound to release her and give her back her life or to reclaim what he'd damaged as his own responsibility, like a cracked vase, mending it as best he could. He wasn't even sure which he preferred. After decades of chronic introspection, he didn't know himself very well either.

Coming out of the turn onto Barnard Road, the Chrysler hit another patch of ice and began to spin its wheels again. Corinne pumped the brakes and held the car steady, but it began turning anyway. Time seemed to slow as houses and trees and parked cars moved in the opposite direction. Instinctively, Roger reached for Corinne, as if his mere arm might protect her from the threat of hurtling steel and glass. He wondered if they were both about to die. If when they crashed into another car or a tree or a telephone pole their lives would instantly end and he'd never be able to tell her the truth about the raid at Caesar's, why he'd been there, what had happened afterward, and how he'd tried so desperately to fix everything. But then the car came to a sudden stop in the middle of the road, facing in exactly the same direction they'd been driving, having turned two full circles without hitting anything at all.

◎ ◎ ◎

In their garage on Rockledge Place, her eyes widened and drifted upward several times while he spoke, as if they were sweeping away the dust of a thousand old doubts. He reminded her of the day they'd met, how attractive he'd found her, and how important it had been to him to marry and have a family. Although he didn't use any words he thought might compound his disgrace, he told her that he wasn't like most men, that he'd never been a real husband. He said he was very sorry to have deceived her, that he'd done it with the best of intentions but now understood that it had been deeply wrong. Corinne didn't cry when he said these things, nor did she seem surprised by them. And when he thought he'd said enough, he stopped talking, listened to the hum of the idling Chrysler and the peppering of ice pellets on the roof of the house. He felt light-headed and queasy but not unhappy.

"I've always loved you," he added, knowing it was the other, no less real truth, but hating how pointless it sounded.

"But you never wanted me," she said.

"Not in the way I should have. Maybe I hoped you'd teach me how."

"Did you really think I had such extraordinary powers?"

To be unwanted or unable to want. Roger didn't know which was worse.

Corinne suddenly let out a bitter, mocking laugh that shook the air between them and then devolved into a guttural, agonized wail. Roger felt all the force of her sorrow not only because he knew he'd caused it but also because it seemed like the distilled converse of all the pain he'd endured himself. But when he reached for her, she slapped him away.

319

Then she threw her head back and he watched as tears spilled from her beautiful eyes, down her smooth tan cheek, and past her unassuming ears, mingling in the downy chestnut hair at the top of her neck. And for the first time, his sense of her beauty felt like a purely disinterested verdict. There was no admixture of contrived desire, no alloy of need or fear. It was merely an experience of good taste.

After she dried her tears and blew her nose into Roger's handkerchief, he explained the events of the past two weeks while she listened patiently. She didn't want to know all the macabre details, but at times she seemed as sensible of his suffering as she was of her own. She cried a second time when he told her about Andy, and she let him hold her hand as she did. The only question she asked was about Julian Prince, whether Roger expected to see him again, and when he said he doubted it, she turned off the ignition.

"I had an affair with Schuyler last fall," she said, solemnly.

Roger felt a strange stillness as she spoke, which might have been relief that he hadn't been the only one with a secret, though he suspected it was more than that.

"It started on a Friday. You were in Washington—at least that's what you told me. Schuyler stopped by to drop off your skis. He'd waxed them for you, I think, or repaired a binding or something. I made coffee and we talked about this and that. Eventually, we talked about you. He said he thought you'd always had some secret demons. I told him I didn't think you adored me. He didn't seem surprised. But when he told me that *he* adored me—that he always had—well, I was certainly surprised by that. He kissed me, and then apologized, and then kissed me again. Do you want to hear more?"

"Yes, of course," Roger said, too transfixed to know how he felt about it.

"Well, we made love from eleven-thirty to twelve forty-five in the guest room while the children were at school. I didn't mean for it to happen—not the first time, anyway. But it did happen four more times, and I definitely meant it then. Maybe I thought the only way to feel loved by you was to make love to your best friend. I really don't know. Though we both saw that nothing could come of it. Which is why we stopped, about a week before Thanksgiving."

Instead of the outrage and humiliation Roger thought he was supposed to feel, there was only gratitude. He was glad that Corinne had known at least a few moments of reciprocated passion and with someone she could trust. It was right that Schuyler had, once again, stepped in to help when Roger had stumbled. He thought about them in bed together, her body entwined in his, and wondered if the alternate version of himself that he'd always imagined whenever he made love to her hadn't been Schuyler after all.

"So I think we have some big decisions to make," she said.

She got out of the car and gave Roger a stoic nod that seemed to say she had every intention of being all right in the end. Then she looked briefly around at the walls of the garage—at the great many seasonal accessories of their life together hanging on hooks—and disappeared behind the mudroom door.

He stayed in his seat and stared at the dashboard—the stubby radio buttons, quilted red vinyl, sleek chrome trim—as if it might help him make a dead reckoning of his turbulent, drifting life. The cold night air began to seep through the steel doors and rubber gaskets of the car, and he felt a thrilling shiver on his arms and neck. He could almost see all the things he'd cared about for so long falling away, like shingles from a roof in a storm. As they dropped and gathered, they became undifferentiated sorrows, one great pile of pain and regret. But they seemed to fall at a distance and not on top of him, and his body somehow felt lighter for the loss. Getting out of the car, he went to close the garage door and saw that the sleet had stopped, the dark clouds were scudding away, and a few doughty stars were already peeking out from the East. There would be no ice storm. The elm would be safe, at least.

He looked up at the beloved tree, water trickling down its trunk, its shadowy canopy bleeding into the night. Then at the house, with the white clapboard and black shutters and the scarlet door, the beacon that hadn't prevented his wreck. And then at the yew hedge, glistening like a wall of black diamonds he'd never been able to afford. He tried to imagine the man who'd live here next—handsome, quiet, a lover of women, impenetrable of secrets—and how much better suited to the place he'd be. Then he blew a great billow of steam into the relenting air, pulled the garage door closed, and went inside, carrying his ruined briefcase in both arms, like a newborn baby.

29

When cathedral bells, construction noise, and a pounding headache made it impossible to stay in bed any longer, Julian rose and lumbered to the bathroom, hoping that a hot shower would prolong his oblivion for another quarter hour. After an indifferent breakfast of coffee and toast, he tried to lose himself in his manuscript, but in the face of actual unrequited love, poetry seemed a taunt and a tease. Paging through a copy of *ARTnews* that Gus had left on the coffee table for Julian's edification only made him think of the horrors of Riker's Island. When he pulled an unwashed bedsheet from the bottom of the laundry hamper—there since well before Pen's visit—and held it to his nose, all he smelled was mildew.

The next day, he canceled his appointment with Ziegler and passed the time in another miserable funk. But that evening, he let Hugh drag him from his brooding to take some air and eat a decent meal. On the way down Broadway to Romano's, their regular Italian place, they walked single-file between snow berms while Hugh waxed fervent about his latest obsessions—the Abstract Imagists show at the Guggenheim, Balanchine's plans for a ballet of *Midsummer*, and two or three other things Julian immediately forgot.

"It's wickedly droll!" Hugh chirped about one of them. "But—and I want to say this without sounding in any way earnest—deeply moving, too."

When they sat down at their table, Julian finally stopped him with an open-handed protest. "Gus and I are through," he said.

Hugh dipped his head and let his glasses fall to the tip of his nose. "Oh, sweetie," he said. "What on earth did you do to upset him?"

Then Julian told him the whole awful story. About the raid, the police station, and the blackmailer; the beating of Danny and the suicide of Roger's young friend; and—saving the worst for last because he didn't want to hear himself say the words—Gus's week in jail and his return to Loosli's. Mercifully, Hugh held his tongue until he'd finished.

"You poor kids!" he finally said. "What crummy luck! When you first called, it never occurred to me that—and when you called again, I was just happy to see you were so smitten. Oh, but my heart aches for you both!"

"I should've told you sooner," Julian said.

"Sometimes it's hard to know whether to hoard our troubles or share them with the world. But as you know, my dear, I prefer extreme philanthropy."

There was something a bit theatrical in Hugh's turn of phrase and dancing eyes, as if he saw Julian's catastrophe as just another poignant drama to be appreciated at a distance. At thirty-two, he'd had countless affairs, though few that outlasted the night. He was clever and cultivated and had taught Julian so much about the world, not least of which was how to appreciate opera and mix a perfect Aviation cocktail. But Julian had hesitated to tell Hugh about Gus's disappearance because he didn't think Hugh knew what it felt like to lose so much. Of course, Julian himself hadn't known until it happened to him. More than a decade of studying Renaissance poetry apparently hadn't taught him much about love. He'd been so focused on the poetic power to revive the image of the beloved that he'd never understood how excruciating it would be to lose him in the first place.

Hugh suddenly looked at him with a frown and gave a short, impatient laugh, as if he understood that Julian had dismissed him as ignorant and unfeeling.

"You know, you're in excellent company," he said.

"Am I?" Julian asked, annoyed to be deprived of his miserable singularity and chagrined for having apparently claimed it in the first place.

"I'd have to resort to the toes on my feet to count the number of fellows I know who've been through the wringer like that."

Julian didn't find his words particularly comforting but knew he was probably right. Raids and arrests, firings and beatings, shakedowns and suicides—they happened all the time, even if nobody talked about them. Either way, Julian's case wasn't as extraordinary or as personal as it had seemed. Only crummy luck.

As they ignored their spaghetti and polished off two carafes of cheap red wine, Julian explained all about Roger Moorhouse, Caspar Donovan, and their plan, which supposedly had been set in motion that morning. There was no guarantee it would work, he said. And even if it did, Julian's meddlesome colleagues might still be depraved enough to act on their suspicions and try to bring him down with them one way or another. If the truth got out, he wondered if Dean Cavanaugh would ask him to leave immediately or let him stay on until the end of the term.

Hugh offered him a cigarette, but Julian decided it was time to quit. It was a habit that had suited the crisis, but the crisis had passed. As they paid the bill and filed back up Broadway in uncharacteristic silence, he caught himself once more taking an inventory of his life. What he had and didn't have, and whether it all added up to something good or was somehow wanting. It was, in fact, very bourgeois of him, another bad habit, much worse than smoking, and another one he'd have to give up. He thought again of Danny and Andy and the other men who'd shared his jail cell and might already have had their lives wrecked beyond repair. If Julian was fired, he knew he'd still have the wherewithal to earn a paycheck—private high schools, he'd heard, often looked the other way when the pedigree warranted it. But even if life went back to something like normal again, it would all be weary, stale, flat, and unprofitable without Gus.

The night was clear and cold, and the third-quarter moon shone above the city like a Chinese junk on a dark ocean. Hugh began chatting again—something about Nureyev and Margot Fonteyn— and as Julian nodded blankly, he gathered up his resolutions. He'd commit to at least another year in analysis. He'd stop measuring himself against the standards of perfection that had always dubiously promised but invariably failed to justify his existence. He'd never again lie about who he was, no matter the circumstances. And then, if Gus changed his mind, at least he'd find Julian a better man than he'd left him.

As they parted at 113th Street, Hugh patted him on the shoulder and squeezed his hand.

"You read about Atlas 6, didn't you?" he said. "After so many delays and doubts, they orbited the earth three times and landed safely in the North Atlantic earlier today."

"What's your point, my dear?" Julian asked.

"Be patient with him," Hugh said. "Even demigods need time to heal."

❂ ❂ ❂

On the sidewalk about twenty yards from his building, standing out against the dull grit of road salt and dirty snow, Julian saw two odd bits of paper. One of them, he realized on closer inspection, was Roger's business card with Donovan's address written neatly on the back. The other was Julian's Con Ed bill. When he hurried inside and raced up the three flights, the open apartment door confirmed his suspicion.

The place was a mess. In the living room, sofa cushions had been overturned, books ripped from their shelves. The contents of an overfilled ashtray defiled the Danish shag rug as if a small artillery shell had detonated. Julian's desk had been thoroughly rifled, his papers scattered across the floor. Although the Aalto chaise lay untouched, the eye clock was gone, along with the Buffet print, the hi-fi system, and the record albums—all except Rosemary Clooney's still unopened *Hollywood Hits*. In the bedroom, dresser drawers had been ransacked, clothes covered the carpet like hapless murder victims, and the mattress lay rudely askew. The kitchen, with all its cupboard doors flown open, looked like a used-up Advent calendar, and the floor was littered with boxes, tins, and shattered dishes. The thieves had taken the toaster, the Vitamix, and even the bottle of Dom Perignon Julian been saving for a special occasion. The complete chaos of the place was an inescapable symbol of his chaotic life and seemed to mock his blessed rage for order. As he dropped his face into his hands, he laughed and sighed, perhaps to keep from crying.

The window near the fire escape, its broken casement lock lying in a pile of plaster on the floor near the philodendrons, had clearly been their way in. The number of items stolen and the speed of the operation all pointed to experienced criminals. Or was it the little mustachioed man or the Charles Street desk sergeant, hell-bent on revenge? Or Harcourt and Sterne, looking for incriminating evidence and staging a burglary to disguise their intent? Or just some drug-addled punks who'd chosen Julian's apartment at random? He'd probably never know. Fortunately, he owned little of real value, except for a few replaceable household gods. He had no money hidden away, no rare books or priceless art, no fancy watches or cameras or jewelry. The Fouquet Medusa was still safe on his finger. As he closed the window, he remembered that, according to something Gus had read in the *Times*, break-ins were on the rise in Morningside Heights, and so there was probably nothing special about his. Just more bad luck.

Then Julian thought of his manuscript and ran to the side of his desk where he'd left his book bag. But the bag and all that had been inside it—his *Inferno*, his *Kittredge*, and the cardboard box that contained the work of many years—were gone, too. Every hour of reading and writing, every ingenious thought, every felicitous sentence, all vanished, along with his prospects for tenure. He considered running straight to Philosophy Hall to begin typing from memory and trying to recover as much as possible. But the idea of separating substantial wheat from misguided chaff soon began to seem overwhelming. In fact, the more he thought about it, the less he found it mattered at all. He wondered why the thieves had taken the book bag, whether it had been spontaneous and arbitrary or planned and intentional. He couldn't imagine how anyone might profit from heavily annotated copies of Dante and Shakespeare and an unpublished work of literary criticism. Millie had pressed him several times to make a carbon copy of the manuscript, but that would have taken precious days and nights, and lately Julian had preferred to spend that time with his lover.

He knew the two things were somehow connected. Losing the man had been the result of his timidity, his book the expression of it. But as he looked around at the mess in the living room and debated whether to call the police, he felt his highly wrought sense of unfairness giving way to a new and strange feeling of possibility. The eye clock, after all, had been a fatuous keeper of the time, wholly ignorant of the real changes that had taken place under its watch. The Buffet print might as well have been a self-portrait. Perhaps their theft, and the wrecking of the stylish apartment Julian had so foolishly cherished, had only stripped him of encumbrances. Even losing the manuscript, he thought, might turn out to be a gift in the end, since without sacrificing the beauty of the *Sonnets*, it would save him from the vanity of them.

❂ ❂ ❂

His Wednesday lecture on *Much Ado* was a total failure. Not even the veiled reunion of the lovers in Act Five seemed to move any of his hard-hearted auditors. But for reasons he couldn't quite explain, Lit Hum, taught with an old library copy of the *Inferno*, went as well as he'd ever remembered a class going. Julian tangled with Carter and a few other boys over the definition of "lust," the difference between Augustine's idea of "incontinence" and Dante's, and what it meant for those poor "wearied souls" in the Second Circle to be blown about by the "fierce winds" of judgment. Then he asked them why lust was the least offensive of the mortal sins and whether this wasn't evidence of Dante's ambivalence about sex.

"Might it not suggest that while his hands were tied by Christian orthodoxy, he went easiest on the fornicators because he felt a little sorry for them?"

Carter, now a self-proclaimed Papist, raised his hand and insisted it didn't matter. "A perversion of divine love is still a perversion," he said.

Then Brockden, a burly athlete from Bucks County, unwilling to be outdone by a squirt, spoke without raising his hand. "So how come he and Beatrice never even got to first base?" he asked to a chorus of appreciation.

"Fine," Julian said. "But give me a show of hands. If forced to choose one circle from among the nine, not including Limbo, wherein to spend all eternity, who among you wouldn't choose the Second Circle?"

Not a single hand in the room went up, not even Carter's.

"Cleopatra and Helen of Troy might be some good consolation," Brockden said to another round of laughs.

"Don't forget Paris and Achilles," Julian added. "Consolation comes in many forms."

He said it spontaneously, almost thoughtlessly, and suddenly all eyes were on him. The old bookcases in the seminar room seemed to pull back, even as the space between him and the boys—now silent with bug-eyed consternation—seemed to shrink. An invisible line had been moved, and everyone seemed to be doing his best to figure out where it now lay.

Whether he lost his job or not, Julian was sure he'd found his work.

"So why are the sodomites condemned to the Seventh Circle, Professor?" Carter asked, reaching for the day's laurel.

"Ah, excellent question, Carter," Julian said. "Probably because in those prudish and benighted times even Dante's imagination had its limits."

◎ ◎ ◎

When he got back to Philosophy Hall, he found two "While You Were Out" messages waiting for him. One was from Dean Cavanaugh, requesting a meeting in half an hour. The other was from Roger Harrington, advising Julian to read that day's edition of the *Times*. Although he was nearly certain the dean's note promised to end his career, he found himself more interested in Roger's.

"You can borrow mine, Professor Prince," Millie said, peeping from behind her silver cat-eyes as she passed him her newspaper. The front page confirmed that Glenn was alive and well and Kennedy aglow with pride.

"You're very kind, Millie," Julian said.

After he sat down at his desk, it didn't take long to find what he was looking for. Sandwiched between ads for Whirlpool dryers and a sale at Sam Goody's was an article about the "Scourge of Violence" lately committed against the New York Police Department. The past weekend alone, it read, three officers had been attacked in separate incidents. One was now in a coma, having been stabbed five times with a knife after he pulled over a late-model Chevrolet in Cobble Hill on Friday night. Another had been found dead on Sunday afternoon in the Bayonne wetlands, shot twice in the back of the head. And early Monday, a third officer was discovered unconscious near Pier 45 and hospitalized with hypothermia, broken bones, and a severe concussion, though he was expected to recover. There were no photos, but Julian wondered if the third cop was the sadist who'd attacked Danny. Whether the second one was the Charles Street desk sergeant, punished by his associates for excessive zeal, was anyone's guess.

Although Julian felt hopeful for both Roger and himself, the beating of one man and the death of another seemed like bad omens. He worried that others might suffer in retaliation and that Danny might be among them. He also knew that further demands for money might still come when he least expected them and the threatened telegrams might still be sent. In fact, it was possible he wasn't any freer now than he'd been the day before. As he folded the *Times*, he thought of Ivan Fischer, the new assistant chief, so self-possessed in his black coat and red scarf, so safe from all the violence he'd ordered, and no doubt pleased with his managerial acumen but probably already focused on more pressing matters. Calculating men had always ruled the world and always would.

While Julian waited in the anteroom of the dean's office in Low Library fifteen minutes later, scrutinized by a dozen portraits of illustrious, silver-haired emeriti on the walls around him, he reconciled himself to the likelihood that his own face would never hang among them. Dean Cavanaugh was a circumspect historian who'd probably explain Julian's predicament in precise and thorough detail. He wondered if he could insist on his right to due process and ridicule the obfuscations of the university's morality clause and still manage to leave the meeting with his dignity intact. But he felt more resigned to the outcome than he'd expected.

As he mused on his murky future, Sterne suddenly burst into the room, his face flushed and his hands fluttering like moths. "Thank goodness you're here!" he cried.

Julian was surprised more by the timing than the frenzy. He felt a twinge of embarrassment as his colleague struggled to steady himself. If Julian idealized handsome young men like Gus, he knew he probably had an unconscious aversion to older, prissier, lonelier men like Sterne and Loosli. Maybe it came from a fear of women or of weakness or simply of becoming old, prissy, and lonely himself. Either way, he'd bring it up with Ziegler.

"Prince, you must forgive all my teasing," Sterne said. "Perfectly boorish of me, I'll admit it. But the truth is I'm at a loss."

When Julian invited him to explain, he didn't waste a breath before continuing.

"Tristan's been suspended! Pending further inquiry but suspended! In the middle of the term! He's so much more naïve than he seems. And he's got nowhere else to go!"

Julian was about to ask what it was that he wanted, but Sterne anticipated him.

"Call me sentimental," he said, pulling himself together a little, "but I must ask—implore you, really—to speak a kind word to Cavanaugh on his behalf. He's a brilliant young man who only wants a bit of guidance and encouragement. Don't you see?"

"Was he involved with students?" Julian asked.

"Oh, pooh!" Sterne said. "No, it was the term papers! And all so well-intended!"

He went on for another five minutes, defending and explaining, but Julian already knew he wouldn't be fired that day. There was no case against him, probably not even a cloud of suspicion. Harcourt had merely recommended him to the dean as a character witness, and the meeting between the two parties was now about to occur. All their lurking and insinuations had been mere prurience and guess-work, a distraction from their own self-inflicted troubles. Sterne was more of a gossip than an extortionist, and he was obviously smitten. But his petition seemed honorable enough on the whole. When asked his opinion about it a few minutes later, Julian told Dean Cavanaugh that, though he knew nothing about Harcourt's case, he could vouch for his youth, his energy, and his resilience. It therefore wouldn't be unreasonable, he added, to consider clemency.

After the meeting, he ducked out of Low Library, left the campus, and turned South onto Amsterdam, his eyes trained on its dusky southern vanishing point. He thought of Gus, abed in Loosli's maid's room, wrapped in his coverlet, his body rising and falling in the steadiest, sleep-loving breaths, and it made him smile. He'd certainly proven himself inferior to his lover, but even after all that had happened, he somehow still felt he deserved him. And as he approached 113th Street, he yielded again, lark-like, to the gravity-defying idea that had swelled his head and roiled his feelings all day. That when he arrived at his building that afternoon, Gus would be standing out in front with his suitcase at his feet, a large canvas wrapped in brown paper under his arm, and his freckled cheeks not yet restored to their natural color but still beaming in the twilight. He'd smile his ready forgiveness, admitting both disappointments and regrets and blaming the systole and diastole of the heart for each. That evening, they'd hang the messy, moving painting where the Buffet print had been, and Julian would nurse Gus back to health by kissing the tender tracery of his ears. At one point, Gus would laugh at Julian's sudden seriousness and bended-knee formality, and when Julian offered him the Fouquet Medusa, he'd blink his eyes a few times and smile, then slip it on his finger and call it a very handsome ring, even though it wasn't.

30

The clink of forks and knives on Margaret Duffy's battered china only made the silence at the table more awkward. Danny watched as she pushed cauliflower around her plate and then, for just a few seconds, forced her face into a thin, pale quarter-smile. Though she seemed genuinely glad to have him back at home for a visit, she looked stunned to her stays by the manner of his return. In between mouthfuls, Michael shook his head in moody disapproval. Mavis seemed unable to look up at all, let alone eat, and only rubbed her swollen belly like a fortune-teller's crystal ball. Ciaran occasionally turned his big slack eyes on Margaret Duffy and cheered her with a compliment about the meal, but as generalissimo of the evening he was failing to reassure the troops. Even Danny, who'd expected a cool reception, felt edgy. For while they weren't a large party that night, they weren't a typical one either. Bill had been sent back to Fort Bragg a week before, Quinn was working late and not expected to come at all, and Rafael, in his best suit and tie, sat at Danny's left, looking a lot surer of what to make of the Duffy family than it was to make of him.

Just being there felt like a kind of victory. If anybody was going to refuse them, it would've happened at the front door. Now that they were sitting down, he had inertia on his side. They must have assumed that, as his guest, Raf was the same unmentionable thing the *Post* had said Danny was. But though he'd brought him along to provoke them a little, it was also to offer the hard terms of a truce.

He knew he couldn't keep both his family and his self-respect unless something changed. It wasn't an apology he wanted so much as an admission—spoken or not—of the truth. Now that he and Raf were lovers—and had been since early Monday morning—he'd no sooner come to a Thursday-night family dinner without him than Ciaran would come without Mavis.

As he chewed his food and looked around the room, he was struck by the strangeness of everything. The lace curtains, the Christmas sofa, the old gilt Madonna. None of it had ever shown up in his dreams. In fact, all of it seemed like cheap window dressing covering over all the conspiracy of unfairness that he'd grown up with, and he wondered how he'd ever lived in such a place. By the way Margaret Duffy looked at him—like he'd been away for years, traveling in parts unknown and picking up outlandish habits—it seemed she was wondering the same thing. He wore his leather jacket and purple tie to make a point about his new independence, and he counted on lingering traces of his black eye to reinforce it.

"How's life at the post office, Rafael?" Ciaran suddenly asked. It was the first time anyone but Danny had spoken his name.

Margaret Duffy inhaled a quick breath and Michael scoffed and rolled his eyes.

"Business is booming," Raf said with an easy smile, which reminded Danny that family dinners were his specialty. "Stamps are very popular this year."

It seemed a good sign that everyone but Michael smiled back, though cautiously, like they weren't sure if Raf was making a joke or not but had decided to give him the benefit of the doubt. Puerto Ricans certainly weren't exotics in the Bronx, but they weren't allowed to live in Parkchester and they weren't often visitors there either.

Danny remembered coming home from the Keller Bar late Sunday night, feeling restless and lonely, and leaving his chilly sofa for the warmth of Raf's bed. Then the quick gulp of surprise, the unflinching reach of long, strong arms, and the instant, wordless understanding. He felt greedy for Raf's dark and lean body, slick mouth, and a-little-bigger-than-average dick—everything he'd been wanting without knowing it. But then he remembered that Raf had only been giving giving giving since he'd moved in, and so instead of taking more,

333

Danny had kissed him softly, smiled his surrender and—saving his own dick, which still required special handling—offered him everything he had.

"Actually, I bought stamps just this morning," Ciaran finally said.

"See what I mean?" Raf said.

Everyone laughed except Michael, who scoffed again, though whether at Ciaran or Raf, Danny wasn't sure.

"Did we really have to do this tonight?" Michael muttered. "I've had a long day."

Margaret Duffy and Ciaran glowered at him, and Danny quietly flipped him the bird while scratching his temple. He figured dinner would now go one of two ways. Either everyone would settle into normal, mostly boring conversation about postage stamps and winter weather and decide it was easier to accept Raf as a fellow human being than risk giving themselves a case of indigestion. Or Michael would decide to take that risk and force their mother to choose sides once again. Danny knew history no longer favored him, but this time he wouldn't let anyone reject him in silence. He'd make sure their choice was as obvious as a dinner-table fart.

Raf gave Danny a look that said he felt pity for any family that could eat without talking. And to show that Danny appreciated his patience, he reached for another of the pasteles Raf had brought along that night that no one but Danny had yet touched.

"Any luck finding a new job, Danny?" Ciaran asked.

"Funny you should ask, Ciaran," Danny said. "In fact, on Monday I start as an ordinary produce clerk at the D'Agostino's near Stuy Town. I'll be making fifty cents an hour less than I used to and my boss will be a kid who used to worked for me at Sloan's."

He hadn't meant to sound so bitter. But if anyone heard it, their looks only said that, like Raf, they thought any job was better than none.

"It's a good store," Raf chimed in. "Six types of squash in February."

Margaret Duffy seemed to brighten at the idea of such variety. "Six types," she said, before giving Mavis an approving look. "Isn't that something?"

Michael scoffed a third time and shook his head.

"You know, you could participate in the conversation," Ciaran said.

"Well, you could suggest more interesting topics," Michael said.

"And you could mind your manners," Danny said to Michael, thinking it wise to use the leverage he had. "We have a guest tonight."

"How could I have missed him?" Michael said, giving Raf a rude look that quickly sank into a sorry, shame-faced one.

"Lord help us," Margaret Duffy said.

Raf suddenly laughed out loud, probably not so much at Michael or Margaret Duffy but because he'd never before been the innocent subject of Irish people's bickering. Then Danny laughed, too, to take Raf's side, of course, but also because he knew laughter was good for people's nerves. And after a few yuks of his own, Ciaran cracked a goofy, gap-toothed smile that made him look like Marty Piletti. And when Margaret Duffy smiled too—a full, pink one that reminded you she'd once been considered pretty—it almost felt like a Thursday-night family dinner from time immemorial.

But then the front door slammed shut and there was Quinn, flinging his coat and hat on the sofa.

"What do we have here?" he asked, eyeing Danny and Raf.

When he'd heard Quinn wouldn't be coming to dinner, Danny told himself he didn't care either way, that he wasn't afraid of him anymore and never would be again. But now that he *was* here, Danny wasn't so sure it was true. Quinn was spiteful by nature. Always mocking and teasing, ever since they were kids. Never once a favor or a kind word. He bullied and tortured and humiliated until it no longer suited him, then he moved on, like a killer shark or a backyard cat. It had been happening for nearly a quarter century, and though sitting next to Raf made Danny feel braver and stronger, he worried that the shame he thought he'd banished was somehow still there, thick in his reflexes.

"Come sit down before everything gets cold," Margaret Duffy told Quinn.

Ciaran shot him a look that said there'd be trouble if he didn't.

But Quinn ignored them both and pointed his finger at Danny like he was picking a criminal out of a lineup. "I know all about you!" he said.

"Oh, and what is it that you think you know, dahling?" Danny said, producing a cluck from Raf and blinking bewilderment from Mavis.

"I read the article in the *Post*!" Quinn said with a foul smirk.

Danny again remembered him as a kid dancing around the apartment on St. Ann's Avenue with the *Daily Mirror* in his hand and shouting the other F-word. He'd seemed glad that, even after the war's end, there were still people you were supposed to hate.

"You've never read a newspaper in your life," Danny said.

"You'd better mind yourself," Ciaran warned Quinn.

But he only wheeled around the table, dropped into the empty seat between Mavis and Raf without looking at either of them, then started piling food on his plate.

Everyone seemed to be waiting for Quinn to make good on his threat, except Margaret Duffy, who looked like she might revolt against her feelings and leave the table.

"Now what sort of establishment is Caesar's, Danny?" Quinn said as he cut into his chop. "Sure, I know full well what a disorderly house is. But what exactly is a 'pervert nest'? And how is it you were found 'loitering' there?"

Danny cringed at the ugly words and might have said something even uglier if Raf hadn't warned him against it with a gentle squeeze of his leg that somehow made him stiff, despite his fury. But then Margaret Duffy, who knew exactly what a pervert was, looked up.

"That's enough," she said to Quinn, louder than anyone expected. "Lord help us."

The table went quiet again. Danny straightened his tie and watched his mother, searching the creases of her frown for signs of strength. Ciaran huffed and puffed, while Quinn sniggered between mouthfuls. Everyone knew what he might say, but no one wanted him to say it, even though they all knew it was true.

"Another word and you'll pay for it," Ciaran said, standing up.

Danny's eldest brother was meek as a lamb nine times out of ten. But Quinn knew he'd get far more than a charley horse in the shoulder if he kept it up, and Danny felt the threat as proof that Ciaran hadn't abandoned him after all.

"Never mind, you old ogre," Quinn said, putting down his fork and getting up from the table. "I've lost my appetite."

He circled back around Ciaran and looked pointedly at Michael, as if expecting him to get up and leave, too. But Michael only looked at Margaret Duffy and threw his hands in the air.

"Really, Ma, how are we supposed to—deal with *this*—whatever it is?" he said, glancing at Danny and Raf. "'Cause frankly I'm stumped!"

Danny had never liked Michael. He was selfish and a scoffer. But he had a point. It was one of the great mysteries of the world why some boys were different from others, though nobody talked about it. Maybe it was like death, ordinary and unstoppable but too scary to think about unless you were on its doorstep. People seemed to think if you said certain words the world would come apart at its zippers.

"Just figure it out, Michael!" Danny said, as he slathered gravy on a slice of Wonder Bread to show how unfazed he was. "Christ Almighty, *we* had to!"

When Raf squeezed Danny's leg again his whole body shivered with love. Margaret Duffy said nothing about his profanity and looked like she might actually be thinking about what he'd said. Everyone else dropped their eyes to the safer mid-distance of candlesticks and serving dishes.

But then Quinn's hazel eyes suddenly gleamed with last-chance madness. "What'd you figure out?" he said to Danny. "That you're a cocksucker? That you like to take it up the ass?" Then he looked at Raf. "That you like spic dick?"

Danny jumped up from his chair and might have leapt across the table if Raf hadn't grabbed him firmly by the shoulder. As Quinn waited for his bombs to explode, the others stared in stony disbelief that anyone would ever speak such unholy words at Margaret Duffy's dinner table. Mavis crossed herself and Ciaran, still standing, turned red and bit his lip, like he was pondering the wisdom of killing Quinn in front of his mother and his pregnant wife.

Instead, he slapped Quinn's face with the back of his hand, grabbed him by the collar, and pushed him over the Christmas sofa. Then he pulled him back up, spun him into a hammerlock, and marched him toward the door.

"You ungrateful skunk!" Ciaran cried.

As Danny watched, he realized that Quinn's bombs hadn't exploded and the world remained zipped. Raf seemed to take it all in stride and even looked sadly at Quinn, like he was a mental case. What he'd said had poked at Danny's dignity a little, but mostly it sounded clumsy and stupid, like a schoolyard taunt. The fight that rose up in him was only on the surface, like an itch. In a way, he was even glad that the truth his family had been ignoring for two weeks—maybe for two decades—had finally been served up on the table in front of them, as overcooked and underseasoned as the chops.

"You ugly Sasquatch!" Quinn shouted, as Ciaran forced his arm up his back.

Margaret Duffy, who'd seen her boys fight too many times to take it personally, waited for a pause in the action before turning away and looking at Danny with a serious, searching expression on her face. He knew that once again she had to choose between two of her sons, and between her hatred of vulgarity and her fear for Danny's soul. But after she'd seemed to have thought about it enough, she turned back to see Quinn wriggle out from under Ciaran's grip and strut a little to get back his pride. Then, as he opened his mouth to complain, she stopped him with a shake of her head.

"Go on, Quinn," she said. "Go on home."

He looked like a man who'd accidentally walked into the wrong party.

"But Ma—"

"Just go," she said again with a small sigh of relief, as if she thought the Lord had finally helped them after all.

As Danny relaxed into his chair, relieved to know he was a member of the family once again—now finally, thoroughly un-ghosted—Quinn grabbed his hat and coat, went to the door and turned around to sneer at everyone at the table. Then he finally unburdened himself of the secret weapon he'd held too long in reserve.

"Faggots!" he shouted, before slamming the door behind him.

But like a bullet fired from too far away, the word had lost most of its power by the time it hit them.

Nobody apologized for Quinn's nastiness or even mentioned it. In some ways, it had been the worst Thursday-night family dinner since the time Pat Duffy was too drunk to say grace and, before he'd even gotten to "Bless us, O Lord," shat himself right there at the table. But this time, instead of panicking, they talked as if nothing had happened. Mavis tried a pastele and said it was too spicy for baby but otherwise better than she'd expected. When Raf told them about his cousin who sold frozen meat from a truck in Bay Ridge, Ciaran marveled at all forms of frozen food. Danny explained that it was Clarence Birdseye who'd invented the flash-freezing process, which kept vegetables from getting mushy when you defrosted them, and even Michael seemed to think it wasn't a completely stupid thing to say. Eventually, Margaret Duffy cleaned her plate, which no one had seen her do in years, and as Danny threaded his fingers between Raf's underneath the table, he realized that, without saying it, she'd given them her blessing. In a way, she'd put Raf in his arms herself, though with a little help from Quinn.

Danny hoped that this major adjustment in the Duffy household might be a second step toward the revolution he wanted to see in the world. Knowing his mother and brother still loved him made him feel all the more up to the task. Four days had passed since Harry Blunt's beating at the Keller Bar and every one of them he'd spent wondering if the man was dead or alive, if he'd come seeking his own revenge, and if it had been the right thing to do after all. Though it was as satisfying as any good fight was, it hadn't brought back Gabriel or sent much of a message to anyone but Harry himself. Danny still liked the idea of a worldwide general strike and had plans to give it more thought. But he was beginning to see that the real revolution would have to take place in apartments and detached houses everywhere, most of which were in need of serious reform. Just thinking about it steadied his breath and made his skin tingle.

That night, while he slept burrowed in Raf's armpit, sweaty and satisfied, keeping all questions of love and justice at bay, his dreams started right there in the little Chelsea apartment, though it was bathed in the hazy red and purple lights of Maria's *West Side* bedroom from the movie. He and Raf and Gabriel were drinking beer and camping it up with Judy and Etta and Connie, and no one seemed to care about a shiny pool of cockroaches clicking and hissing in one corner. After a while, the dream shifted to the Catskills, to a house on a hilltop that the three of them had built from pine planks and spike nails, and Raf couldn't stop laughing because everywhere you looked there were fruits and vegetables—apples and peaches, tomatoes and eggplants, calabazas and kabochas—popping up out of nowhere. Then, through some weird dream logic he couldn't remember, they were all back in the city again, dozens of them, Sharks and Jets together, side-kicking up huge piles of white rubble in San Juan Hill, snapping their fingers, knives at the ready, singing music they knew by heart, while above them the afternoon sun tilted toward New Jersey and an impossibly blue sky spread out toward places Danny had never even heard of.

Acknowledgments

For reading, teaching, and inspiring, I owe the greatest debt to Mark Jude Poirier, who never stopped believing in this novel and my ability to write it. Without him, there'd be no book at all.

Many other generous and talented people helped enormously. I'm grateful to my agent, Pamela Malpas, for her guidance and determination, and to my editor, Richard Morrison, my copy editor, Nancy Basmajian, and everyone at Fordham University Press for their commitment and care. Michael Bronski and Amber Dermont offered indispensable comments and suggestions. For feedback on early drafts, I'm indebted to Daniel Contreras, Michael Drexler, Richard Giannone, Corey McEleney, Ben Neihart, Stacey Richter, Gemma Sieff, Ed Sien, Charlie Suisman, and Andy Tuck. For their wisdom and support, thanks to Julia Borcherts, Jack Carroll, Tim Cockey, Jennifer Gilmore, Sands Hall, Owen King, Michael Nava, Ed Sikov, Karl Soehnlein, Julia Strohm, Johnny Temple, and Don Weise.

The history of queer people experiencing injustice under the law begins with the law itself and continues to the present day in a majority of countries around the world. This novel is inspired by many thousands in the United States who were persecuted in the mid-twentieth century. Because of federal, state, and local laws, written under the guise of public morality but enacted and enforced to suppress sexual diversity, they were harassed, beaten, blackmailed, arrested, convicted, fined, incarcerated, fired from jobs, evicted from homes, alienated from families and communities, forced into psychiatric institutions—where they were drugged, electrocuted, sterilized, and lobotomized—and sometimes driven to suicide. All of these *disorderly* queers suffered; some bravely fought back against this injustice in ways that eventually made the world a little better.

The Andy Warhol solo exhibition at the Stable Gallery actually occurred in November 1962, and the historical Sixth Precinct station on Charles Street, now a luxury condo building called Le Gendarme, did not have an alley behind it. But fiction always plays with time and gives us another way out.

Edward Cahill lives in New York City and teaches English at Fordham University. *Disorderly Men* is his first novel.